"I AM PREPARED TO DO MY DUTY AS YOUR WIFE."

A hard smile touched Sloan's lips. "Duty? That's precisely my point. I'm not interested in a cold-blooded mate. Colorado winters get frigid enough without having an icicle in my bed."

The flush that tinged Heather's cheeks told him he'd hit a nerve. "What makes you think I wouldn't enjoy it?" she retorted softly.

"I guess there's only one way to find out." His gaze never leaving hers, he tossed his hat on the settee. She stood helplessly in his power, transfixed by his mesmerizing eyes. He moved closer, letting his body touch hers.

The shock was stunning. She felt blistered by his sudden invading heat, by the hard, masculine contours that branded her.

Through a daze she heard him whisper against her lips. "You really think you're woman enough to handle me, duchess?"

THE HEART BREAKER

NICOLE JORDAN

AVON BOOKS ◆ NEW YORK

AVON BOOKS
A division of
The Hearst Corporation
1350 Avenue of the Americas
New York, New York 10019

Copyright © 1998 by Anne Bushyhead
Inside cover author photo by Wayne Johnson
Published by arrangement with the author
Visit our website at **http://www.AvonBooks.com**
Library of Congress Catalog Card Number: 97-94077
ISBN: 0-380-78561-7

First Avon Books Printing: February 1998

AVON TRADEMARK REG. U.S. PAT. OFF. AND IN OTHER COUNTRIES, MARCA REGISTRADA, HECHO EN U.S.A.

Printed in the U.S.A.

WCD 10 9 8 7 6 5 4 3 2 1

To Jay, who makes my heart whole

With love for always

The wounds invisible
That love's keen arrows make.

WILLIAM SHAKESPEARE

THE HEART BREAKER

Prologue

Colorado
February 1887

Moonlight played over her pale, nude body, silvering her fair hair yet obscuring her delicate features in shadow. Sloan McCord groaned as the woman above him gently lowered herself to straddle his taut thighs.

Her lovely, lush form pearlized by moonglow, she bent closer, her ripe breasts teasing him, the budded nipples begging for the touch of his teeth and tongue.

Sloan squeezed his eyes shut as another hot wave of desire ripped through him. He couldn't see her face. She was a stranger, and yet . . . he knew her touch. He knew her white, satin-smooth skin . . . her proud, lush breasts . . . the lustrous cascade of pale gold hair spilling over her naked shoulders. . . . Knew her with the hungry, intimate knowledge of a lover.

Her breasts overflowed in his palms as he coaxed her willing body down to receive his hard shaft. His blood pulsed feverishly at her enveloping warmth, and he inhaled a harsh breath, welcoming the fierce heat that surged through him.

Here was fire and fantasy.

The woman in his arms trembled as she impaled herself fully on his rigid flesh, sheathing him in silken wet heat. At the exquisite sensation, his hands shifted restlessly upward, his fingers tightening in her glorious hair, burying in the curling golden strands. Yet when he tried to draw her closer—to kiss her lips, to see her face—she held back.

"Slowly, my love. . . ." she whispered, her voice as liquid as the moonlight. "We have forever. . . ."

Forever. The husky word breathed a promise into his soul.

Sinuously she took over riding him, heightening the coiling tension burgeoning in his body, fanning the flames with every soft surge of her hips. His teeth clenching, he strained to keep his explosive need in check, to withstand her tender, sensual assault. He wanted to plunge wildly inside her, wanted to take her with savage lust, to pound into her. . . .

Blindly, helplessly, he raised his hips and thrust deep.

Her back arched and she moaned sharply, shuddering. Her writhing movement excited him beyond bearing. His body shook, and he felt desire, fierce and desperate, spiral through his groin in a sweet agony of pleasure—

With a violent start, Sloan came awake, a rough cry of passion echoing in his mind.

Heart pounding, loins throbbing, he scanned the darkened room. His bedchamber. His ranch house. His bed. *Alone*.

Moonlight filtered through the chintz curtains, reflecting brightly off the snow-blanketed landscape outside.

"A dream," he whispered hoarsely. She was only a dream.

The wrong dream.

It had been too vivid, too seductive. A fine sheen of sweat covered his skin in the wintry night air; his manhood still strained in hot, unrelieved arousal.

Freeing an arm from the tangled covers, Sloan ran his hand raggedly down his face, trying to shake off his dark, fevered imaginings, to forget the way her naked skin had burned against his. Yet he could still feel her lithe, lush body, still feel the treacherous heat of desire.

Dammit to blazes, it was wrong. *She* was wrong. His dream lover had been blonde, not raven-haired like his Cheyenne wife. Pale, not dark-skinned. Voluptuous, not spare and sinewy.

Not like his dead wife.

A dark fist of pain gripped his heart. More than a year had passed since Sleeping Doe had been murdered, another innocent victim of a bloody range war. Haunting memories, dark and bitter, swept over Sloan, clashing with the sensual remnants of his dream. Normally his tormented dreams were of his wife and her final gasping moments in his arms . . . her blood on his hands as he'd sobbed harshly and railed at the heavens and vowed vengeance for her death.

Trying urgently now to forget, he focused instead on the throbbing of his groin. His eyes shutting, Sloan closed his fingers around his rigid flesh and with rough, quick strokes, brought himself physical relief.

He didn't much relish this dispassionate means of release, but it wasn't unnatural for a healthy man to have needs, and he hadn't had a woman in months.

Oh, there were any number of females who'd be willing to scratch his masculine itch, including Doc Farley's pretty daughter and a lively rancher's widow who lived on the outskirts of town. But he'd shied away from them all, avoiding even the doves at the saloon in Greenbriar. They couldn't fill the emptiness inside him since losing the woman he'd loved, or replace what he'd shared with Doe.

Despite what his family said.

His brother Jake was pushing him to get on with his life. His sister-in-law insisted he needed another wife.

With a swift, impatient movement, Sloan threw off the covers and swung his legs over the side of the bed. After wiping his damp hand on the sheet, he bent over tiredly, his corded forearms resting on his thighs, his head bowed.

Ever since Caitlin's marriage to his brother last summer, she'd been intent on playing matchmaker, Sloan reflected somberly. She'd finally worn him down with sheer persistence.

"What in blazes do I want another wife for?" he'd demanded several months ago when Cat first broached the subject, half amused by her gumption, considering that they'd been mortal enemies for years.

"I can think of several excellent reasons," she'd returned stubbornly.

And all her arguments had been sound, Sloan was forced to admit. Shrewdly she'd started with his foray into state politics.

"You want to win your campaign this summer, don't you?" Caitlin asked.

"I have some notion of winning, yes."

Ignoring his wryness, she eased her body, which was beginning to swell with child, into the leather sofa in his study, looking prepared for a long siege.

"Then you'd better start thinking about how to get people on your side. Your maverick ways haven't endeared you to voters, Sloan. Especially to sheep men."

Caitlin was right, he knew. He planned to run for the Colorado senate, but his violence in the long range war had earned him more than a few enemies. Caitlin herself had helped him end the feud, but there was still bad blood between cattle ranchers and sheep farmers.

And then there was his marriage.

A hell-raiser in his youth, he'd earnestly avoided matrimony until he'd fallen for the full-blooded Cheyenne woman he'd met soon after his brother was unjustly branded an outlaw. His marriage had stunned and shocked the community. And it hadn't helped that later, as a widower, he'd continued to evade the local belles.

"It would improve your public image significantly to be married to a well-bred lady," Caitlin persisted.

Sloan didn't bother repressing his scoff. "Your 'well-bred lady' is from St. Louis. A citified Easterner."

"Who would do quite well as a political hostess."

"I'd be better off marrying a Western woman. One suited for ranch life. Somebody who at least knows which end of a steer is which."

"Do you have anyone particular in mind?"

When he hesitated, Caitlin said archly, "Of course you don't. The women here have been chasing you for years, Sloan, and you've never shown the least interest in any of them. But you won't win voters if you keep breaking hearts. And you won't get any respite until you marry again. There are a dozen matrons who will keep smothering you with motherly concern and driving you to distraction until you do."

"Matrons like you, Cat?"

Caitlin smiled sweetly in reply, making Sloan understand once again why his brother was so crazy for her.

Sloan couldn't help but grin back. But then he gave a rebellious shrug. "Maybe I could use a wife, but I can't afford one who needs to be pampered. Or who'd be afraid to dirty her soft hands."

"Heather wouldn't need pampering."

"You said she came from rich roots."

"True, but she'd never let on about it. And she's in dire straits now. Her father left her with a pile of gambling debts to settle. She had to sell his newspaper and her home and move in with my Aunt Winnie. In all likelihood she'll be forced to shut down her school to meet the mortgage."

"Well, I can't afford to bail her out. I'll be lucky to scrape by this winter with two bits to my name."

"Jake and I could help if you'd let us."

Sloan shook his head emphatically. The McCord cattle empire was crumbling; the vast spread he and his father and brother had carved from the shadow of the Rockies was at risk of going under. It had been a hell of a hard winter, with heavy snows and lethal temperatures ravaging herds from Texas to Montana.

His brother hadn't been hit as hard by the brutal winter. Jake was now a county judge with a steady wage. And Caitlin had her late father's sheep ranch to tide them over, raising woollies that could survive frigid weather better than beeves.

But Sloan already owed them enough. He still hadn't fully been able to buy out Jake's share of the ranch. And he refused to become any more obliged to them than he was.

Caitlin, however, let their longstanding argument pass and concentrated on championing her genteel friend from St. Louis.

"If you wait, Sloan, you could miss your chance altogether. Heather might not be available for long. Not with the railroad baron who's been after her to marry him."

"So let her marry him."

"She doesn't want to! She doesn't even *like* the man, let alone want to become his wife. But she may not have much choice."

Sloan frowned skeptically. "Heather Ashford. . . . What kind of fancy name is that?"

"She's not fancy, I tell you," Caitlin insisted. "She's a true lady, but strong in her own way. She'd not afraid of hard work. She built her girls' school from almost nothing."

"What is she like?"

"Oh, her looks are passable enough," Caitlin replied. "She has fair hair . . . and she's rather tall, with a full figure."

Sloan's mouth curled as he envisioned a plump starch-and-tea schoolmarm. Plain and homely, no doubt. An unappealing spinster who couldn't catch a man on her own.

But her looks wouldn't matter to him. He didn't want beauty in a wife . . . as long as she wouldn't drive away the men who would be voting for him.

"But," Caitlin continued with a note of triumph, "you're forgetting the most important reason to take a wife. Janna needs a mother."

Roughly Sloan ran a hand through his hair. Caitlin had astutely saved that argument for last. *That* was the only reason that truly counted. His daughter needed a mother. Janna had been two months old when her Cheyenne mother was killed. For over a year now he'd tried to raise his daughter on his own, but it wasn't easy, what with trying to keep his ranch afloat.

Besides, a baby girl needed a woman to care for her. Yet he was losing his Mexican housekeeper, who planned to return home to look after her younger siblings. And Caitlin had her own family to care for—her four-year-old son Ryan plus another baby on the way. Cat helped out with Janna whenever she could, but he couldn't ask her to take on the responsibility full-time.

Caitlin wasn't about to give up trying to solve his problem, though. "Heather would make a good mother, Sloan, I swear it. She's a born teacher, and no one is better with children. She helped me raise Ryan from a baby when I had no one else but my aunt to turn to."

Sloan felt his jaw harden involuntarily. "What would she think about raising a half-breed? White women have a way of turning up their noses at anything 'Injun'."

"Heather wouldn't do that. I know her, Sloan. And I truly think you couldn't do better. She could teach Janna the social graces, how to handle herself in white society. . . . Prepare her for the slights and outright hostility she'll face with her blood. Especially when Janna gets older, when you won't be there to protect her. You must realize she'll need every advantage you can give her."

Remembering his sister-in-law's words now in the darkness of his bedchamber, Sloan rose abruptly and pulled a blanket around his bare shoulders. Crossing to the pot-bellied stove near where his young daughter lay sleeping in her cradle, he added a scoop of coal and then hunkered down beside her, gazing at her dark-skinned features relaxed in sleep, soft with innocence.

Intense feelings of protectiveness and tenderness

swept over him, while fierce love twisted powerfully, painfully in his chest.

This slip of a child had been his salvation. After
losing his wife, he'd been so crazed with vengeance
that he'd gone on a relentless rampage against his
enemies. He'd made Doe's murderers pay, but for
a long while afterward, he'd felt as if he had nothing left to lose, including his own life. He'd felt
empty, as if his heart and lungs and guts had all
been torn out. Sealed off by grief from everyone
around him.

Janna was all that had kept him alive. She'd been
the only thing worth living for.

In the past months since the range war was ten-
uously settled, his rage had eased somewhat, but
guilt still burned inside him. His enemies had
killed his wife to get at him. Doe had been all that
was good and strong and gentle in his life. And he
hadn't been able to save her.

Guilt had burned a searing brand on his soul,
leaving him with tortured dreams. The nights were
the hardest. In the darkest hours before dawn,
when the long, bitter years of loneliness stretched
endlessly before him, he found himself craving the
time when vengeance and hatred had been his closest friends.

He didn't want another woman to share his life.
Hell, for that matter, what right did he have to ask
someone to shoulder his burdens? There were only
shadows and sorrow in his past, hardship in his
future. His hands were stained with blood and violence, while a cold blackness surrounded his soul.

But his child needed a mother.

And he'd pay any price, go to any lengths, to
help his young daughter.

With infinite care Sloan tucked the covers under

Janna's small chin and stood. He resented it like hell, but he needed a wife.

In any event, the time for debating was over. He was committed now. Yesterday, by letter, he'd made Miss Heather Ashford a formal offer of marriage. In it he'd pledged to pay her remaining debts—fifteen hundred precious dollars he would have to scrape together somehow—to free her of her obligations in St. Louis. It was too late for him to honorably back out.

He hated the thought of marrying again. He much preferred to let his wounds scar over with time, if that were even possible.

But Miss Ashford wouldn't be a true wife to him. He would settle for a female body to warm his bed and someone to care for his child. A woman of refinement who could give Janna the advantages he couldn't give her. That his bride also possessed the poise and breeding to help him get elected this September would only be an added benefit. No, theirs would be a marriage of convenience, nothing more. A business arrangement, pure and simple.

Heather Ashford.

He closed his eyes, trying to envision the genteel lady who would soon bear his name.

When the wanton angel of his recent dream drifted into his mind, Sloan cursed. The memory of her sensual lovemaking was dark and sweet . . . her flesh pale in the moonlight, her fair hair, wild and glorious, spilling over her naked shoulders, her ripe breasts straining for his touch. . . . To his disgust, he felt himself getting hard again.

It had been one hell of a dream. Nothing like reality would be, he was certain. But then, he didn't want a real woman, or a real marriage. If he had to wed again, he would rather his bride be a prim, starched-up schoolmarm like Miss Ashford. A total

stranger who couldn't touch the inner core of him. Who wouldn't get any foolish notions about things like love.

Love wouldn't be part of their bargain.

He could never give his heart again. It had died with his wife.

Chapter 1

St. Louis
March 1887

The telegram burned a hole in her skirt pocket, its message brusque and to the point:

ARRIVING TRAIN WEDNESDAY AFTERNOON—CEREMONY THURSDAY EARLY—MUST RETURN COLORADO DIRECTLY—SLOAN MCCORD.

For a wedding arrangement, it lacked all sense of romantic flair, Heather reflected with dismay, and only served to increase her growing feeling of panic. On the morrow she would wed a total stranger.

She must be mad to consider such a step.

But if her head had once been filled with dreams of romance, she could no longer afford such luxuries. She had no one else to turn to. No one to depend on but herself.

A sheen of tears she couldn't repress blurred her vision as she made the final rounds of her school. It had taken her years, but the conservatory for young ladies had developed an exclusive reputa-

12

tion, where well-bred girls learned deportment, elocution, music, and geography, as well as how to figure sums and to set a fine stitch. The elegant little clapboard house was quartered in one of the better St. Louis neighborhoods—an endeavor she had begun with such excitement and optimism what seemed like a lifetime ago.

With regret and sadness, Heather let her hazel eyes sweep the comfortable parlor one last time, remembering the laughter and sorrows of the past five years. A fierce ache tightened her throat as she recalled the tearful good-byes of this morning, when she'd said farewell to the last of her pupils, a dozen girls ranging from ages nine to sixteen.

"Pray don't go, Miss Ashford, we don't want you to leave!"

"Mamma has been perfectly horrid! She intends to enroll me in Mrs. Underwood's Academy. Please, you can't let her, Miss Ashford. I'll die there!"

"Can you not take us with you to Colorado, Miss Ashford?"

Heather had faced their pleas and embraces stoically, refusing to cry—until the youngest presented her with an ivory lace shawl crocheted by all the students with their own labors. Despite an occasional uneven stitch and unsightly knot, the garment seemed beautiful to her.

She had lost her composure then, breaking down with a total uncustomary lack of grace and poise. Tears shimmered now in her eyes as she ran her fingers over the polished mahogany surface of the long-suffering pianoforte.

This chapter of her life had ended. She had been compelled to close her school, but she would not let herself see it as a failure. Merely, the time had come for her to move on. In truth, she would be grateful to have a strong shoulder to lean upon, to help ease the burden she had carried for so long.

And at least she would no longer have to put up with the carping of snobbish mamas, Heather thought defiantly, forcing a halfhearted smile.

Her smile faded as she remembered the telegram in her pocket. Tomorrow she would wed a stranger. Yet *she* was making the choice, she tried to remind herself. *She* was taking control of her fate.

Still, she had never felt so alone.

Caitlin's congratulatory letter gave her some small measure of reassurance. Her friend had staunchly vouched for her future husband's character, and told her something of Sloan McCord's past.

A powerful cattle baron who had carved an empire from the majestic Colorado foothills, McCord was known as a maverick. He was cherishing a bitter sorrow—the murder of his beloved Cheyenne wife during a bloody land war.

His tragic story had touched her heart, even though she'd also been warned of his darker side.

Heather had her own reasons for wishing to marry. Her father's recent death from heart failure had left her alone, with large gambling debts she felt honor-bound to settle. And her sole other choice of suitor was not a man with whom she cared to spend the rest of her life.

There remained only the task of convincing Evan of the soundness of her decision.

Squaring her shoulders, she found her charcoal-gray wool coat and slipped it on over her black bombazine gown, for protection against the chill of the winter afternoon. She was still in mourning for her father, and would have only a limited wardrobe for her wedding. The black bonnet she donned next was one she'd borrowed from Caitlin's Aunt

Winifred, and made her complexion look sallow and her hazel eyes far too large for her face.

Her hand trembled slightly as she locked the front door for the last time. Tomorrow the bank would take possession of the school.

Evan Randolf's bank.

Negotiating the icy steps with care, Heather turned west, toward home. Evan thought he had won, but he was due for an unpleasant surprise. And she would find more than a measure of satisfaction in informing him she would no longer be a target for his determined designs.

The street widened some three blocks later, to become a thoroughfare lined with barren oaks and flanked by rows of attractive false-front stores. Deep in contemplation, Heather had just reached the corner and started to cross to the opposite side when a commotion to her right jolted her from her thoughts: a woman's scream, followed by the pounding of horses' hooves. With alarm she saw a pair of chestnuts galloping pell-mell directly toward her, dragging a closed carriage. The team had no driver, but the passengers within were evidently female, their cries for help echoing with pure terror.

Momentarily frozen with horror, her heart pounding as the out-of-control vehicle bore down on her, Heather could do no more than raise her hands in an instinctive attempt to slow the panicked horses. She barely had time to register how fruitless and foolish her effort was before suddenly she felt herself being wrenched backward by her arm and flung to the cobblestones.

Too stunned even to gasp, she watched dazedly as a man wearing a wide-brimmed Stetson and buckskin overcoat propelled himself past her and lunged at the side of the careening carriage. Benumbed, she saw the superhuman effort he exerted as he hauled himself on board the brougham, into the driver's seat.

The desperate action seemed to unfold in slow motion. . . . His hat flying off in the wind, the man flung himself on the back of the near horse and, in a herculean feat of athleticism, stretched down and grabbed one dangling rein, while the passengers within clung fearfully to the straps.

Long miraculous moments later, he managed to wrestle the pair of chestnuts to a trembling halt, nearly a block down the street from where Heather lay sprawled.

"Thank God," she whispered hoarsely.

She exhaled the ragged breath she'd been holding and unsteadily struggled to her feet. Absently brushing her disheveled skirts with her soiled gloves, she moved forward to offer aid as other bystanders were doing. By the time she came abreast of the brougham, though, a crowd had already formed.

Onlookers helped the two female passengers—a well-dressed woman and a young lady—alight from the carriage. Bonnets askew, shaken and sobbing, they appeared barely able to stand. Their rescuer, after sliding to the ground with easy grace, had gone to the horses' heads and was speaking in a low crooning voice to soothe the animals' fright.

Arrested by the husky sound, Heather froze where she stood, her gaze transfixed by the tall, rugged stranger. There was something compelling about him, an aura of toughness and strength that stemmed from more than simply his height or lean, muscular build. His overlong hair was the color of dusty wheat and brushed the collar of his buckskin coat. She found herself staring at an unruly strand that curled around his hard, stubble-shadowed jaw—

The carriage's Negro driver came running down the street just then, apologizing profusely to his mistress for letting the horses bolt, even as he took a firm hold of the reins.

Relinquishing responsibility, the stranger ran a hand through his waving hair and glanced back up the street, as if he'd just realized his hat was missing. He started to turn, as if to fetch it, but the elder lady would not permit him to leave.

"Oh, sir . . . I cannot thank you enough. . . . My daughter and I were terrified!"

"It was nothing, ma'am," he replied, his voice low and edged with a natural, rough huskiness.

"Nothing! Why, I declare, you saved our very lives!"

"So brave," the pretty daughter murmured.

Heather concurred wholeheartedly. His heroic action had taken extraordinary courage. She knew of few men who would willingly step into the path of an onrushing vehicle, and fewer still who could manage to intercede so skillfully. He had very likely prevented a tragedy—and saved *her* from possible injury as well.

He looked reluctant to accept their praise, though, and murmured a brief pardon, obviously intending to take his leave. But the girl reached out a trembling hand and swayed toward him as if she might fall.

He had no option but to catch her. His hands came up to clasp her upper arms, supporting her unwillingly.

Heather could see why the girl might swoon. Lean and sinewed, the stranger possessed a powerful ruggedness that was unusual in the gentlemen of St. Louis. His hard, chiseled features were remarkably handsome, his sensual mouth clean-cut and bracketed by twin grooves, his complexion tanned a deep bronze by the elements. His unruly, sun-streaked hair looked as if he hadn't visited a barber in a great while, yet it was his eyes that were most striking. Even from a distance, she could see they were a light, startling shade of sky-blue.

Then, as if he sensed her watching, his gaze lifted slowly, meeting hers across the street. Heather found herself riveted by his stare. The cool intensity of his gaze unnerved her and made her pulse beat faster.

His gaze swept her form slowly, with a vague suggestion of scorn, as though he recognized her as the helpless, inept widgeon he'd rescued from the path of a runaway carriage. Heather flushed, hoping the wide brim of her bonnet hid her mortification.

"You are my hero, sir," the young lady murmured in breathless praise, demanding his attention.

Suddenly an ironic half-smile curled the corner of his mouth. It was the kind of smile that made sensible women do foolish things, Heather realized, one that softened his hard features with breathtaking effect and invited others to share his amusement.

He was evidently accustomed to females swooning at his feet. That rueful, rough charm called out to her, even across the crowded thoroughfare, and she found her heart skipping a violent beat.

"I declare, Mama, I cannot walk another step," the girl complained faintly, even as she gazed slyly up at her rescuer and fluttered her eyelashes at him. "You cannot make me get into that carriage again. I couldn't bear it."

"Is there a doctor nearby?" the stranger asked, his voice holding only the slightest hint of resignation.

"At the next corner," the girl's mother proclaimed.

"Then allow me, miss."

With little effort, he swung the girl up in his arms. She looked perfectly happy to cling to his neck as he strode off with a long purposeful stride, not glancing back.

Heather stood there a moment, willing her heart to calm down. She was about to move on when an elegant landau drew up beside her.

She needed no one to tell her the stunning pair of matched grays belonged to Evan Randolf. The wealthy railroad magnate prized good horseflesh even more than beautiful women, and his stables were the finest in three states.

Evan was a handsome man, with dark hair and eyes, fashionably luxuriant sideburns, and a well-trimmed mustache. When he opened the carriage door for her, she saw that he wore an exquisitely tailored fawn frock coat. But then, he was never seen in public without being impeccably attired. An acquaintance of her late father, Evan was a spoiled and arrogant millionaire who was saved from sheer ruthlessness by a genuine charm and a keen intelligence she knew better than to underestimate. Although he moved in the most elevated circles of St. Louis society and could have his pick of beautiful socialites, he had struck on the misguided notion that she, Heather Ashford, would make him an ideal wife.

Descending from the carriage with elegant grace, he tipped his bowler to her in greeting. "Are you on your way home, my dear?" he asked with a hint of a British accent that betrayed his aristocratic origins. "Permit me to escort you."

"That won't be necessary, Evan," Heather replied politely. "It is only a few blocks more."

"Please, I insist," he urged with a gentle smile that held every confidence he would get his way. And he usually did—through sheer charm and persistence. It was what made him so dangerous.

"I cannot leave you to trudge home in the cold, my dear, unaccompanied by a maidservant. Though I must say the chill has brightened your lovely eyes and put roses in your cheeks. You have been far too pale of late."

Heather bit back the response on the tip of her tongue—that she was no longer in a position to afford a maidservant. Or that Evan himself had been the one to encourage her father's disastrous gambling habits after her mother's death, so that he'd squandered whatever remained of his wife's inherited fortune at the poker tables.

She could have refused Evan's offer of escort, but she did wish to speak to him alone. And she preferred to do so in private, on her own terms. He would not be happy with her decision, and a displeased Evan Randolf was not a man to be taken lightly.

Reluctantly she allowed him to hand her into the landau and settled into the plush leather cushions. During the short journey, her companion conversed about general pleasantries, but Heather remained unusually silent, uneasy with his proprietary air.

The landau drew to a stop before the modest house she now shared with Caitlin's Aunt Winifred. Heather had sold her own home to pay her father's gambling debts, and was living off Winnie's charity.

"Will you come in?" she asked quietly. "There is a matter of importance I wished to discuss with you."

Evan smiled benevolently, as if knowing she intended to discuss his suit. He obviously expected a favorable outcome.

Winnie would not be home, Heather knew, for she was shopping for tomorrow's wedding breakfast, but Bridget should be. The young woman she'd employed in past years to help with her school was also living with Winnie until she found a new position.

Heather accepted Evan's assistance in removing her coat and hung it on the rack in the hall. She did the same with her guest's coat and hat, stored his gold-handled cane in the umbrella stand, and then led him into the front parlor.

The small house was not as elegant or spacious as the one she'd grown up in, but the clutter of lace doilies and sepia daguerreotypes and china figurines was attractively arranged to provide an atmosphere of homey cheer.

"Please have a seat. May I offer you tea?" Heather asked as Evan settled himself on the chintz settee.

"Thank you, I would enjoy some."

She had to repress the impulse to reach for a rope-pull and ring for tea, for Winnie's house was unequipped with such luxuries. Instead, she excused herself and went to the kitchen in the rear of the house, where she asked Bridget to prepare the refreshments.

Then, chiding herself for being a coward, Heather went upstairs to her bedchamber to remove her bonnet, an action she knew was only a delaying tactic.

She was reluctant to begin this interview, even a bit fearful. Not only had she refused Evan's suit more than once, but now she intended to wed another man entirely.

Evan Randolf was not accustomed to being

spurned. The British capitalist had made a fortune in railroad stocks and mining ventures and was intent on winning every battle he chose to fight. In this instance, *her*.

For a long time she'd thought his pursuit of her merely the action of a bored profligate. It was common knowledge that he kept a mistress, a flamboyant stage actress, and that he enjoyed sporting a different woman on his arm each evening.

But she knew now that what Randolf cared about was power and how to wield it to further his own ends. He fancied Heather as an ornament for his empire, and was not above using his vast wealth to pressure her to accept his marriage proposal—including taking over her late father's newspaper and buying up the mortgage for her school.

He'd mistakenly thought desperation would drive her into his arms, Heather reflected. He had offered to assume all her financial burdens, to protect her from worry and grief and settle her in the lap of luxury. And there *had* been moments during the past difficult six months when his offer seemed tempting.

Dismayingly, his determined pursuit of her had led to some unsavory gossip at first—when she couldn't afford even a hint of scandal if she hoped to maintain her school's exclusive reputation. One highbrowed matron had actually withdrawn her daughter from the school, before Evan let it be known he was courting her with honorable intentions, that of making her his wife. And of course then none of the other pupils' mothers wished to offend the future Mrs. Randolf.

Heather could not understand his obsession with her. Though her mother's family had been wealthy, she had never aspired to join the circles in which Evan moved, and made no secret of her discomfort with his scandalous life-style. Perhaps, though, her prime appeal was her reticence. Evan was not accustomed to being denied, and her refusal of his hand had only whetted his appetite for the chase. For several months now, she'd tried to walk a nerve-wracking line of warding off his pursuit without making an outright enemy of him.

But even had she not been discomfited by his character and his excesses, she had no desire for the role she would lead as Mrs. Evan Randolf—a useless socialite whose prime function was to host elaborate dinner parties and attend charity functions with self-important people. She wanted to do some good in her life, something meaningful. Unlike her mother, she wanted her most pressing decision to be more momentous than which gown to wear.

Taking a deep breath, Heather withdrew from her bureau drawer the letter Sloan McCord had written in a bold, slashing hand. At least being a rancher's wife would present all the challenge she could possibly wish for. More importantly, she could provide valuable service in exchange.

Reluctantly then, she returned downstairs to the parlor and went to stand near the hearth, hoping to draw warmth from the meager fire as she faced her guest. Evan was still seated on the settee, one leg elegantly crossed over the other.

"Evan," she began with less confidence than she would have wished. "I do not quite know how to put this. . . ."

Again that patronizing smile. "I understand, my dear. You have changed your mind. That is a lady's prerogative, of course. And in this instance, entirely welcome. I will be the most fortunate of men."

"No, you mistake the matter," she said hastily.

"I have not changed my mind. Indeed . . . but . . . perhaps you should read this."

It might be cowardly to let Sloan's proposal of marriage speak for her, but she was sorely lacking in eloquence at the moment.

She handed Evan the well-perused letter, and then watched his expression turn from boredom to curiosity, to disbelief, to outright anger as he read.

"I have accepted Mr. McCord's suit," she said quietly, wishing she were anywhere but here.

Evan's dark gaze rose from the letter to pin her with blistering force.

"I think I understand, my dear," he replied tersely, biting off his words. "This is a ploy to force my hand. You wish me to settle a larger sum upon you at our marriage."

Heather opened her mouth to protest, but he cut her off.

"You disappoint me. I never anticipated that you might resort to such sly stratagems. But . . . very well. Will a half-million be adequate?"

A half-million dollars.

Heather shook her head, desperation and dismay battling within her. "No, you mistake me entirely. I assure you, Evan, it is no ploy. I truly do not wish to wed you. A marriage between us would never succeed. I could not be the sort of wife you desire. You want a different woman every night—"

He waved an impatient hand. "This is utter foolishness. You are a virtual pauper. Do you honestly expect me to believe you would turn down so vast a sum?"

She clasped her fingers together to still their unsteadiness. How could she convince him she was serious? "I expect . . . I hope you will do me the honor of believing me. I am speaking the truth. I am flattered by your interest and sorry to cause you any pain—though I cannot believe your heart is truly engaged. But you will recall I told you from the first that I never desired your attentions. You chose not to take me at my word, just as you are doing now."

His hand slowly clenching, Evan crumpled the letter in his fist. "I have not wasted all these months courting you simply to have you make me a laughingstock."

"That was not my intention—"

He rose abruptly. Flinging the letter to the floor, he took a stride toward her. "I was willing to offer you *marriage*. I have never offered my hand to any woman, and you think to spurn me?"

Heather swallowed hard, repressing a twinge of alarm. How could she make him understand? She might be the woman he thought he wanted, but she could not reciprocate his feelings. It would have solved her direst problems if she could have loved Evan, but while she bore him a wary respect, a life of ease with a man of his ruthless ambition would not satisfy her chief goal in life. It was only his wounded pride that made him react as he did now.

She shook her head. Perhaps it was *her* pride that was driving her to refuse him; heaven knew she had abundance of that human failing. Perhaps she was a fool to reject his magnanimous offer. But she didn't want to be bought and trapped in an elite but idle society. Evan would never have allowed her to keep her school after their union in any case. Saints forbid that his wife should *work*. She couldn't bear to be set on a shelf like some hothouse flower and trotted out for display upon occasion.

She considered Sloan McCord's proposal a far more equitable bargain. She could bring something of value to their marriage. It would be a worthwhile endeavor, raising his baby daughter. And she could aid his state senatorial campaign, as well. He truly *needed* her.

Evan Randolf didn't.

"It . . . is not you I am spurning. It is just that . . . we are too different. Our goals are too different. What we want out of life is not the same. I cannot be your wife."

Randolf took another step toward her. "I intend to change your mind."

Heather felt renewed alarm. "It is too late for that. I . . . am to be married tomorrow."

"*Tomorrow?*" For a moment he looked stunned. Then he reached for her, grasping her upper arms in a tight hold. "You forget one small detail, my dear. No one denies me."

His complexion flushed with anger, he resembled a spoiled boy in the midst of a temper tantrum. Except that Evan Randolf was no boy. He was a powerful man, and his grip on her arms was painful.

"Evan . . . you are hurting me."

"Indeed?" The fury in his tone frightened her. "Perhaps that is the answer. I shall have to teach you that it is a mistake to thwart me. If you think I shall simply let you walk away now. . . . If you think I will permit you to choose some common cowman from the savage West over me. . . ."

"Please. . . ."

He crowded her with his body. "I should have taken matters into my own hands from the first. Confound you, I could have closed down your bloody school anytime in the last six months, but I vowed to let you come to me of your own accord. No more!"

His arms forcibly drawing her into his embrace, Evan brought his lips crashing down on hers. Unprepared for his assault, Heather could only struggle impotently. She had been kissed only twice in her life, both times by young gentlemen her own age. Evan's violence stunned and frightened her.

When at last he raised his head, still keeping her imprisoned, his dark eyes glittered with anger and something else she was woman enough to recognize as savage lust.

"There is a remedy for your reticence, my dear. One night in my bed, and you will be singing a far different tune. Your paragon will not want you then. No man wants damaged goods for his wife. I might not even have you then."

Her heart leapt in fear at the look in his eyes. She tried again to pull away, but he was too strong for her, too fierce. "No . . . don't!" When Evan bent to her again, she fought back a scream.

She tasted rage in his kiss, rage and ruthless determination. Her hands came up to pummel his chest futilely.

She was suffocating; she couldn't breathe.

Through her daze, she heard a low warning growl, like that of a predatory animal.

Then suddenly Evan was no longer holding her.

"What the—" he uttered as he was wrenched off her.

Her release was so abrupt, Heather's knees almost gave way. Out of the corner of her eye, she watched, stunned, as Evan was flung across the parlor to land face-first with a thud on the carpeted floor, barely missing the tea table.

Feeling faint, she clutched at the mantel to keep from falling. Evan rolled over and lay holding his jaw, staring up at his assailant.

Shaking, light-headed with relief, Heather shifted her gaze to her savior.

Her eyes went wide. It was *he*. The bold stranger who had rescued the runaway carriage in the street a short while earlier. He wore his hat now, and the dark brim shadowed his eyes as he stared down at Randolf.

"I believe the lady told you to let her go."

"Who the devil are you?" Evan demanded.

The stranger tipped his hat back, his eyes as hard as ice. "The name's McCord." He shot a glance at Heather, who stood trembling, one hand still gripping the mantel. "I believe I'm the lady's fiancé."

Heather's heart seemed to trip over itself.

Her future husband.

There was almost a visible force about him. He looked dangerous and intense as he gazed fixedly down at Randolf.

Then Evan made the mistake of reaching in his coat pocket to withdraw a derringer. Swiftly McCord's hand brushed back the front flap of his buckskin overcoat to reveal the revolver strapped to his thigh.

Randolf froze as he eyed the Colt six-shooter.

"I wouldn't try it." McCord's voice was low, deadly, while danger jumped and pulsed around him like fire. "Where I come from, a man doesn't draw unless he's willing to die. And he sure as blazes doesn't manhandle a woman without her permission."

Wisely Evan eased the weapon back into his pocket.

"Now . . . I suggest you take your leave before I forget I'm in the presence of a lady."

Evan seemed to shake himself then. He appeared dazed, disoriented as he sat up. His gaze shifted slowly to Heather, where she still stood unsteadily by the hearth.

"Heather, my dear . . . forgive me. . . . I never meant to hurt you." He seemed honestly contrite.

She swallowed. It seemed incongruous for a man

of Evan Randolf's stature and elegance to be sprawling on a parlor floor in defeat. But he deserved worse after his unwarranted attack on her. Evan was no villain, but he had threatened to destroy her because she refused to become his wife. She would find that difficult to forgive or forget.

"Evan . . . I think it best if you leave."

"Yes. . . ."

She saw pain in his eyes, and shame. For the first time in her long relationship with him, she wondered if she might have mistaken his feelings for her. Perhaps Evan truly did feel a deeper attachment than possessiveness.

He climbed slowly to his feet. Giving her a long, last glance, he finally turned and quit the parlor, brushing past the young woman who was hovering in the doorway holding a tea tray.

"Oh, miss, are you all right?" Bridget asked faintly.

With a start, Heather realized the maid was watching the scene with wide-eyed dismay, and probably had witnessed the entire incident.

Heather raised a hand to her temple. The situation might have been farcical were it not so serious. It was fortunate she had already closed her school. She would never live down the scandal otherwise.

"Y-Yes . . . I'm fine. Thank you for the tea, Bridget. Will you set it on the table, please?"

The girl did as she was bid and bobbed a curtsy before withdrawing, leaving Heather alone with the fierce stranger.

Sweet heaven, her future husband.

The parlor seemed too small to hold him. He was more intimidating up close, the sense of hardness, of danger about him, overwhelming. Lean, muscular, and long-limbed, he radiated a vital intensity that made her feel fragile and acutely feminine.

Yet he had given her his protection. Twice. Surely he would not harm her?

She watched nervously as Sloan McCord let his coat close back over his gun. He resembled no gentleman of her acquaintance. His features were all sinewed planes and angles, while beneath high, hard cheekbones, his jaw was shadowed by a hint of stubble. And those eyes. . . . Those remarkable eyes were the color of blue ice, and yet at just this moment, they held concern, an incongruous softness that startled her.

She tensed as he took a step closer.

His gaze dropping to her mouth, he reached up to grasp her chin between a callused thumb and forefinger. His grip was light yet made her skin burn. Protective, infinitely tender, his gaze held a gentleness that reached inside her to touch her soul.

"You okay?" he murmured, his voice so low and husky it made her want to tremble.

She could only nod in answer, wetting her lips in instinctive response.

Almost absently his thumb brushed her bruised mouth with a delicate pressure. Heather flinched involuntarily at the spark he ignited with simply a touch.

At her reaction, he went absolutely still. It was as if a mask descended over his face. His concern suddenly vanished, to be replaced by cool wariness.

His hand falling away, he stepped back to put a less intimate distance between them. The silence once again became tense, awkward, at least on her part.

Sloan McCord stood staring at her from beneath the low-riding brim of his dusty black Stetson, assessing her blatantly with those remarkable eyes— eyes that were a shade lighter than the faded chambray shirt showing beneath the open collar of his coat. Once again they were strangers.

"You *are* Miss Ashford, I take it?"

Heather could scarcely find her voice. "Yes . . . I am."

"You seem to make a habit of getting into scrapes, don't you?"

Any hope that he hadn't recognized her from their earlier encounter on the street, when she'd worn her bonnet and coat, died a swift death.

Heather felt shame wash through her. Merciful saints, why did her first meeting with Sloan McCord have to be so . . . humiliating? Not only had he rescued her from being run down by a carriage, he'd saved her from a railroad magnate's possessive lust.

Mortification stung her cheeks. She was grateful for this man's intervention, yet ashamed to be so helpless.

His gaze, narrowed and measuring, swept her black gown, her disheveled bodice. She fought the urge to smooth her skirts or rearrange her hair, certain there would be a dozen wisps slipping their pins.

She should have offered her hand for him to shake, yet Heather stood uncertainly, clasping her fingers together.

"How . . . d-did you get in?" She stumbled over the inane question.

His hard, sensual mouth curled sardonically. "Your maid showed me in."

"Oh, of course."

He tilted back his hat further, his expression grim as he gave her the full force of his blue-ice gaze. "Tell me, ma'am, did I interrupt anything important with your gentleman friend?"

"No . . . Evan . . . he was merely . . . disappointed when I refused his offer of marriage."

McCord seemed to consider her reply. "Cat told me I had competition. But I have to say . . ." His mouth pressed together in a tight line. "My sister-in-law neglected to tell me one hell of a lot else."

Chapter 2

〜♥〜

It was all Sloan could do to rein in his rioting emotions as he stared at his promised bride. The longing he'd felt when he'd finally gotten a good look at her had been instantaneous, blinding, overpowering. Her familiarity was baffling.

She was his sensual dream lover in the flesh.

Except that in his dream those pale, champagne-blonde tresses had cascaded over her bare shoulders, caressing her luscious breasts, her taut nipples. Now that silky hair was sculpted in a sleek chignon. And now her face was no longer obscured by the night shadows of a dream, or the concealing brim of a bonnet.

He intended to throttle his sister-in-law, Sloan thought grimly. *Passable*, hell. If Heather Ashford's looks were merely passable, he was the king of England.

He was stunned by her beauty. She was exquisite in the cool, ethereal way of a goddess, with that delicate, oval-shaped face, that slender, patrician nose, that perfect, porcelain skin.

Lust coiled and tightened in his gut. He couldn't blame that bastard Randolf for wanting her.

Her eyes were alluring, the shade not quite

33

brown but the rich gold of sherry. Her lips were red and lush and velvety as rose petals. And her smile . . . soft, tentative, vulnerable. Sloan felt his heart kick against his ribs as she offered him an apologetic smile.

"Forgive me for my rudeness, sir. I . . . I'm afraid you find me at a loss. Would you care to be seated?"

Sloan swore under his breath. She was still quivering with fear, her cheeks flushed with mortification, yet she was trying to put *him* at ease. He would rather see her flushed with passion.

The thought came unbidden: *Would she make love the way she had in his dream?* The memory of her moving over him, her lush, silken body surrounding him, made him hard in an instant as another tide of unexpected, unwanted arousal hit him.

Damn, he'd gone too long without a woman. And this wasn't just any woman. Miss Heather Ashford was a lady of breeding all the way down to her lace drawers. She reminded him of royalty, with her gracious manners and her precise, elegant voice. Proud, aristocratic, no doubt very cold and correct. And as helpless as a newborn calf. She couldn't even cross a city street or fend off an unwanted suitor on her own. Sure as hell *not* what he was looking for in a wife.

Damn Cat for tricking him.

Sloan tugged off his hat and ran his hand roughly through his hair as he fought the urge to turn and run. What the devil was he doing here? What did he need with a blue blood on his ranch? He was going to kill Cat when he saw her.

Heather was experiencing similar sentiments regarding her friend as she floundered in a sea of agonized embarrassment. This had never happened to her before, this debilitating loss of composure.

Yet as Sloan McCord's silence deepened, somehow she found the courage to let her eyes graze his. He was giving her a thorough scrutiny, his look almost offensive in its bold assessment of her femininity.

She was supposed to *marry* this man?

Caitlin had plainly mislead her. As had Winnie. She had expected a gentleman. Mr. McCord was evidently no gentleman. His unruly hair, a rich tawny gold heavily streaked by the sun, was too long to be fashionable. His lean, bronzed features looked as if he'd never seen the inside of a genteel parlor. Yet it was his hardness, his intensity, that unsettled her. He seemed as uncompromising as the Rocky Mountains he called home.

A lifetime of reserve hadn't prepared her for Sloan McCord. Those light, breathtaking eyes were slightly narrowed, as if permanently squinting against the sun, but there was a coldness, a distrust lurking behind their emotionless gaze. And his hard, chiseled face was set like granite.

"Would you care ... for tea?" Heather asked, striving to conceal her distraction.

His sensual mouth curled, whether in amusement or disdain she couldn't tell. It had been the wrong thing to say, she concluded.

"I think maybe this situation calls for something stronger than tea," he said, his tone lightly mocking.

"I ... believe Winifred keeps some whiskey in the kitchen."

"Don't bother. Ma'am," he added almost as an afterthought. He made no move to sit down, although at least he had removed his hat. "You didn't seem to be expecting me. Maybe you didn't get my telegram?"

"Yes. ... I received it yesterday."

McCord's frost-filled gaze swept slowly over her again. "You don't look ready."

"My belongings are packed. And I have closed my school."

"What about Randolf? That looked like unfinished business to me."

Heather took a shaky breath. "Evan labors under a mistaken assumption. He thinks that because I'm indebted to him, he owns me." Her chin rose the slightest degree. "I happen to disagree."

McCord hesitated, as if debating what to say. Then he blew out a long breath and fixed her with those intense, ice-blue eyes. "Well, I've been thinking . . . I might have been rushing you. In fact . . . maybe this whole thing is a mistake."

"Mistake?"

When he remained silent, Heather said awkwardly, "Forgive me, I am not usually so dull-witted. What is a mistake?"

"Our getting married."

Her uncertain expression held a hint of distress. "Have your circumstances changed, then? Caitlin said you needed a mother for your daughter . . . and a political hostess for your campaign this summer."

"I do."

"Then you . . . find me . . . objectionable in some way?"

Hell, yes, Sloan wanted to reply. "Let's just say you aren't what I expected."

"What . . . did you expect?"

"Someone more suited to be a rancher's wife. Someone less . . . helpless, less upper-crust."

The faintest glimmer of wounded vulnerability shone in her beautiful golden eyes. "I know what it must look like, Mr. McCord . . . but despite present appearances, I am not entirely helpless. For the past five years I've worked for my living, running my own school."

Sloan felt something twist in his chest and did his best to ignore it. Duchess Ashford *did* look helpless. That ebony silk gown made her seem fragile, in need of a man's strength. She looked exquisitely delicate, like expensive crystal. And yet, unwillingly, he had to admire her aplomb, her dignified manner. She had recovered from an assault that would have had some ladies whimpering on the floor. And according to his sister-in-law, Heather Ashford was gamely scraping out an honest living—and repaying her father's crushing debts to boot.

Sloan slapped his hat impatiently against his thigh. "Sure, you've run a fancy finishing school. But knowing how to pour tea and play the pianoforte won't get you very far out West."

Her chin lifted. "I can cook and sew and care for a child as well as hold teas."

"That doesn't change the fact that I'm not the proper husband for you. I'm a cattle rancher. You're a blue-blooded city woman. I don't need a duchess for a wife."

"A . . . duchess? I am hardly that."

"Caitlin tells me you come from a wealthy family."

Heather pressed her lips together as he struck a nerve. "My mother's family was well-to-do, but that has little to say to my present circumstances. I have been living quite meagerly since my father's passing, I assure you. Most of my worldly possessions went to pay his debts."

Sloan frowned. "You say you still owe Randolf fifteen hundred dollars?"

"Yes . . . or rather, his bank."

He winced at the reminder. He'd been forced to

take out a mortgage on his ranch to raise the sum—an obligation that would put him in one hell of a precarious financial position until spring roundup when he could sell some of his beeves. But money, as big a problem as it was, wasn't his prime worry regarding Heather Ashford. The chief problem was . . . *her*.

He felt unaccountably vulnerable with her. He didn't like the feelings she shook loose inside him, with her grace and beauty and touch-me-not air. He felt like the rawest cowhand around her. He had no right to be lusting after this satin-skinned duchess. He owed more to the memory of his late wife.

His guard stayed up as he studied Miss Ashford closely. "You do realize that my daughter is half Cheyenne Indian?"

"Yes. You made that clear in your letters."

"Her half-breed blood wouldn't sit too well with most ladies."

"I assure you, it will hold no weight with me."

He made no reply, but one heavy, dark-gold eyebrow rose skeptically.

"You don't wish to marry me after all, is that what you are trying to tell me?"

Sloan hesitated. As a gentleman, he couldn't say such a thing. As a gentleman he wanted to take her in his arms and erase that wounded look in her eyes. As a *man*, he wanted to loosen that sleek knot and let her hair stream down all pale and silken, like it had in his dream. He wondered if she would clench and shiver around him in climax as she'd done in his dream. . . . Sloan drew a sharp breath as fresh desire knifed through him.

He cursed again, telling himself the ache in his groin would pass. What he felt for Miss Ashford was simply healthy lust, nothing more complex.

She had a cool, untapped sensuality any man would find challenging. He just didn't want the challenge.

Hell, his mind was only playing tricks on him. Along with his body. The duchess was doubtless a missish prude, nothing like his dream. She wouldn't possess the uninhibited passion of his late wife, either. Doe's favorite place to make love was a grassy meadow under the hot sun. This crystal-and-lace figurine would probably cower under the covers.

Yet he couldn't honorably back out of the marriage now. Still, that didn't mean he couldn't try to convince Miss Ashford to turn him down.

He took a deep breath. "What I'm saying is that maybe you should reconsider. A soft woman like you isn't cut out for the kind of life I live. Working a ranch is tough on the hardest folks."

"I am stronger than I look," Heather argued stubbornly. "And I am in excellent health."

His mouth twisted cynically. "Are you now?"

"Would you care to inspect my teeth, sir?"

He grinned unwillingly at the way she lifted her chin with evident pride. The impression he'd had of inner fragility was evidently misleading. The duchess had steel in her backbone. She was no shrinking violet. But that didn't mean she was cut out to be a rancher's wife, or the mother of his daughter. He felt a fierce, protective love for his child. He couldn't entrust Janna to a woman who couldn't even take of herself.

Sloan shook his head. "Good health or not, in one day I've had to save you twice. What makes you think you can survive out West if you have trouble managing here in civilization? What makes you think you can look after my daughter? I won't have time to devote to pulling you out of scrapes.

I sure won't be able to protect you every minute of the day."

"You won't be required to."

"Look . . . Miss Ashford." He took another tack. "I don't believe you know the whole truth about me. Caitlin wasn't completely forthright about my situation. I'm not wealthy like Randolf. I'm holding on to my ranch by my fingernails. I can't afford to support a wife with fancy tastes."

Heather felt anger lap at her, driving away her nervousness. "I am not looking for wealth in marriage, Mr. McCord. If I were, I would have accepted Evan Randolf's proposal long ago. Indeed, I fully intend to carry my own weight. I won't be a burden to you."

"Just having to keep you decked out in silk gowns will be a burden."

His words slashed at her pride. "I assure you, I do *not* expect silk gowns—or anything else besides food and shelter."

When he remained silently doubtful, Heather asked tightly, "Once and for all, are you withdrawing your offer of marriage?"

Feeling trapped, Sloan exhaled a breath of frustration. "No. I just want you to be damn sure about what you're letting yourself in for. The work is not only backbreaking, but dangerous. There's been a range war going on for decades."

"Caitlin told me something about the feud, but she said it had ended for the most part."

"Did she tell you about all the innocents who've died?"

"She . . . told me about your wife."

The pain was swift and sharp. Sloan shut his eyes so that the duchess wouldn't see his own private hell. He didn't want another woman to get hurt the way Doe had been hurt. He couldn't bear the guilt.

Yet if Heather became his wife, the violence could touch her.

She didn't look the sort to cotton to violence— which might be an argument he could use in his favor.

"I'm not blameless myself. I've killed when I had to, more men than I care to count. I have blood on my hands."

His frank admission disturbed her, yet she couldn't believe he could kill indiscriminately. She looked down at his hands. They were not a gentleman's hands. The hard fingers were work-roughened, the palms callused, injured— Heather winced as she saw the fresh blood welling there. The fingers of his left hand oozed red, while the palm was scraped raw.

"You do indeed have blood on your hands," she said somewhat tartly. "You must have hurt yourself when you climbed aboard that carriage. Those cuts should be dressed."

When she reached for his injured hand, though, Sloan pulled it back, keeping it out of reach. "I don't need a nursemaid, any more than I need a duchess."

Her head snapped up at that, and he saw the flash of fire in her golden eyes. She looked as if she wanted to tell him to go to the devil but was too well-schooled in social niceties to be so blunt.

Sloan pressed his argument. "You would do better with Randolf. He's more your style."

"I believe," she responded a bit testily, "that I am in a better position to decide what sort of husband Evan would make me."

Sloan shrugged his muscular shoulders. "Maybe so. But I know what sort *I* would make. You wouldn't be happy with me."

Probably not, Heather thought, although she gritted her teeth and restrained herself from saying so. Happiness was a dream she could no longer afford. As long as her debts remained, she would be obliged to settle for a marriage of convenience, with the chance to do some good in her life.

She would not beg Sloan McCord to take her, though. Nor would she be the one to back out. If he meant to withdraw his offer, he would have to do so without help from her.

"I am sorry," she replied coolly, "if you traveled all this way merely to dissuade me from marrying you, but I haven't changed my mind. The advantages to us both outweigh the drawbacks. Indeed, I see no reason we cannot have a relationship based on mutual respect and shared goals."

That seemed to stop him momentarily, but then his hard mouth curled.

"Some ladies have misguided notions about love." His bright eyes pinned her, challenging her. "I loved my wife, duchess. I'm not looking for anyone to take her place."

Her chin lifted again. "I would not *dream* of trying."

"And then, we haven't even discussed the matter of carnal relations yet." His tone held a faint hint of warning as he moved toward her.

His closeness brought with it the animal heat of his body. Heather froze, her senses assailed by his potent male presence.

When Sloan reached up to brush her lower lip again with his thumb, another strange, warm sensation jolted her. She had never had such a primal reaction to a man. He made her very aware of her femaleness. He made her feel as if her corset was laced too tight. As if she couldn't take a deep breath. Sweet heaven, she was acting no better than that foolish girl from the carriage—practically swooning at his feet.

"Are you afraid of me?" he demanded, his voice suddenly low and husky.

Perhaps a little, Heather reflected silently.

"Aren't you afraid I might hurt you?"

Slowly she shook her head. With an instinct as strong as it was inexplicable, she knew Sloan McCord wouldn't harm her physically. Caitlin had said he was a good man, and although he looked dangerous, even a bit uncivilized, his violence was somehow leashed. No, she'd seen for herself his concern for others . . . that flash of tenderness in his eyes earlier when she'd stood trembling in fear from Evan's assault, the protectiveness when he spoke of his daughter. . . . "A . . . man who would risk his life to stop a runaway carriage does not seem the kind to harm women."

"Appearances can be deceiving."

Her spine stiffened at the threat in his tone. He was testing her, she suspected. Trying to get her to back down. But she would not be cowed. "That is *my* point precisely. You are judging me based solely on appearances."

The sharp tension was back in the air between them. She could feel his intensity, the raw, powerful vitality that hummed around him.

His gaze bored into her, penetrating in a way that was disturbingly intimate. "Maybe you don't understand. I'm not interested in merely a business arrangement. You wouldn't be my wife in name only."

"I . . . am aware of that."

Sloan smiled. "Are you now? Are you aware that I'm a man of great carnal need?"

"What . . . do you mean?"

"Shall I be blunt, duchess? I'll want sex with you.

Regularly and often. Do you know what sex is? You'll share my bed, and give me your body whenever I want it."

She flinched at his bluntness, Sloan saw with satisfaction. He no doubt had offended her ladylike sensibilities. Then she raised her eyes to meet his fearlessly. He liked that even more.

"I am prepared to do my duty as your wife."

A hard smile touched his lips. "Duty? That's precisely *my* point. I'm not interested in a cold-blooded mate. Colorado winters get frigid enough without having an icicle in my bed."

The flush that tinged her cheeks told Sloan he'd struck a nerve. His ma, had she been alive, would have taken a strip off his hide for talking that way to a lady. But it wasn't bad manners driving him to be so crude. He was fighting for his own survival.

He kept up the attack. "You didn't appear to be enjoying Randolf's attentions. What makes you think you would enjoy mine any better?"

Heather felt herself tense nervously as he took a step closer. She had no experience with a man like Sloan McCord. But she knew instinctively, with a woman's elemental intuition, that she wouldn't respond to his attentions the same way she had with Evan. This man made her feel hot and shivery inside, with his hard-eyed gaze and his vital maleness. Surrendering to him would be like getting swept up in a dust storm, all heat and power and compelling force.

Deliberately she tried to brace herself for the impact. Heather was aware he was trying to intimidate her. Yet rationally she could understand his actions. Any father worth his salt would be reluctant to entrust his daughter's care and protection to a woman who'd shown the inadequacy she'd shown today.

But Sloan McCord was wrong about her. And he would learn that attempts at coercion only roused her courage and made her rise to the challenge.

"What makes you think I *wouldn't* enjoy them?" she retorted softly.

The taunting smile slipped from his features, and he stared at her hard.

"I guess there's only one way to find out," he said finally. His gaze never leaving hers, he tossed his hat on the settee.

His hands rose to grasp her shoulders then, holding her with a featherlight pressure. She could have pulled away had she wished to. Yet she didn't wish it.

She stood helplessly in his power, transfixed by his mesmerizing eyes. There was something hot and dangerous in those intense depths, something that inexplicably thrilled and excited her.

He moved closer, letting his body touch hers.

The shock was stunning. She felt blistered by his sudden invading heat, by the hard, masculine contours that branded her.

Her heart beat in a wild pulse of alarm and need as he bent his head to her.

Through a daze she heard him whisper against her lips. "You really think you're woman enough to handle me, duchess?"

She couldn't answer that; her throat was too dry. Her eyes fluttered shut as his mouth lowered slowly to settle over hers.

His lips were warm and hard, like the man . . . threatening, dominating . . . yet somehow gentle. In response, something deep within her body quivered in purely sensual reaction.

His kiss deepened into a bold invasion, his

tongue parting her lips and thrusting inside. The intimate intrusion shocked her for an instant. She hadn't known a man's kiss could be so blatant, so devastating. Hadn't known she could respond this way . . . that she could feel so weak and hot . . . so wanton.

Heather shuddered helplessly against him as primal instinct took over. Her body was aching shamelessly for him. The warm thrust and stroke of his tongue against hers made her tighten inside, made her breasts throb, while hunger spread through her with unsettling speed.

She gasped softly when she felt his hand glide down to cover her left breast. An underlying fire that was totally foreign to her caught her by surprise, yet she didn't want his tender assault to end. Her arms lifted weakly of their own accord to twine around his neck. . . .

When he pulled back abruptly, she almost cried out. She opened her eyes, disoriented, bewildered, to stare at him. She was shaking, her breath coming in soft pants, yet he appeared totally unaffected. His face was set like granite. The fierce sensuality she'd glimpsed so briefly had evidently been her imagination.

Her heart sank with dismay. His kiss had shattered her, yet she had only disappointed him.

Sloan stared back at her, holding her at arm's length. When she swayed, he tightened his grip to steady her. He cursed silently as desire twisted anew inside him. Her lips had been so damned soft and warm beneath his, the taste of her intoxicating, hot and sweet like wild honey.

Damn, but he hadn't scared her off. He'd only made himself hungrier. The instant he'd touched his mouth to hers, he'd been wild to get inside her.

The duchess had felt the same passion, he was

certain. He recognized all the signs of an aroused woman. He could still feel her trembling. Inexperienced or not, she wanted him. Just as he wanted her.

His dream woman.

The thought of having all that cool beauty and inner heat beneath him, around him, made his cock cramp and throb with need.

He sucked in a sharp breath.

"You sure you won't change your mind about marrying me?" he asked gruffly, his voice still husky with want.

Heather gazed up at him, not at all certain her knees wouldn't give out. Could she go through with it?

This was nothing like the tender union she'd long ago envisioned when she'd contemplated marriage, nor was this man—this stranger with eyes as hard as ice and a take-no-prisoners bluntness. She had dreamed of a man she could love, but Sloan McCord didn't want her love.

Despite his stark virility, he seemed emotionally untouchable. At least by her. His heart still belonged to his late wife, it seemed. She'd seen the flash of pain in his eyes, heard the rawness in his voice, when he spoke of his wife.

She, on the other hand, was merely a necessary complication in his life. He felt nothing for her other than perhaps irritation and disdain. He'd made it clear he wanted her only as a housekeeper and an asset to his political ambitions. And a carnal bed partner.

Heather took a step backward, where it was safer, clasping her fingers to quiet their trembling. She wanted to tell him to go to the devil, but she bit back the words. She had always possessed too much pride. Pride which she could no longer afford. She had little choice now. She had given up her school, and in the conflict with Evan a short while ago, she had burned the last of her bridges.

Besides, she was offering Sloan McCord a fair bargain.

"No," she said shakily. "I don't intend to change my mind."

His jaw hardened for a moment. Then he gave a sigh of resignation. "All right then. Where can I find Randolf?"

The unexpected question took her aback. "Why would you wish to find him?"

"To pay him the fifteen hundred dollars you owe him."

She stared. "You can't mean to pay the entire debt now."

"Can't I?" The blue of his eyes was almost chilling. "I won't have my wife owing money to another man."

"Mr. McCord. . . ." She shrugged helplessly. "I wasn't aware of your circumstances before, but now. . . . I can't allow you to be so generous. You just told me you couldn't afford—"

"I said I'll take care of it."

His reply, low and grim, put an end to the debate.

Heather felt her cheeks flush with mortification. She didn't like being in this man's debt. It seemed worse somehow than owing Evan Randolf. But she would pay back every last penny, she vowed.

Pride kicking her like a hobnailed boot, she said with great reluctance, "Very well. But I intend to repay you someday."

She was grateful when he didn't ask her how she could possibly manage such a feat but instead repeated impatiently, "Where can I find Randolf?"

"He's often at his bank on Tenth Street, or his house on Washington Avenue."

Sloan nodded brusquely and turned to pick up his hat.

Just then Heather heard the front door open. She gave a start and moved away from her visitor, putting a safer distance between them. Self-consciously she reached up to smooth her disheveled hair as Winifred Truscott called out, "Heather?"

"I'm in the parlor, Winnie. We . . . have a guest."

A moment later, a plump, gray-haired woman came bustling in, her cheeks flushed with cold as she removed her bonnet. Her eyes lit up when she saw Sloan. "You've finally come!"

The widow had met him on her visit to Colorado last summer, Heather remembered. Like Caitlin, Winnie had sung Sloan McCord's praises and supported him staunchly while promoting the marriage. And like Caitlin, Winnie had neglected to mention the most vital details when Heather had questioned her intently about Sloan and pressed her for information.

"Welcome, dear," Winnie told him warmly. "I'm delighted to see you at last."

She gave Sloan a motherly hug and offered her cheek for him to kiss—which he did with surprising willingness.

"Mercy, I heard about your heroics this afternoon from a score of people, Sloan McCord. The handsome cowboy coming to the rescue of two helpless ladies. Well done! I declare, you're just like your brother Jake, setting the town on its ear before you've been here two minutes. Speaking of your scapegrace brother . . . how is Caitlin and my grandnephew-to-be?"

The chiseled planes of Sloan's face seemed to soften at the mention of his sister-in-law. "She's doing well, if you call being big and round as a pumpkin well. She swears the baby isn't due for two more months, but she looks ready to drop any minute."

"She'll be fine, then. Ryan was a big baby, too."

Heather felt herself flush at such plain speaking, but Winnie seemed to consider it natural.

The older lady went on blithely. "You don't know how delighted I am about this match between you and Heather. We'll be family twice over now. I suppose you two have been getting acquainted?"

At the ensuing silence, Winnie looked from one to the other, apparently catching the undercurrents between them. She cleared her throat. "I see Heather has offered you tea, Sloan. Would you care to sit down?"

Heather interrupted. "I believe Mr. McCord was just leaving."

"Yes, I was," he seconded.

A frown appeared between Winnie's brows. "Is the wedding still set for tomorrow morning, then?"

Heather glanced hesitantly at Sloan, leaving the decision to him.

His jaw flexed for an instant, but then he forced a pained smile. "I suppose it is."

Looking relieved, Winifred beamed. "Splendid! You just leave all the preparations to me."

"I trust it's nothing fancy, Winnie."

"No, no. We'll hold the ceremony here in the parlor, at ten o'clock. I've invited just a few friends, with a breakfast afterward. The train leaves tomorrow afternoon, I understand?"

"At one."

"Do you have a place to stay, Sloan? You're welcome here, of course, although it *is* bad luck for a groom to see his bride before the wedding."

"I'm bunking not too far from the rail station. The Muleskinner Hotel." He settled his Stetson on his head. "I'll see you tomorrow morning, then," he said, tipping his hat to Winifred yet scarcely glancing at his bride.

Heather politely accompanied him to the front door. She thought he might leave without a word, but he paused with his hand on the latch, looking down at her.

"I'll be here tomorrow at eight sharp to collect your trunks and take them to the station."

Her heart sank as she met his hard gaze. He was so cold . . . so businesslike. Far from the sensual man whose passionate kiss moments ago had set her head spinning and her body aching for some unnamed fulfillment.

"They will be ready."

With no more than a brusque nod then, he left.

It took all Heather's willpower not to slam the door behind him. She felt herself trembling, whether in outrage or nerves or self-disdain, she wasn't certain. She couldn't explain the effect Sloan McCord had on her, or why a man she barely knew had the power to rouse such fierce emotions in her.

Heather returned to the parlor reluctantly, unwilling to face the curiosity in Winnie's blue eyes. The older lady had poured them each a cup of tea. Heather accepted her cup gratefully and sat beside her on the settee.

With her usual frankness, Winnie voiced her thoughts at once. "I declare, that man is potent."

Heather let out her breath. He was indeed. She was still shivering from his embrace. However would her senses survive a lifetime with him? She shook herself mentally, not wanting to remember the sensation of his body pressed against hers, or the taste of his kiss. Or her own wanton response.

It was shameful, the way her body had betrayed her.

She flushed as she felt Winifred's penetrating gaze on her.

"You're not having second thoughts, are you, dear?"

"A few," Heather admitted truthfully.

"It's only to be expected. All brides have wedding jitters. But this is the perfect solution for you both. It will solve your problems and his. You get your debts paid while he gains the ideal wife."

"Winnie . . . I believe you misled me about his financial situation. Mr. McCord isn't nearly as well off as I understood."

The older woman's blue eyes widened innocently. "Is he not?"

"No. But he insists on paying the money I owe Evan, even though he can't afford it."

Winnie considered that as she sipped her tea. "It's only right that a husband take responsibility for his family. And the McCords are a proud bunch. Reminds me of someone else I know," she added with a pointed glance at Heather. "You should let Sloan act as he sees fit."

Heather's gaze was troubled. "But it isn't his debt."

"It wasn't yours, either," Winnie said tartly. "It was your father's. If Evan Randolf was half the gentleman he claims to be, he would have forgiven you those debts. Instead he used them to oblige you to him. I think you should count your blessings and consider yourself well out of it."

Heather nodded slowly, remembering Evan's shameful assault on her earlier. At last she was now free of his control.

It should have been liberating. Yet all she could feel was a sense of trepidation.

Had she merely exchanged one problem for another? At least with Evan she had managed to maintain some measure of independence. But after tomorrow, she would be tied to Sloan McCord in holy matrimony . . . for life.

There would be no turning back.

"It will work out for the best, you'll see," Winnie murmured, patting her hand.

Heather wished she could be so certain. Her mouth twisted in a faint smile. "Mr. McCord doesn't believe that I'm . . . woman enough to handle him."

Winifred's eyebrow rose. "Doesn't he, now?"

"I expect he's right."

Affectionately the elderly widow tucked her arm into Heather's. "Well, we'll just have to do something about that, won't we? Gentlemen like innocence in their brides, but *ignorance* is another thing entirely. We can't have you going to your bridal bower without any notion of how to go on."

Winnie smiled, her blue eyes twinkling. "I think an intimate little talk about men is in order, dear."

Chapter 3

❧⟳♡♡♡⟳

Sloan lay awake in the darkened hotel room, only half listening to the unaccustomed night sounds of the nearby train depot and river docks. His mind was focused unwillingly on his bride-to-be . . . the sweetness of her taste, the lush softness of her body . . . her total unsuitability to be his wife.

Damn it to hell, how had he gotten himself into this fix? This time tomorrow he would be saddled with a woman he had no business marrying. And he was fifteen hundred dollars poorer to boot—

A creaking floorboard from out in the hallway alerted him to the presence of a visitor. Cautiously Sloan reached for his revolver, his instincts roused in warning.

A soft rap sounded on the door. "Mr. McCord?" an aristocratic male voice called out.

The accent was vaguely familiar. Sloan rose from the bed and opened the door. A gentleman in black evening attire and satin opera cape stood there, looking doubtful. He eyed the six-shooter with mild surprise.

"You are a difficult man to find," Evan Randolf said dryly. "I've made inquiries at nearly every hotel and tavern in town."

Sloan caught the subtle disdain in his visitor's tone. The Muleskinner Hotel was not the lodging a rich railroad baron would have chosen, he knew. But he'd settled for it because it was cheaper. Tomorrow morning he would visit the bathhouse down the street in order to spruce up for his wedding. Other than his boots and hat, he was still fully dressed, both to ward off the chill of the unheated room and to be prepared for any trouble.

"I'm a cattleman. I'm used to roughing it," Sloan replied casually. "Now that you've found me, what can I do for you . . . Randolf, is it?"

"Yes, Evan Randolf. May I come in?"

Sloan stepped aside, allowing his visitor into the darkened room.

"Would you mind lighting a lamp, so that we might hold a conversation in a civilized fashion?"

Sloan preferred to keep Randolf at a disadvantage, but he struck a match and set it to the wick of the lamp beside the bed. A yellow glow burgeoned in the darkness, casting flickering shadows against the bare walls.

"The Claridge or the Warwick Hotel both offer far better accommodations, you know," Randolf drawled in that same mocking tone.

"Have a seat," Sloan replied, ignoring the comment. He gestured toward the single chair in the room, a wooden rocker.

There was a moment's hesitation before Randolf gave a grudging sigh and moved forward to settle there. Sloan took the bed. He propped his back against the wall while keeping his revolver in his lap.

"I understand you visited my bank today and made a payment in Miss Ashford's name, to close out her account."

"What if I did?" Sloan said unhelpfully.

Evan Randolf's dark eyes narrowed slightly. "I've made inquiries by telegram about you, sir. And I must say I am . . . concerned by what I discovered."

"Are you now." It wasn't a question.

"Indeed. You are in rather difficult financial straits, which undoubtedly will grow worse if the cattle markets collapse this spring, as many expect."

"I hardly think my finances are your concern, Randolf," Sloan said softly, keeping his anger tightly leashed.

"You plan to marry the woman I love. Therefore I'm making it my business. You can ill-afford to lose such a sum— But I did not come to quarrel with you. I am here to put a proposition before you."

"I'm listening."

"As I understand it, your prospective union with Miss Ashford is but a marriage of convenience. I propose to make it more convenient for you to terminate the arrangement than to execute it."

Sloan waited in silence for him to continue.

"I am a very wealthy man, Mr. McCord. What would it take to persuade you to return to Colorado alone? Without holding the ceremony? Would a hundred thousand dollars be sufficient?"

Sloan raised an eyebrow. "Would you perhaps be offering me a *bribe?*"

"I prefer to think of it as an investment. We are both rivals for Miss Ashford's hand. And I do not like to lose."

His mouth curled in genuine amusement. "You really expect me to sneak out of town and leave my bride waiting at the altar?"

"I can make your apologies to Miss Ashford. She need only know that you changed your mind."

For an instant, Sloan even considered the proposition. Reneging on the marriage would solve his immediate problems. He could pay back the bank, and he wouldn't be shackled to a tea-and-china duchess for life. There was no denying Heather Ashford was the wrong wife for him.

But then he remembered the proud lift of her chin, the defiant flash of her golden eyes, and he shook his head. "I can see why she was disinclined to marry you if you throw your weight around with her like this," he said, amused. "Tell me, Randolf, did you try to buy her, too?"

The baron's jaw tightened. "I should think carefully before you refuse me, Mr. McCord."

"I don't need to think about it. You can keep your money. I've given my word. Where I come from, that means something."

The baron took a deep breath. "My motives are not merely selfish. I can offer her the life she deserves. Tell me, Mr. McCord, can you say the same?"

Sloan shrugged. "I can offer her the life she *wants*. That should be enough. It's her choice to make, and I think she's made it."

Randolf's dark eyes smoldered with fury at being thwarted, and Sloan knew he'd made an enemy of the man.

"I give you fair warning," the baron said softly. "I intend to follow your affairs closely. You had best take exquisite care of her, or you will have me to answer to."

Sloan wisely kept silent.

Randolf rose to his feet. "Don't bother to exert yourself," he remarked. "I can show myself out."

With the air of a man struggling to contain his anger, he turned and let himself from the room. The door shut quietly behind him.

Sloan muttered an oath, then ran a hand roughly through his hair. He had sealed his fate with his refusal. He would have to marry Duchess Ashford now. He was not about to leave her to the likes of Evan Randolf.

But now at least he could understand her determination to hold him to their bargain. Hell, he could almost sympathize with her.

She was so eager to be free of Randolf, she was willing to marry a stranger who didn't want her.

Her wedding was not likely to make the society columns, Heather reflected somberly as she took her place beside the groom. The event was too small, too quiet and informal to merit attention.

It was to be a brief ceremony, with only a minister and her closest friends in attendance. Heather was glad for the simplicity, not certain she could bear the turmoil of a large crowd. Outwardly, she knew, she appeared calm and controlled, yet her heart hammered as if she'd run a quarter-mile race to the altar.

Sloan McCord stood tall and intimidating beside her, the most prominent figure in the hushed parlor. At least he was clean-shaven now, as well as appropriately attired in a tailored, dark-gray suit, starched white shirt, and string tie. He looked dismayingly handsome, with his lean, muscular frame and rugged features. Handsome enough to make her breath catch.

Yet those striking blue eyes held a hard touch of frost. He'd said perhaps three words to her since his arrival. It had remained for Winnie to keep the small company entertained with pleasant chatter and reminiscences.

Heather's three friends had seemed surprisingly awed and fascinated by her betrothed and disappointed by his insistence on catching the next train back to Colorado. Heather had been forced to explain that Sloan wished to return to his daughter and his ranch. She couldn't, however, help but resent him a little for rushing her through the ceremony. Even if at the same time she wanted to get it over and done with.

Her friends had exclaimed in delight over her wedding dress, a Worth gown from Paris which had belonged to her mother. Designed for a fashionable society wedding in New York, the fabulous full-skirted creation was made of ivory satin with an exquisite lace bodice and train, as well as a gossamer veil to crown her upswept hair.

Sloan McCord's disapproval of it was rather evident, however. And his hard, handsome face was set like granite as she murmured the words that would make her his wife. When she stole another glance at him, Heather felt her heart sink.

She should feel excitement on this, the most special day in a woman's life. Excitement and hope and delight. Yet all she felt was trepidation.

She wished her father could have been present, and her mother as well. But were her father still alive, she would never have come to this difficult turning point in her life. And her mother had succumbed to an epidemic of pneumonia when Heather was fourteen, which had begun her father's downhill spiral into despair—

Realizing how negative and disjointed her thoughts had become, Heather raised her chin and stiffened her spine. Women had been making this sort of bargain for centuries. She would not start complaining about her lot now.

A short while later she heard the minister pronounce them man and wife and give the groom permission to kiss the bride. Heather turned slowly, as if in a daze.

When her new husband raised her veil, her heart seemed to stop beating. She had almost forgotten this hard man's intensity, his potency. For a moment those mesmerizing ice-blue eyes held hers in cool challenge.

Heather felt herself tense with nerves. She was too aware of Sloan's body, the size and strength of it, the heat of his nearness.

The memory of his last devastating embrace.

She held her breath, wondering if he might repeat the episode, out of spite. She wouldn't put it past him to create a scene to publicly embarrass her by forcing his passionate attentions on her rather than the chaste salutation expected of him.

The brush of his lips on hers, however, was remote and impersonal, and blessedly brief.

It was a further relief to be able to turn away and receive the congratulations of her friends.

Winnie was smiling through tears as she hugged Heather fervently. "I am so happy for you, dear," she whispered. "This will be for the best, you'll see."

At the moment, Heather could see nothing of the kind, but she forced a smile and let Winnie lead the way to the dining room.

The wedding breakfast was delicious—ham and fried chicken and flaky croissants, hothouse strawberries, and clotted cream. Heather, however, scarcely tasted a bite as she sat beside her new husband at the lace-covered dining table. From time to time she glanced covertly at Sloan.

Her mother would not have approved of him, although her father might. Charles Ashford had liked independent, strong-minded men.

Her own feelings were more nebulous and confused. Despite his remoteness toward her, she felt an attraction she could not explain. She was drawn to Sloan McCord against her will. There was something about him that called to her, something untamed and elemental.

He had a similar effect on other females, apparently. To her dismay, her friends sat awed and spellbound as Sloan politely described some of the sights out West and recounted the dangers of a cattle drive.

The breakfast was concluded with coffee and slices of wedding cake—an iced confection crowned with a delicate china figurine of a bridal couple. Afterward, the female guests rose to help Winnie clear the table, while the minister departed.

Heather found herself momentarily alone with her new husband. She risked a glance at him, wondering if he felt as strange and awkward as she did. His expression was unsmiling, with no sign of warmth in those remarkable eyes.

"Do you need help to finish packing?" he asked without inflection.

"No, I can manage, thank you."

"I'll harness Winnie's buggy and wait for you outside, then."

Heather heaved a soft sigh as she watched him leave. If their marriage was to be this chilly, this polite and distant, the years ahead would be long indeed.

Sloan escaped the stifling atmosphere of the house for the chill of the winter air. Out on the porch, he took a deep gulp as he struggled to breathe.

The ache in his chest had started this morning even before he'd laid eyes on his stunning bride— an ache that had only grown tighter as the minister droned the fateful words that would bind him to Heather Ashford in marriage. The ceremony itself resembled his first wedding, but he'd felt none of the love, the joy, the intimacy he'd known the first time.

This time he had wed a stranger. They had less than nothing in common, starting with their social stations. Hell, that fancy wedding gown of Heather's must have cost a fortune, a far cry from Doe's simple white buckskin dress embroidered with beads. . . .

Sloan shut his eyes, missing Doe as if a knife were buried in his chest. But that part of his life had ended brutally the day she died. All he could do now was hoard his precious memories and try to make it through each day. With his new bride.

Sloan clenched his teeth. He badly needed a stiff whiskey, but he would have to wait till they boarded the train and he could find the smoking car. For now he was stuck, he thought bleakly as he headed for the livery down the street where Winnie's buggy and team were stabled.

The duchess was now his wife, for better or worse.

Surprisingly she did not take long to change. By the time he returned, she wore a traveling suit of black velvet relieved only by a small spray of dried white flowers on the lapel.

He collected her two valises and secured them to the back of the buggy, then forced himself to wait patiently while she said tearful good-byes to her friends. Since Winifred was to accompany them to the train depot, he helped the elderly lady into the vehicle, then did the same with Heather, before taking his own place next to her in the driver's seat.

With the three of them, it was a snug fit, and he

didn't like the close proximity to his bride. The sweet scent of her rose up to tease his nostrils, and he couldn't control his physical response as his loins clenched.

Sloan set his jaw hard. This woman was his wife now. He had a right to touch her if he wanted. But he didn't want to.

It was barely a half mile to the station. He'd bought tickets for the bottom berth of a Pullman sleeper, yet the conductor intercepted them as they started to board the train.

"You are Mr. Sloan McCord?"

"Yes."

"Sir, ma'am, I've a personal message from Mr. Randolf." When Sloan reached for it, the conductor held back. "Mr. Randolf told me to give it to the lady directly."

Curious, Heather accepted the envelope of hot-pressed blue paper, addressed to Mrs. Sloan McCord. She faltered at the strange title, but then broke the seal and read the note penned in a bold, elegant hand.

Mrs. McCord,

My behavior toward you yesterday was reprehensible and inexcusable, I freely admit. Indeed, I deserve to be horsewhipped. Perhaps it is too much to ask your forgiveness, but I would be honored if you would accept the use of my private car as a wedding gift, by way of apology.

I must respect your choice, my dearest Heather, though I fear I am not yet sanguine enough to wish you joy in your marriage. I can only trust he will be as good to you as I would have striven to be. However, I shall count myself your friend always

*and beg you to call on me should ever you find
yourself in need.*

*Yours forever fondly,
Evan Randolf*

Heather felt her expression soften. Evan was ac-
knowledging her marriage and asking her forgiveness, showing far more generosity than she
expected of him.

"What does he say?" Winnie asked.

Realizing both Winnie and Sloan McCord were
watching her, she looked up to find those arresting
blue eyes fixed intently on her. "Mr. Randolf
wishes to loan us his private car."

"How thoughtful," Winnie remarked.

"Tell Mr. Randolf," Sloan said to the conductor,
"that my wife and I cannot accept."

Heather felt herself stiffen at his peremptory
tone. "It is a wedding gift. He means it as an apology."

Winnie's brow wrinkled. "Actually, it might be
rude to refuse."

"Indeed it would," Heather insisted, "which is
why I don't intend to."

Sloan visibly clenched his teeth. "Then we'll pay
for its use."

Heather stared at him in bewilderment, but received only a cold glance in return.

"Can you see Mrs. McCord to her quarters?"
Sloan asked the conductor. Without waiting for a
reply, he turned and strode off toward the ticket
office.

"Oh, dear," Winnie said worriedly. "Perhaps
that was a mistake. I forgot how stubborn male
pride can be."

Heather repressed an even sharper remark, unwilling to discuss her conflict with her husband with the conductor looking on.

The conductor escorted them to a car toward the rear of the train. Once inside, Heather caught her breath at the ornate decoration. Gold wall sconces and gilded mirrors adorned the beige silk walls, while the brocade bed hangings and velvet chaise longue were hued a deep crimson.

"Oh, my," was all Winnie said about such decadence.

Heather could only stare at the huge bed, thinking of her wedding night still to come.

The conductor set down her valises. "The train will depart in half an hour, ma'am."

When he was gone, Winifred toured the car's length, inspecting the furnishings in detail.

"I must admit this is a treat for me," she said, shaking her head. "It isn't often I get to board an iron horse, and even more rare that I get to see such riches. That Randolf *does* have excellent taste—but what a waste of good money."

She kept up a trivial chatter to set Heather at ease, for which Heather was infinitely grateful. She regretted when the time came for Winnie to go.

They both shed tears as they clung to each other, knowing they would not see each other for a long while.

"I don't like to leave you like this," Winnie said, sniffing.

"I'll be fine, truly."

"I'll miss you dreadfully, dear."

"And I you, Winnie. I can never repay you for all you've done for me."

"Pooh, it was nothing more than you would have done for me."

When the train whistle blew another long and piercing blast, Winnie stepped down from the car and stood on the platform, hand raised to wave good-bye.

The smell of cinders hung in the air as the huge engine strained forward. For an instant Heather experienced a moment of panic as she wondered where Sloan was, fearing that he had neglected to board the train. But then she remembered how determined he was to return to Colorado right away. He would not have missed this train, even if it meant sharing the company of an unwanted wife.

With a sigh of resignation and perhaps wistfulness, Heather went to the car window to watch as the huge iron vehicle slowly gathered speed, carrying her to a new life. Filled with sadness and misgiving, she waved until her dear friend was out of sight.

Then she turned away from the window and sat down to await her new husband.

Chapter 4

He was a long while in coming. By the time Sloan deigned to join her in the private car, dusk had fallen. The porter had lit the lamps and cleared away the tea tray he'd obligingly brought earlier.

Heather was quietly reading while occasionally sipping a glass of wine to steady her nerves, which thrummed like the vibrating iron wheels of the train.

As she looked up, her husband of a few hours shut the car door gingerly, muffling the whistle of the wind and the groaning chug-chug of the steam engine. He still wore his wedding suit, but he'd draped his buckskin overcoat over one arm and carried his hat. When Sloan turned to face her, she recognized the half-empty bottle of whiskey dangling from his fingers.

Heather tensed. Sloan was staring at her watchfully, his eyes narrowed and cool. Filled with dismay, she forced her own gaze back to the leather-bound volume in her lap. Apparently he was still angry at her for accepting the use of Randolf's private car.

Without a word, Sloan tossed his coat and hat

aside and sauntered past her to settle in a crimson armchair, opposite the chaise longue where she sat. Heather caught the scent of whiskey and cigar smoke, not unpleasant, and tried to ignore it.

Several moments later, she started when his cool voice broke the silence.

"Care to tell me what you find such fascinating reading?"

She did not look up. "*Émile* by Rousseau. It is a treatise on education."

"In French?" His eyebrow lifted. "So, I married a bluestocking as well as a duchess?"

Heather felt herself stiffen at the derogatory term. "Merely because a woman possesses a measure of scholarship and intellectual curiosity is no reason to be disparaging."

"Your taste doesn't surprise me. I didn't think you'd be the type to prefer novels."

She shrugged. "It serves to pass the time—considering the present lack of congenial company."

At her barb, Sloan took a swig from the whiskey bottle.

"Should you be drinking so much?" Heather commented as she finally lifted her gaze to his.

His mouth curled mockingly at her question. "Not only a bluestocking, a reformer in the bargain."

"They mean to serve dinner in a short while."

"I know. It comes with the car. I paid for it."

She fell silent, but Sloan felt her gaze searching his face. Still riled at the unnecessary expense of the private car, he averted his own gaze to survey his surroundings. The fancy accommodations had put him further in debt, to the tune of several hundred dollars. It was masculine pride that had spurred him to refuse Randolf's gift. That, and a desire to quash the baron's efforts at manipulation.

He wanted to be rid of the man for good, to get him out of Heather's life entirely. Didn't want him having anything to do with his wife. Heather belonged to *him* now. Whether he wanted her or not.

She was still looking at him, her brow furrowed with concern. "How much did you spend for the car?"

"What does it matter?"

"I want to know how much more I'm obligated to you."

"Three hundred dollars."

She made a small sound of dismay. "So much?"

"You're the one who insisted on accepting it."

"But you didn't have to pay for it. There was no need."

"There was every need. I won't be indebted to a man like Randolf."

"Evan meant the use of his car as a wedding gift, an acknowledgment of our long acquaintance."

"No. He meant it to keep you bound to him. He still thinks he has a claim to you." Sloan's gaze scorched her. "You're my wife now, duchess, and I'll thank you to remember it."

Heather's spine straightened. "I thought *you* were the one who wished to forget it."

"I don't reckon I can manage that, considering I paid fifteen hundred dollars for the privilege of marrying you."

"How *kind* of you to remind me."

Their gazes clashed, blue warring with gold.

"I intend to repay every penny of my debt to you," Heather replied tautly.

Sloan's mouth curled with skepticism. "And just how do you mean to do that?"

"Perhaps I can take in sewing or mending, or tutor ranchers' children."

"You'll be too busy with my ranch and my

daughter to think about doing chores for anyone else. And come summer, the senate race will be starting."

"That may be so. But I have no intention of letting that debt hang over my head forever—or having you think I mean to live off your charity."

Fortunately for the sake of peace, two porters arrived just then bearing silver trays with their dinner. Heather would have preferred to eat in the dining car to avoid being alone with her disagreeable husband, but short of creating a scene, she would have to endure his company.

Sloan inspected the dishes the porters uncovered. Then, with a gallantry she was certain mocked her, he held out her chair for her. "Will you join me, darlin'?"

Forcing a smile for the benefit of the railroad employees, she rose and went to the small table, dismayingly set for an elegant and intimate dinner for two. Heather tensed as Sloan seated her. The weight of his hand on her shoulder was heavy for a moment, like an explicit demonstration of ownership. Then he dismissed the porters and took the chair opposite her.

The fare was ample and delicious—venison cutlets in mushroom sauce, pheasant casserole, sautéed root vegetables, potatoes au gratin, green peas, and for dessert, chilled custard pudding with stewed apples and French coffee.

She should have been hungry after having eaten so little at her wedding breakfast, yet Heather merely toyed with her food, filled with nerves and tension and concern about the night to come—as well as worry about the current disastrous state of her relationship with Sloan McCord.

Their marriage had started badly from their first meeting, and didn't seem to be improving upon further acquaintance, she reflected somberly. She found it difficult to maintain even a semblance of civility when Sloan seemed determined to keep them at dagger's point. It rankled to have him throw her debts in her face, especially when she was already smarting from the necessity of accepting his sacrifice. A woman of fierce pride, she had vowed not to be a burden to him.

Sweet heaven, this was not the bargain she'd anticipated when she'd agreed to the marriage arrangement. Nor was Sloan McCord the kind of man she had hoped to wed.

But then . . . it was too much to ask for a husband who cherished her with all his soul. She had relinquished that dream long ago. And she had made her bed, so to speak. It was now time to lie in it.

Her glance went to the huge bed draped in crimson hangings. She couldn't help but feel a twinge of trepidation.

Sloan saw the direction of her gaze. Clenching his jaw, he took a final swallow of coffee, then tossed aside his napkin and rose. "If you'll excuse me. . . ."

She gave him a startled glance as he crossed to the door. "Where are you going?"

"The smoking car," he threw over his shoulder. "There's a poker game in progress."

Her look of dismay made Sloan recall her father's disastrous gambling habits. "I thought I might win back some of the money I paid Randolf," he added defensively. "You can read your treatise. I doubt you'll miss me."

"Will you be coming back?"

His blue gaze sharpened. "You're not worried that I might try to skip out on you?"

"The thought had occurred to me."

"I'm a man of my word, duchess. I'm not planning to abandon you."

Dropping her gaze, Heather shifted the food on her plate with her fork. "Actually, I was . . . wondering about . . . appearances. How will it look if we . . . if you . . ."

"If I leave my bride alone on our wedding night? Who's to know that we're newly wedded?"

"I would know. I thought . . . you . . . we . . ."

"You thought we would consummate our union, is that it?"

Her cheeks flushed at his plain speaking. "It *is* customary for a married couple, I understand."

Sloan muttered a curse under his breath. With such unsettling feelings of guilt and disloyalty churning inside him, he'd hoped to avoid the consummation tonight—maybe give them both time to come to terms with the strangeness of this situation, this unwanted union. But in fact, there was no real reason not to go through with it. Randolf's car had ample space, where an ordinary sleeping berth would have been crowded. And the large bed was as inviting as any he'd seen, well-suited to the purpose of lovemaking.

Perhaps it *was* best to get it over with now. If only to put it behind them and help the duchess get over her obvious apprehension. She kept glancing at him like a nervous filly, like she expected him to tie her to the bed and rape her.

Hell, he was just as uneasy with her, Sloan reflected, though he doubted she would believe it. He'd never felt so uncomfortable with a woman; this proper lady with her elegant airs and treatises written in French was so different from his late wife. He didn't like the memories of the past the duchess dredged up, or his unwanted attraction for her. Didn't like what she made him feel, how raw she made his emotions.

And yet walking out on her now might be considered a bit cruel. She would doubtless find it humiliating to be left alone on her wedding night.

Could he stay? Could he take her body and bind her to him in marriage? Could he make the fact of their union irrevocable?

Truth to tell, it wouldn't really be a hardship to make love to her . . . except for the danger to his own defenses. He didn't *want* to be tempted by that white, silken skin, that lush, cool beauty of hers. He was scared as hell he would enjoy the experience too much, when all he wanted was to remain true to the memory of his late wife. Desiring the duchess the way he did seemed somehow traitorous.

He couldn't ignore the powerful need she aroused in him. Couldn't stop remembering their kiss yesterday, the way her mouth had softened and shaped itself to his . . . how they'd almost lit a brushfire between them. At the thought, his manhood began to stir.

Angry at his body's reaction, Sloan leaned back against the door and crossed his arms over his chest, determined to keep his hands to himself for as long as possible. "I suppose we *should* get it over with."

"If you don't wish to go through with the marriage—"

"What I wish is beside the point at this late date." Sloan cocked his head, considering her. "Do you know how a consummation is conducted?"

He intended to make this difficult for her, Heather suspected. "Not . . . precisely."

He seemed unsurprised by her inexperience, she noted. Yet thanks to Winnie, she was not totally unaware of what was expected of her. Still, she'd never before felt so vulnerable. She had no experience dealing with this situation, with this kind of man. A ruthless stranger who was too tough, too remote, to show much in the way of understanding or compassion or sympathy for her nervousness.

"However," Heather added stubbornly, "I am not entirely ignorant about . . . about the mating act."

One dark-gold eyebrow shot up. "How'd you learn? You read about it in a book?"

"No. Winnie advised me."

"Did she now? And just what did she tell you?"

"She said . . . to trust you. That you would know what to do. She said tonight . . . might hurt the first time, but if you were a . . . considerate lover, the act would be pleasurable."

"Is that all she said?"

Her flush deepened. "Well . . . she also said I should try to . . . give you pleasure in return."

Heather thought she caught the faint ghost of a grin. "I fail to understand why that should amuse you," she retorted tersely.

His expression sobered. "Believe me, duchess, nothing about this situation amuses me. I just find it hard to think of Winnie as an expert on carnal relations."

"Well, she seemed to know what she was talking about."

"And just how are you supposed to accomplish giving me pleasure?"

"She said . . . that you would show me."

Heather heard Sloan take a deep, slow breath. Then he exhaled in a sigh. "Okay, duchess. Come here."

She eyed him warily. "Why?"

"So we can get on with it. Unless you want this to take all night?"

Rising from the table, Heather forced herself to cross the car and stand before him. She could feel the train's vibration coming up from the floor, running through her limbs and heightening the sensation in all her nerve endings.

"I think maybe you should have the honors."

"What do you mean?"

"You kiss me this time—unless you're not woman enough after all."

He was taunting her, challenging her . . . intentionally, she suspected. He knew she would rise to the challenge. But at least it made her less afraid and gave her the courage to lift her mouth and press it to his.

He tasted of whiskey and his own highly arousing, masculine flavor. When he made no move to help her, Heather drew back to eye him with annoyance.

"I cannot manage it alone," she said stiffly. "Perhaps you might condescend to instruct me."

"You're doing all right." His hard, sensual mouth curved in a half-smile. "Give it a chance."

This time she increased the pressure of her kiss and felt a feminine flood of heat shiver through her in response.

Dazed at the pleasure she felt, Heather shut her eyes and savored the taste of him. How a man as cold as he could have such warm, enticing lips was beyond imagination. As the gentle kiss went on, she felt herself tremble. Her hands rose to his shoulders of their own accord, but then she hesitated, uncertain what to do next.

When she faltered, he whispered against her lips, "Open your mouth this time. Use your tongue."

"I . . . don't know how."

"Like this. . . ."

He proceeded to show her, the warm stroke of his tongue inside her mouth nearly making her melt.

"This," Sloan murmured, "is like what I'll do to you when I have you in bed."

His demonstration was explicit enough that she couldn't mistake his meaning. She could feel the hard bulge at his loins through their layers of clothing, could feel his hard belly and slim hips pressing against her. The rocking motion of the train only made it worse, for it rubbed their bodies together.

Sloan was keenly aware of his physical condition as well. He drew back to stare reluctantly down at her. "Sure you don't want to back out, duchess? If you mean to, now's the time."

In response, she unconsciously moistened her lower lip with the tip of her tongue.

Desire hit him in the gut. Damn, he didn't want this, Sloan thought defiantly. He wanted to remember Doe. Doe was the wife of his heart. *This* stranger could never take her place.

Yet it had gone too far to stop. His late wife was merely a fading memory now. Painful, poignant, yet distant all the same. As insubstantial as a dream. This woman was flesh and blood, lush, warm, and very, very real. The fever in his blood needed appeasement *now*.

"No. . . ." she said softly, echoing his thoughts. "I don't want to back out."

His sigh was long and slow as desire warred with regret and won. "We'd best take off our clothes then."

She froze, staring at him.

"Do you need help undressing?"

"No. It's just . . . the light. . . ."

He looked at her with something like tenderness

softening his hard features. "You don't have any charms I haven't seen before on a woman, duchess, but if it'll make you feel better. . . ."

Quietly he moved about the car snuffing the lamp wicks, banishing the harsh, revealing light, leaving only the one beside the bed burning with a low flame. "That better?"

"Yes."

"You don't need to look so worried. I'm not about to murder you."

With a skeptical smile at his intended reassurance, Heather turned slowly and moved away from him. Keeping her back to Sloan, she carefully removed her bodice jacket and skirt and laid them on the chaise longue. Her shirtwaist followed, then petticoat and corset, half-boots and stockings. Finally her linen shift. She shivered as the cool air touched her bare skin.

Gathering her nerve, she turned back to face Sloan. The remaining lamplight was still too bright to be merciful, and so were his eyes. They ruthlessly surveyed her as she stood naked before him. Every ounce of modesty she possessed was outraged, and yet she felt a strange excitement as well. The mere feel of his eyes on her naked breasts made her quiver with sensation, made her heart beat far too rapidly.

This man was her husband, she had to remember that. He had a right to look at her if he wanted. To touch her. To have her body.

He looked his fill, taking his time, while the silence stretched thickly between them, accentuated by the steady grinding throb of the train wheels.

He seemed entirely dispassionate. Yet despite outward appearances, it was all Sloan could do to conceal his physical response to her beauty. She had a perfect body, he thought resentfully. More perfect than his dream.

She was nothing like his late wife. With her ripe, white curves, her proud thrusting breasts, the pale curls at the vee of her silken thighs, his new bride was every inch a duchess, elegant and proper, ladylike and shy.

But she had courage, he'd give her that. She was returning his gaze defiantly, her chin raised at an angle he was beginning to recognize. He reached for his belt buckle.

He proceeded to undress slowly, first his frock coat, then his tie and starched linen shirt, and finally his trousers and long johns.

Heather watched with bated breath. His potent masculinity was even more apparent as Sloan shed the last of his clothing. For all his leanness, he was unexpectedly muscular, his naked torso roped with long, smooth cords that rippled when he moved. His arms and back particularly were bronzed from the sun, while the center of his chest was covered with a triangle of silky dark-gold hair.

She could not deny there was a wild, primitive beauty to his body. He had long, lean legs and a horseman's powerful thighs and calves, his belly ridged with muscle. . . .

Heather drew a sharp breath. Her gaze locked on his loins, heavy and aroused. Rising there from the swirls of hair was that pulsing awesome maleness she'd felt burning through their clothing.

A fine shaking seized her legs. Winnie had said a considerate lover would make the act enjoyable for a woman. But would Sloan McCord believe she deserved consideration?

His expression was shuttered, no emotion showing in those bright, compelling eyes, the hard planes of his face. When he took a step toward her, a wild sensation fluttered in her middle, a deep primal fear.

Sloan came to an abrupt halt. Her eyes were clear and huge, her mouth soft and vulnerable. He cursed silently. He'd spent half the night dreaming about that mouth, that softness. He clenched his teeth at the heavy surge in his loins. He could simply take her, with no emotion, no tenderness, no passion. A brief, impersonal coupling, all business. Or he could make her first time good for her.

Damn, but he really had no choice. He didn't want to hurt Heather. Didn't want her to fear him.

"I won't do anything you don't want me to," he murmured, his voice hoarser than he liked.

He stood very still, letting her take in every detail of his body, giving her time to grow accustomed to the prospect of nudity between them, aware that she was getting her first eyeful of a naked man. And he was a highly sexed man at that. Desire pulsed in his groin with a sweet, almost unendurable ache, yet he tried to repress it. He would have to go slow with her. He couldn't treat Duchess Ashford like a saloon whore. She was nothing like the experienced women he used to enjoy before his first marriage. She was nothing like the women of the Cheyenne, who found great pleasure in open, uninhibited sex, mating like wild animals.

Only when her look of alarm faded did he stir a muscle. Then silently Sloan drew down the brocade coverlet to expose ivory satin sheets. Then, without a word, he took her hand and led her to the bed.

She moved stiffly, and he could feel the tension in her slender fingers as she followed hesitantly. Yet she made no protest as he held the sheet for her to climb into bed.

Sliding in after her, Sloan untied the near sash of the bed hangings and let the curtain fall, enveloping them in semidarkness. When he turned on his side, he could see the soft gold-red glow of her skin cast by the crimson brocade. She lay watching him, clutching the sheet to her breasts, her eyes wide, bottomless pools.

"You're not afraid of me, are you, duchess?"

"Perhaps . . . just a little."

"There's no need to be. You were right. I'm not the sort to hurt women."

"Not intentionally, I suppose."

An unconsciously tender smile touched his mouth. "I promise, I'm not going to do anything you don't ask me for. Now why don't you relax and roll over."

"What?"

"Turn over. Give me your back."

She stared at him a moment, then warily did as she was bid. His arms came around her, drawing her close, into the warm curve of his body. Heather caught her breath at the stunning contact. She could feel Sloan's muscled body at her back, sleek and hard. Could feel his heat, his heartbeat.

He held her that way for a long while, cradling her, silent in the darkness. Heather remained rigid, flinching when his hand moved ever so slowly beneath the sheet to cover her bare midriff.

"Does this hurt?"

"N-No."

She remained tense under his hand as he began to caress her skin. He pressed closer to nuzzle the nape of her neck. "What about this?"

"No."

His hand slid upward to cup her breast. "And this?"

She could feel her nipple throb against his palm. "No, it doesn't hurt."

"Good. I don't want it to hurt. I want it to feel good."

He stroked her for a long time, until finally she started to relax. When he touched her shoulder, urging her onto her back, she obeyed helplessly, making no protest even when he drew the sheet down to bare her body.

Heather held her breath as he bent over her, as his lips found the soft underside of her throat. But when he moved lower to close his mouth over a tightly budded nipple, she gasped and clutched at his shoulders.

"I want you to see," he murmured against the fullness of her breast, "just how much pleasure your body can give you."

She was beginning to understand. She could scarcely bear the incredible sensations streaking through her at the feel of his hard, hot, arousing mouth softly sucking. She shifted restlessly at the vibrant heat that burned inside her. Never before had she realized how sensitive her woman's breasts were. Never before had she felt this fierce, pulsing ache, deep in the pit of her stomach.

He drew back, his eyes touching her more intimately than his hands and mouth had done. She'd been wrong about his lack of emotion. It was there, fiery and intense, not so much banked as carefully hidden. His raw sensuality was a potent force. Yet there was gentleness in him after all. His hands were tender, delicate . . . deliberate, as they stroked her with skillful rhythm. The welcome warmth he was arousing in her began to blur the edges of her fear.

Her gaze locked with his as his mesmerizing caresses moved lower. Then slowly his fingers brushed the golden curls crowning her thighs. Her body shivered in a silken tremor.

He smiled as her frown reflected her need and confusion. Gently he parted her thighs. "Open for me, sweetheart. . . ."

With his fingers he caressed her, stroking her to quiescence, till he felt her soft folds grow moist and slick, till her embarrassment gave way to a vibrating, throbbing sensation that grew and built.

When he settled his body between her parted thighs, though, Heather went rigid again.

"Easy now, easy. . . ." He whispered gentle, calming words until she warmed and softened against him. All the while his manhood pulsed between her legs. He remained unmoving, letting her become accustomed to the feel of his rigid arousal, allowing her to respond at her own pace.

Heather quivered as the heat and power of his naked chest pressed down on her, his flesh smooth and hot. She wanted to escape the threat he posed, yet something deep and primal pulled her to him. Her woman's body craved the maleness of him, his hard heaviness. Closing her eyes, she strained upward shamelessly, seeking his heat.

Sloan gritted his teeth, fighting the heavy throbbing sensation of his flesh. It had been so very long since he had touched a woman. Forcing himself to go slowly, he lowered his weight and arched his hips, pressing himself into her. Sweet Christ, she was tight.

Her eyes flew wide.

He saw the pain and panic in them, but he thrust inexorably, smothering her gasp of surprise with a deep kiss as he sheathed himself in her body. Then he held himself completely still, waiting for the pain to dissipate, waiting for her to feel the pleasure of a man's fullness stretching her.

Her breath was coming in shallow pants, yet

gradually it slowed, while her rigid body relaxed somewhat.

"All right?" he asked hoarsely.

"Yes," Heather whispered, amazed that she could say so.

He was staring down at her, his eyes intensely blue, burning and tender.

She shifted her hips tentatively and saw him flinch. "I . . . don't know what to do," she whispered.

"Wrap your legs around me."

She did so tentatively.

"That's right, honey, let me feel you move." He arched over her, probing deep.

Heather moaned, clutching at him. The pain was gone now, leaving nothing but a dark, secret pleasure. He was taking her someplace she'd never been before, somewhere brilliant and terrifying.

"Don't fight it," he said in her ear as she arched against him. "Let it happen."

Heather whimpered, colors and blinding light blurring before her eyes. It was like being swept up in a storm, unable to do anything but go along for the ride.

The first tiny convulsions swelled to shafts of fire. She strained against him, burning, pulsating, spinning away into a netherworld of shooting flames.

Her writhing frenzy nearly shattered Sloan's tenuous control. He clenched his teeth at the powerful hunger streaking through him, while her frantic cries filled the air. When the woman beneath him splintered into ecstasy, he groaned with a savage need held barely in check. At the rhythmic clenching of her loins, desire shot through his groin, white-hot and explosive.

Unable to restrain his agonized arousal any longer, he surged into her, deep into the tight, wet welcoming of her body. With a final groan, he thrust into her fiercely one last time, before shuddering and collapsing against her, his body pulsing inside hers.

For a long moment, while his ragged breathing slowed, he held her trembling form. Shutting his eyes, he inhaled her scent, silently cursing her for her desirability. Then he rolled away to lie on his back, staring up at the crimson canopy overhead.

The desire that had blazed between them had caught him off guard. Blood still surged thick and hot through his veins, while guilt knotted his chest.

He hadn't once thought about his wife. When he closed his eyes now, he saw a ghost with dark liquid eyes and raven silk hair. *Forgive me, Doe.*

Forcing his eyes open, he turned his head on the pillow, to face his new bride. She was watching him, her eyes large and questioning.

"Was that . . . usual?" Heather asked quietly.

"Usual?"

"That powerful. . . ."

She couldn't seem to find the words to describe the explosive fire that had ignited between them. Sloan shrugged, not wanting to acknowledge how unusual it had been.

"Did I do something wrong?" Her voice was soft, uncertain.

He cursed silently. What was *wrong* was him wanting this woman so much. He was grateful the shadows covered his reaction to her. "No. You did nothing wrong."

"But I disappointed you."

Disappointed him? Startled was a better word. The searing pleasure of their first joining had shocked him.

Sloan shook his head. There was a clear explanation for the passion that had ripped through him.

What he'd felt for Heather was carnal desire, plain and simple. A slaking of lust for a man who'd gone without for too long. Purely a physical reaction, nothing spiritual. It hadn't touched his soul. There'd been none of the tender joy, none of the overwhelming love that had filled his heart when he'd made Doe his wife.

"You surprised me, that's all. Ladies aren't supposed to feel such pleasure."

Her smile was soft, tentative. "But then, you are a great expert with ladies, I understand."

Sloan felt a fresh stirring of desire and a dangerous tenderness. Damn, but he needed to get out of here before he lost his head and crawled back between her legs and spent the night ravishing her body.

"I guess you aren't as cold and untouchable as you look," he muttered. Sitting up, he pushed open the bed curtain and swung his legs over the side, giving her his back. "You won't mind if I leave you now?"

His question had the effect he wanted; he could tell by her shocked silence. He inhaled sharply. "I've done my duty. And that poker game won't wait."

Heather flinched as if he'd struck her. Nothing he could have said could have hurt more.

She bit her lower lip hard, holding back sudden tears, as he stood and crossed the car to his clothing. Feeling too vulnerable, too fragile to move, she remained silent as Sloan dressed with swift efficiency.

He gave her one final glance, his expression shuttered and enigmatic. "I'll see you in the morning," he murmured before letting himself out of the car.

When he was gone, she lay there numb and bewildered by what had just transpired. Her husband—her lover—had walked out on her on this, her wedding night.

And Sloan McCord had called *her* cold.

He had a heart of ice, Heather thought bitterly.

She shut her eyes, willing herself not to cry. If not for his incredible tenderness and patience earlier, she would have called him cruel.

But he *had* been a considerate lover after all. Her initiation into lovemaking had been breathtaking. She was slightly shocked by the intimacies he'd insisted on, dazed by the strangeness of it all. The initial pain had given way to a sensation so intense she'd almost wept, a rapture so stunning she still trembled.

But it was Sloan's remoteness afterward that had left her aching. She'd felt his withdrawal from her as if he'd physically raised a wall between them.

She didn't know what she'd expected afterward. Perhaps for Sloan to hold her and cherish her and reassure her. To explain what had happened to her.

She hadn't known her body could take control like that. Hadn't known she could behave so wantonly, or feel such shameless joy. Hadn't known she could come apart in his arms. The shattering experience had left her shaken . . . and filled with impossible longings for her new husband.

Heaven help her.

Heather drew the pillow to her body, breathing in his masculine scent and calling herself all kinds of fool. She had to resign herself to reality. Their marriage was a business arrangement, nothing more. She had to learn to still the wild pendulum of her emotions. Had to learn to guard her heart more closely. She had already exposed much more of her vulnerability to him than she could stand.

Hardening her jaw with determination, she rose from the bed. Dragging the sheet around her body,

Heather went to the mirror which hung on one wall.

She didn't look like a wife. She looked like a woman who'd just been pleasured—wanton and wild, with pale wisps of her hair escaping their pins, her mouth slightly swollen, her skin flushed.

Her fingers wandered to her lips, where Sloan's kisses still burned like a brand. For a moment she closed her eyes and relived his taking of her, remembering the feel of his hard body against hers. Every line and plane of muscle had etched itself into her memory, never to be forgotten. His incredible tenderness had etched itself onto her heart.

The feverish madness that had seized them both had been remarkable; every womanly instinct she possessed told her so. She hadn't been mistaken. The intimacy of their joining had gone beyond the physical. For the briefest moment she had felt so close to Sloan . . . as if she were a part of him, and he a part of her.

But he was determined to push her away, to keep his heart closed to her.

Heather let out her breath in a sigh. Sloan McCord didn't want a true wife, she had to remember that. She had to crush the fledgling emotions she was beginning to feel for him and make the best of an awkward situation.

She had to uphold her end of the business arrangement—and protect herself from heartache, if she could.

Chapter 5

～っとの～

The Denver train depot was a bustle of activity despite the winter season, Heather noted with surprise. While she waited for Sloan to collect his buckboard from the livery and load her trunks, she watched curiously as passengers scurried along the platform.

The station seemed less genteel than the one in St. Louis, with fewer ladies and frock-coated gentlemen and more cowboys sporting low-brimmed Stetsons and spurs with six-guns riding their lean hips. The stockyards in the distance marked the terminal as a main cattle-shipping center, while the buildings boasted painted clapboard instead of brick.

It was perhaps colder here, as well, she thought. Snow covered the ground in patches, glittering in the bright afternoon sunshine.

Heather was grateful for the added warmth of the sun. With her emotions so raw, she'd slept little last night and was weary after twenty-six hours on the train, with the prospect of a thirty-mile trip to the McCord ranch in the foothills of the Rocky Mountains still to come. Sloan had warned her they would arrive well after dark.

Otherwise he'd spoken little to her since the consummation of their wedding vows. Shortly after breakfast this morning, he'd returned to the car and lain down on the bed to sleep. A porter woke him when the train was a half hour outside of Denver, and he'd shaved and changed clothes with scarcely a glance at Heather. It was all she could do to concentrate on her book. She felt bare, exposed, far too vulnerable in his presence, especially with him performing such intimate tasks, the way a real husband might in front of his wife.

That defenseless feeling rose again unbidden as she saw Sloan pushing through the crowd, his tall, lean body moving with athletic grace. When she stepped down from the train, carrying her carpetbag, their gazes locked.

"You ready, duchess?"

His expression was cautious, wary, distant. Heather was the first to look away. It hurt to see that remote, impersonal look in his eyes, as if their explosive joining had never happened. As if she'd never lain beneath his body and cried out with the wonder of it. She was still desperately fighting the emotions he'd unleased in her last night.

She had been a stranger to herself. No one had ever told her about the madness, the fever, the blindness of desire. She never expected to feel sensations so sweet, so powerful, that she would shatter in a million pieces. She never expected, either, to feel such conflicting sentiments for this hard man, one part of her wanting to burrow into his arms and reclaim the tenderness he'd given so unwillingly last night; another wanting to rail at him for shutting her out so coldly; another yearning to understand the deep sorrow she sensed in him, the complex forces that had made him the uncompromising stranger he was.

Taking her bag, Sloan led her to the buckboard and handed her up. When he considerately tucked a blanket over her skirts, she thought of those hands touching her last night.

"Thank you," she murmured, her face flushing from the vivid recollection.

"It'll be cold," he replied matter-of-factly. Climbing up beside her, he gave her a single glance before the brim of his hat shaded his face. "Jake and Cat will be expecting us. I sent them a telegram."

She nodded, trying to forget the memory of his hard fingers and soft mouth, of his heated lips on her skin.

Sloan slapped the reins and the team moved forward. Leaving the crowded depot behind, they traveled along streets lined with ornate false-fronted buildings and bustling stores and less refined saloons.

As they left the city, they maintained a mutual silence, Sloan concentrating on driving over roads patched with ice and mud, while Heather studied the scenery. The land surrounding Denver was flat prairie dotted with shrub, yet the snow-covered mountains seemed quite close, shining in the distance.

Eventually the level grassland gave way to rugged hills flecked with cattle and the occasional ranch. The cold air had a cleaner, sweeter smell here, it seemed, while the view from the ridgetops was utterly spectacular. Beyond the foothills the main range of the Rockies rose up in jagged splendor, their snowy peaks glistening in the sunlight, their slopes covered with frosted ponderosa pine and tall spruce and bare, white-trunked aspen.

Heather found herself staring in awe. It was an unbelievably beautiful country, splendorous and wild, with a sheer vastness that was breathtaking.

Once toward sunset, Sloan drew the team to a halt and sat for a moment in silence, regarding the panorama. Heather could understand his reverence for the untamed grandeur. The mountains had turned purple and gold as the sun slid down their massive shoulders.

When he glanced at her to gage her reaction, she offered him a quiet smile. "It's beautiful."

"God's country," he said simply.

A while later they heard the staccato sound of hoofbeats behind them. With one hand Sloan reached for the rifle stowed in the scabbard beside the wagon seat. He kept the weapon slung across his knees until the three riders, all older cowboys, passed with a greeting and a tip of their hats.

"Are you expecting trouble?" Heather asked in a low voice when they were alone.

"No, but the range war hasn't been over long enough to go around unarmed. I want you to always carry a gun with you when you travel."

Hearing his grim tone, Heather recalled soberly what Caitlin had told her—that Sloan's Indian wife had been killed by gunmen while simply driving home.

The road became rougher as it grew dark, with boulders and ruts and broken snow choking the trail. Sloan made frequent use of the brake on the steep inclines and had to dismount several times to lead the horses through particularly treacherous patches. Shortly, though, a full moon rose to bathe the countryside in pale luminescence, lighting the way. As they edged alongside dangerous precipices, Heather clung to the rocking buckboard, yet somehow she felt safe in Sloan's care.

The bitter cold was another question. She buried her face in the wool blanket as she found herself shivering.

"Not much farther," Sloan said sympathetically. "We'll turn off before we reach Greenbriar."

Heather nodded. Caitlin had told her about the town that was the local watering hole for ranchers and miners.

"Is Greenbriar part of the district you would represent if you run for the state senate?" she asked.

Sloan gave her an odd look, as if surprised she would concern herself with such details. "Yes. The district's large—stretches from a few miles back to twenty miles into the mountains, and nearly a hundred miles north to south. Part of the problem has always been balancing ranching and mining interests."

Some ten minutes later they left the main road and traveled along a rocky trail that wound through the foothills. The McCord ranch was nestled in a moonlit valley, at the base of a dark, pine-clad slope. Welcoming lights shone in the distance as they drove through a gate marked Bar M.

In the moon's silver glow, Heather could see a handsome split-timber house, two stories tall, flanked by corrals and outbuildings. A lantern illuminated the front porch of the ranch house, while wood smoke curled from several chimneys.

Sloan had scarcely pulled the team to a stop in the yard when a raven-haired woman came hurrying out of the house, her slender form now bulky with pregnancy.

Heather felt a surge of joy at seeing Caitlin, yet a bit alarmed when she negotiated the slippery porch steps in order to greet them.

Without waiting for Sloan to help her, Heather climbed down from the wagon seat and found herself drawn into her friend's warm embrace.

"At last," Caitlin exclaimed. "You don't know how much I've missed you."

"I, too. I didn't expect to find you here."

"We wanted to welcome you to your new home. Sloan, you should be roped and tied for making her endure such a hard journey," Caitlin scolded. "I'll do it myself if you don't bring her inside *at once*."

Sloan's mouth curved in a reluctant grin. "Yes, ma'am."

Heather's brows rose in surprise at their easy rapport. She suspected few people had the nerve to order Sloan McCord around, much less threaten him.

"You must be frozen," Caitlin remarked. "Come warm yourself by the fire. Supper's heating in the oven."

When Heather had collected her carpetbag from the back of the buckboard, the two women went up the steps arm-in-arm and encountered a man dressed in a chambray shirt and denims.

"Heather, this is my husband Jake—Ryan's father."

In the lantern light, Heather regarded the former outlaw curiously. Like Sloan, he was tall and rugged, with the same lean-muscled build and roughly chiseled good looks. His hair, too, was the color of dusty wheat, but his eyes were a vivid green, lacking the frost that glittered in his brother's ice-blue ones.

Just now those striking eyes were inquisitive yet cautious, as if Jake McCord intended to withhold judgment of her. His work-hardened hand, however, felt warm and strong as he offered it to her to shake.

Heather smiled. "I'm pleased to meet you at last. Caitlin has told me a great deal about you, Judge McCord."

"Call me Jake. Cat told me about you, too, but she didn't warn me I'd be getting such a handsome

woman for a sister." His easy grin was as unconsciously seductive as it was dangerous, with the potent masculinity his brother possessed in full
measure. "Welcome to the family."

"Where's Janna?" Sloan asked from behind
them.

"In your study," Caitlin replied. "She wanted to
stay up to see her papa and meet her new
mamma."

At the remark, Sloan went still for an instant. But
then he moved past them and entered the house.

At the urging of her friend, Heather followed.
She caught a glimpse on her left of a darkened parlor, with brocade furniture and flocked wallpaper
that looked surprisingly modern. On the right,
however, was where Sloan disappeared.

Her first impression of the study was one of
warmth and comfort and enduring solidness. Rus-
tic beams stretched across the ceiling of the large
room, while colorful woven rugs covered the floor
and bookshelves lined one wall. The furniture was
masculine, overstuffed tanned leather of black or
rust hues—far less formal than that in the parlor
and a good deal more inviting.

A cheerful fire blazed in the fireplace. The young
ebony-haired boy playing on the bearskin rug before the hearth jumped to his feet and ran to greet
them.

"Aunt Heather, you've come!" he exclaimed as
he threw his small arms around her skirts.

With a laugh, she returned Ryan's hug. "My,
how you've grown."

"Yes," he boasted in delight, gazing up at her
with his father's green eyes. "I'm quite big now."

"You are indeed."

"I have a pony now, Aunt Heather. His name is

Snoops, because he always puts his nose where it doesn't belong."

Heather ruffled his dark hair. "He sounds much like another mischievous fellow I know."

While Ryan chattered on about his most cherished possession, her gaze lifted to find Sloan. He had bent to scoop up a young child from the blanket in front of the fire. The toddler had straight, coal-black hair, with skin several shades darker than Sloan's and features that were decidedly Indian.

She was grinning happily and mouthing disjointed phrases like "Papa home" as she patted her father's hard face.

When she gave his cheek a faint kiss and said, "Love Papa," Sloan flashed the most incredibly disarming smile Heather had ever seen on a man.

She felt her heart twist, recognizing the tenderness he had shown her so briefly last night. There was no question that he adored his daughter.

Distracted, Heather allowed Caitlin to collect her coat and bonnet and gloves, but she kept her carpetbag and returned her attention to her godson. "I've brought something for you, Ryan." Digging inside, she gave the boy a wrapped parcel, which he promptly ripped open.

"Ohhhh," he exclaimed in awe at the painted toy soldiers. "Pa, look what Aunt Heather gave me!"

When Ryan scurried off to show Jake his new prize, Heather moved forward to meet her new stepdaughter.

The black eyes, bright and luminous, turned solemn when she spied her; like most children, the tiny girl was apparently shy in the presence of a stranger.

Sloan held her protectively while Heather stretched out her fingers, palm up. "You must be

Janna," she said softly. "I am very pleased to make your acquaintance."

Safe in her father's arms, the child gazed back at her curiously. After a moment's hesitation, the small fingers curled around Heather's slender ones.

"My name is Heather," she said, knowing it would be too much to ask to be called "Mama." "Can you say that?"

Janna shook her head and buried her face in Sloan's shoulder.

Not giving up, Heather sank to her knees and fished in her carpetbag for another parcel. "I've brought you something, too."

Sloan set the toddler on the floor but stood over her, watchful and wary. When Heather unwrapped a raven-haired doll with a porcelain face and blue calico skirts, Janna's dark eyes widened with delight.

"She's not as pretty as you are, I think, but she needs a friend. Would you like to be her friend?"

Nodding vigorously, Janna took the doll carefully and stroked her rosy-cheeked face. Then, turning, she reached up to touch Heather's pale hair, which was pinned back in a sleek chignon.

"Pretty," Janna echoed.

Heather smiled warmly. "Why, thank you, sweetheart."

Beside her, she could actually feel Sloan's tension ease; his relief was palpable. Yet she too was grateful that she would be accepted by his young daughter.

Just then Janna gave a huge yawn and rubbed her eyes.

"Come on, darlin'," Sloan said gently as he swung the child up in his arms. "It's way past your bedtime. Say good night to your aunt and uncle."

"I can put her to bed," Caitlin offered.

"Thanks, but I want to."

With another yawn, Janna mumbled " 'Nite," and, clutching her doll, allowed herself to be carried upstairs.

"I'll see to the horses and get the boys to bring in Heather's trunks," Jake told his wife, retrieving his coat from the stand beside the front door.

Heather flashed him a grateful smile. When he had gone, Caitlin said, "Come to the kitchen with me while I get supper on the table."

"I'll help you."

"No you will not. After the grueling trip you had, you deserve to be treated as a guest. Tomorrow will be soon enough for you to take charge of the household."

They left Ryan by the fire to play with his new toys. The large kitchen at the rear of the house was warm and welcoming, Heather decided. The copper pots and pans on the walls gleamed, the walnut breakfront cabinet shone with a high polish, while the modern range put out a steady heat. The rectangular table was set for two with white and blue patterned china.

"Sit down," Caitlin said, donning an apron. "We've eaten already, but I thought you might appreciate a meal of hot roast beef."

"I think I could eat an entire cow, hooves and all."

Her friend smiled. "Beef usually comes from a steer, not a cow. You have to be careful what you say now that you'll be living around cattlemen. A cow is only a cow if it's a female bovine which has borne two calves."

"Ah," Heather said wryly. "Thank you for the enlightenment."

She sat at the table while her friend went about

slicing the roast and arranging carrots and potatoes and gravy on two plates.

"That seemed to go well, your meeting Janna," Caitlin mused.

"As well as can be expected, I imagine. I'm a stranger to her. It will take time for her to accept me as a friend."

"I know she'll love you when she gets to know you. You seem to be getting along well enough with Sloan, at least."

Heather hesitated, frowning. "Appearances are sometimes deceiving."

Caitlin shot her a glance. "It's not easy living with the McCord men, I know."

"Sloan wasn't at all what you led me to believe." Her tone was slightly accusing.

"If you mean you find him hard and intimidating, I won't dispute you."

"You might have warned me."

"Perhaps I hedged a bit, but it was for a good cause. If I'd told you the bald truth about him, you might never have agreed to marry him."

Heather bit back a retort, unable to condemn her friend for meddling. Caitlin cared deeply for them both, and thought her prevarications justified.

"You should at least have told me he couldn't afford to pay my debts. You made it sound as if his ranch was quite prosperous."

"It was, until recently. For twenty years the Bar M has been the biggest outfit around here. But beef prices have fallen hard the last couple of years. And it's been a brutal winter. Like a lot of the cattlemen, Sloan has already lost a quarter of his herds or more—and the snows aren't over yet."

And *she* had only compounded his troubles by driving him further into debt, Heather reflected with remorse. She sighed. "I know you meant well,

Caitlin, but I expect our marriage might have been a mistake."

"You're just tired, dearest. Things will look better in the morning, after you get a good night's sleep. Once you settle in, you'll like it here, I'm sure of it. It's different from St. Louis—wilder and harder— but this land gets in your blood." From across the kitchen, Caitlin gave her a penetrating glance. "This *is* what you wanted, wasn't it? A fresh start?"

Heather nodded. The loss of her father had been a huge blow, while the responsibility of repaying his debts and keeping her school afloat and avoiding Evan Randolf's maneuvering had proved a heavy burden. She had hoped to ease her grief by beginning a new life. . . . *This* was just not quite the life she'd expected.

"I'm not certain I'm cut out to be a rancher's wife," Heather replied unhappily. "Sloan doesn't think so, at any rate."

"You'll learn, and soon, I have no doubt. Besides, your ranching skills aren't what really matters to him. This spread is a lot of things to Sloan— mother, mistress, duty—but his daughter means more. If you can help Janna, he won't care if you don't know a cow from a steer."

Heather's chin rose. "Well, I mean to earn my keep—and to repay him if I can." She knew she was overly proud, but it was mortifying to be so indebted to him. Owing Sloan left her too vulnerable. "I don't like being so obligated to anyone. I've never been inclined to take charity."

"Good heavens, it won't be charity! Sloan will be getting the better end of the bargain, if you ask me. Janna desperately needs a mother—and Sloan needs you, too, whether he realizes it or not."

"Still . . . he's so . . ." Several descriptions came to mind: Forceful. Dangerous. Overpowering. He was all of those and more. "Frightening. . . ." she finished lamely. "I have no notion how to deal with him."

Caitlin set the plates on the range to keep warm and sat down at the table. Staunchly she took Heather's hands. "You're not really afraid of him, are you?"

She *was* afraid. Afraid of his power over her. In three days, Sloan not only managed to rake her emotions raw, he'd created a storm of rebellion and discontent within her. He stirred the deep lonely places inside her and made her ache for things she'd only dreamed of until now.

Passion and tenderness and love.

A pained smile twisted her mouth. She wasn't likely to find such gentle sentiments with Sloan McCord. He wasn't capable of showing them.

Caitlin was regarding her with sympathy. "I know he's not an easy man, Heather. You look into his eyes and see things you wished you never had to."

Heather nodded. She had felt it, that haunted bitterness beneath the cold mask. The bleakness.

"But you have to understand him. I told you about the range war, how long and bloody and savage it was. But Sloan suffered more than most of us. First he lost his father, who was shot in the back in a cowardly ambush. Then his brother was branded an outlaw and forced into hiding. Then his wife was assaulted and murdered by my father and his hirelings. It changed him, Heather. Sloan made vengeance his life."

"He said he had blood on his hands," Heather murmured.

"He does. Rumor has it that he killed my father for what they did to Doe, and I believe it."

Heather shivered. Sloan seemed entirely capable

of taking the law into his hands and dispensing justice unremittingly.

"There was a time when Sloan was my greatest enemy," Caitlin added seriously. "I think he might even have liked to see me dead."

"You seem to have put aside your differences now."

"Yes, but it took months of pushing and prodding. Making him trust me and accept me. It was like peeling an onion, layer by thin layer. No . . . more like prying open the rigid shell of an oyster. He would only budge a fraction of an inch at a time." Her blue eyes darkened with concern. "The pity of it is, Sloan is still only a shell of the man he could be. He won't give up the darkness. He can't let go of the past, especially his wife's death. I'm worried about him, and so is Jake."

Heather searched her friend's face. "What was she like, Sloan's Indian wife?"

"I never met her. But Jake did, years ago when he was recuperating from his wounds after the gun battle with my brother. I told you that Wolf Logan rescued him and took him to his mining camp up in the mountains? Well, Doe was Wolf's half-sister, a full-blooded Cheyenne. She was keeping her brother's cabin when Sloan visited for the first time. Jake said she had this quiet way about her . . . peaceful and serene like a mountain lake."

"Sloan loved her a great deal, didn't he?"

"So I understand. But worse than losing her, he blames himself for Doe's death. He believes he should have been able to save her. I think he can't forgive himself for letting her die."

When Heather remained silent, Caitlin squeezed her fingers. "Sloan is hurting, Heather. Surely you can see that."

She nodded. His grief was real; the torment she

sensed in him was a tangible thing. And he had shrouded himself in isolation and loneliness.

"I think you can change that."

"What do you mean?"

"If anyone can help Sloan, it's you."

Heather smiled wanly. First she would have to get past the granite wall of remoteness and reserve he'd erected—and that would likely be an impossible task. "I fear your faith in me is greatly misplaced."

"No," Caitlin said earnestly. "You'll be his salvation. I'm sure of it."

Supper was mostly a one-sided affair, with Caitlin and Jake and a chattering Ryan carrying the weight of the conversation. Afterward the two women washed up while the brothers went out to the barn to check on the animals and hitch up Jake's spring wagon.

"Thanks for seeing to things while I was away, little brother," Sloan said as they led the horses into the yard.

"Don't mention it. The boys handled everything."

Sloan glanced toward the bunkhouse where lights shone from chinks in the shutters. He kept a half-dozen cowboys, including a range cook, on the payroll during the winter months. Come spring roundup, that number would increase tenfold.

"It's good you made it home tonight," Jake observed. "Feels like a storm moving in. Probably hit tomorrow night."

Sloan nodded as he gazed out over the winter-ravaged land. His senses honed by past experience, he could smell the threat of snow in the air. The night sky was a sheet of black velvet studded with ice crystals for stars, while beyond the corrals, the foothills rose stark in the cold moonlight.

Despite the promise of more hardship, though, the sight was beautiful. The rugged majesty of the land never failed to touch him, no matter how brutal or dangerous. This was home. He'd had to fight for every inch of it—against sheep farmers, bigoted whites, the elements. . . . He could endure another snowstorm.

It was his marriage that he didn't want to face.

"So how are you cottoning to wedded life?" Jake asked curiously, interrupting his thoughts.

Feeling himself tense, Sloan forced himself to shrug. "Not so well. I think marrying her was a mistake."

"Are you complaining?"

Yes, he was complaining. It had hurt, seeing the duchess sitting at his table tonight, as mistress of his home. Taking Doe's place.

He sucked in a deep breath to ease the raw ache of memory. "Cat tricked me, saddling me with a tenderfoot. Duchess Ashford doesn't know a mule's tail about ranching."

"She seems a game one, though."

"Game enough, I suppose."

"And she seems to like kids."

Sloan nodded unwillingly. His fears had eased a bit, watching Heather's gentle smile when she'd greeted his daughter. She was good with Janna, he'd give her that much. He'd been worried as hell that she'd hold the same prejudice most white women had against Indian blood.

"She's not your usual type, I'll admit," Jake added with a fond note of humor. "A mite above your touch, I'd say. You don't find a combination like that often—a lady who's such a prime eyeful."

It *was* a puzzle, Sloan reflected, how a well-bred gentlewoman of such grace and elegance could arouse a man's lustful urges. His unwanted bride had the kind of looks that made a man think of rustling silk and fragile crystal . . . and hot sex.

She was a grown man's fantasy. Everything about her was profoundly sensual, from her champagne locks, to the chiseled perfection of her exquisite face, to her ripe, luscious body.

"You can't tell me you found your wedding night a hardship," Jake prodded.

"I can," Sloan retorted.

As if to make a liar of him, his body responded powerfully to the remembrance of Heather naked and writhing beneath him. He wanted to deny the fierce passion that had exploded between them, but the memory of how she tasted, how she felt, how she responded, wouldn't fade.

The consummation had been a mistake, he knew that now. He'd thought he could bed Heather and be done with it. Yet he hadn't counted on his own lack of control. Hadn't realized that after taking her, he'd want her even more.

Thank God he'd been able to mask his want. With the anguish of the past year, he had plenty of experience hiding his thoughts behind a hard face and expressionless eyes. Even if he couldn't detach himself from the dull throb of guilt that reverted in his chest afterward.

"I'm not sure I see what the trouble is," Jake kept up.

"She's not Doe," Sloan replied, his tone brusque. "That's the trouble."

Jake's gloved hands stilled on the harness. "You may not want my advice, big brother," he said slowly, "but I think Doe would be the first to tell you to let go of the past. She'd want you to forget about her and get on with your life."

Sloan's head came up sharply. *"Forget?"* His jaw

clenched. "Can you imagine forgetting *your* wife?" he demanded. "Can you imagine loving any woman but Caitlin?"

Jake shook his head. "No. Hell, no. But then, Cat's not buried under six feet of dirt and rock."

Sloan winced at the brutal observation. Pulling off his hat, he shoved his hand roughly through his hair, his jaw set like granite.

"Don't you think you're being a bit hard on her?" his brother pressed. "You brought her all this way. She deserves a fair shake. Give her a chance."

Sloan let out his breath in a weary sigh. Jake was right, he knew. He had no right to take his anger and bitterness out on Heather. She was his wife now and deserved to be welcomed into his home.

But he wanted no repeat of their wedding night, when his passion had gotten out of hand. He couldn't share his bed with her.

Or even his bedchamber.

That room was his sanctuary, the one place where he could find some measure of peace. Where he could remember Doe and the love they had shared.

The duchess could have no claim to that part of him.

She would just have to accept that.

They said good night to Caitlin and Jake and a sleepy Ryan, and watched from the back porch as the wagon rumbled away into the darkness. In the moonlit silence, Heather could hear the muted sounds of male laughter coming from the bunkhouse, could see her breath in the frigid air.

When she shivered, Sloan gave her a swift glance. "You'd best go inside before you freeze."

To her surprise, he followed her into the warmth

of the kitchen. "You must be tired," Sloan said evenly, bolting the door behind them.

"A little."

"You should go to bed. You can see the rest of the house in the morning."

"I would like that, if you don't mind."

"I'll show you to your room, then."

When he picked up an oil lamp, she searched his face, a rough-hewn sculpture of masculinity. Recalling his dark past, Heather fought the urge to lay her palm against his lean cheek. Something in her wanted to offer comfort, but she fought it down. She doubted Sloan would accept any such tender sentiments from her.

She followed him upstairs to the hallway and the first room on the right. It was a small bedchamber, with a brass bedstead and a white counterpane embroidered with blue columbines. A water pitcher and washbasin sat on the bureau, while a pile of woolen blankets were stacked neatly in a wooden rocking chair. A small cast-iron stove stood in one corner, giving off a welcome warmth.

"The house has no central furnace," Sloan said, "but this stove works well enough. And you can heat a brick for your feet if you need it. The bathroom's down the hall. I improved the plumbing a few years ago, so there's hot running water."

"I'm sure I will be fine."

"Well then . . . good night." He set the lamp on the bureau and started to turn away.

Heather's question, low and uncertain, stopped him. "Where . . . will you sleep?"

His blue eyes remained narrowed and cool, his stance guarded. She recognized the all-too-familiar aura of impenetrability about him.

"My room is across the hall. Janna sleeps there

by the big stove so she'll keep warm, and so I can hear her if she wakes up."

He meant for them to have separate bedrooms, Heather realized. She fought back the wave of disappointment that threatened to crush her and summoned her faltering pride.

"You have a problem with that, duchess?" her husband asked evenly when she hesitated.

Heather raised her chin with a touch of defiance. "Not at all. These arrangements will suit me perfectly."

Chapter 6

⟨~⟩⟨⟩⟨~⟩

She was up before dawn, even before Sloan stirred. Determined to prove her worth, Heather dressed quickly and made her way downstairs to prepare breakfast. She was standing at the range when Sloan entered the kitchen carrying his daughter.

Heather flashed Janna a gentle smile and surveyed her husband. He wore a faded chambray work shirt and denims, and his tawny, sunstreaked hair was still slightly tousled from sleep. She felt her heart twist.

"Breakfast is almost ready, if you would care to sit down," she forced herself to say easily.

He stared at her a moment, then slung his gun belt over a chair back and settled at the table with his daughter on his lap.

Janna clung to her new doll and watched Heather curiously. So did Sloan, for that matter, as he sipped the cup of coffee she poured for him.

He seemed surprised by the meal of flapjacks and sausage she set before him.

"What is the matter?" Heather asked hesitantly. "Don't you like flapjacks?"

The corner of his mouth curved upward reluctantly. "Yeah, a lot. I just don't eat them as often as I'd like. Doe never could get the hang of fixing them."

Heather bit back the response that came to her tongue. Doubtless she would have to become accustomed to being compared to his late wife. But Sloan would have to learn another fact as well. She was not Sleeping Doe.

She served him butter and honey for his pancakes and then saw to Janna's breakfast—a bowl of hot porridge sweetened with molasses and bits of dried apple mixed in. Caitlin was right, Heather thought optimistically. Her situation did look better this morning. She intended to make a place for herself, if not in Sloan's life then on his ranch. She would not live on his charity. She would salvage her tattered pride by providing something of value to their relationship. Starting with his daughter.

"Come, sweetheart, why don't we let your papa eat his breakfast? You can sit on my lap. Would you like that? I'll wager you're hungry, aren't you?"

With unexpected willingness Janna allowed herself to be transferred onto Heather's lap. Sloan watched guardedly as the duchess fed his daughter and pretended to feed the doll. She showed not a trace of awkwardness with the child, he noted with surprise, until he remembered that she'd helped raise his nephew Ryan from a baby. He felt his tension ease. Still, it hurt to see her holding Janna, her blonde head so close to the small raven one.

Sloan took a swig of coffee, strong and scalding just the way he liked it. She could cook, too, just as she'd promised—a far cry from the monotonous range food he'd gotten used to eating on the run during the past year.

"When we're through with breakfast," he said

more gruffly than he intended, "I'll show you the house."

Heather shook her head. "I'm certain you have work to do. I can find my way around."

A pleasant silence filled the kitchen for a time. Sloan cleaned his plate and then rose to strap on his gun belt.

"Can you handle a gun?" he asked, seeing her eyeing his Colt revolvers.

"I can shoot a derringer. My father taught me."

"A peashooter won't do you much good here. I'll teach you to use a rifle."

"Are you certain that's necessary—"

"You'll learn," he said brutally, not inviting debate on the subject. "My daughter will be under your care, remember?"

"My memory is quite adequate," Heather returned coolly, raising her chin. She might have surrendered any dreams of love, but she would not be Sloan McCord's doormat.

He shrugged on his coat. "I'm leaving one of the hired hands behind for your protection. Rusty will be within shouting distance if you need anything. And in case of real trouble, the signal is to fire two quick shots in the air. There's a loaded rifle in the pantry." Sloan hesitated. "Will you be all right here? I may be gone all day."

"We'll be fine." Heather smiled down at his daughter. "Won't we, love?"

Janna gave a toothy grin.

"What about dinner this afternoon?" Heather asked him.

"I'll eat with the boys out on the range. You could keep supper warm, if it's not too much trouble."

"No, it's no trouble at all."

He bent to kiss his daughter's cheek, then settled

his hat firmly on his head, his hard countenance shadowed by the brim.

Then, turning, he walked out the door, into the cold dark morning, leaving Heather to become acquainted with her new stepdaughter and her new life.

It was a pattern that repeated itself often during the following week—meeting for breakfast, then seeing little of each other until late at night.

A storm moved in that first evening, leaving a blanket of fresh snow covering the range. Before it hit, Sloan and his hands worked feverishly hauling hay they'd put up last summer out to the cattle. In a bad winter beeves were as likely to starve as freeze, for they were unable to get at the stubby grass beneath the heavy, crusted snow.

It took Heather only a day to discover how bitter a Colorado winter could be. When the winds swept down off the mountains, the snow swirled so thick she couldn't see her hand in front of her face. Even shut up in the house, it was impossible to ward off the cold. She wore three pairs of drawers and bundled Janna in a woolen suit she fashioned out of a worn blanket, complete with mittens and hood.

The frigid weather was only one of the grueling challenges of her new life. Sloan had warned her what to expect, but she discovered firsthand how hard ranch life was. And how isolated. She kept busy with the endless chores—cooking and cleaning and washing, as well as caring for Janna—but loneliness gripped her heart like a fist, especially in the long hours after dusk while she waited for Sloan to return home.

Janna at least was a treasure. Heather cherished the little girl, who had the sweetest disposition of any child she'd ever known. But it was a struggle to keep her own spirits up. She crawled into bed each night, weary and sore and heartsick.

She made no complaint, though, particularly to Sloan. She doubted he would offer her anything in the way of sympathy. Indeed, he might just offer to buy her a train ticket back to St. Louis.

In any case, he had his own troubles to occupy him—chiefly, trying to save his herds from the crippling weather. He seemed to be fighting a losing battle.

It hurt to watch his exhausting campaign against the uncontrollable elements, to see him bear his defeats in grim, stoic silence. Once or twice when he came home long after dark, half frozen and ravenous, she saw the vulnerability in the hard, shuttered face. In those moments something painful caught at her heart. She wanted to offer him comfort, but she labeled the feeling as foolishness and shoved it aside. Sloan would not want her sympathy, any more than he would give it.

She would not be his salvation, as Caitlin had prophesied. She would never have the chance. He was a man torn by a terrible grief, but he would never let her near enough to help him with the demons that haunted him.

When the snow let up later in the week, she met his ranch foreman and several of his half-dozen hired hands, including the range cook named Cookie. Some of the boys, Heather learned, lived in line camps—isolated cabins from which they patrolled the ranch's distant reaches, but the rest lived in the bunkhouse. There were countless winter chores to keep them busy. Besides helping the cattle stay alive by hauling out hay or driving the herds onto snow-free grass, they had to cut ice in water holes, bring in sick cows or calves, find strays that had drifted, repair corral poles and barbed-wire fences, chop firewood, mend gear ... an endless monotony of work.

The ranch hands seemed to welcome her presence and were eager to help her settle in, particularly Rusty, the tall, ginger-haired young man Sloan had designated to protect her and Janna.

"We're right glad you've come, ma'am," Rusty said shyly one laundry day as he helped Heather carry buckets from the barn to the kitchen. "Janna needs a real ma. Especially since Maria left."

"That was Sloan's housekeeper?"

"Yes'm, a Mex woman. But she had family troubles of her own to see to. All the boys try to help with Janna, but we can't take the place of a woman."

"You seem to care for Janna a great deal."

"We're all a mite protective of her."

"Have you worked here long?"

"Goin' on ten years, I reckon." He set down the buckets on the back porch and brushed a forelock of red hair away from his eyes. "Sloan's pa hired me straight from Texas, when I was still wet behind the ears. I was here when Sloan got hitched and when Ben McCord died and when Janna was born and when Miz Doe was killed. . . ." His brown eyes darkened.

Heather waited, wondering if Rusty would say more about the tragedy, but he didn't. Not wanting to sound as if she was prying, she asked a different question. "Janna is rather an unusual name, isn't it?"

"It's short for her Cheyenne name—Aiyanna. Means eternal blossom, or some such thing. Miz Doe's name was a lot harder to say. . . . E-naaotse mehe-vaotseva. Sounds like Natsy Me Vava." He grinned. "My tongue always got twisted around it. We all just called her Miz Doe."

Sloan himself was not nearly so forthcoming as his ranch hands at informing Heather about his past. True to his word, though, he found time to give her a shooting lesson. Heather thought she acquitted herself adequately firing a rifle. She was less proficient with a revolver; her slender hands had difficulty controlling the kick of the weapon. And she was hopeless with a shotgun, which nearly knocked the breath out of her. At Sloan's insistence, however, she learned how to load and use each type of firearm, and she paid careful attention when he showed her the half-dozen loaded rifles and shotguns he kept hidden about the house. The savage decades-old feud between cattlemen and sheep men had been over scarcely six months, and Sloan was deadly serious about her learning to protect herself and his daughter.

She also learned new skills vital to ranch life. Cookie taught her how to milk a cow, so there would be fresh milk for Janna and for making butter. In St. Louis she had always ordered milk and butter from the delivery wagon that came twice a week, but Bar M Ranch couldn't afford such luxuries. Her first attempt at churning butter blistered her hands, yet Heather was proud of her effort.

And no matter how weary she became, despite the frustrations that often rubbed her temper raw, she tackled her chores with fierce determination. She wanted to prove to Sloan she was more than a useless society ornament. And though he seemed reluctant to show any gratitude toward her, she suspected she at least was starting to earn his grudging respect.

Even so, Heather often sensed herself being compared to his late wife and coming up short. Sometimes she would find Sloan's ice-blue eyes on her, narrowed and intent, as if he were measuring her against the past.

She was nothing like Sleeping Doe, Heather suspected. In Sloan's bedroom, she'd seen a daguerreotype of him with the raven-haired Cheyenne woman. Her dark-skinned Indian features were more striking than beautiful, but there was a serenity to her that seemed almost tangible. In the scene, Sloan looked happy and at peace, with a glint in his arresting eyes that spoke of devilish mischief. He must not always have been the hard, bitter man he was now, Heather realized.

She spent long moments staring at the portrait, trying to fathom what had made the woman so special to Sloan. He clearly saw his first wife as a saint, and she, Heather, would never come close to such perfection.

The only time he truly let down his guard around her was when he played with his daughter. Only then did she glimpse the rare, brilliant smile he reserved strictly for Janna. Heather was always unprepared for the stab of envy that pierced her at that smile. She wished just once Sloan would look at her that way, as if she were the light of his life, the sun around which his entire life revolved.

Instead he remained wary and terrifyingly remote. Once he even frightened her. It was late afternoon toward the beginning of her second week in Colorado. She'd found a beaded buckskin coat in the corner of a closet, stained with what might have been blood. She was scrubbing the garment at the kitchen sink, using a recipe of Winnie's, when Sloan came up silently behind her.

Heather nearly jumped out of her skin when she heard his savage bark. "What the *hell* do you think you're doing?"

She whirled, startled to see the seething fury on

his face. "I was t-trying to clean away the stain."

He ripped the coat from her grasp. "Don't. Don't dare touch this again, do I make myself clear?"

Too astonished to reply, she simply stared. Sloan spun on his heel and disappeared upstairs without even stopping to greet his daughter.

On rare occasions, however, there were moments when they seemed almost like a married couple. It was always late at night in his study, when she would sew or quietly read while he worked on the account books. He had never actually invited her into the masculine domain of his study, but neither did he refuse her entrance. Perhaps it was stubbornness, or merely a way to ward off the stark loneliness, but Heather made a habit of retiring there after putting Janna to bed, to await his coming. Unexpectedly she found a wide selection of leather-bound books on the shelves that lined one side of the room, some with the McCord brothers' names inscribed inside, others which had belonged to their father Ben or their mother Elizabeth.

When at last the weather thawed a little, Heather met some of her neighbors. Several of the women came to call, bringing favorite dishes or small homemade gifts to welcome the new Mrs. McCord to the community. Heather found their open frankness surprising but a welcome respite from the stifling, shallow society in which she'd been raised.

She also met Caitlin's friend Sarah Baxter when Rusty drove her into town to buy supplies at the general store. Greenbriar was much like Caitlin had described. Nestled in the rugged foothills, it boasted a saloon and jail, a barber and bathhouse, a blacksmith and livery, a church, and several clapboard storefronts. Main Street was unpaved and six inches deep in mud and melting snow, but wooden boardwalks lined both sides.

When Rusty had helped her down from the buckboard, Heather negotiated the slippery planks with Janna in her arms and hurried inside the store, grateful for the warmth of the woodstove in the far corner.

"Don't tell me—you're Heather," the brown-haired woman behind the counter said affably.

Heather returned her smile. "How did you know?"

"You're the talk of Greenbriar, that's how. And I see rumor didn't exaggerate in the slightest. You're every bit as beautiful as I heard tell. But honestly, you're no giant like one old cat claimed. 'A tall, decidedly elegant figure' is how I would put it." Before Heather could become uncomfortable, the woman grinned. "I'm Sarah Baxter, by the way. My husband Harvey and I own the store. I hope you'll forgive me for not paying you a visit first thing, but the weather was so bad, and the minute it let up, the store was swamped. . . ."

"Of course," Heather replied politely.

"I just know we'll be friends. Caitlin has spoken so highly of you. Don't be upset, though, if the other ladies of Greenbriar don't welcome you with open arms. You're sure to be a target of envy."

"Envy?"

"For snaring Sloan." Sarah's brown eyes filled with wry laughter. "You must realize women find him attractive—a handsome widower with a cattle empire the size of the Bar M. And with that dangerous air about him. . . . Well, he's a mite hard to resist."

Heather understood quite well what Sarah meant. *She'd* always been keenly aware how vulnerable she was to Sloan's potent masculinity, and that aura of brooding sensuality of his only increased his appeal.

"His first wife wasn't decently buried in her grave," Sarah explained, "when the local gals started hounding him again. I fear it's always been that way," she added wistfully. "The McCord boys were a hell-raising pair when they were younger. Jake was the charmer, but Sloan . . . well, Sloan was the real heartbreaker. Half the women around here were in love with him, but he paid them no mind. Wanted nothing to do with them. And then he up and married Sleeping Doe. Shocked the entire community, I can tell you. And now he's gone and done it again—disappointed all the belles by taking another stranger for a wife."

Heather repressed a pained smile. It struck her as ironic to be envied by her female neighbors for capturing the elusive Sloan McCord. Doubtless they would be surprised to learn she and Sloan had a marriage in name only.

"I don't know that *I* envy you," Sarah added thoughtfully. "Sloan McCord is a hardheaded maverick if there ever was one. Being his wife can't be easy. You have a real job on your hands, I'm certain."

Heather's silence was eloquent.

As their eyes met, Sarah nodded in accord. "I imagine he's grateful to you at least for keeping the females away. And for looking after Janna. A lot of women want to be the one to help Sloan recover from his grief, or simply become mistress of all that land, but there aren't too many anxious to mother a half-breed daughter."

Reflexively Heather's arms tightened around Janna. "I don't much care for that term," she replied coolly, "and I'll thank you not to use it in her hearing."

Sarah's grin only broadened. "Good, you've got steel in your backbone, just as Caitlin said. I'm afraid you'll need every ounce of it, with what you'll have to face. But I want you to know, if you ever need my help, you have only to ask.''

Heather cherished little hope of improving her relationship with her husband, and the long years of loneliness stretched out before her like a frozen river. Yet despite Sloan's cold reserve toward her, she knew he must have a softer side. She'd seen for herself his extreme gentleness with his daughter, his passion for the wild land, his devotion to his ranch hands . . . the love he still harbored for his first wife.

She'd seen the vulnerability in those bleak, world-weary eyes when he thought she wasn't watching. She was learning to look beyond his man's hard face, into the raw places in his heart.

She wanted to reach out to him, to offer him a touch, some comfort, even though she knew instinctively he wouldn't want it. The knowledge made her heart ache, and she vowed to do everything in her power to aid Sloan in his struggle to keep his ranch solvent.

The devastating winter hung on with a vengeance, bitter with cold and enough snow to bury a steer chest deep. Sloan drove himself till he was dizzy with pain and fatigue. He was a man who wouldn't admit defeat; he didn't know what it was, Heather realized. But even she, who knew nothing about cattle, could see the kingdom he had built was crumbling. His very way of life was threatened.

It was during her third week that she sensed a small crack in Sloan's granite exterior—the night she was awakened by Janna's mewling cries. Leaping out of bed without even taking the time to put on a wrapper or slippers, Heather hurried down the hall to Sloan's room, to find him cradling his daughter against his bare chest, pacing the floor by the light of a lantern, wearing only red long johns.

He gazed at her with a helpless expression. "She won't stop crying."

"She's probably teething," Heather said soothingly. "I thought I saw a tooth breaking through when I fed her this evening. There's nothing to worry about. It happens all the time." She reached out her arms. "Let me have her."

"Can you help her?" he asked as he reluctantly entrusted the baby to Heather.

"I think so. Why don't you go back to sleep? I'm sure you have a hard day ahead of you tomorrow. I'll care for Janna, I promise."

"I know you will. But I can't sleep, knowing she's hurting."

Heather felt another chunk of her heart crumble at Sloan's concern for his daughter. He refused to rest, even though he must be exhausted after the grueling day he'd put in. But he wouldn't be easy until Janna was sleeping soundly.

"Do you have any oil of cloves? It would help to rub it on her sore gums."

"I don't know."

"If you can't find any, then fetch some snow. Cold serves to dull the pain."

While he went to find the remedies she'd recommended, Heather wrapped the fretful child in a blanket and picked up the towel by the washbasin. Slipping a corner of the cloth in Janna's mouth for her to chew on, she settled in the rocking chair before the stove and began to rock to and fro, humming softly.

When Sloan returned, he came to a complete standstill, staring at the scene they made: the dark child and the golden woman, softly lit by lamplight. Heather in her virginal nightdress, her pale hair twisted in a thick braid, her milk-white skin a contrast to the bronzed hue of the tiny girl's.

Janna had quieted and was mouthing the cloth while Heather crooned a lullaby. Sloan's heart twisted with remembered pain. Doe had sung to their daughter like that, though in a different language. This golden image of mother and child seemed wrong ... and yet at the same time, somehow *right*.

These past three weeks, he had thrown himself into his work, not only to save the Bar M, the heritage he would fight to the death to preserve, but in a stubborn attempt to forget the woman who now shared his home, who was now nurturing his daughter.

It was a futile effort. Heather was the kind of woman who got under a man's skin in a heartbeat.

He hadn't found the oblivion he'd sought in physical exertion. And no matter where he was in the house, he was always aware of her. She made her presence known in subtle ways: the lavender scent of the feminine soap she used, the quiet rustle of her skirts, her gentle laughter when she played with his daughter.... Consciously or not, she'd found the surest way to slip under his guard. His daughter.

He shouldn't complain, Sloan tried to remind himself. He'd married Heather so Janna could have a mother. The duchess was only fulfilling her part of the bargain. But though wild horses couldn't get him to admit it to her, when she was near, the sense of stark loneliness dulled a bit.

Hell, the truth was, he was grateful for her presence. She was surprisingly tough, tougher than he'd hoped for. This land had broken weak men. The ones who survived had to be strong. And he was beginning to suspect that elegant lady or no, the duchess had the kind of grit a Western woman needed to have, the kind of inner strength his ma had possessed, or Caitlin, or Sleeping Doe, or any of the countless ranchers' wives and daughters who'd fought beside their men, carving out homesteads from the rugged, unforgiving foothills of the Rockies.

Reluctant to shatter the scene, Sloan moved forward. "I found the oil of cloves," he murmured.

Heather glanced up at him with a faint smile. "I think she might go to sleep without it. I'm hesitant to disturb her now."

He nodded, suddenly aware of his state of undress, of *her* state of undress. Of their location—his bedchamber.

Sloan felt his heart kick painfully against his ribs, felt his lower body quicken with need.

With a silent oath, he turned away. The duchess didn't belong in this room. She had invaded his own private sanctuary, where his memories of Doe remained inviolate.

Still, she *was* caring for his daughter. . . .

Grimly, he fetched another blanket from the bed and draped it around Heather's shoulders.

At the solicitous gesture, she looked up, lips parted in surprise.

"You don't need to catch cold," he explained gruffly.

Yet it wasn't the cold he was afraid of. It was the images in his mind. The trouble was, he knew what lay beneath that virginal nightdress. He knew how Heather could look, that radiant hair tangled by the wildness of their passion, her mouth red and swollen from his kisses.

All too easily he could remember her beneath him, writhing in the throes of desire he'd awakened in her, that cool refinement melted into primitive heat.

All too easily he could forget Doe.

His jaw clenched. No, by God. He had no intention of giving in to his urges this time. He would keep his hands off the duchess and maintain his distance. For his own survival.

He couldn't bear the sense of vulnerability that came with letting her too close. He couldn't bear the guilt.

Two nights later his resolve was tested severely. The hour was late, during a harsh new snowstorm. Having long since put Janna to bed and changed her gown for a nightdress and woolen wrapper, Heather sat in the kitchen mending clothing and watching worriedly for Sloan to ride in from the range.

Her unease grew when sleet began spitting against the glass windows. She knew she shouldn't fret. Sloan had lived here his entire life. He knew this land and its savage challenges. He would survive the danger.

She was unprepared, however, when at last the door burst open and Sloan stumbled inside, ushered in by a shrieking, biting gust of wind.

With a start, Heather rose abruptly to her feet. When he forced the door shut and sagged heavily against it, Heather realized he was half frozen and shaking with fatigue. Ice encrusted his heavy shearling coat and wool chaps, while snow crystals frosted his lashes.

He had driven himself to the limit of his endurance.

"You need to get out of those wet clothes," she urged, going to him.

"Yeah," he agreed simply, too tired to argue.

He made no protest when she took his hat and gloves and hung them on wall pegs to dry. With difficulty she unfastened the buttons of his coat and dragged the heavy garment free of his arms. The chambray work shirt beneath was damp at the collar and shoulders, and he shuddered with terrible, numbing cold.

Swiftly Heather poured a mug of steaming coffee and wrapped a dishcloth around it, then forced it into his hands. His frozen fingers curled stiffly around the cup, seeking warmth.

"Let me get some blankets," she murmured.

When she returned from upstairs, however, Sloan still hadn't managed to pull off his chaps or boots but had collapsed in a chair beside the table. Evidently he would need help undressing.

She knelt beside his chair and worked to unfasten the hooks that ran down the outer seams of his chaps. When she had unbuckled the belt, the garment fell to the floor in a puddle. With effort she dragged off his boots, then his denim trousers, leaving only his woolen drawers and undershirt and socks.

Solicitously Heather wrapped two blankets around his shoulders and took his hand as she would a child's. His flesh was so cold, it frightened her.

"Come to the study, Sloan. The fire will warm you."

Surprisingly he allowed her to lead him. When he reached the hearth, he sank to his knees on the bearskin rug. For a long moment he stared into the flames. In the firelight she could see the stark lines of weariness etched into his face.

"We found two dozen dead steers today," he said, his low tone dark with despair.

Heather didn't know how to reply. Her heart ached for him.

"The hell of it is, I can't do one goddamn thing to save them." He laughed harshly. "If this keeps up, there won't be anything left of the Bar M."

Unbidden, a fierce protectiveness welled up inside her. Sloan didn't deserve such hardship. He'd been hurt too much already.

The need to reach out to him was strong. Kneeling beside him, she hesitantly raised a hand to his face, her fingertips brushing the shadow of stubble on his lean cheek. "I wish I could help."

Wincing, he turned to look at her, his eyes dark and distrustful. He was too proud to accept pity, too bitter to accept compassion. She longed to rid him of that bitterness. She longed to offer him comfort. Her palm softly cradled his jaw.

Every muscle in his body tensed in rejection, the sinews cording his neck so rigid they stood out visibly.

A stillness came into the room as their gazes locked, a sense of breathless waiting.

Heather watched him, her urge for self-protection vanishing. This was a man in need.

To his dismay, Sloan couldn't break the connection with her golden eyes, so warm with concern. He wanted to move away from her, away from the dangerous seduction of her compassion. He was too vulnerable just now. He felt so raw, so tired from the war he was waging. He couldn't bear to have her this near.

"You'd best go," he whispered, his voice raw and cracked.

She didn't stir.

Nor did he. He couldn't manage it. In his chest he felt that strange swelling, twisting sensation again. He didn't like it. It *hurt* to feel. It was easier, safer, to keep himself isolated, remote, his rampaging emotions under tight control.

Yet he had no defense against her. He couldn't save himself.

He remained perfectly still, a terrible tension vibrating through him. He didn't want to acknowledge the need tightening in his belly and churning in his soul. Her feminine scent taunted him. His hands actually hurt from wanting to touch her.

Sloan swore a silent oath. He couldn't stop himself from wanting her.

Raising his hand, he touched her face. That was all he meant to do, and yet. . . . He found himself following the sensual line of her mouth with his fingers. She had the face of an angel but lush lips made for sinning.

They were parted now in unconscious invitation, so damned tempting. . . .

He wanted to accept. God, how he wanted to.

Telling himself he just needed a taste of her, he bent his head. When their breaths mingled, though, he knew he was lost.

Closing his eyes, Sloan inhaled sharply at the powerful desire streaking through him. He wanted to pull her beneath him and drive himself into her body until he was mindless. He wanted to take until the ache in his soul had been eased.

This was what he needed tonight. A willing woman. This woman. The solace of her body.

"Warm me, Heather," he whispered hoarsely before his lips covered hers.

Chapter 7

◯◯

The fire crackled as he pressed her down upon the bearskin rug. Heather wrapped her arms around Sloan, sharing her body heat, pleading silently with him to take the comfort she longed to offer.

He was shaking, this beautiful man with his hardened soul. She could feel the tension in his body, the tightly leashed power in his muscles as he raised himself up. She could see the raw emotion in his eyes. His face was hard, taut, like a man on the verge of agony.

His hand slid under her nightdress. Wordlessly, he pushed up the skirt, bunching the fabric at her waist, and encountered the barrier of lacy drawers she wore for warmth. Without pause he tugged down the layers of underwear, stripping them from her legs along with her slippers and stockings.

Stretching over her again, he covered her with his weight. His mouth took hers feverishly, in a kiss that plunged something sharp and searing into her soul. Her body responded at once, flaming with sudden heat.

Sloan heard her low moan, but he was blind to

127

any need but his own as he sought solace in her body.

Just tonight, he promised himself. Just tonight he needed to ease himself in the soft magic of a woman's flesh. With one hand he tore at the folds of his own drawers, setting his stiffened shaft free. Spreading her legs, he put himself between them.

Heather stirred uneasily as his powerful thighs pushed her own apart, her body tensing as she felt his probing shaft tease her entrance. When he pressed harder, pushing deep, she gasped at the shock of his naked flesh penetrating her.

"Am I hurting you?" he rasped.

"No," she said, a lie. She bit her lip to hold back a moan as she tried to accustom herself to his sudden invasion, his unexpected size.

As if realizing his fierceness, Sloan halted. He held himself still inside her, until the line between pain and pleasure blurred, until desire suddenly rippled through her body, flaring and tightening every nerve ending.

His eyes burned into hers as he began slowly to move. Heather's breath shallowed as her flesh responded with quickening need, throbbing with heated sensation, her skin aflame. Closing her eyes, she fought to hold back a ragged sob. Her body was straining to open for him, while wanton sounds of urgency came from her throat.

Sloan gritted his teeth as he tried to keep a grip on his fierce need. His heart was pounding in his chest, and he feared that if he lost control, he would never get it back.

When the impassioned woman beneath him twisted helplessly, the fever escalated, gathering and surging relentlessly, enveloping him in tumult. He felt himself going under, losing himself. Burying his hands in her hair, he ground his mouth against hers, catching her soft, wild sounds, ruthlessly driving her on and on, until she clawed at his back, frantic for release. Until with a cry, she arched and convulsed around him, finding her own trembling ecstasy.

There was no way he could restrain himself now. He was beyond words, driven by savage need. He kept thrusting heavily into her, again and again, until with a hoarse groan of desperation, he exploded within her, embers bursting, white-hot with light. For an instant, all the darkness was banished from his soul.

Afterward it was she who held him. She felt the shudders ripple through him, felt the clenching and unclenching of his muscles, felt the pain-sharp breaths he dragged in.

When he tried to withdraw, Heather tightened her arms around him, despite his crushing weight, despite the ache between her thighs and in her heart.

She counted his heartbeats as they slowed to beat in rhythm with hers.

"Ah, damn. . . ." His curse was quiet, raw.

For a long moment he was silent. When he shifted his weight, Heather winced.

"Are you all right?"

She couldn't answer honestly; he wouldn't want to hear the truth. She lay there, frightened and stunned by what she felt for this enigmatic man. She was not afraid of *him*. She was afraid of herself, her shameless response to him. She hadn't expected that wild hunger in herself, that wanton need. With barely a touch, Sloan had ignited the same fierce passion that had blazed between them once before.

When she gave no reply, Sloan withdrew himself from her and rolled on his back, one arm covering his eyes.

"That was unforgivable," he said, his voice low and rusty. "It won't happen again, I swear it." It was the best he could offer. A promise not to touch her again.

He had never acted so savagely with a woman, never lost control like that. His need had been blind, desperate.

He should never have taken her that way, with such raw, unbridled lust. He had fucked her on the floor, with no pretense at finesse, with no thought to her pleasure or inexperience. Hell, he would show a whore more respect.

Cursing himself for his weakness, Sloan drew a ragged breath. He should never have let himself get so near. He'd promised himself he would keep his distance. What had happened to him that he should lose himself in her arms? That he should turn into a savage animal? With Doe he had never lost command of himself—

Doe.

He squeezed his eyes shut. He tried to summon Doe's face, but only succeeded in gaining a hazy, indistinct image. An empty ache throbbed in his chest. Why couldn't he remember?

His anger at himself shifted to the woman lying beside him. His new bride.

Damn her, how had she made him forget his beloved wife, even for an instant?

Suddenly he was unreasonably angry with her. She didn't belong here, and he didn't want her here. Didn't want her in his life. Didn't want the savage reminders of the past she brought him.

He turned his head to find Heather watching him, her golden eyes wide with uncertainty. That look smote him. Her lips were still dampened and reddened from his mouth, her naked thighs glistening with the sheen of his seed. Even now, after he'd sated himself with her, her pale sensuality made his loins swell. He could smell her scent . . . heated feminine flesh mingled with the musk of their coupling.

With an oath, Sloan reached over and roughly tugged the hem of her nightdress down to cover her bareness. Averting his gaze, he pushed himself unsteadily to his feet.

He needed to get away. One hand over his eyes, he stumbled from the room, seeking escape from his devils and the ghost that haunted him. Seeking escape from *her*.

Stunned, Heather lay there unmoving. She tried to tell herself not to feel wounded. Sloan was hurting, and lashing out was a natural response. Yet any slim hope she'd held out for closeness had just been shattered. It made her ache with sadness.

Shivering, Heather turned to stare at the fire. She had to make allowances for the haunted, complex man she had wed. For the anger and bitterness and hatred she knew he harbored inside.

But it wasn't easy.

A hard chill shook her. Self-protectively, she curled herself into a ball, wrapping her arms tightly around herself, trying desperately to get warm.

The stone-piled grave was buried under two feet of snow, but by dawn's first light, Sloan unerringly directed his bay saddle horse to the place beneath the giant fir. The gelding's frosted breath came in puffs of steam as he struggled through the uneven drifts.

The winter blizzard had vanished with the night, but the bitter cold remained. The rising sun hung low in an ice-blue sky, casting glittering rays over a meadow that glistened pristine white, the reflection brilliant enough to hurt the eyes.

This was a private place, a hidden glade secreted in the foothills of the Rockies, surrounded by bare, white-trunked aspens. Doe had first brought him here on their wedding day. In summer, Sloan knew, the meadow would be blanketed with blue columbine; in autumn it would shimmer with the fiery gold of the aspens.

They had consummated their love here. Doe was buried here.

Reining to a halt, Sloan dismounted slowly and hunkered down beside the concealed grave. With his gloved fingers he gently brushed the snow from the granite headstone, reading the inscription carved there:

> *Here lies Doe Who Sleeps*
> *Beloved wife of S. McCord*

Tugging off his hat, Sloan bowed his head. The pressure in his chest was heavy; his heart ached with a sense of loss.

He shut his eyes, trying to recall Doe's smile. It was her shy smile that had captured his heart from the first. So soft and gentle and filled with promise, it touched something deep inside him.

Yet, hard as he tried, he couldn't picture her face, her smile. All he could see was her grimace of pain from the bullets that riddled her slim body.

Suddenly he was awash in memories, the savage images assailing him, razor-sharp, as if it had been yesterday.

The last moments of Doe's life, when her shallow breaths had dwindled to nothing. The bright blood that soaked the ripped bodice of her gown and seeped between her legs. The harsh sobs that tore out of his body in great shudders as he clutched her still form to his chest.

His soul had been stripped away from him that day. The bleakness and grief had closed around him, enveloping him in blackness. It was the darkest time of his life.

With a raw curse, Sloan rose to his feet and turned away from the grave. Would he ever be free of the haunting memories? Of the guilt that hounded him?

He ran a hand raggedly down his face. Taking a deep, shuddering breath, he lifted his gaze to the rocky, pine-clad slope above the meadow. These mountains, this ranch, the cattle and horses, were all he'd ever wanted before he met Doe. He'd never imagined he would come to cherish a woman above his heritage. Even above his own life.

He would have died in her place if he could. Instead he'd had to live with a bitter knowledge: *he* was the reason Doe was dead. If he hadn't been so set on protecting his herds, his land, if he hadn't been so determined to continue the feud. . . .

To get back at him, his enemies had made his wife their target. They'd found Doe alone, driving back from town, and shot her team in its traces. She'd put up a valiant fight, Sloan learned later. The buckboard was riddled with bullet holes, while the rifles she'd carried were empty of ammunition. But when the last bullets were spent, Adam Kingsly and his confederates had set upon her like a pack of rabid wolves.

By the time Sloan found her, he was helpless to save her. Doc Farley told him afterward that if she hadn't died from the gunshot wounds, the blood loss from the savage rape would have taken her.

His vengeance had been swift. With cold-blooded efficiency he'd tracked every last man down, all seven of them, and made them plead for their miserable lives, before ending them with more mercy than his wife had been shown.

But he couldn't bring Doe back.

His tortured eyes slid closed. For a few moments Sloan allowed himself to hurt. He let the ache rise up inside him, fierce and overwhelming, as he relived tormenting memories he wanted to shut away.

Then he inhaled another shuddering breath and forced himself to turn back to the grave.

"Doe, there's something I have to tell you," Sloan murmured in a voice that was low, ragged. "I married again. A stranger from back East. But I want you to know, it doesn't mean anything to me. *She* doesn't mean anything. I did it for Janna. Our daughter needed someone to care for her and raise her to be a lady. I know that's what you would have wanted."

He paused, unwillingly remembering the woman who'd lain unprotesting beneath him last night, allowing him the hot sweet comfort of her body while he pounded into her.

"She can't take your place, Doe. I can't think of her as my wife, or even mistress of the Bar M. Hell, she doesn't know beans about ranch work. She's never tanned a hide or driven a herd through a snowstorm. But she's not as green as I first feared. And Janna has taken to her. She's good with Janna, Doe. I think you'd approve.

"Still . . . it's hard, seeing her in your place. The other day she found your buckskin coat, the one you were wearing the day you. . . . She was washing out the bloodstains." His mouth twisted. "I yelled at her. Scared the daylights out of her. But I didn't want her touching your blood."

Sloan stopped, distractedly fingering the brim of his hat as he remembered his fury at Heather that day. It wasn't just her interference that had riled him so unreasonably. It was the insidious effect she had on him. For the past year his heart had been encased in ice, yet the duchess kept finding cracks in his defensive armor.

He despised the emotion she roused in him. He resented her fiercely for all he felt, all she made him feel. He resented his weakness for her.

He didn't want to want her. Yet he couldn't get the taste of her out of his mouth, or the feel of her off his skin, or her voice out of his mind. His attraction for Heather was getting out of hand. Last night had shown him his own frightening vulnerability—

With a harsh oath, Sloan pulled some semblance of control around himself. What the hell was he doing, thinking such profane thoughts over Doe's grave, for crissakes?

Clenching his teeth, he gave one last glance at the headstone and jammed his hat on his head. Then, turning away, Sloan gathered the bay's reins and swung himself into the saddle.

He was halfway across the meadow before a measure of equanimity returned, and his resolve along with it. He had no intention of being led around by his groin. He would get his craving for his new bride under control if it killed him.

He knew what he wanted from Heather, and it didn't include love or even passion. He would never feel for her what he'd felt for Doe. He never wanted to care that deeply for a woman again. He couldn't stand the pain.

Not that it would come even close to that.

Last night had sure as hell been a mistake, but the simple truth was, it had meant nothing to him. He had used Heather's body, that's all.

It was a basic tale of man wanting woman, male

needing female. Only sex. Desire in its basest, rawest form. The kind that had nothing to do with love or tenderness, and everything to do with physical need. Their lovemaking could never be like what he'd known with Doe, tender and gentle and . . . meaningful.

The duchess could never be anything more to him than temptation, Sloan swore. He damned sure wouldn't let her.

Chapter 8

His vow to keep away from Heather proved easier once the spring thaws finally came in mid-April. Sloan was able to bury himself in ranch work—the hell with her wary eyes and soft mouth and silken body. The exertion focused his mind and made certain the overriding pain was in his muscles.

With the melting of the snows, he could take stock of the disastrous damages the brutal winter had wrought. Few folks could remember a season whose bitter cold lasted so deep into April, or one so devastating. Fully a third of the Bar M herds had perished, and the steers remaining were more bones than beef.

Heather knew Sloan was avoiding her, yet she tried to bear his neglect with stoicism. She was still inclined to make excuses for him, and during the days at least she had her own work to keep her busy. If during the long nights she had to battle wrenching loneliness, well then, it was the price she had to pay for choosing this life, as the wife of a cattle baron who cared for nothing but his ranch and his daughter.

At least her relationship with Janna continued to

137

develop. Her fondness for the young child grew, as did the bonds of trust and affection between them. Beginning to shed her quiet shyness, Janna often could be heard chattering to her doll in baby language, before setting off on hands and knees, crawling into corners to explore. Yet for the most part she stayed close to Heather, as if reluctant to let her out of sight.

Heather's acquaintance with the Bar M ranch hands improved as well. She had never known men quite like these cowboys—ones so honest and direct, who took pleasure in simple joys. They treated her with respect, indeed almost reverence, but lived such rugged lives, she wanted to help ease their hardships if she could.

One afternoon as she stood at the kitchen window, Heather saw several of the hands ride in. She donned her coat and carried a tray out to the bunkhouse, laden with two golden-crusted pies still warm from the oven.

The cowboys were unsaddling their horses at the corral, and when they saw the pies, they tugged off their hats and greeted her with whoops and "Thankee ma'am's."

While they teased Cookie good-naturedly about the inadequacy of his cooking, Heather followed the tall, ginger-haired Rusty into the bunkhouse and deposited the pies on a wooden table. She had just stepped outside again when she came to an abrupt halt.

Her husband had ridden up on his rangy bay and sat staring down at her from beneath the brim of his hat.

To her dismay, Heather heard herself stammering. "I b-brought the men some rhubarb pies. Caitlin told me cowboys are wild for it."

His silence, along with his hard, unwavering gaze, unnerved her.

"Did I do something wrong?" she murmured.

It was all Sloan could do to repress a savage reply. He shut his eyes briefly as a memory pierced him. Doe laughing quietly at herself as she poked at a pie crust, burnt to a crisp around the edges and raw in the middle. Her dismal failure as a cook had frustrated her, only because she'd wanted to please him. She'd never gotten the hang of baking the white way, fixing biscuits like rocks and flapjacks like leather. . . .

The tormenting memory faded, leaving him with a bittersweet, lingering sense of loss.

"No," Sloan forced himself to say to his present wife, more gruffly than was warranted. "You did right, duchess. The way to a cowboy's heart has always been through his stomach."

Heather bit her lip hard, refraining from making the reply that sprang to her tongue. *Is that the way to your heart, Sloan? Do you even have a heart?*

She watched, unsurprised, as without another word, he whirled his bay and rode off at a lope, leaving her to stare after him.

He seemed somewhat repentant, however, when he joined her in the study late that evening for the first time in over a week. After asking her how Janna had fared, Sloan went to his desk and pulled out the account books. For a time, the only sound in the room was the crackling of the fire in the hearth and the occasional scratch of his quill pen.

When his heavy sigh broke the silence, Heather couldn't tell whether it was due to frustration or despair. She looked up from her book to see Sloan roughly run a hand through his tawny hair.

"What is it?" she asked quietly.

"It's going to be a skinning season." She waited. When he explained, his tone held an edge of bleakness. "It's what they call a bust year for cattle. When there's no market for beef, a rancher can only make money selling his steers for the hides."

"And there is no market for beef this year?"

"That's putting it mildly. The price has been dropping for the past two or three years, and it's at rock bottom now. Add to that the fact that I have fewer head to sell because so many were lost to the cold. Even worse, I'll have to compete with the big cattle outfits up north. Word is, a lot of them are selling out. If they dump their beeves on the market all at once, it'll only send prices lower. Even selling the hides won't recoup my expenses." He laughed without humor. "At least with smaller herds I won't have to hire as many hands for spring roundup."

Heather watched him helplessly, wanting to offer comfort. "You can rebuild your herds, can you not?"

"What would be the point?" His lip curled cynically. "The days of the big cattle dynasties are over. Jake saw it coming. He's been pushing me to diversify since he came back last summer."

"Then what do you plan to do?"

Sloan shrugged. "Convert some of the land to raising hay. I started last year. That's the only way we survived this winter. I don't much like the idea of becoming a hay farmer, but the demand for hay is growing. And it takes money to keep a ranch going."

Money he didn't have. "You still have a great deal of land. Can you not sell some of it?"

His head shot up, and he looked at her, his expression hard and protected. "I don't think you understand. The Bar M isn't for sale and never will be."

Heather returned his gaze steadily. "Perhaps I *don't* understand, but I would like to. Very much."

Sloan took a deep breath, as if realizing her sincerity. "Nearly forty years ago, my father came to Colorado during the gold rush days. But instead of digging for gold, he and Ma carved the Bar M out of rock and timberland. Pa died defending it, and left it to me and Jake. I'd cut off my hands before I willingly sell an ounce of dirt of this place."

Heather heard the passion in his voice and could no longer question his fierce desire to protect the legacy left to him. Sloan had been entrusted with the land and everything on it, and he would keep it or die trying.

He must have realized how harsh he sounded, though, for his tone softened. "I'm better off than some of my neighbors; any of the larger cattle companies are. In the past few years several big Eastern conglomerates have pushed their way into Colorado, buying up small family ranches, taking advantage of bad times, foreclosing on mortgages and the like. And the U.S. government's policies have supported the outsiders. In fact, the laws they've made lately are downright hostile to homesteaders." Sloan made a scoffing sound deep in his throat. "Hell, half the politicians in our own legislature don't know the first thing about ranching. They're miners or railroad magnates who don't give a damn about the folks who built this state with their own sweat and blood."

"Like you," Heather murmured.

"Me and all the ranchers like me, whether cattle or sheep." He sought her eyes. "That's the real reason I decided to run in September's election. As a state senator I could make a stand for the ranchers

. . . maybe make a difference. The man I'll be challenging sure as hell won't help them. Quinn Lovell has represented this district for two years, but he doesn't know beans about ranching or about what Colorado really needs. He's a mining baron who only cares about raping the land for gold and silver. Lining his pockets. Expanding his rule."

She understood men like that. And after knowing Evan Randolf, Heather was all too well-acquainted with their methods of acquisition. Whether driven by greed, a hunger for power, or simply the glory of challenge, there would always be men who had to conquer the world by whatever means, fair or foul.

"Lovell's worse even than the conglomerates," Sloan observed grimly. "He's bought out more homesteads than the other Easterners combined— and he's got his sights on the Bar M."

"What do you mean?"

"He'd like nothing more than to drive me under. I'm all that's standing in the way of him owning the entire north range." Sloan looked away. "I'll be damned if I want to sell, but with a bust market, I'll be lucky to hold out through the spring."

"But . . . you just said you would never give up any of your land."

"Not willingly. But I may not have a choice. I'm vulnerable. I took out a bank mortgage on the ranch last month when I married you."

He didn't have to be more explicit. To pay her debts, was what he meant.

"Sloan . . . I'm sorry."

His shoulders lifted in a shrug. "It couldn't be helped. But I'm likely to be cash-poor for a long while."

He bent his head to pore over the accounts again, while Heather stared at him with dismay and regret. If he hadn't wed her, he would not have been obliged to shoulder her debts and put his ranch at risk. . . .

She hadn't known the plight of the ranchers was so dire, or that Sloan might be facing financial ruin. She wished she knew how to help. She wished he would allow her close enough to try. She wished . . .

What exactly? That she could control the conflicting turmoil Sloan roused in her?

She was finding it more and more difficult to sort out her feelings for him, Heather reflected. He was as hard and untamable as the land he loved, frequently impossible to deal with, even hostile at times, and yet. . . .

Yet she couldn't explain the yearning Sloan stirred in her. Couldn't understand the strange, gnawing restlessness that plagued her since becoming his wife. It struck her hardest when she was weary and lonely, yet the need was always there, shimmering beneath the surface of their relationship.

What she felt for him was far more than sympathy or compassion. A big part was attraction. An awareness of Sloan as a man. A keen *sexual* awareness.

That made sense, perhaps. As her husband, Sloan had initiated her to carnal relations, had awakened her to passion. After such stunning intimacy of the flesh, it was natural that she experience a physical affinity toward him. Especially with his potent masculinity. She understood why her pulse quickened to a drumbeat whenever he was near, why her breath shallowed and her skin flushed. She was responding primally to him, as a woman.

But she was also his wife. And she yearned for something deeper, something softer between them.

She longed for the elemental emotions that were missing entirely from their marriage: closeness, tenderness, laughter. Affection.

Yet tragedy had destroyed the laughter in him. Sloan cared for no one but his daughter and the hallowed memory of his late wife.

Heather couldn't repress a wistful sigh. He intended to keep her shut out of his life.

Still, he had shared something of himself tonight. He had opened up to her in some small measure, more than he ever had in the past.

It gave her reason for hope.

It was the following day when they first quarreled over Janna. Heather's afternoon began pleasantly enough, for the local schoolmaster came to call. Vernon Whitfield was a handsome bachelor with curling, dark-brown hair and a gentle manner that contrasted sharply with the rough and rugged cowboys of her recent acquaintance. He was also a good friend of Caitlin's.

Heather liked him from the first. Originally hailing from Chicago, Vernon was obviously well-read. Over tea, they discussed their favorite authors and the peculiar differences between Easterners and Westerners, before Heather broached a subject of prime concern for her: Janna's education.

Vernon was driving away in his buggy when Sloan returned home early.

"What did Whitfield want?" he asked as he entered the kitchen where Heather was making biscuits for dinner. There was little inflection in his voice, but she had the distinct impression he disapproved.

"He wished to welcome me to the community." She wouldn't admit to Sloan how much she had enjoyed Vernon's visit. Not only had it provided her respite from the aching loneliness, but she had found a kindred spirit. "I was glad to meet him. Particularly since I wanted to discuss Janna's schooling with him."

"Schooling?" Sloan asked sharply. "What do you mean?"

"I thought I would take Janna to visit the schoolhouse this week and let her meet the other children. Ryan will be there and he can help introduce her. If she is to attend school in a few years—"

"Just a minute. I married you so you could teach her."

Heather took a deep breath. "I intend to, of course, at least at first. But Vernon and I agreed it would be beneficial if—"

"Did you, now?" Sloan's tone hardened dangerously. "Let me set one thing straight. No one is going to tell me what's best for my daughter, least of all a bookish city fellow who can't tell a rifle from a revolver."

Summoning patience, Heather tried to ignore Sloan's anger. "Before you reject his advice out of hand, you might consider this for a moment. If Janna is to be accepted in the white world, she needs to grow up in that world. It's essential that she learn how to deal with other children—and they with her. I know she is just a baby, but it isn't too early to start her acclimation. If I take her to school now and then, it will give the children a chance to grow accustomed to one other."

Just then Janna looked up from where she was playing on her blanket and stretched out her arm toward Heather. "Ma-ma . . . Ma-ma. . . . Eat. . . ."

"You can eat in a few minutes, darling, just as soon as I finish the biscuits."

Sloan went rigid as his gaze shot to Heather. "You aren't her ma." His tone was icy.

"No, of course not. I've never encouraged her to think so. I suppose she picked up the word because she's heard Ryan call Caitlin mama."

"I don't want her calling you that!"

For Janna's sake, Heather fought down an angry reply. "Would you please lower your voice in Janna's presence?" she said calmly. "You're frightening her."

Sloan spun around to find his daughter watching him anxiously, her brow wrinkled with alarm. In two strides he reached her and scooped Janna up into his arms.

"I didn't mean to scare you, sweetheart," he said soothingly. He planted gentle kisses over her cheeks until the toddler gave a gurgle of laughter and patted his face.

Holding Janna protectively, he returned his attention to Heather. "I don't want her calling you mama. Is that clear?"

"Perfectly." Heather sent him the sweetest of smiles, yet a hint of steel edged her voice. "But allow *me* to make something understood. You might be my husband, Sloan McCord, but you will not bully or browbeat me. Is *that* clear?"

He stared at her, as if gauging her defiance. When he replied, it was not directly. "You'll be the one to teach her, not Whitfield?"

"Yes, certainly. And I shall begin with polite manners. Janna obviously will not learn them from her uncivil, ill-tempered ogre of a father, who cannot seem to master even the basic social graces."

His expression froze for an instant, before his eyes turned a cool blue that reflected nothing.

"I assure you," Heather added tightly, her own temper roused, "I am not attempting to shirk my duties. Janna's well-being is my only concern. I intend to do my utmost to give her every possible advantage. But it isn't necessary to come to a decision just now. We have ample time to discuss her future and decide what's best for her."

Sloan gritted his teeth, an apology lodging in his throat like a chicken bone. "Maybe . . . I tend to be a bit protective where Janna's concerned."

"You do indeed—and it's perfectly understandable. But I am *not* your enemy, Sloan. Nor is Vernon Whitfield. He can be a valuable ally in educating her."

"Maybe," he replied grudgingly.

"Furthermore, you can't shield Janna from every unpleasantry in life. Certainly you can't do it by wrapping her in a cocoon and never letting her out of the house."

"I realize that." She watched Sloan's blue eyes grow dark and shadowy. "Still . . . I don't want her to forget her ma, or her heritage."

"Well. . . ." Heather shrugged, wishing she hadn't seen the raw pain in his eyes when he spoke of his late wife. "I don't know how to teach Janna about her Indian heritage. I'll have to leave that to you."

Stiffly Heather turned away to resume her baking.

"Heather?" Sloan said after a moment, as if forcing the words out.

"Yes?" she replied woodenly, punching the biscuit dough.

"I . . . I'm glad you're here for Janna. You have the right of it. I don't know how to raise a baby girl. She needs you to help her." Tenderly he kissed the top of his daughter's ebony head. "I don't know how."

Heather felt her anger drain away, felt herself weaken helplessly. Sloan's admission was an apology of sorts, and it touched her in the most tender corner of her heart. She couldn't fight him when he was being humble and reasonable, or when he was showing such unconditional love for his daughter.

She nodded, accepting his apology, resuming their unspoken truce. For now, at least.

He had overreacted, Sloan knew. He'd had no cause to jump down Heather's throat when she was simply trying to help his daughter. She was right. She wasn't his enemy.

A whole host of uncomfortable emotions crawled like ants inside Sloan's skin when he considered the way he'd treated Heather since her arrival in Colorado. She was his wife, but he'd shown her less regard than an unpaid servant, shunning her like a rabid animal.

To her credit, Heather had stood up to him better than most men did. That sure as hell had surprised him. The duchess wasn't the helpless widgeon he'd feared. Truth was, she was adapting to the lonely, hard life of a rancher's wife better than he could have hoped for. She was well on her way to winning the hearts of his daughter, his ranch hands, his neighbors . . . hell, anyone who got to know her. And with each victory his defenses grew harder to sustain.

While he might resent her for fitting in so well, he found himself admiring her grit. She was strong in her own way—tough and fragile at the same time. A combination that touched him in a way he didn't want to admit. He didn't like having to deal with her. Yet each time he lashed out at her, he only wound up feeling more vulnerable.

But he wasn't going to drive her out of his life, Sloan conceded. It was time he accepted that.

He had married her, and he had to live with her. She still unnerved him, though. Like the morning he heard gunshots coming from the north side of the house as he repaired tack in the barn while waiting for a sick cow to calve.

His heart thudding with alarm, Sloan broke into a run, drawing his Colts along the way. He slowed as he reached the corner of the house and edged his way around cautiously, every nerve alert for danger.

He took in the scene in an instant: The empty fruit tins standing upright on the ground. Heather picking herself up off the ground, muttering to herself. The shotgun lying where she had dropped it.

Relief flooded Sloan with such overwhelming force that he had to lean weakly against the timber siding. Evidently she'd only been practicing shooting and had been knocked on her elegant backside. The only thing in any danger was the split-rail fence some twenty yards beyond her target cans.

It might have been relief making him light-headed, but the sight of the duchess cussing so inadequately as she dusted off her skirts was somehow humorous.

"You dratted, ornery, son-of-a . . . of a *blue-bell.* . . ."

Sloan holstered his guns. "Remind me to teach you some real swear words sometime," he said, chuckling.

Heather spun around, to find him leaning lazily against the house, hands on hips, dry amusement kicking up one corner of his mouth.

"You aiming for a target in the next county, duchess?"

She flushed but retorted with dignity, "I was simply practicing as you suggested. You expressed disdain for Mr. Whitfield because he didn't know a 'rifle from a revolver,' so I thought it best if I tried to become proficient."

"I told you to hold the butt tight against your shoulder."

"I did. It still kicked like a bullheaded mule."

Sloan laughed, a sound that was rusty from disuse, and moved to her side. "You're mixing your critters." Bending, he picked up the shotgun. "Here, let me show you again before you blow the fence to bits."

Heather froze as Sloan turned her around and slid his arms around her waist. It was a strangely intimate thing, his teasing. Almost as intimate as his nearness. Immediately she began to experience a shortness of breath.

"Now concentrate," Sloan ordered. Fitting the shotgun to her shoulder, he placed his finger over hers and squeezed the trigger smoothly and efficiently. The gun blasted in Heather's ears, but amazingly the recoil only smarted a little. Three tin cans jumped it the air and came down with a clatter.

"I think maybe," Sloan said, his tone suspiciously unsteady, "you better have me or one of the boys around to help you. When you learn to hit the side of a barn, you can practice on your own."

Heather glanced back up at him to find his bright eyes dancing. He was obviously still laughing at her. Her shoulder would likely be black and blue tomorrow, but her pride had suffered more.

"Sloan," she said sweetly, "did I mention we are having turnips for supper tonight?"

His laughter faded as he observed her warily. "You know I hate turnips. I told you that the last time you served them."

"So you did," she replied, taking the gun from him and turning back toward the house with a swish of her skirts.

*   *   *

She didn't make good her threat to feed him turnips that night, but instead served a delicious chicken pie that made his mouth water, with stewed sweet peaches for desert.

Surprisingly content, Sloan sat at the table, holding his sleepy daughter and savoring his coffee while Heather washed up after supper. His relaxed mood was shattered, however, when she leaned around him to retrieve the empty peach dish.

When her arm brushed his shoulder, they both felt the shock of the contact like a jolt of lightning. Heather jumped back as if burned, giving him that nervous-filly look.

Sloan gritted his teeth. Her touch, however innocent, however unintentional, had reminded him just how soft and tempting a woman could be.

He steeled himself against that small weakening, yet he couldn't tamp down the lingering sense of sexual awareness—not then, nor two nights later, when they sat in his study, Sloan at his desk and Heather on the settee, quietly reading.

He couldn't seem to ignore her presence, even though the account books should have held his complete attention. The future of the Bar M looked grim, and he needed to focus all his efforts on bringing the operation to solvency.

At least his daughter's prospects seemed to be improving. Heather had reported that Janna's visit to the schoolroom this morning had gone well. Some of the younger children had actually been delighted to play with a baby, even one of Cheyenne heritage. And the older kids had refrained from showing any outright hostility. Sloan suspected that Heather's presence had greatly influenced their behavior. She had that way with folks; you wound up wanting to please her, to live up to her high expectations.

Hell, he should be glad to have Heather at his side. She was succeeding with Janna better than he could have hoped. And she would likely be able to help with his campaign this summer—another prime reason he'd married her. The election wouldn't be held till the first week in September, but he needed all the help he could get if he stood a chance of beating Lovell. Once spring roundup was over, he could devote more time and energy to the race. Until then he would have to keep his distance from her. . . .

Sloan forced his mind back to the books.

Several moments passed before Heather spoke quietly. "Perhaps I could help."

Realizing he had sighed with frustration, he looked up to find her watching him. "Help?"

"With the accounts. I might be hopeless with a shotgun, but I'm rather skilled with figures. I managed the books for my school for years. If you would like, I can take over the bookkeeping for the ranch."

He stared at her, wondering if she meant her offer. "I couldn't put you to such trouble."

"It wouldn't be any trouble. I wouldn't mind, truly."

Sloan hesitated. She did seem truly interested in the fate of the Bar M, and not just because the ranch was now her only livelihood. He knew her well enough now to recognize she was a woman of great pride. She wanted to be useful, to carry her own weight.

Relenting, he favored her with that same brilliant smile he hoarded like gold for his daughter. "I'd be much obliged. I hate ciphering almost as much as I hate turnips."

Heather blinked, as if taken aback. Sloan realized his grin was what was affecting her. He didn't often smile.

"You can start tonight, if you like," he said, tempering his look. "Come here, and I'll show you what entries I've made recently."

She seemed to collect herself. Laying down her book, she rose and went to the desk. Sloan let her take his seat.

He watched her as she studied the credits and debits, but he found his thoughts wandering. The curve of her neck beckoned to him to lower his head and sample a taste of her. . . .

Careful, cowboy, Sloan warned himself, feeling the blood pool hot and thick at his groin.

Heather must have felt a similar awareness, for just then she glanced up. When she caught him staring, her lips parted.

Sloan was glad he was so skilled at hiding his expression behind a cold mask. The tension was back between them, so thick he could almost cut it.

Clearing his throat, he took a safe step away from her, trying to distance himself from the scent of her, the heat of her.

It was hard, living in such close proximity, never touching. Especially while sharing the intimacy of raising a child and running a ranch. The situation was explosive, like a powder keg with a short fuse.

The fuse caught fire several days later, in a manner neither of them could have predicted.

Heather was seated at Sloan's desk, engaged in reviewing the past year's accounts, when she heard the sounds of galloping hoofbeats accompanied by a shout coming from behind the house. Catching up a rifle as a precaution, she went out on the back porch.

At the same moment Rusty came running from the corral, also carrying a rifle; as usual Sloan had left the cowboy behind to provide protection for his daughter.

Skidding to a halt, the rider never dismounted from his winded horse, but tipped his hat to her hurriedly and identified himself as one of Jake McCord's ranch hands. "I'm on my way to fetch Doc Farley in town, ma'am. Seems Miss Caitlin's time is near. Jake asked if you would come. He's a mite worried about the missus, since she's early."

"Of course," Heather replied immediately, "I'll come at once."

Nodding, the rider whirled his mount and galloped away.

"I'll hitch up the buggy," Rusty said quickly. "But I'd best drive you to Jake's place, Miz McCord. Looks like it means to storm."

Heather scanned the horizon, torn between her duty to Janna and concern for her dearest friend. The sky over the foothills was ominously dark, portending a thunderstorm, while a chill wind blew from the west.

"Perhaps it would be better if I drove myself and you stayed here to look after Janna till Sloan returns from the range. I would rather not expose her to the inclement weather unnecessarily."

The cowhand nodded. "Reckon that would be best."

Heather was already turning back to the house. "I'll get Janna's supper ready if you'll bring the buggy around."

She went inside and quickly mashed some potatoes she'd boiled earlier and scrambled an egg. After donning her coat and bonnet, she paused long enough to write Sloan a note, saying she meant to attend Caitlin's lying-in and would be back as soon as she could.

Moments later, she was back and stowing the rifle in the buggy. As Rusty helped her into the driver's seat, she gave him some last-minute instructions.

"Janna is upstairs napping and should remain asleep for another hour or so. When she wakes, she can have the supper I left on the table. If she's . . . wet, you will have to change her napkin. There are clean ones in the bureau beside her cradle. They fit like . . . underdrawers. Try to fashion a replacement like the one she's wearing." Heather felt herself blushing a little at such plain speaking, but Rusty nodded solemnly, as if he'd been entrusted with the most sacred of tasks. "Sloan will take care of the rest when he gets home."

Slapping the reins against the horse's rump then, Heather drove down the drive. She shivered as a cold gust of wind buffeted her. It was nearly the end of April, and the magnificent land had only just begun to come alive with hints of green— shoots of grass pushing their way up through the brown earth, buds sprouting along barren tree limbs—but winter still seemed inclined to linger on.

She was glad she was driving in daylight, and gladder still that she remembered the way. She'd only been to Caitlin's home once since her arrival in Colorado, and the rutted road that wound through the foothills was not well-marked.

She accomplished the journey without mishap, however, and surrendered the buggy to one of the hands in the yard.

The ranch house was nearly brand-new—a handsome timber-frame, one-story dwelling that boasted the modern conveniences of a central furnace and hot running water. Jake had refused to live permanently in the house Caitlin's father had built—the man who had unjustly branded him an outlaw and later murdered his sister-in-law, Sloan's Indian wife.

No one greeted Heather when she entered the kitchen, so she followed the sounds, making her own way to the master bedchamber toward the rear of the house.

Caitlin's time was indeed near, Heather realized, hearing a cry of pain. Her labor had begun, while her pale face was soaked in perspiration. It was no wonder. The room was like an oven, since the fire had been stoked to a roaring blaze. At the same time Jake was creating his own tempest as he frantically paced the floor.

Heather took one look at him and banished him from the bedchamber.

"I promise you, Caitlin will be fine," Heather assured him. "I'll look after her until the doctor arrives."

"What if he doesn't come in time?"

"Then we'll see your new son or daughter into the world ourselves. I've a little experience at these things. I was present at the birth of your first child—didn't Caitlin tell you?" Heather wasn't at all as confident as she let on, but Jake desperately seemed to need reassurance.

When he was gone, she removed her coat and cracked a window, then drew a chair beside her friend's bed.

Caitlin smiled wanly. "I'm glad you're here," she murmured weakly as Heather took her hand. "Jake was driving me to distraction. I told him I was warm enough, but he wouldn't listen."

"Hush, dearest. Save your strength for the baby." Smoothing Caitlin's raven hair back from her

forehead, Heather bathed her face with cool water—
a process that was repeated countless times during
the following hours. Night had fallen before the
doctor finally arrived, and several more hours of
painful labor passed before a squalling baby girl
was delivered into the world. The child seemed in
perfect health, although a bit premature.

Watching the miracle of birth, Heather found
herself blinking back tears of joy. She nearly cried
again when she had the honor of placing the newborn in her papa's arms for the first time.

Jake's expression was one of stunned wonder as
he gazed down at the tiny, squirming scrap of hu-
manity.

"She's beautiful," he whispered, staring with
awe at the red puckered flesh and thatch of raven
hair.

Heather couldn't help but smile. "She is, indeed.
Perhaps you should tell your wife so."

Cautiously, as if his new daughter might break,
Jake knelt beside the bed and gazed into Caitlin's
eyes. His look was nakedly intimate, declaring
more explicitly than words the love he bore for her
and their new child.

Heather had to turn away from the disturbingly
private moment. Hoping her envy wouldn't show,
she wondered wistfully if she would ever know the
joy of bearing a child . . . Sloan's child. It didn't
seem likely, since he continued to keep his distance.

Both mother and child were sleeping soundly
when Heather finally took her leave at half past
midnight. Jake, keeping watch over them, was too
preoccupied to offer her an escort home, and
Heather didn't think of it till she was a half mile
down the road. The night seemed ominously dark
as well as damp and frigid, but she needed to get
back to Janna and thus decided against turning

around—a decision she regretted when it began to sleet.

Visibility grew worse the longer she drove, and so did the wind. Blinding gusts drove icy needles into her face. Then just as suddenly as the storm hit, the world quieted, and the sleet turned to snow, dusting the road with eerie white. In only moments the landmarks Heather had committed to memory disappeared.

Shivering with cold, she closed her frozen fingers stiffly around the reins and drew the horse to a halt, fearing that she was lost. After long moments of indecision, she clambered down from the buggy and took the horse by the bridle, meaning to lead it home. At least by walking she could see the outline of the road.

Determinedly she hunched her shoulders and trudged forward through the dark night, fighting the bitter cold as well as alarm. Her face was numb, and she could no longer feel her fingers within her gloves or her feet inside her half-boots. Occasionally a gust of wind blew stinging, biting flakes right through her.

Once, the horse whinnied and began to resist her, pulling back as if he might bolt. Heather managed to regain control and urged him to the left, where the road seemed to fork.

Sometime later, however, she realized she must have made the wrong choice. She halted in her tracks, fighting the panic that gripped her throat. Every landmark looked unfamiliar, while walls of rock rose on either side of the narrowing trail. She had led them into a canyon.

Swallowing fear, she struggled to back the horse and turn the buggy around—and then gasped as an apparition appeared out of the black night.

The horseman came riding toward her, shrouded

in white. When she recognized Sloan, her relief was so profound, Heather nearly sank to her knees.

He gave her no word of greeting as he dismounted, but treated her to total silence. Trembling, she stood to one side as he unharnessed her horse from the buggy and slapped its rump. It took off at a gallop.

In the dark, she couldn't make out Sloan's expression, but his grip on her arm was painful as he led her to his mount. She realized then why he hadn't said a word. He was furious with her.

Sloan tossed her up on his horse and swung up behind her. Heather was grateful when his arms came around her shivering form.

"How did you m-manage to find me?" she asked weakly, her teeth chattering.

She wasn't certain he would answer. "Pure luck," he gritted out. "Your tracks had nearly disappeared. A few minutes more and I wouldn't have been able to see them."

"I l-lost my way."

"You should have given the horse his head. He would have found the way home."

"I didn't t-think of t-that."

"No, that's the trouble, duchess. You didn't think at all." His tone was savage.

"I d-didn't know it would sn-snow in late April!"

"Hell, it snows in the Rockies in *June*."

Sloan bit back any further comment, not trusting himself to speak as he urged the bay through the deepening snow. Brutally he clamped down on the emotion he refused to recognize as protectiveness. He didn't want to examine any of his emotions too closely. What he wanted was to punish Heather for scaring him so. His relief at finding her unhurt was no compensation for the stark terror she had put him through.

When at last they reached the house, Sloan set her down none too gently. "Get inside and get warm. I'll see to the horse."

Heather could barely move, she was so cold, but she forced herself to climb the back porch. Rusty was waiting for her inside, a worried frown on his weathered face.

Gently, yet fussy as a mother hen, the cowboy helped her remove her wet coat and bonnet and gloves and led her to the stove. Solicitously, he poured her a steaming mug of coffee, but her frozen fingers couldn't bear the heat. She took a sip and gave it back. Instead she held her icy hands out to the stove and stood there trembling as painful feeling began to return to her numb limbs.

She hadn't moved when Sloan came in a moment later. He took one look at his wife, then nodded to his hired hand.

"Thanks, Rusty, I'll handle things now. You can go back to bed."

The silence when he was gone was terrible. Left alone with Sloan, she risked a glance at him. He was watching her, his blue eyes icy and lethal.

"I . . . I'm s-sorry," she murmured.

His jaw hardened. "Sorry isn't good enough, duchess. What the hell were you thinking? You could have died out there."

She shuddered and swayed weakly. His hands were there—rough, impersonal, catching her.

"C-Caitlin needed me," she replied, tears crowding her throat like jagged rocks.

"So did Janna! You left her alone with no one but a cowhand to care for her."

"Would you r-rather I'd exposed her to the snowstorm?"

Sloan ground his teeth. Janna's welfare wasn't what really worried him—Rusty had seen to her well enough. It was Heather who had scared the hell out of him. He had feared for her life.

He was furious that she should endanger herself that way. He couldn't forgive her either for the anguished memories she'd aroused, the helpless, suffocating feeling of panic that had risen like bile in his throat. She might have died and he would have been helpless to prevent it. Just like Doe.

His fear took the form of anger; the rise of his protective instincts made him even angrier.

His eyes were a hard, glittering smoke. "I would rather," he ground out, "you have the sense not to go out alone in a snowstorm. I warned you about the dangers here. Goddammit, do I have to play nursemaid to you every minute of the day?"

The words erupted between them with soft violence.

Despite her shudders, Heather stiffened, her spine going rigid. Backhanding the tears from her cheeks, she turned her face away. She didn't want him to see her cry.

"No," she managed hoarsely, "you are not required to play nursemaid."

Forcing her feet to move, she retrieved her coat from the wall peg. When she went to the door, Sloan gave a start.

"Dammit, where do you think you're going?"

"Somewhere where I'm wanted—where I'm n-not considered a th-threat to your daughter...."

Behind her, Sloan cursed. Moving swiftly, he put a hand against the door and shoved it shut. Heather struggled to open it again, but he was too strong for her, and she was too weak with fatigue and cold.

"Dammit, duchess, don't be a fool. You can't go back out there. You'll freeze to death."

"What do you care?"

Her voice caught on a sob. She was shaking; her head was bowed.

He steeled himself against her tears. At her back, his hands rose to her shoulders, gripping tightly.

She flinched. "Damn you, leave me be!"

She tried to draw away, but he forced her to turn around. The tears streamed down her face, yet she refused to look at him.

Those tears kicked him square and hard in the chest. Sloan inhaled a sharp breath, surveying her beautiful face, vainly trying to ignore the heat that surged through him. He tightened his grasp and found himself bringing her closer, imprisoning her. He wanted to erase those tears. He wanted to shelter her, to hold her, to warm her with his body, his lips . . . even as he wanted to punish her.

With another vivid curse, he brought his mouth down hard on hers.

Chapter 9

〜⌒⊙⊙⌒〜

Heat leapt between them, shocking and primal. Relief, anger, need, all came pouring out of Sloan, into his kiss. His temper was frayed from the strain of weeks of wanting her, from the emotions that fought and tangled inside him ... fear and passion and pent-up desire.

He felt Heather attempt to pull away as his mouth took hers fiercely. It triggered in him a primal, violent response to subdue and conquer. He deepened his kiss, refusing to release her—until she made a soft, despairing sound that broke through his blind haze of lust and anger and tore at his heart.

Lifting his head, Sloan took a deep breath, fighting the savage heat of his body. It was like a knife in him to see those tears on her face.

"Don't," he whispered, his voice low and rough. "Don't cry."

Something twisted painfully in his chest and made him reach out to touch her wet cheek. She turned her face away, her body racked by shuddering.

Remorse squeezed his heart like a fist; her vulnerability pierced him as nothing else could.

163

His anger turning to tenderness against his will, Sloan slid his arms around her and gathered her into him, this time gently, wrapping her carefully in his strength. She leaned weakly against him and sobbed quietly against his shoulder.

The last of his defenses crumbled. She was soft and trembling against him; her tears seemed to soak through his shirt and into his heart.

He didn't want to let her go. He wanted, he realized with dismay, to hold her and touch her, to keep her close and protect her. He wanted to make love to her.

"I'm sorry," he murmured.

Hearing the rough contrition in his voice, Heather fought to hold back a ragged sob. The hand that stroked her back and smoothed her gown along the curve of her bottom was soothing, gentle. She couldn't understand Sloan's sudden compassion, yet she needed whatever comfort she could find.

Drawing back, she looked up into his eyes. Her tears arrested at his expression—three parts concern and one of tenderness.

The night trembled around them as Sloan brought his hands up to cradle her tearstained face. He pressed the lightest of kisses on her lips, then bent and lifted her into his arms.

Wordlessly he carried her from the kitchen and up the stairs to her bedchamber. The room was dark but warmed by the steady heat of the woodstove. Sloan set her on her feet and lit a lamp. In the sudden pale glow, Heather shivered.

Watching her, Sloan hesitated. Desire knifed through him, sharp and insistent; his body was hard with need. Yet seeing her standing there, looking so proud and vulnerable, gave him pause. She had wrapped her arms around herself, protecting herself from him. Her eyes were wary.

He knew she wouldn't come willingly to him. He'd seen to that. He had pushed her away at every opportunity. He had made her cry. Her very gentleness had goaded him to hurt her. Now he was filled with the desire to offer solace, the need to comfort, as well as other primal feelings more basic and male. Still, he intended to give her the choice.

"Do you want me to leave?"

The air between them trembled, raw with tension.

"No," Heather whispered.

His gaze heated to molten pewter. His hand came up to touch her, because he could no longer bear a moment of not touching her. The hell with waiting. He wanted her, wanted to lose himself in her body, the taste of her, the smell of her, the feel of her.

The combs that held her heavy hair were the first casualty. Then Sloan bent his head, tangling his hands in her silver tresses and holding her mouth still for his kiss. It seemed foolish that a simple touch could give birth to intense need, intense hunger, yet just this small contact made him want her more.

Her quivering seemed to echo in him, sending tremors that shivered across his own skin. It brought him back to reality just a little.

"You're freezing," he murmured. "We have to get you out of these damp clothes."

Tugging back the bedcovers, he pressed her down to sit on the edge of the mattress. Then Sloan knelt to unlace her half-boots and remove her wet stockings. Her feet were like ice. He wrapped his hands around one at a time, massaging gently, until she made a soft sound that was half pain, half relief.

Her underdrawers came first, then her gown. Finally her corset and chemise. Her skin gleamed like ivory, the ripe breasts tumbling forward, lushly made, the nipples tightened in automatic response.

The need that had gripped Sloan in its talons for days now tightened its hold ruthlessly. He was hard and throbbing with it. He wanted to fill his hands with her breasts, his mouth with her taste, wanted to feel her softness enveloping his man's heat. He wanted to watch her when she went wild beneath him. . . .

"Lie down," he urged hoarsely, helping her into bed, the foot of which was warmed by hot, flannel-covered bricks. Pressing her back on the feather mattress, he drew the piles of covers over her naked body. Then swiftly he pulled off his own clothes, tossing them haphazardly on the floor.

Heather watched him wordlessly, bracing herself for what was to come. Sloan would hurt her, just as he had in the past. Not physically, of course. He wouldn't be rough with her. But her wounded heart would be the worse for this night.

She tensed as he came toward her, one corner of her mind registering the sheer physical splendor of his naked body. Starkly masculine, he moved with athletic grace, his body rippling with fluid strength. Her gaze wandered lower, to the tempered-steel thighs and the thick erection rising from the dark curls at his groin. She drew a sharp breath as a hot shameless need filled her.

She fought against it for a moment, her heart slamming painfully against her rib cage.

Sloan stood over her, waiting. "Heather?"

Was she imagining that hoarseness in his voice that hinted of desire? That spoke of primal need, of want? That echoed the need inside her?

Could she deny him? Could she deny herself?

But no, Heather reflected with silent misery. She had only one choice. The time for self-protection was long past. She wanted his hands, his mouth, his hard body, wanted him with a raw, reckless hunger. He made her want him.

He could see in her expressive eyes she was his for the taking. He slid beneath the covers, pressing against her, letting her feel his heat and hardness.

His hands stealing upward, he threaded his fingers through her tangled hair. "I want to make love to you," he murmured, his voice silky and rough.

His lips found her throat and her back arched, her taut nipples scraping his chest. Her shyness vanished as it always did when he touched her, while a shallow gasp broke from her lips. Then he lowered his head to her breast. His tongue circled the dusky crest, now pebbled and urgent. When his hot mouth closed over her nipple, sucking it strongly, Heather whimpered at the searing wet heat.

Sweet God, how could he affect her so? Why did her heart lurch so wildly at his touch? Her newly sensitized body thrummed with panic and desire, her senses spun wildly.

Yet Sloan seemed totally in control. His sensual assault was slow and unhurried and careful. He lingered over her, deliberately branding her flesh as his, while his hand slid between her thighs. He was touching her there now, intimately stroking, arousing the slick flesh with exquisite caresses.

Her head thrashed on the pillow as the torment continued. Once she'd thought he lacked tenderness. That he was dark and hard and dangerous. She'd been wrong about the tenderness. His touch was smoke and fire, making her burn with the pleasure he was giving her. Her skin was fevered, her senses singed by brazen heat. She could scarcely bear the savage magic he was working with his hands and lips.

Raw heartbeats later, Sloan eased his body between her thighs. His naked arousal pulsed hard between her legs.

"Look at me, darlin'." He gazed down at her, his smoky eyes suddenly very blue as he pressed into her.

She gasped aloud at the feel of him, huge and hot and urgent. Desire, savage and blinding, rippled through her as he slowly thrust home. She heard his voice, raw silk, coming from far away as he whispered to her, sensual, carnal words, telling her how good he felt entering her, stretching her, filling her. His dark words only inflamed her more.

Then he began to move inside her, reaching deep with every stroke. Heather moaned and clutched his shoulders, her nails scoring his skin.

Sloan felt the same exquisite torment. The breathless need that spiked through his body was fierce and overwhelming. He was a man who prided himself on control, but the sweetness of her hot, tight flesh drove out all logical thought. The urgency built and built, on and on, until the savage pleasure engulfed them both.

Racked by ecstasy, she cried out and twisted to meet his thrusts. As she shuddered around him, Sloan shoved her face against his sweat-slicked shoulder and buried her scream. Each tremor burned through him relentlessly, melting reality into oblivion. His straining thighs pressing hers wide, he drove into her with pent-up wildness. In only moments, fiery talons of sensation ripped through him in a harsh, convulsive climax . . . frenzied . . . tumultuous . . . violent. Groaning, gasping for breath, he plunged into her, feeling his body explode inside her, pulses of fire flowing between them.

When it was over, he held her shaking body while the heated tremors faded. His quick, hard breathing feathered her face as he willed his pulse to slow.

He was stunned by the primordial possessiveness that had overcome him, by the very rawness of his male hunger. He couldn't understand his restless, aching need to possess her. The pleasure he'd had with Heather had been shattering, totally wiping out the memories that usually plagued him during sex.

He raised his head. She was limp and trembling, her eyes dark and dazed with remembered passion, her pale cheeks framed in a wild tangle of glorious silver-gold hair. His heart twisted in his chest.

Sloan stirred, easing the crush of his weight off her.

"Don't leave me—" Her whisper of alarm was a plea as her fingers tightened on his bare shoulder.

"I'm not leaving." Shifting his body, he drew the rumpled covers up over them both and settled her against him. "I should check on Janna and close up the house for the night, but that can wait."

Relief flooding her, Heather burrowed into the heat and strength of him. He hadn't left her this time. He'd remained with her, holding her tight against his warmth, his muscle-corded arms wrapped around her, his lean, sinewy hands absently stroking her naked skin.

It was not that Sloan truly cared about her, she knew that well enough, despite his present tender regard. But she would take what comfort he would give her. She sighed, feeling his heart beat strongly against her breast. She wanted him to go on holding her like this forever. She wanted to feel this close, this safe, always.

Sloan lay beside her, his thoughts in turmoil, his passion spent. He knew he should return to his own bed. It wasn't wise to stay—not when they were both so vulnerable. But he couldn't walk away. He wasn't strong enough.

He'd considered himself invincible, yet he couldn't steel his heart against the insidious desire to keep Heather close and just hold her.

He breathed her in, savoring the sweet warm fragrance of her skin. The taste of her clung to his mouth, and he pressed his lips against the silk of her hair.

He closed his eyes, remembering the recent moments of raw torment and searing pleasure. He had been wild to have her, but the duchess had been just as wild for him. He was still stunned by the contrast of her cool, elegant image and the moaning, writhing woman in his arms. She was so astonishingly sensual, she had the power to shatter his hard-won control.

He was crazy to have let himself go so far, yet his relief to find her unhurt had affected his judgment disastrously. He'd needed to reassure himself that she was really okay. . . . And then he'd wound up savaging her with his temper again.

"Heather?" His voice was a hoarse murmur. "If I was angry at you tonight, if I went over the line . . . it's because I was afraid."

"Afraid?"

He turned his head slowly on the pillow to look at her, his unreadable eyes sliding over her face. "I've already lost one wife. I was afraid I would find you . . ." He didn't finish.

Dead, was what he meant, she realized. He was thinking of Doe. She could see the bleak sorrow in his eyes. A new coldness crept through her body.

She didn't want the tragedy of the past to intrude on the peace of the moment, yet it was the first part of his inner self Sloan had shared with her willingly. The vulnerability he'd revealed to her was all the more shattering, because she knew how rare it was.

"You weren't to blame for her death, Sloan," she whispered.

At her murmur, the fingers stroking her arm suddenly went still. He was silent for so long, she thought he wasn't going to answer.

"I was to blame," he said, his tone devoid of emotion.

"No, you can't condemn yourself for what happened."

"You weren't there. You don't know."

"Tell me about it," she urged.

His gaze turned distant. He didn't want to talk about it. He didn't want to remember that day. Doe's pain, his rage, his despair. He couldn't save her. . . . Guilt rose in his throat, almost choking him. "She died in my arms. Christ, there was so much blood. . . ."

His voice had dropped to a husk of a whisper, but Heather heard the raw pain at its depths.

"The buckskin coat," she said quietly, suddenly making the connection. "The one I tried to wash. You were upset at me for touching it."

He heaved a shuddering breath before he nodded. "Doe was wearing it that day. I couldn't bring myself to throw it away. I didn't want to forget."

He had saved the bloodstained coat like some grisly trophy—or worse, a reminder of his guilt. She stared into his eyes, absorbing his pain. Her throat hurt with the need to cry. "You must have loved her very much."

"Yes, I loved her," he said hoarsely. "So much I ached with it. She was ... She was like the sun, warm and nurturing. She was my life." There was a pause. "I died that day, along with her."

"No," Heather replied urgently, "you didn't die. You lived to care for your daughter."

The words reached inside him and cradled a part of him he didn't want anyone near. Sloan winced, wanting to curse Heather and her damned interference. She didn't understand the bleakness of his soul, the great gaping hole where his heart should have been.

Then he made the mistake of looking into her eyes. It was like stripping his soul bare. He saw quiet compassion there, and sheltering, tender solace. A solace he didn't want, couldn't accept. He gathered his shattered defenses around him like armor, drawing into himself. He turned his face away to stare up at the ceiling.

In the silence Heather felt his withdrawal like an icy wind. Once again Sloan was the remote, cold stranger, though he held her against his warm, naked body.

Tears stung her eyes at the loss. Gazing at his chiseled profile, she wondered what it was like to love someone that much, so much that death meant the death of one's own heart.

Instinctively her hand reached up, her fingers touching his lean cheek, but Sloan might have been a marble statue for all the warmth or emotion he showed.

She closed her eyes against the longing that welled up in her. She couldn't ease his torment or heal the deep sorrow that tortured him, heart and soul. Perhaps Sloan was right. He had been mortally wounded that day, just as surely as if his enemies had plunged a knife into his chest.

Her own heart constricting with pain and regret, Heather swallowed the ache that rose in her throat. She was mistaken. Sloan's heart was not made of ice. The reality was far worse. His heart belonged to his late wife.

She had a dead woman for a rival.

Chapter 10

He stayed with her the entire night, holding her, warming her, comforting her with his strength when she needed so badly to have his arms around her. He left before dawn, telling her to sleep a while longer.

Already missing him, Heather lay there in the early-morning darkness, remembering.

She had tried to imagine what Sloan's lovemaking would be like, with heat and need and hunger. But never had she envisioned the sensual power of his burning lips and magical hands and lithe body. His lovemaking was as intense and elemental as he was, like getting caught up in a storm. Yet for all the violence and power of their coupling, there had been a gentleness as well.

She should be grateful for that small victory. Sloan McCord was a hard man, brooding and remote and untouchable. A man who gave no hint of feeling anything for her beyond resentment and raw, male lust. Yet for a brief moment last night, she had broken through his granite shell.

He had wanted her, she was certain of it. The memory of how he had looked in the throes of passion, his hair damp with sweat, his eyes burning in his taut face, gave her reason to hope. The intimacy between them had been sexual, true, but it was still intimacy of a sort. Sloan had allowed her closer than he'd ever done in the past.

As Heather rose to wash and dress, her heart was lighter than at any time since her marriage. The weather matched her mood. The spring sun came out, bright and benevolent, warming the land and melting all traces of snow by noon. It was as if the late-winter storm had never blown through, endangering her life and her tenuous relationship with her husband.

She tackled her chores with renewed energy, wondering if Sloan would return home early, and if so, whether there would be a repeat of last night's passion. As the day wore on, needles of anticipation and excitement pricked her nerve endings.

Sloan, however, was determined to delay the moment of his return as long as possible, at least until he got himself under control. After paying a visit to his brother and his new niece, he rode the range for hours, rounding up strays and moving one of his larger herds to lower pastures—all the while cursing for letting himself desire his new bride.

At the same time another part of his mind rationally argued with his tangled emotions. He had no reason to flay himself with guilt. Hell, Heather was his wife. He had the right to take her body if he wanted.

The trouble was, he was becoming obsessed with her. He couldn't get enough of her, of the powerful, addictive pleasure that being inside her brought. His simple male hunger had become a restless, aching need—hurting and painful.

Denying himself wasn't working, Sloan realized grimly. Maybe if he changed tactics, he could get Heather out of his blood. If he had her body over and over again, then maybe he could rid himself of these explosions of passion and craving and relief that were driving him crazy.

That would be the extent of their relationship. Carnal gratification. There would be no pretense of love or affection between them. Love wouldn't enter into it. He wanted her body, not her heart. All he wanted was to get the ache in his groin taken care of.

And as long as he held himself remote—no emotion, just uncomplicated lust—then he could take what he wanted. He wouldn't let himself drown in her. Yet he would offer her wild, hot, mind-numbing sex in return.

The duchess wouldn't like being used that way, he suspected, but he wouldn't give her reason to complain. He would have his fill of her, until the blazing heat in his body was sated. He would have her whenever and however he wanted. But he'd make damn certain she enjoyed it.

Anticipation and arousal riding him hard, he returned home in the mood to wrestle grizzlies. Heather was at work fixing Janna's supper, but looked up as Sloan entered the kitchen. His hat was pulled down low over his eyes when his gaze locked with hers.

An invisible skein of lightning wrapped around them, catching them fast.

The spell was broken when Janna threw her spoon on the floor in a rare fit of impatience.

"I didn't expect you so early," Heather murmured, trying to quell her rapid pulse.

With a shrug, Sloan rescued his daughter's spoon and picked her up in his arms.

"Are you hungry?" Heather asked him.

"I could eat," he prevaricated.

He took Janna with him when he went to wash up for supper, while Heather finished cooking. When they returned, Sloan's tawny hair was still damp, with curling tendrils falling over his ears and shirt collar, making him look younger, less forbidding. The angles and planes of his face, however, were set in their usual rigid lines. Any tenderness or regard she'd evoked in him had gone the way of the storm, Heather suspected.

And despite the presence of his daughter, there was a new tension in the air, along with a sense of heightened danger. Sloan's brooding sensuality was as potent as a bonfire. When she moved close enough to serve his supper, she could feel the heat emanating from his body, smell the warm musky male scent of his skin.

It was all Heather could do to take her place at the table and act normally, as if her heart was not racing a mile a minute.

"You haven't yet asked how Caitlin fared last night," she managed to remark. "You have a new niece."

"I know. I rode over at first light. Cat and the baby are doing fine," Sloan answered at her inquiring look. "I gave Jake hell for letting you go out in the storm."

"He wasn't to blame, I was. I didn't think it necessary to have an escort."

Sloan sent her a hard look that clearly conveyed what he thought of such foolishness. Heather fell silent and applied herself to her supper, barely tasting what she ate.

"Leave the dishes," he murmured when she started to clear the table.

She felt her heart skip a beat. He was watching her. His gaze dropped to her breasts. His eyes were so intense, so hot, she felt their invading heat burn right through to bare flesh underneath.

They ascended the stairs and put Janna to bed together. When the young child's eyelids grew heavy, Sloan turned down the lamp wick to a low glow.

Moments later Heather felt a shock of pleasure when his arms slid around her from behind. Her back arched involuntarily when his lean hands moved to cup her full breasts—those knowledgeable hands that knew a woman's body so well. When his lips brushed the side of her throat, she felt the familiar treacherous warmth filling her.

"Let's go to bed."

His voice was husky and low as he turned her around. His blue eyes were narrowed in a look of sexual intent as old as time. Her breath caught in her throat. She hadn't thought much beyond the simple, burning need to be close to him.

She glanced at his bed, the one he had shared with his beloved wife.

"Not here," Sloan added in a low voice. "I don't want to wake Janna."

Heather disbelieved his explanation, but let it pass. She wanted him, wanted to comfort him and offer him something soft and gentle. She wanted to heal him.

Healing did not seem to be on Sloan's mind as he led her to her bedchamber. He left the door partially open behind them as she turned to face him.

"Take off your dress," he ordered quietly.

The room was dark but for the moonglow spilling through the open curtains. He didn't light a lamp, but instead stood silent as she undressed, his features cast in a mix of silver light and black shadow, his expression hard and sensual as he watched her. Heather felt the rise of heat inside her, a coiling tension, a need so palpable it throbbed and pulsed with a life of its own.

He said not a word until her bodice and skirt fell to the floor. "Now the rest."

With fumbling fingers she obeyed. When finally she stood naked before him, Sloan drank in his fill of her. He could feel the reckless hunger begin, slow and insidious, his loins growing heavy with desire.

She was a woman, lush and full, her body white and wanton, her skin smooth and flawless in the moonlight. Yet even nude she maintained that aura of elegance, of poise. He wanted her for that cool composure, wanted to shatter it with passion. He wanted her all soft and melted beneath him as he took her. He wanted to see wonder and blind pleasure in her eyes.

"Come here, duchess," he murmured, "and take off my shirt."

She hesitated only a moment before moving toward him, as if drawn by an invisible force, the same inexorable force that was driving him. She drew off his leather vest first, then his shirt and undershirt. Then she raised her face to his.

"Taste me. . . ." he muttered thickly.

She came willingly into his arms. His fingers threading through her moon-silvered hair, he took her mouth, needing her taste, her touch. He craved the silky softness of her body. He wanted to stroke her, get her wet, make her want him. He wanted to set her afire, until she turned hot and wild in his arms, until she burned, until she couldn't bear the fierce arousal any longer.

Deliberately clamping down on his male urges, Sloan pulled back. Her lips were wet from his kiss, her eyes dazed. Without giving her chance to protest, he lifted her in his arms and laid her on the bed. Shadows danced across the tumbled sheets, caressing her lovely body. His breath came hard and heavy with the need to cover her with his own body. He could imagine himself thrusting inside her, could almost feel her tight, wet heat.

Desire knifed through him, but he held back, settling beside her on the mattress instead.

His thumb brushed across her nipples that budded hard and tight, reminding her of the pleasure he could give her. When she drew a sharp breath, he slowed his assault even more, caressing this time.

Heat flared inside her as his dark hands played over her white skin, his calloused thumbs teasing and tormenting by turns. Then he lowered his head to her breast, and Heather whimpered. When he sucked strongly, she shuddered at the blatant carnality of it, helpless with desire.

His lips moved relentlessly over her body. He was gentle but he wasn't loving. His exploration was slow and ruthlessly thorough, his hot mouth raising chills wherever it grazed. Shameful pleasure flared wherever he touched her. She felt his mark everywhere. Only the shredded remains of her pride kept her from crying out in wild delight.

"Sloan. . . ." Her back arched, her body begging for his conquest. It was unlike anything she had experienced, this feeling of intense excitement that grew like a whirling flame inside her.

When he lifted his head, his hard eyes were filled with masculine satisfaction, and there was a ghost of a smile on his mouth . . . that incredibly sensuous, beautifully carved mouth.

Shifting his body, he parted her thighs so that her slick, swollen folds were completely exposed to his gaze. When she felt his hot breath on her, she moaned, her body trying to twist away.

"Be still. I want to enjoy you."

Kneeling, he lifted her legs onto his shoulders. Scandalized, Heather went rigid.

When his cheek brushed the inside of her thigh, her breath suddenly ceased. Then she felt the silken probe of his tongue parting her, and a strangled pleading sounded deep in her throat.

"No . . . don't. . . ." Yet she wanted him to kiss her there; her body was craving it, begging for it.

As if he understood her need, his hard hands cupped her soft, rounded cheeks, and he bent his mouth to her, his tongue dipping and circling.

A choked sob tore from her throat. "Oh, God, please . . . Sloan. . . ." She was dimly appalled to realize she was begging.

He kissed her as though he were kissing her mouth, while her hips restlessly strained against the velvet torment. Heather quivered at the feel as his dazzling mouth branded her with his caresses. She couldn't stand the fiery throbbing.

Desperately she dug her fingers into the tawny pelt of his hair. His hot, open mouth sank deeper and she cried out as he buried his face between her thighs.

His tongue savored her sweetness in long, hot strokes, probing, lapping, suckling. His mouth devoured her, taking her ever closer to the forbidden, throbbing pleasure he promised her, dredging another broken sob from deep within her as he held her surging hips down with his hands.

"Let it go, sweetheart."

Her body aflame, she surrendered to his demands, yielding, exploding with a scream of pleasure. He drew back slowly, leaving her weak and trembling. With a final kiss to her dewy, throbbing center, he lifted his head.

Heather lay panting in shock, her tongue wetting

her dry lips, while Sloan shifted his weight to un-buckle his belt and free his erection.

Heather couldn't find the energy to move . . . not until he eased between her thighs and positioned the thick head of his shaft at the entrance of her womanhood . . . not until his hard, hot sex slowly glided into her.

Another tremor shook her and Sloan bent to kiss her high brow beneath her wild hair, feeling her ripple and contract in latent ecstasy. One hard thrust and she would be twisting beneath him again, panting and mindless.

"Look at me, duchess."

She obeyed. The expression in his eyes was sud-denly shockingly intense; she felt she might melt from the blistering heat, from his smoldering sen-suality. His face was so rigid he looked brutal. He sank in hard, filling her, his teeth clenched against the fierce storm that was sweeping them in its wake.

Suddenly he couldn't hold back, and neither could she. Her body craving his heat and strength, she moved against him, with him, caught up in a spiraling hunger and desire that was out of control.

There was no tenderness. It was a savage reckless coupling, one of incredible urgency. There was a wildness about him as he drove hard into her fully aroused body. He made her shake inside as he hur-tled her to the heavens. She clawed at his back, her cries melding with his raw moans as the violent, shattering release found them both.

The liquid tremors went on and on and on. In the harsh aftermath she lay struggling for breath in his arms. She could smell the hot musk of his arousal, feel the warm wetness of tears on her cheeks from the tumultuous force of their lovemak-ing.

When finally he raised his head to gaze down at her, Heather averted her face, unable to meet his gaze. More disturbing than the heat and intensity of those ice-blue eyes was the aching knowledge deep in her heart.

She could love this man, this moody, powerful man with his hard eyes and tender hands. But love was no part of their bargain. She would have to settle for hot, blinding pleasure, for that was all Sloan would give her.

He woke slowly, his body alive with desire. The bedroom was bright and warm with sunrise. Still sleeping, Heather was curled into the curve of his thighs, her warm, soft fanny pressed against his groin, making his morning erection that much harder.

He pressed his mouth against the pale mass of her burnished hair, his lungs filled with the rich, tormenting scent. His hand stole beneath the covers to cup a lush bare breast. A sensual sigh escaped her lips as she stirred, but she didn't awaken.

Fierce impatience seized him. He was hard and ready for her. His blood surging thick and hot, Sloan caught her hips and eased between her thighs from behind, pushing inside her before she'd managed to come fully awake. She moaned helplessly and arched her back.

Driven by a savage, nameless hunger, he found his pleasure and took Heather along for the wild ride.

It was long moments later before she roused from the incredible dream she'd been having, feeling limp as if drugged, her limbs heavy, her body replete. Sloan was at her back. She lay unmoving, savoring his heat, the incredible lean toughness of his body, the work-hardened hands that were still stroking her skin.

"Morning." His early-morning voice was dark and rough as he whispered in her ear.

Her eyes opened slowly as awareness returned. Heather flushed, remembering the carnal excesses of last night. He'd made love to her over and over again, and each time the pleasure had intensified. Her own behavior was shameful. She'd rutted, lain beneath Sloan and begged him. And this morning, she'd let him . . .

She glanced in puzzlement at the bright sunshine streaming in the window. "It's daylight."

"So it is."

She turned over to face him. Sloan felt his breath catch at her beauty. She looked soft and sleep-rumpled and sensual enough to eat.

"It's late. . . . Shouldn't you be leaving for the range?"

He shrugged. "The boys won't wait for me. I told them I'd be up at the house all day."

"All day?" She flushed again. "They'll know what . . . we . . . you. . . ."

A grin tugged at the corner of his mouth. "Maybe they will. And they'll likely be jealous as hell."

Heather pulled the sheet over her breasts, a gesture that struck him as sweetly incongruous, considering everything they had done last night. He'd explored and savored every secret of her body, some more than once.

"There's no need to be so modest, duchess." Sloan caught her hand and turned her palm against his cheek, warm and beard-rough. "You're my wife. You've committed no crime. It's just sex."

She turned her face away. She didn't want him

to deny he'd felt all the things she had in their mating.

She rose from the bed and drew on a wrapper to fend off the morning chill. Catching a glance of her wanton image in the mirror, Heather sat at the small dressing table and picked up a brush in order to bring some semblance of order to her wild hair.

Sloan spoke lazily from the bed. "There's no need for you to get dressed yet. We won't be finished for a while."

She glanced at the bed to find him watching her, his hands laced behind his head, the pale sheets barely covering his narrow hips. Her pulse leapt at the sight. He looked like a ruffian, his tawny hair tousled, jaw hardened by darker stubble—thoroughly disreputable and oh so sexually compelling. As tender as she felt in certain parts of her body, Heather could still feel herself growing warm and liquid as she looked at him. "But Janna . . . the chores."

"The chores can wait. And I'll take care of Janna when she wakes."

"Sloan . . . it's broad daylight," she protested, half in dismay at his insatiable hunger, half at her own unassuaged arousal.

The tension suddenly returned between them.

"What if it is? I warned you before we married, I'm a man of great carnal need. You agreed to give me your body whenever and wherever I want you. You backing out on our bargain, duchess?"

Their gazes locked and warred, hers cool, his burning with intensity. "No, not at all."

"Then take off your robe. I want to see you."

His hard, raspy, early-morning voice was sensual enough to make her shiver, for it brought to mind the rawly sexual things he had murmured in her ear throughout the dark hours of the night.

Heather briefly shut her eyes. She was not about to back down, but there was only one way she could keep her composure—by pretending Sloan wasn't watching her so brazenly, by acting as if they had never made love with frantic, explosive need.

Keeping her back rigid, she unfastened the clasps of her wrapper and let it fall off her shoulders. Then, squaring her shoulders, she faced him proudly, challenging him with her eyes.

He didn't smile as he gave her a thorough inspection, with acutely masculine appraisal. She could feel his gaze like a tangible caress, drifting insolently over her breasts, her bare thighs, the pale curls between. . . . Trying to quell the excitement flaring low in her belly, she resumed her brushing, determined not to lose this war of wills between them.

Sloan watched her as she drew the bristles through the long, glorious tresses. She was achingly beautiful, and as proud and regal as any queen.

"You look as untouchable as an ice princess," he observed casually. "Seeing you now would dare any man to try melting you."

"I feel like ice," Heather retorted, ignoring his provocation. "The air in this room is chilly. No one in his right mind would sit naked like this."

"That depends on how you were raised, I reckon. Doe never wore a wrapper, or a nightdress," Sloan observed thoughtfully. "The Cheyenne are unashamed of their bodies, of sex."

It stung her, his casual reference to his beloved wife. "I fail to see how it does either of us any good to make comparisons."

It did *him* good. It made him remember where his loyalties lay. "The Cheyenne don't wear corsets or drawers either. Maybe in the coldest weather they might wear buckskin leggings under their dresses, but that's all."

Heather turned to meet his gaze directly. "I was brought up differently—but I am not in competition with your first wife. Indeed, I'm certain no woman could ever measure up, so I won't presume to try."

He smiled and some of the chill was back between them. "No, you're nothing like Doe. She was a proper wife."

"Proper?"

"Accommodating and obedient. An obedient wife doesn't hide her body from her husband. She would keep herself ready and waiting for him any time he wants her."

"It is unfortunate then," Heather replied with cool defiance at his taunting, "that I have never been considered particularly obedient."

His return smile was lazy, although there was nothing casual about the glitter in his smoky eyes. "A proper wife isn't cold to her husband, either. Then again, you weren't cold last night. You were hot as a firecracker, out of control."

Her cheeks warmed with color. "You are deliberately being crude."

"What if I am? You could do with a little shaking up." He was studying her intently, his heated eyes lingering on her naked breasts. "At least those prudish notions of yours disappear in bed."

"I hardly think it prudish to be a bit shocked by your wickedness. Any lady would have been scandalized by the things you did last night."

"You enjoyed the wicked things I did to you, admit it." Sloan shifted on the mattress, wincing slightly. "I can feel the nail cuts you left all over my back and shoulders."

"Perhaps . . . I did enjoy them, but that doesn't

mean I care to repeat the experience this morning. I have work to do, duties to attend to."

"One of your main duties is pleasing your husband. Come here and please me, duchess."

Her spine stiffened. "My name is not *'duchess.'* "

"Heather, then. Come here, sweetheart." His voice dropped to a caress, infused with masculine charm. "Please."

She eyed him archly. "You can't possibly be eager to make love again."

"Oh, yes, I can. I want you, Heather. I want you beneath me, your legs wrapped tight around me as I lie buried hard and deep inside you."

Every low, husky word stroked her. Almost against her will, Heather rose and went to stand before him.

At the nearness of her luscious, naked body, Sloan began to harden as desire heated his loins. He'd taken her four times last night and again this morning, but it hadn't been enough. He wanted her still, more powerfully than before. He wanted to make her lose the last of her inhibitions.

Her hesitation just now, however, was not simply due to modesty or ladylike reserve. "Sloan . . . I'm not certain I can . . . bear any more just now."

His hard gaze suddenly softened. "I should have realized you'd be sore."

He could think of nothing he'd like better than to bury his fingers in that silvery mane and stretch Heather naked on this bed and have her over and over again. But he had to remember the fierce demands he had already made on her body.

Still, that didn't mean he couldn't employ other methods. He wanted to teach her what it was like to enjoy a man. He wanted to bring out the sensual side of her nature—and drive her mindless with unbearable pleasure at the same time. The woman he wanted in his bed was the incredible lover he'd known in his dreams.

He drew the sheet aside, an invitation for her to join him in bed. "We won't do anything that hurts you. In fact, I won't do a thing. You can have all the honors."

She gazed at him uncertainly, at his body rippling with muscles. The center of his chest was sparsely furred with a silky gold triangle of hair that narrowed over his hard, flat belly to his groin. Her gaze dropped lower. His upthrust sex was already thick and swollen, reaching almost to his navel. That exciting hardness made her blood race.

"I don't know what to do," she murmured, her voice holding a strange huskiness.

"Use your imagination."

Slowly, she climbed onto the bed and knelt naked beside him. His magnificent masculinity no longer shocked her. Instead, it left her tingling with sexual awareness. She wanted to reach out and satisfy her natural curiosity about his body. She actually ached to touch him.

"Touch me," he murmured, echoing her thoughts. His eyes were hot and held dark promises. "Take my cock in your hands and hold me."

Gently, he captured her hand to encourage and guide her. When her fingers closed around him, he winced slightly.

"Does that hurt?" she asked.

He gave a strangled laugh. "A good hurt." His fingers wrapped about hers so she held him tightly. With a soft groan, he shut his eyes.

For the first time in their stormy relationship, Heather understood the effect she was having on him, and it soothed her initial panic. She took a deep breath. She had not given Sloan much pleasure during their first sexual encounters; she'd been too nervous and inexperienced even to try. But now he was giving her the chance.

And she wanted to take it. She wanted to make this man, as remote and icily detached as he was, feel the same hot, uncontrollable pleasure he aroused in her.

Her fingers cupped him tentatively as she watched his face. The bronzed skin was pulled taut across lean cheekbones while the pulse beat so strongly in his throat, she could see its throbbing rhythm. Her exploration grew bolder, learning the feel of him, the sensations of swollen sacks nestled in soft dark hair, the long, thick shaft that was hot and silken to the touch, the flushed, bulbous head with the encircling ridge. . . .

With effort, Sloan lay completely still, allowing her to set the pace. Only his hand moved, guiding her, showing her how to stroke and arouse him.

"Like this?" she whispered.

"Exactly . . . like that. . . ." he agreed, his voice an uneven gasp.

In fascination she fondled him, caressing until he arched his hips in fitful need. Yet Heather was not inclined to satisfy him just yet. She wanted to draw out the intimate moment, to drive Sloan as mad with desire as he did her.

Following her intuition, she rose up on her knees. She wanted to taste him. Daringly, she bent over him, her long hair caressing his body as she pressed her lips to his engorged flesh. Sloan groaned.

Her own body aching shamelessly for him, she placed a questioning kiss on the velvet-smooth head. His every muscle went rigid. Greatly encouraged, she touched him with her tongue, tasting salt and musk and male sweetness. His head moved restlessly on the pillow. Her tongue traced the rigid length, and she felt a surge of triumph when his fists gripped the sheets.

The last remnants of shyness fading, she continued her sensual assault, sliding her lips down over the swollen crown as her fingers caressed him.

It was the startling boldness of her next intimacy, however, that made him shudder. She sucked gently, drawing him into her mouth with an innocent passion that inflamed him.

Pulsating wildly, Sloan let the male ache wash over him in ripples of pleasure-pain. "Duchess. . . ."

"My name is Heather," she whispered against his hot flesh. "Say it, Sloan."

He laughed softly and then groaned. "Heather . . . ahh . . . sweet Jesus, what are you doing to me?"

She was reveling in her sensual power—but suddenly it wasn't enough for her. She wanted to take him inside her body. "Sloan . . . please. . . . I want you."

It was all the encouragement he needed. Reaching for her arms, he pulled Heather on top of him. The soft warmth of her naked breasts met the hardness of his chest with the impact of a brand. Their eyes met, his hot, hers dazed.

Trying to quell the raging lust that rippled through his body, Sloan lifted her up till she sat astride his sinewed thighs. Instinctively her back arched, her breasts filling his palms, hardening and thrusting out to seek his touch, his mouth—but he held her still.

His eyes had sharpened to a glittering awareness. In a soft guttural tone he demanded, "You sure I won't hurt you?"

"Yes," she gasped.

She was breathless and ready for him, hot and

dripping wet. In a single swift motion, he raised her up and lowered her on his shaft.

The sensation of her sleek, heated flesh sheathing him was so exquisite he nearly came right then; his hunger was that raw, that explosive.

"Ride me," he rasped, and she obeyed. Her soft thighs settled over him and she began to move, seeking an urgent rhythm, her hips undulating in search of the hot pleasure he had taught her.

Desire flared hot and bright inside him, a desire he couldn't hold back. The frantic rhythm became a frenzied hunger. He bucked wildly beneath her, driving relentlessly. Her fingers dug into his shoulders as she cried out, her head thrown back in ecstasy as her climax came. His release followed instantly in a fiery explosion, and he spilled his seed in pulsing spasms.

Panting, she collapsed against him, her lush body flushed and dewy with perspiration.

This was how he wanted her, Sloan thought weakly, with her elegant, aloof image shattered. And yet remorse tinged his triumph. He'd been way too rough with her. But then ... he couldn't have controlled himself, any more than he could have stopped a wildfire racing up a dry canyon in the heat of summer.

"Is it always like this?" she whispered long moments later.

When he didn't answer, she drew back a little to look down at him.

His eyes grew hooded. He didn't want to meet her searching gaze.

Just then, they heard the sound of a child's gurgling laugh through the partially open door. Janna was awake.

Grateful for the interruption, Sloan eased himself from beneath her and left the bed. Giving her a glimpse of taut, bare buttocks, he bent to pull on his denims.

"Hell, it's just sex, duchess," he lied. "Happens all the time. Nothing to get worked up about."

Chapter 11

Their relationship changed that day, at least physically. Where once Sloan had ignored her, now he couldn't seem to get enough of her. He took her whenever and wherever he pleased.

Helpless to resist, overwhelmed by his heat and sexuality, Heather gave him everything, her body, her honor, her pride.

He became master of her body. Under his tutelage she discovered a wild, uninhibited side of herself she never suspected existed. To her dismay, she reveled in her liberation, appalled yet renewed at the same time.

He showed her the many different facets of passion. She'd never realized that lovemaking could be a slow, languorous tangle of bodies, or a feverish battle of wills. She never felt so alive as she did in his arms, losing herself in a pleasure so intense she became mindless.

Sloan, however, appeared to escape the devastating impact of their smoldering encounters. The words he whispered to her in the heat of passion were of lust and carnal need, merely that. She could put no stock in them.

Oh, he wanted her body, of that she was certain.

She couldn't mistake the taut, savage look on his face as he took her. But their lovemaking was raw and hot and purely sexual, nothing more.

Heather tried not to let it wound her. She tried to ignore the fact that Sloan's bedchamber was still off limits to her. He never took her there, although any other location in the house seemed acceptable— her bedchamber, the kitchen, his study in front of the hearth, the spare room upstairs that was used for sewing and storage and extra overnight guests. Each time, she desperately fought the feelings he unleashed inside her. If she was to survive, she would have to keep her distance emotionally. She would have to try her level best to hold herself aloof.

But she feared she was fighting a battle she could never win.

The battle proved easier once spring roundup began in mid-May. She'd heard tales of the West, thrilling stories of cattle drives and gunfights, but the reality of a ranch was endless days of grueling, mundane work as Sloan and his cowboys brought the cattle down from the hills to mark them with the Bar M brand.

Several times Heather drove out with Janna to observe the operation at a safe distance. The scene looked chaotic, the air filled with the smells of dust and smoke and burning hide, as well as the lowing of hundreds of cattle and the singing and calling of the drivers at their flanks.

Watching, she thought she understood how cowpunchers got their name. There were several members of a branding crew. First a cowboy on a racing horse would cut out a calf from the herd, rope it, then drag to closer to the fire, where a bulldogger would throw it to the ground and tie it. Then the brander would shove a hot iron into its rump, all in a matter of seconds. Lastly the ears were marked with a sharp knife, and if the animal was male, the testicles were castrated and the fries thrown into a pile to be cooked later.

Heather felt for the poor calves. Their pitiful bawling as they ran crying back to their mamas wrung her heart. But Rusty assured her it wasn't as brutal an ordeal as it looked.

"Their hides are tough," he insisted, "and they're more scared than wounded."

On her first visit with Janna, Sloan broke away from the branding operation and rode over to greet them. His smile was chiefly for his daughter, but his gaze held Heather's for a long, sensually charged moment. "Glad you could come." When he bent near, she caught the hot, earthy scents of sweat, sun, leather, and man, and her blood quickened.

The spell was over in a moment. Sloan scooped Janna up in his arms and set her before him on his horse.

"Come on, darlin'. It's time you got a look at your heritage." Much to the child's awed delight, he rode slowly around the camp, showing her the sights.

Except for the few sojourns to the range, however, Heather saw little of Sloan during the weeks of roundup. After putting in a long day branding calves, he came home late and fell wearily into bed each night, only to rise before dawn to begin all over again.

She found herself missing his presence. There were no longer any quiet cozes in his study, or homey, peaceful meals with Janna between them, or pulsing nights of darkness and desire.

She kept herself occupied, though, as spring slipped into early summer, and was not discontented with her lot. In helping to raise Janna, she'd found a sense of renewed purpose in life, and her former existence in St. Louis began to seem like a distant dream.

Until, that is, she encountered Quinn Lovell.

For the past month or more she'd heard various accounts of Sloan's political opponent, but she first met him face-to-face one morning when she drove into Greenbriar for supplies. The wealthy mining baron had already begun campaigning for state senator, it seemed, and Heather discovered him holding sway on a street corner before a small crowd of townspeople, explaining the bleakness of the future of Colorado's cattle industry.

She drew the buggy to a halt and pulled Janna onto her lap as she listened curiously. The intent crowd was questioning him about his plan to start new silver mines in the district. The few hecklers apparently were cattlemen, but the town marshal, Luther Netherson, stood to one side, keeping the peace, his pair of six-guns prominently visible.

Mr. Lovell seemed a persuasive speaker, with a powerful, booming voice any Shakespearean actor would envy. He ran to portliness perhaps, but he was tall enough to carry the bulk, and the superbly tailored suit he wore helped to disguise his paunch. He might be considered handsome, Heather reflected, but he reminded her of Evan Randolf, not merely because of his dark-chestnut hair and sideburns and curling mustache, but his suave manner.

The discussion ended with Lovell appealing for votes, and the crowd dispersed. Before Heather could drive on, though, she found her buggy approached by Lovell himself, accompanied by Marshal Netherson.

When the marshal introduced them, Mr. Lovell tipped his hat to her. "Ah, the lovely Mrs. McCord.

I understand you are the wife of my political opponent."

Heather nodded politely. "How do you do, sir."

"I am delighted to meet you at last," he returned, displaying a graceful social address. "We share a common acquaintance, I believe. Evan Randolf thinks very highly of you. He asked me to look you up."

"You know Mr. Randolf?"

"We are both on the board of the Union Pacific Railroad. I travel to St. Louis frequently on business. I understand you recently quitted that fine city. You must find it vastly different from the state of Colorado."

"Different, yes, but pleasantly so."

His eyes swept her body, taking in her jacquard bodice and skirt, as well as the half-Cheyenne child she held on her lap. "This is the little Indian child I've so much heard about?"

Protectively, Heather wrapped her arm more tightly around Janna. "This is my stepdaughter, Janna McCord."

"Her features are more pronounced than I expected."

His tone conveyed the slightest hint of triumph, and he had no need to explain his rationale aloud to Heather: Janna's lineage would likely prove a disadvantage to Sloan's campaign. The good citizens of Colorado would not be able to forget who her mother was.

"Yes, isn't it fortunate?" Heather replied evenly. "With her fine bone structure, she will doubtless grow up to be a real beauty. And she has the sweetest disposition. . . . Anyone who meets her, loves her at once."

"Perhaps." His smile was patronizing, but he seemed to tire of sparring with her. "A pity you are supporting the wrong candidate, Mrs. McCord."

Heather smiled coolly in return. "I don't believe my husband is the wrong candidate, sir."

"Well, we shall see. . . ."

Quinn Lovell tipped his hat again and politely took his leave, while Heather breathed a sigh of relief. Normally she reserved judgment until she knew someone better, but instinctively she did not like Mr. Lovell. She had the uncomfortable suspicion he possessed the same ruthless ambition as Evan Randolf.

Sarah Baxter seemed to agree with her assessment. Sarah was behind the counter of the general store when Heather entered, and wasn't at all shy in giving her opinion about Quinn Lovell.

"He's a low-down sidewinder, that's what."

"A sidewinder?"

"A rattlesnake," Sarah explained. "Pure poison— preying on decent folk down on their luck."

When Heather eyed her quizzically, Sarah explained. "Lovell's been buying up cattle ranches hereabouts. He offers the owners a pittance, but with the terrible winter we had and the price of beef so low, they have no choice but to sell. And that isn't the worst of it," she added darkly. "I've heard he's assayed a dozen sites and means to start digging new mines any day now."

"He suggested as much in the speech he gave just now. But why is that a problem?"

"Have you ever seen a slag heap? Mine tailings are about the ugliest thing you could ever lay eyes on. It's going to destroy this beautiful land."

"If that's so, then I should think the voters would object to having Lovell as their representative."

Sarah gave a ladylike snort and shook her head. "He already has a lot of support. A good third of the business in this town comes from miners, and

they want someone who'll look out for their interests. And folks who lose their ranches could find
work in Lovell's mines. . . . It's a prime pickle for
sure. We have to stop him, Heather," Sarah said
earnestly. "We have to do our darnedest to make
sure Sloan gets elected."

Late that night, though, when Heather told Sloan
about Lovell's speech in town, he only nodded with
grim resignation.

"Lovell is getting a head start on the campaign,"
she pointed out. "If you're not careful, the election
will be over before it's even begun—and he will
have won."

"Even so, I can't afford to spend time campaigning just now. I have a ranch to see to. When
roundup's over, I can concentrate on the race."

"Could you not let your foreman run things for
a while now? You could hire more hands to replace
you, could you not?"

"I can't spare the cash."

"But there must be something you can do."

Sloan sighed, his frustration evident. "It takes
money to fight men like Lovell. Money I don't
have."

Heather winced silently, remembering precisely
why Sloan was short on resources: because he'd
paid her debts. She dropped the subject for the moment, but the issue gnawed at her.

She would have to ask Vernon Whitfield what
jobs might be available for a woman with her skills.
Perhaps the schoolteacher would know where she
could find work as a part-time tutor. But this was
not the best time to begin looking. School would be
letting out shortly and not resume until the fall.

Meanwhile, however, she would do what she
could to help Sloan's senatorial campaign. She

needed no convincing to know he was the better candidate. Sloan's political aspirations were different from his opponent's. His was not a search for power or wealth, but a fervent desire to make life better for the ranchers.

The roundup ended the second week in June. Sloan and his cowpunchers drove a herd to the railhead in Denver, a short distance compared to the long treks of most cattle drives. He left Rusty as guard and general handyman.

While he was in Denver, Sloan planned to meet with a group of politicians who were interested in seeing him beat Lovell. He intended to be gone only three days, but Heather missed him more than she cared to admit. The day after his departure, she was gathering Sloan's clothing to launder when she found the chambray shirt he'd worn when they'd first met in St. Louis.

Wistfully, she rubbed the soft collar between her fingertips. Bunching the fabric in her hands, she brought it up to her face. She could still smell his male scent. Unbidden, the vulnerability, the loneliness, the longing rose up in her like a tide. She longed for a true marriage, a husband who cherished her. She longed for Sloan.

Her heart aching, Heather shook her head. She was a fool for wasting her emotions on an impossibility. Sloan had made it clear he didn't want love. She yearned for a man beyond her reach. Despite the intensity of his passion, he kept himself shut off from her, elusive and terrifyingly remote, guarding what was left of his soul like a miser.

And yet when she looked into his haunted eyes, she could almost forgive him. He still grieved for his first wife. Still loved the ghost of another woman.

She couldn't fight a ghost, or compete with such

a hallowed memory. Yet she would not, could not, stop trying to get close to him. Even though she greatly feared he would break her heart in the end.

He came home on Thursday, in mid-afternoon, just after she had put Janna down for a nap. Heather's heart did a somersault when she descended the stairs to find Sloan in the kitchen.

He seemed to be waiting for her, one hip lounging casually against the wooden table. He looked dangerous and a bit disreputable with his sleeves pushed up to expose corded, tanned forearms, his thumbs hooked into the gun belt riding low on his hips. A rough stubble shadowed his lean cheeks, while his skin seemed very bronzed. He exuded raw male attraction, every hard male inch of him.

Heather felt her pulse leap with sexual awareness, while all her senses honed to him. The air was suddenly fraught with dark undercurrents of passion.

He watched her, his ice-blue eyes intense, as he slowly unbuckled his guns and dropped them on the table. Her mouth went dry.

"Janna asleep?" he asked, his voice low, husky.

"Yes. I just put her to bed."

"Good. Come here."

That was all he said, all he needed to say. Her heart alive with excitement, she went to him. Almost roughly Sloan drew her into the hard cradle of his thighs. In response, hunger flared inside her, fanned into instant life at his touch. The heat of his body seared her through their clothing.

Heather closed her eyes, savoring the smell of horse and man rising from that seductive heat. Eagerly she raised her mouth to his.

Sloan held himself back for only an instant. He'd told himself he wasn't going to attack her the minute he got home, but for the last ten miles, all he could think of was her naked body, pale and frenzied as he took her. He wanted to be locked deep inside her, feeling her heat, making her moan for him. He wanted her clawing at his back and arching her hips for him.

His arousal was hot and throbbing. He could feel his cock pressing against the rough denim of his pants, a pleasure-pain.

"I've been hard since I left you," he muttered. "And all day today...." He pressed her hand to the straining fabric of his jeans. "I'm so hard now, my guts are hurting. I want to be inside you."

"Yes," she breathed in reply.

His lips seized hers in a kiss as darkly intimate as the mating of their bodies had once been, while his fingers fumbled with the buttons of her shirtwaist. Her clothes were in his way. He wanted to strip every stitch of them from her body. He needed to get between her long legs and make her feel things she'd never felt before. He needed to make her as hungry for him as he was for her.

He managed to pull her blouse down over her shoulders and free her flesh from the top lacy edge of her corset. Her jutting, naked breasts rose above the tight whalebone, bared to his heated gaze. His fingers closed over the pale, high-swelling curves like they were his property. She was so damn beautiful that looking at her made him ache.

He rubbed her budded nipples to hard little points of fire, so that she arched into his touch with a whimper.

"I have to taste you," he muttered.

Turning her, he lay Heather back on the kitchen table and bent over her hungrily. She gasped as his lips traced burning kisses around her full swells. His mouth was hot, his tongue rough and wet on her sensitive skin, arousing the peak to a pebble-hard point of pleasure, setting the rest of her body on fire. With a hard sucking motion, he assaulted her, his devouring lips dragging across her breasts, pulling at her flesh, nipping softly. He was tasting her to his ruthless satisfaction, staking a claim.

But it wasn't enough, for either of them. Still suckling her fiercely, Sloan pushed her skirts up to her waist. He felt a shock as he realized she wasn't wearing drawers. She was naked from the waist down, open for his pleasure. When her bare legs parted, the sweet scent of woman rose to his nostrils.

Raw need bolted through him like a wild horse. His gaze lifted abruptly, silver-blue smoke.

"Such an accommodating wife," he murmured hoarsely in approval.

He slipped a finger into her cleft, feeling the heat and dampness and need of her. She was so wet, so trigger-hot, she nearly came right then. She made a soft whimpering sound of need as she reached for him, but Sloan clenched his teeth and held back. She made him shudder with the urge to pound deep and pour his hot seed inside her, but he wanted her to plead.

His hard lips closed wetly over her nipple. His hot mouth seared her with a lash of pleasure that was almost cruel, while his fingers stroked fiercely.

"Sloannnnn. . . ." His name was a keening moan which changed to a strangled cry. The orgasm that shook her was powerful, instantaneous, shattering.

Sloan held himself still as tremors shook her lush, magnificent body, fighting the raw lust that ran rampant through him. His body pulsed against hers while his hardened shaft cramped beneath his pants. He wanted her, wanted to impale her until he drowned in her.

Abruptly he rose above her, tearing at his pants until they opened and he could push them out of the way. He had to have her or go crazy. In a rush of heated flesh, he plunged into her.

When Heather cried out again and wrapped her legs around him, he spread his fingers and clasped her bare buttocks hard to draw her closer. Her breathy whimpers were driving him mad. He'd never been so hungry for a woman before, so hot. He'd never felt this kind of need, mindless, relentless, endless.

He rode her hard and fast. Wildly, he drove himself into her, big and hard, his lean, powerful body trembling with almost angry need. His lips drank in her wild moans as she clawed at his back.

In only a moment, fire exploded where her slick, heated flesh sheathed him. When in the same moment she began to convulse around him once more, his body contracted. He shook violently, shuddering with a pleasure so piercing it was almost unbearable.

In the breathless aftermath, Sloan collapsed, sinking his head on her breast in panting surrender. He could still feel the ripples caressing him.

God, he wanted her still. It would only be a minute before her warmth could make him hard and ready again, but he didn't want it to be here, like this.

He would take a bath first and wash away the grime of the trail. Then he would take her to bed and do it all over again, slower this time, using his mouth on her breasts, between her legs, till she was hot and wild and sweet and burning up with wanting him.

He raised his head. She looked lush and wanton and well-loved.

"Now that," he said, a grin playing at one corner

of his hard mouth, "was one hell of a welcome. No drawers. Seems like you're learning to be a proper wife after all."

She flushed a delicate rose.

Sloan chuckled at the ladylike display. The duchess still hadn't shed her modesty—but he would work on it.

He kissed her again, refamiliarizing himself with the dark recesses of her mouth. Then, easing away from her, he smoothed down her skirts and helped her to stand. "Why don't you come upstairs with me and join me in a bath?"

"You want me to bathe with you?" Heather repeated rather weakly.

"It'll be a tight fit, but the tub's big enough for two." He turned and sauntered to the door. Pausing to cast a glance over his shoulder, Sloan smiled, a slow sexual smile that burned right through her. "If we're lucky, we have another hour till Janna wakes. And that new plumbing cost a fortune. We need to make good use of it if I'm to get my money's worth."

Once roundup was over, Sloan had more time to devote to his campaign, and they often discussed the subject over supper. Heather cherished those private moments with him, for it usually meant that he let down his guard.

To her surprise and gratification, though, Sloan earnestly sought her opinions.

"I want your advice," he said two nights after he'd returned from Denver. "Cat and Jake have offered to host a meeting between cattle ranchers and sheep men to let me present my views on the issues. It might be wise. I've made some enemies over the years," he admitted, "and it would give me a chance to mend some fences."

"I think it's a marvelous opportunity," Heather replied. "Perhaps you could pay a call on all your neighbors beforehand to issue an invitation to the meeting. You could talk to them personally . . . find out their concerns and tell them your aspirations."

"Will you come with me?"

Her eyes widened. "If you like."

Sloan nodded. "I think it would help my cause. The ranchers here never could resist a beautiful woman. They'll be more willing to attend the meeting if the invitation comes from you."

It was some consolation that Sloan thought her beautiful, even if he saw her primarily as a political advantage. But she didn't intend to quibble. "That makes sense, but as long as we're talking about persuasion . . . you shouldn't neglect the ranchers' wives. Even if only men can vote in Colorado, women can influence the outcome of an election."

His eyebrows rose thoughtfully, as if he recognized the truth to her observation. In addition to offering advice, though, Heather encouraged him to talk about his plans and tried to help him frame his ideas.

"People respect passion and conviction, Sloan. They need to understand why the election is so important to you, that you want to protect the land and help salvage people's ranches. You know what it's like to live with hardship. If you simply tell them the truth, if you speak from the heart, they'll listen."

For a rare moment, his smile reached those bright, unreadable eyes. A thatch of wheat-colored hair fell over his forehead, making him look boyish and incredibly masculine at the same time. She felt her heart melt.

Heather swallowed, trying to ignore the sensation. When he brushed it back out of his eyes, she suggested thoughtfully, "If you mean to start making public speeches, you might consider getting a haircut."

He gave her a long, vaguely amused look. "My hair isn't fancy enough for your tastes?"

"For a cowpuncher it is perfectly adequate, but a shorter style would look better if you don a suit. I doubt a shaggy bear is the image you want to portray with voters."

"You're the fashion expert, duchess."

She trimmed his hair in the kitchen the next morning, and greatly enjoyed the task. At just that moment, Sloan looked carefree and relaxed. There was no sign of the dark, brooding stranger she had wed. Indeed, as she drew a comb through his longish hair, he even began flirting with her, showing the reckless, charming side that had won the hearts of all the local belles.

"I hope you've had more practice with those things than you have with a shotgun," Sloan murmured, eyeing the shears. "You don't mean to scalp me, do you?"

"I only hope to give you an air of refinement— no small task for a rugged cowboy, I must admit."

Sloan shifted in the chair like a small boy.

"Would you please hold still?"

"What if I don't?" The corners of his mouth kicked up in amusement. "You gonna rap my knuckles and send me off to the woodshed like one of your wayward pupils?"

"I might at that."

He crossed his arms over his chest but obediently stopped moving. "Very well, your highness, I'll be good."

"Your grace."

"What?"

"I believe the proper form of address for a duchess is 'your grace.' Not that you give a fig about proper social deportment, but if you're elected senator, you'll likely find yourself in situations which will require you to exercise polite manners."

Sloan chuckled. "I can be polite if I have to. Even if you think I'm an ... uncivil, ill-tempered ogre. Isn't that what you once called me?"

"I suppose you have managed to improve on further acquaintance."

"So have you. You're not so full of starch and vinegar." He reached around her and palmed the bustle of her skirt. "You wearing drawers today?"

Heather jerked the scissors back. "Yes!"

"Too bad." Sloan regarded the table where he'd taken her with such sizzling passion. "A bare bottom might make this ordeal more fun."

Trying to steel herself against the insidious warmth curling around her heart, Heather glanced at his young daughter, who was playing quietly in her corner. *"Will* you behave, Sloan McCord?"

"Yes, ma'am, if you insist." He grinned and the effect was dazzling. "But I get a reward afterward."

Heather turned away in dismay. His lighthearted mood was more dangerous than his savage temper. When he was like this, it was too easy to love him, to need him, to want his arms around her.

And yet finding those small chinks in Sloan's defensive armor heartened her. She desperately wanted to counter his reserve and chip away at his coldness, to draw out his softer side and win his trust.

At least he no longer saw her as his enemy. He actually seemed grateful for her efforts with Janna. And surprisingly, he didn't fly into a rage when he was reminded poignantly of his beloved late wife.

That afternoon, they were leaving to pay calls at all the neighboring ranches when Janna insisted on carrying the raven-haired doll Heather had brought her from St. Louis.

"Want Va-va," Janna babbled when Sloan picked her up, reaching down toward her basket of toys.

"What's she saying?" he asked. "She wants water?"

"No," Heather replied. "Her doll. We named it after her mother, but she can't pronounce the words fully."

When Sloan went rigid, Heather regarded him warily.

"Mehe-vaotseva . . . that was Doe's Cheyenne name, was it not?"

His gaze hardened. "Who told you that?"

"Rusty."

Sloan stared at her, and she could see pain in his eyes at some long-ago memory.

"You said," she added softly, "that you didn't want Janna to forget her heritage."

"No." His whisper had a raw edge. Bending to retrieve the doll for his daughter, he tightened his hold on Janna and kissed the top of her raven head. "Thank you," he said, his eyes shut.

Heather swallowed the ache in her throat as Sloan stole another piece of her heart. He was trying, she realized. He was endeavoring to put the past behind him and move on with his life.

She had to hold on to that—and hope that his future included her.

The personal visits to neighboring ranches paid off for Sloan's campaign. Nearly everyone they called on agreed to attend the political meeting to be held Sunday afternoon at Jake's place. Heeding Heather's advice, Sloan invited the ranchers' wives as well.

Sunday morning dawned bright and clear. Sloan

drove his family over early, so that he and Heather could help set up.

The carriage ride through the rugged foothills was breathtaking, with a warm blue sky that heralded the onset of summer. A golden eagle soared high overhead, the slopes covered with Douglas fir and lodgepole pine, while blue columbine had begun to blossom in the emerald-green meadows.

Holding a bright-eyed Janna on her lap, Heather realized she was glad she was here rather than St. Louis. She didn't miss the stifling existence of her past life in the least. The wildness of this land had conquered her heart, and so had the man sitting beside her.

Caitlin and Jake were waiting proudly with their tiny but healthy new daughter, whom they'd named Elizabeth after Jake's mother. Janna was fascinated with the baby, and a boisterous Ryan happily entertained both young ones. He took his cousin to the back porch to play while the grownups discussed the arrangements for the meeting, which was to be held picnic-style in the yard.

Heather had brought several pies and she busied herself arranging tables for the food, as did Sarah Baxter and her husband Harvey, who were among the first arrivals. They all helped Sloan greet the ranchers, who came in droves. The men mostly wore Sunday trousers and good boots, the women dresses and fancy bonnets, and the gathering took on the festive air of a holiday.

Heather, passing out lemonade along with Caitlin and Sarah, watched as Sloan moved easily through the growing crowd, shaking the men's hands and working his rugged charm on the ladies.

"It's a shame women don't have the vote," Caitlin suggested.

Sarah laughed and nodded. "If they did, Sloan could get elected president."

Heather had to agree. He exuded raw male attraction, and she couldn't suppress a thrill of pride that he was her husband.

When the crowd finally settled on blankets in the yard, Jake, still holding his baby daughter, called the meeting to order. He said a few words to introduce his brother, before Caitlin stepped forward to address the sheep men in the crowd.

"I know we've had our differences in the past," she observed earnestly, "but that's all over now, thanks in large part to Sloan McCord. As you all know, he had a big hand in ending the feud. Now he's running for state senator and he needs your vote. This is your opportunity to learn about his views. All we ask is that you give him a fair hearing."

The first question was thrown out by a stalwart, red-bearded man in almost a hostile tone. "Why in tarnation should we vote for you, McCord? For twenty years your pa tried to run our sheep out of the territory. How do we know you ain't got the same notion up your sleeve?"

Sloan smiled and replied easily, "I've got nothing up my sleeve, John. You've known that for over twenty years, ever since we first went skinny-dipping together in Bear Creek when we were eight."

Several men in the crowd guffawed, while the women tittered.

Sloan's expression grew serious. "We'd be fools to turn our backs on sheep. The hard truth is, the cattle industry is going bust, and sheep are still profitable enough to support our county."

"You aren't suggestin' we all become woolly-boys, are you?" a cattleman called out incredulously.

"No. But we have to face reality. Our way of life is changing, and we have to change with it if we hope to survive. It's hard even for the big outfits like mine to make ends meet. The small ones don't have a chance unless we all stick together. And that requires going against the mining barons who've taken over the Colorado legislature. We need laws that will give us a square deal. We need someone in the government who'll look out for our interests."

"I hear Quinn Lovell plans to bring mines into the area," someone else said. "That'll mean good jobs for some of us."

"Leaving aside the fact that mines will destroy the land, wouldn't you rather hold on to your ranch than risk your life underground? Mining is a dangerous business. You know how many men make it to see forty without getting seriously hurt? And if so, they find their lungs eaten away by disease."

"But turning Lovell away won't put food on the table, Sloan. I hear he's paying good money for scrap acres, and he'll pay double if he wins the election."

Frowning, Sarah Baxter leaned toward Heather and said in a furious undertone, "The gall of that sidewinder Lovell. He's trying to buy votes!"

Sloan's mouth curled dryly. "I can't match Lovell's offer to buy your land. All I can do is promise to fight for all of us equally."

"That still don't mean we should trust you," another man muttered. "You turned your back on your own kind, taking a Injun squaw to wife."

A muscle in Sloan's jaw hardened, but he answered evenly, if quietly. "You can't always pick and choose who you love, Cirus. You of all people should know that. I loved Doe, just like you love Molly. I recall your pa raising Cain when you married an Irishwoman.''

The pretty ebony-haired woman at Cirus's side elbowed his ribs. "Aye, ye great galoot, ye'd best be remembering how smitten ye were wi' me, or I'll be reminding ye wi' a skillet upside the head.''

The crowd's laughter was more strained this time.

"I don't like this,'' Sarah muttered loudly, perhaps to distract Heather from the subject of Sloan's late wife. "They're listening, but they're still not convinced Sloan would be a better candidate than Quinn Lovell.''

"Maybe we need to take another approach,'' Caitlin whispered.

"What did you have in mind?'' Heather murmured.

"I think we should talk to the ladies.'' Her blue eyes were narrowed thoughtfully. "If we can convince them how bad Lovell would be for us, then *they* can persuade their husbands to vote for Sloan.''

Chapter 12

Sloan shook his head in chagrin as the last of the ladies drove away dressed in their Sunday finery. A *tea party*. The duchess had turned a stuffy afternoon ritual into a political tactic, inviting all their female neighbors to tea to discuss the upcoming election. And damned if it wasn't working. Heather and her cohort in crime, Caitlin, had persuaded over three dozen women to crusade for him. This was the third tea they'd held at the Bar M in the past week, and each time they'd barred him from the premises.

With a wry snort of amusement, Sloan stamped his dusty boots on the back porch stoop before opening the kitchen door. Now that the gaggle of guests were finally gone, he was able to enter his own house.

Cat was just leaving. She smiled at Sloan and kissed Heather's cheek before picking up her new daughter. "I'll call on you tomorrow morning at ten," she said to Heather.

Sloan accompanied Caitlin outside and handed her into her buggy. When he returned, Heather had just made a final trip to the parlor to retrieve the remaining teacups and dishes. Sloan cleared a place at the kitchen table for her to set down the tray.

"The tea went well, I think," she said brightly. "Better even than the first two."

"That was the last of them, I hope. Why is Cat coming back tomorrow?" he asked curiously.

"Oh, I meant to tell you, I'll be gone for a few hours tomorrow morning. Caitlin and I have an errand in town."

"Errand?"

She hesitated an instant. "We have a strategy session with Sarah regarding your campaign."

A grin curled his mouth. "Don't you think you're taking this campaign thing a mite too far?"

"No, I don't. In my opinion, Caitlin's plan is brilliant. Organizing the women of the community to campaign for you is the surest way to gain the support of their husbands—which you badly need if you're to beat Lovell and win the election."

"Seems like a lot of trouble to me, dressing up for a tea party."

"Most women enjoy dressing up and being involved in a worthy cause. Believe me, they like to feel useful and appreciated. Besides, a tea party allows them to escape from a drab life for a short while."

Sloan gave her a penetrating look, wondering if she was looking to escape. "Is your life so drab then, duchess?"

Heather returned his intense gaze steadily. "I wasn't speaking of my situation, but since you ask, I've attended enough tea parties to last me a lifetime."

He wasn't certain he could believe her, but he let it pass and picked up a round, flat cake. "What's this?"

"A crumpet. Try one, why don't you? Janna loves them with strawberry jam."

Sloan raised an eyebrow but bit into it experimentally. "Ummm, it's good, even with such a highfalutin name. Tastes a lot like pancakes."

"I know." Heather smiled wryly. "Simply because it has a fancy name is no reason to turn up your nose at it. Would you mind looking after Janna a moment while I go upstairs and change my gown?"

At her smile, Sloan felt his heart kick against his ribs. Letting his gaze sweep over her figure, he felt the pulse lower down as well, in the vicinity of his groin. How could she look so sexy in a prim, long-sleeved, high-necked afternoon dress? The duchess was garbed rather plainly in dark-blue gaberdine, so as not to outshine the other women, he suspected.

"You need any help getting undressed?" he murmured, a husky catch to his voice.

Her skin took on a faint color. "Thank you, no. I have dozens of dishes to wash, and then I must fix Janna's supper."

Sloan reached up to tuck a stray tendril behind her ear. "Too bad. I thought maybe we might have our own private tea party and I could see how strawberry jam tastes on you."

Her color deepened to an appealing flush, but she shook her head and left the kitchen.

The scent of her lingered in the air when she was gone. Sloan munched on the crumpet thoughtfully, regretting his impulse. Heather's hair had looked fine. It hadn't needed smoothing back into place. He'd done it merely to have an excuse to touch her. And her smile. . . . That lovely smile had damned near taken his breath away.

Watch yourself, cowboy, he thought sternly. It was all well and good, her charming the men of the community with her beauty and wit and sensual appeal. *They* were the ones who could vote. But it was dangerous as hell, letting Heather charm *him*. It was safer to keep his distance. Better if the only bond between them was sex.

Sloan shook his head. The trouble was, Heather was infecting his life. Mostly for the good, he had to admit. Her social skills had already come in handy in his campaign, as had her talent for saying just the right thing. She was helping him polish the speech he intended to give at the Fourth of July celebration next week.

All right, so he had misjudged her at first. The duchess was far from the helpless, genteel widgeon he'd first thought her. . . .

Sloan frowned as he recalled her comment about the drab life of a rancher's wife. Did she regret the choice she'd made?

The duchess might have been burdened by debt, but she was accustomed to a life of ease, with teas and soirees and fancy parties to fill her social calendar. With her marriage to him, she'd exchanged her silk dresses for calico, savaged her pretty white hands with blisters and her ivory complexion with sunburn. Did she miss her former life?

If she was unhappy, she was careful not to let it show. By all appearances, Heather had taken to ranch life like a steer to range grass. The endless hard work hadn't seemed to put her off. She never complained about the rough conditions—the bitter cold and snow of winter, the bluster and muck of spring, the dust and heat and smells of summer.

She'd put up with his foul moods as well. He hadn't been able to drive her away. No matter how he tried to antagonize her or push her, Heather came back fighting. It was that grit that drew him, that he'd come to admire. . . .

She did the damnedest things, things that caught

him off guard. It had hurt when she'd named that doll after Doe—reminding him of his great loss—and yet he had to appreciate the gesture.

No, it was his own self-control that was the problem.

Sloan muttered an oath. When he was near her, he was no better than a randy buck—or a fractious stallion scenting a mare in heat. When he was away, her memory stayed with him. He couldn't stop thinking of her, remembering the taste of her skin, the scent of her hair, the texture of her nipples. He couldn't stop remembering his dream lover—the pagan goddess with the pale, voluptuous skin and lush body, the silvery hair that made a wild cloud of waves over his pillow.

He had wanted Heather to shed her ladylike primness in bed, and he'd succeeded far beyond his expectations. Making love, she was a wildcat, turning all sweet and hot in his arms, naked and vibrant and alive with need for him. But when he was locked deep inside her, mindless with sensation, he was as much at the mercy of his body as she was to hers.

He'd never been so hungry for a woman before. He couldn't get enough of her. The depth of his need astonished him. With Doe sex had been uninhibited, but not wild and urgent and violent. With Heather he was ravenous.

It was crazy to feel as hungry and obsessed as he did. He knew all about obsession. For months after Doe's murder, he'd been driven by the need for revenge. But this hot, fierce wanting that ate at his reason—there was no excuse for it. She had only to enter a room and lust began tightening his body. She had only to touch him and she brought him to instant uncomfortable arousal.

It was damned embarrassing sometimes. When

he was on the range with the boys, the smallest
things made him think of Heather—of falling into
bed and easing into her or tossing her on the
kitchen table and riding her hard and fast. He'd get
so hard, he had to find some way of disguising it.

The hell of it was, Heather was getting under his
skin. When he was away, he spent much of his
waking hours fighting with himself. When he was
near, he found it harder and harder to keep his distance.

And even if he got his craving under control, he
wouldn't be any less vulnerable to her. The truth
was, he needed her. For his daughter. For his campaign.

For himself.

Heather had never before been inside a saloon,
so her gloved palms felt damp with nervousness as
she followed Caitlin through the alleyway to the
back door of the Stirrup & Pick Saloon. It was mid-
morning, and they'd left Janna and baby Elizabeth
in Sarah's tender care at the general store.

The saloon was quiet. They made their way
down a hallway to a barroom, which fortunately
was nearly deserted, but which smelled of whiskey
and cigars.

Staying close behind Caitlin, Heather found her
attention riveted by the gaudy furnishings. A long
gilt-edged mirror adorned the wall behind the li-
quor-stained mahogany bar, while on the opposite
wall, beneath the stairway, hung a huge oil paint-
ing of a voluptuous, pink-fleshed female in a state
of near-undress. There were also dozens of scarred
poker tables and wooden chairs and a shallow
stage that boasted red velvet curtains and an upright piano.

Heather felt herself torn by curiosity and an instinctive sense of dismay. She'd been raised to think of saloons as dens of iniquity, where men gambled and caroused and drank to excess, where the women sold their bodies for money.

An uncomfortable thought prodded her as she shifted her gaze to the woman standing behind the bar. Wasn't that what she herself had done in marrying Sloan? Sell herself for money? Fifteen hundred dollars to be precise. . . .

The woman at the bar had upswept raven hair and large brown eyes, with a painted face that was pretty in a tawdry sort of way. She wore a garish red gown, whose black-fringed bodice was cut scandalously low, exposing much of her full breasts.

She broke into a smile at Caitlin's appearance, showing a chipped front tooth. "Well, I'll be. . . ." Then her eyebrows shot up as she spied Heather.

Heather eyed her curiously in return. There were various unflattering names for females employed at saloons—fancy piece, soiled dove, woman of ill-repute, prostitute . . . all of which seemed to fit this woman. The cheap scent of her perfume clouded the air.

Heather wondered if this was the woman who was reportedly such good friends with Sloan's brother Jake. Keeping quiet, however, she followed Caitlin to the bar and allowed her to take the lead in the introductions.

"Heather, I'd like you to meet Della Perkins. Della, this is Heather McCord, Sloan's new wife."

Della nodded almost warily. "I know who you are, Miz McCord. I've seen you around town."

"It's a pleasure to meet you," Heather murmured with a quiet smile meant to reassure.

"I don't know that I can say the same. Isn't every day we get such fine ladies to visit. Fact is, last time

I can recall, it was a grievance committee set on running us girls out of town." She glanced soberly at Caitlin. "You mind telling me what brings you here?"

"We've come to ask you a favor. You know Sloan's campaigning for senator? Well, we want you to help get him elected."

"Me?"

"You and your friends here," Caitlin explained. "We suspect most of the cowboys will vote for Sloan, *if* they vote, but they'll likely need encouragement to show up at the booths on election day. And the miners could use some persuasion in general if they're to go against Quinn Lovell. We figured, who better to sway their opinions than you and the ladies who see them regularly?"

"Let me get this straight, you want me and the girls to sweet-talk the fellas who visit here and plant the notion in their thick heads that they go vote for Sloan?"

Heather gathered her courage to enter the conversation then. It was rather awkward to ask for help under these circumstances, but Caitlin had persisted. Who better to influence the men of the town than the women who slept with them?

"It might make the difference in the election," she observed. "Sloan could truly use your help."

Della stared. Then she grinned, flashing her broken tooth. "Honey, if there's one thing I know how to do, it's persuadin' a man."

"Do you think it wise for us to speak to your friends as well?"

"Mercy, no. They'll have a conniption if they see such a fancy lady in a whorehouse. You better let me do it."

Heather forcibly swallowed her embarrassment.

"Thank you. I would greatly appreciate any effort you could make."

"Don't mention it." Della regarded her almost admiringly. "You've got some kind of gumption comin' here, I'll say that for you. But if you're a friend of Caitlin's, I reckon I can understand." Her look turned sly. "I must say, I haven't seen much of Sloan since he came back married."

Caitlin smiled. "And you won't, either, if Heather has any say in the matter."

Della laughed. "Too bad."

Heather felt herself wince inwardly. Sloan had no doubt patronized the saloon before their marriage. She wondered if he'd ever come here with the intent of bedding one of the soiled doves—or if he'd ever slept with this woman. It was not a comfortable thought.

Caitlin, however, seemed to take it in stride. "Just you concentrate on getting Sloan elected, if you don't mind," she told Della.

"I'll do my best. And so will the girls. They always did have a soft spot for Sloan McCord."

Those words echoed in Heather's mind the following week as she campaigned earnestly for her husband—and again the morning of July Fourth as she dressed for the picnic and supper-dance to be held on the outskirts of town.

She was standing in her lacy underdrawers, trying to don her corset, when Sloan walked into her bedchamber carrying Janna. When his glance raked over her, a warmth rose inside Heather that had little to do with the heat of the day.

"We're ready," he announced, settling in the armchair by the window with his daughter to wait. "Doesn't Janna look pretty?"

Heather gave the child a warm smile. "Beautiful."

The toddler was garbed in a pale-blue calico dress with a froth of cream ruffles adorning the neck, a dress Heather had lovingly fashioned to complement the one she planned to wear to the celebration.

But it was Sloan who took Heather's breath away. Sunlight was reaching through the window now, turning the dusty blond of his hair to gold, a rich, burnished shade that reminded her of wheat fields in summer. He looked ruggedly masculine and impossibly handsome, dressed in the same dark-gray suit he'd worn at their wedding, a crisp white shirt and string tie setting off his lean features. His mere presence roused in her a sensual memory of the previous night: his tender, relentless hands caressing her, his dark voice murmuring words of praise and pleasure, his hard, driving body taking her to the heights of passion. . . .

Yet this morning he was a different man from the incredible lover of last night. Despite the six-guns strapped to his thighs, he seemed carefree and relaxed. Holding his daughter on his lap, he straightened the blue bow Janna wore in her raven hair, but then glanced at Heather with an easy smile curving his lips.

She loved him most, Heather reflected, at moments like this, when his tenderness for his daughter spilled over to *her*, when he softened toward her and let down his guard.

Heather froze in the act of tying the corset strings.

She was in love with Sloan, she realized with dismay. Despite her efforts to protect her heart from danger, she had fallen in love with her husband.

He apparently misconstrued her hesitation. "You

need help putting on that contraption?"

Taking a deep breath, she shook her head silently.

"Just as well. I don't know the first thing about corsets, except how to take them off." His amused blue eyes grew distant with fond memory. "Neither did Doe, for that matter. She tried to put one on once, and wound up with it upside down. Broke a string, too. I laughed so hard, I thought I would split my sides."

At the soft affection in his tone, Heather swallowed the ache in her throat. She wondered if Sloan's heart could ever be freed from the chains of love he bore his late wife. Should she even try? Until now, she'd been content with winning small victories in her attempt to become indispensable to him—aiding Sloan with running his household and raising Janna and promoting his campaign. But she wanted to mean more to him than a helpmate. More than a lover. Much, much more.

The realization haunted her thoughts and made her unusually quiet during the drive into town, so much so that Sloan commented on her silence.

"You all right?" he asked, giving her a penetrating glance.

Heather forced a bright smile. "Perfectly," she lied. "I'm simply enjoying the beautiful day."

And it *was* beautiful. The foothills were magnificent in summer, the rocky slopes bright with sunshine and richly green with towering pines and firs, aspens and spruce, while the meadows brimmed with wildflowers—delicate blue columbine and lavender phlox and flaming Indian paintbrush.

The Fourth of July was a major holiday in Colorado, Heather had learned, and the day would be filled with picnicking and baseball games and fireworks, to be followed that evening by a dance and late supper. This year's celebration would also include speeches by the two senatorial candidates.

The entire community seemed to be present, Heather decided when they arrived at the meadow on the edge of town—ranchers, cowboys, sheep farmers, miners, and all their families. She deposited her pies on a long table already groaning with food, then remained at Sloan's side, holding Janna, as he mingled with the crowd. She was pleased to recognize so many faces, and more pleased by the number of people who greeted her warmly.

After several athletic events ended, including sack races and ballgames, the picnickers gorged themselves on lemonade and fried chicken and apple pie. For the meal, Heather and Sloan shared a blanket with Jake and Caitlin, while Harvey and Sarah Baxter sat beside them, along with the schoolteacher, Vernon Whitfield. There was much laughter and friendly banter among the families. Afterward the older children took themselves off for more games, while the babies napped and the adults lazed on blankets during the worst heat of the day.

An hour or so later Sloan excused himself to talk to some of the other ranchers, and Vernon moved over to join Heather.

"A few weeks ago you asked me about possibilities for employment," Vernon began, "and I've thought of an idea that would benefit us both. You know that since school let out, I've been reporting on the political races for the *Rocky News*?"

"I know. I've read your articles," Heather said warmly. "They're quite lively and informative."

"Well, there's more work than one person can handle. I hoped you might consider helping me part-time—editing my articles, primarily, but upon occasion, writing up my notes into articles of your own. The salary wouldn't be lucrative, but the hours are flexible and you wouldn't have to leave your ranch. And you might find the intellectual challenge stimulating as well as rewarding."

"I would enjoy it immensely," Heather replied. "As long as it wouldn't interfere with my caring for Janna, it could prove the perfect job."

"Well, then, what do you say I call on you tomorrow and we can go over your duties?"

She smiled at Vernon with warmth and gratitude. She would indeed enjoy the challenge of editing and writing. Certainly she possessed the necessary skills, having been exposed to her father's journalistic world practically since birth. Moreover, Heather reflected silently, with a salary, no matter how meager, she would no longer be so totally dependent on Sloan, and she could even begin repaying some of the debt she owed him.

Despite the congeniality of the day, however, Heather found herself growing nervous as the afternoon waned and the picnic wound down, since the time for speech-giving was fast approaching. She had seen Quinn Lovell across the meadow shaking hands with countless people, and knew he was making the most of the opportunity to ingratiate himself with voters.

Her nervousness increased tenfold, though, when she saw the mining baron make his way toward Sloan. When the two men met, Heather picked up a dozing Janna from the blanket and moved closer, so she could hear what Lovell was saying.

". . . surprises me you can afford the expense when your ranch is mortgaged so heavily."

"Seems to me," Sloan returned with a chilling smile, "your interest in my ranch is misplaced. I have this quaint notion that my finances are my own business."

Lovell gave him a measuring stare, but then he caught sight of Heather and tipped his hat to her. "I've had the privilege of meeting your lovely wife, McCord. You are quite fortunate."

Sloan gave her a brief glance. "Yes, I am," he said coolly.

"Well, then, I shall wish you luck. May the best man win."

Lovell turned away then, toward the platform which had been erected for the speechmakers and the fiddlers.

"What did he want?" Heather asked Sloan curiously.

"To deliver a threat, I expect."

"A threat?"

Sloan's jaw clenched, but then he smiled at his sleepy daughter. "You'd best go back to your nap, darlin'," he murmured, deliberately avoiding Heather's question. "There's no need for you to listen to long, boring speeches."

As the crowd resumed their places before the platform, Lovell was introduced to the crowd by Harvey Baxter, who ran through a long list of the baron's accomplishments, including his stock holdings in railroad companies and mining ventures.

Waiting for the applause to die down, Lovell raised his hand benevolently. "Most of you know me by now," he began with a friendly smile. "And you also know that I want to bring renewed prosperity to this part of Colorado. . . ."

What followed was a long speech—as boring and uninspiring as Sloan had predicted, Heather thought, making no allowances for her decided partiality. The speech garnered a smattering of polite applause, before Lovell stepped down for Sloan to take his place.

Although unsure if her imagination was playing tricks, Heather could feel the sudden rise in tension as the two men passed. Sloan stepped up on the platform then, and faced the crowd, making deliberate eye contact, one by one.

A charge of energy filled the air; the atmosphere was so quiet, it sounded almost like a crack of gunfire when Sloan cleared his throat and raised his voice so as to be heard in back.

"I'd say most of you know me, too. We grew up together. Some of us were enemies in a range war we didn't start. We've shed blood together. We've fought to protect our homes and our families. We've shared some good times as well as bad. But a new fight is just beginning.

"It's no secret that my opponent is wealthy enough to buy half the state of Colorado. Well, fine. But I don't intend to make this a competition to buy your vote. I can't afford it. Like many of you, I'm having trouble making ends meet. And it looks as if the hard times are going to get worse before they get better.

"I'm not about to give up, though. Not in this lifetime. I'll be damned if I'll let all the sweat and blood and tears go for naught. But the fight is bigger than any one man. I can't win it alone. I need your help. I can't promise you a rosy future. I can only promise to try to protect our way of life, to keep this community a good place to raise our families. I can only say that we have to stick together. This is *my* land—mine and yours. And I'm asking you to help me keep it that way."

Heather felt her heart swell with pride as Sloan interrupted the stunned silence to step down from the platform. He hadn't stuck precisely to the script they'd worked out during long hours in his study, but he'd spoken simply and eloquently, from the heart.

And the sparse speech clearly had a powerful impact. He had touched his audience if the reaction of the crowd was any measure. Somebody—a cowboy from one of the neighboring ranches, perhaps—let out a piercing whistle, before the rest of the crowd broke into applause that seemed deafening in contrast to the reception Quinn Lovell had received.

When a chant of "Sloan, Sloan, Sloan . . ." broke out, Harvey Baxter stood up, raising his hands to ask for quiet. "Well now, we thank you two gentlemen for the fine words. But now I think we need to start the dancin'. What do ya say, folks!"

The chants turned to whoops as rowdy cowpunchers tossed their hats in the air and scurried to find a female partner. A half-dozen couples had taken to the grassy floor by the time the fiddles launched into a lively reel, and more followed suit directly.

Throughout the evening, quite a number of people came up to congratulate Sloan for his insightful remarks and promised to support him. Lovell appeared to take his temporary setback with composure, although once Heather caught him studying Sloan with a dark look that disturbed her.

Fortunately, the dance was uneventful, as was the supper afterward. Heather found herself in great demand as a partner, and she had the pleasure of dancing twice with her husband, who proved to be a surprisingly accomplished dancer.

The hour was late when the weary but happy revelers finally dispersed. Sloan drove the buggy home in the dark, while Heather sat silently beside him, holding a sleeping Janna. The night was warm, the sky black as velvet, while the rugged hills towered over them like benevolent giants.

Heather might have been content to enjoy the peaceful interlude but for the disquiet she felt after the obscure threat Quinn Lovell had made earlier.

"Lovell won't like the idea of losing the race, will he?" she asked quietly as they neared the Bar M Ranch.

"I doubt it," Sloan responded.

"What do you think he means to do?"

"I don't know. I figure I'll have to be prepared for just about anything." His jaw hardened. "Don't worry. I'm not going to let him hurt you or Janna."

Heather shook her head. She hadn't really needed such reassurance. She knew Sloan well enough to know he would do everything in his power to protect his own.

When they reached the ranch house, Sloan helped her dismount before driving on to the barn to stable the horses. Heather heard the greeting he gave some of his hired hands, who had arrived home just ahead of them.

Entering the dark kitchen, she laid the sleeping Janna on the blanket in her play corner in order to light a lantern. When she turned back to pick up the child, a harsh buzzing sound suddenly reached her ears.

Heather froze in the act of reaching down for Janna. A rattlesnake lay curled beneath one edge of the blanket, within easy striking distance of them both. Poised to attack, the reptile stared at her, its beady eyes gleaming cold and vicious in the lamplight, its tail issuing a deadly warning.

Fear screamed through Heather, but with an inhuman act of will, she forced herself to remain still. She prayed Janna would remain asleep and not attract the rattler's notice before Sloan could get there.

It seemed like forever before she heard Sloan mounting the back porch steps. She tried to call out to him, but her breath was trapped in her throat. As he pushed open the door, she made another desperate attempt.

"Sloan. . . ." The word came out a hoarse rasp. "Stop. . . ."

He was carrying the empty pie plates from the picnic, but he hesitated at her plea, taking in the scene. He suddenly went rigid as the harsh rattle sounded again. She sensed rather than heard his curse.

"Heather," he whispered, "stay still. Don't move a muscle."

"Yes. . . ."

"I'm going to try and shoot it. I need a clear shot. I'll hit you if you move."

"Don't . . . worry about me. . . . Just . . . kill it . . . before it hurts Janna."

In a lightning-fast motion, Sloan dropped the pie tins and reached for his six-shooter. Bringing the barrel up, he fanned the hammer rapidly, firing off five shots in quick succession. The snake jumped in rhythm with the explosions.

Awakened by the uproar, Janna let out a piercing wail of terror. Even so, the silence afterward seemed deafening. For a moment, Heather stood paralyzed as she stared at the bloody mess that had been the rattlesnake. A sense of unreality kept her immobile; a thin haze of gunsmoke swirled around her, while the stench of powder stung her nostrils.

The baby was crying, she realized dazedly.

With a sudden sob of relief, she scooped Janna up and held her tightly in an almost crushing embrace, feeling a possessiveness so savage, so strong, it made her weak. She was shaking so hard, her knees nearly buckled beneath her.

She was grateful for the support when Sloan came and put his arms around her as she held Janna.

"God . . . I thought . . ." His jagged murmur said everything she was feeling.

She nodded, shuddering, unable to answer.

And instant later they heard footsteps pound up the back steps, before a half-dozen Bar M ranch hands burst through the door in response to the gunshots, many of them in stockinged feet.

Rusty was in front, rifle drawn. He stopped abruptly when he saw Sloan embracing Heather and his wailing daughter.

"What happened, boss?" Rusty demanded breathlessly.

Sloan glanced over his shoulder. "Everything's okay. Heather surprised a rattler, but I shot it before it struck anyone."

"Well, if you're sure you don't need anything. . . ."

"We're okay, thanks."

The boys backed out, shutting the door politely. When they were gone, Heather said hoarsely, "I was so afraid. I thought you might not come in time. It could have . . . killed her."

Sloan rested his forehead on her hair. "But it didn't. We were lucky." His reassurances, however, didn't disguise the tremor that shook his own voice.

"Sloan, I'm sorry. . . . I should have been more careful."

He shook his head. "You couldn't know. . . . You did right to keep still, duchess. Tomorrow we'll turn this place upside down and make sure there aren't any more critters lurking in any dark corners.''

Heather nodded weakly, trembling to realize how close they had come to tragedy. Life was so very precious—but it could be taken away in an instant.

She stood quietly in Sloan's embrace, while Janna's cries died down to whimpers. She understood now, Heather thought, the fierce devotion that had led Sloan to wed a perfect stranger in order to provide a mother for his child. She felt the same overwhelming emotion for Janna herself. She'd grown to love the young girl as if she were her own daughter. She thought she understood, too, the fear Sloan must have felt when his wife was murdered, the helplessness, the rage. . . .

Heather almost cried out when Sloan withdrew the support of his arms and stepped back to gaze down at his sniffling daughter. With infinite tenderness, he bent to press a gentle kiss on the small forehead.

But then he glanced up at Heather. His expression, filled with poignant emotion, was one of gratitude, of appreciation, of love.

Heather felt her heart contract with hope. For while she knew his love was reserved for his daughter, it was possible—just possible—that some of the tenderness she saw brimming in Sloan's bright-blue eyes might just be for her as well.

Chapter 13

The terrifying moment when Janna's life was threatened would forever be branded in Heather's memory, as would Sloan's poignant gratitude afterward. She had never felt so close to him as in that moment, or yearned so deeply to have her love returned.

She wanted to feel that closeness again. In the week that followed, her pride prevented Heather from divulging her growing feelings for Sloan, but she soaked up any hint of tenderness he showed her, hoarding it away in her heart. She told herself she must be content with searing passion, satisfied with any crumbs of affection he tossed her way, yet she wouldn't abandon hope that someday his gratitude could evolve into something more substantial. Behind Sloan's cold mask lived a tender, vital, sensual man. Someday, perhaps, he could put aside the mask and the bitter past and accept the love she longed to lavish on him.

While their relationship seemed at an impasse, at least the political tide seemed to be swinging in Sloan's favor. Shortly after the July Fourth celebration, he received an invitation from the governor of Colorado—the same governor who a year earlier had pardoned Jake McCord for the crime of killing Caitlin's brother. A political dinner was to be held three weeks hence at the governor's home, in honor of the state's legislators, and several candidates were invited.

Although summer was a relatively slow time on a cattle ranch, Sloan didn't want to spare the time or expense for an overnight sojourn in Denver, but Heather urged him to go.

"It will benefit you to meet the men you'll have to deal with if you're elected," she advised.

They left Janna behind, in Caitlin's tender care, and made the journey in the afternoon, arriving in time to book a room at a modest hotel and then bathe and dress for the dinner.

For the occasion, Heather had unearthed a gown of dark-blue and rose silk from her wardrobe. The square-cut décolletage was filled with a frilled collar, high in back, while the overskirt was drawn up at the sides and draped behind to emphasize her narrow waist and curving hips. To complete the picture, she wore a slender choker of pearls around her throat and pearl-studded earrings in her ears—the few pieces of jewelry belonging to her late mother which she hadn't sold to pay her father's gambling debts.

The effect was one of quiet elegance, but from the narrowed look Sloan gave her when she came out from behind the dressing screen, Heather wondered if she had struck an unsuitable note with her attire.

"Is something wrong?" she asked uncertainly.

He shook his head, yet his expression remained cool, remote. "No. I just wondered where that fancy dress came from."

"I had it made up a few years ago, before my father . . . became mired in financial difficulties. I suppose it's a bit out of fashion by now. I thought this an appropriate occasion to wear it, but if you don't like it. . . ."

"It's fine," Sloan said rather abruptly, without really reassuring her. His brusqueness reminded her uncomfortably that money was still a troubling issue between them.

The governor's residence was within walking distance of the hotel, merely two blocks away. The sumptuous decor might have been imposing to many Westerners, with its gilt-and-crystal embellishments and lush carpets and rich brocade furnishings, but the display of wealth was a familiar world to Heather, one her mother's upper-crust family had enjoyed. The social setting was familiar as well, a milieu she had been thoroughly trained for. Attending formal dinners with high-powered politicians and wealthy magnates, offering charming, gracious conversation while remaining self-effacing, had been her mother's forte. It was a role *she* might have played had she wed Evan Randolf. . . .

That unwelcome thought crossed Heather's mind as she went through the reception line on her husband's arm. Yet she didn't miss this stifling life in the least, she reflected. Nor would she exchange the riches of this mansion for her present circumstances, despite her uncertain status as Mrs. Sloan McCord.

She could feel Sloan's eyes on her as she met the portly Governor Payne and his attractive wife, Ruth, and again when they joined a small group of gentlemen who were discussing the fate of a legislative bill in the last congressional session. When Sloan had introduced those he knew, Heather accepted a tall-stemmed glass of champagne from a passing waiter and slipped into her new role as a political wife.

She was eminently successful. Sloan watched Heather enchant the company, torn between admiration for her social graces and a vague sense of guilt. The duchess was in her element here, radiating elegance and charm and aristocratic breeding. Yet by marrying her, he'd taken her away from her rightful world—the lavish social sphere of teas and balls and soirees. She deserved to be gowned in silk and diamonds, rather than the calico and crystal beads he could afford.

He was obliged to her for relinquishing that life so willingly, yet he didn't like the obligation. Nor did he like the comparisons his mind insisted on making. In this setting at least, Heather outshone his late wife by miles. He couldn't imagine Doe campaigning for him or holding court in a gathering of wealthy white gentlemen—or aiding the local schoolteacher's journalistic efforts, for that matter.

Twice since the July Fourth celebration, Sloan had come home to find Heather and Vernon with their heads together, involved in a spirited discussion regarding the principles of democracy or the ramifications of a particular turn of phrase. Though intimate, there was nothing in the least sexual about their encounters. Yet on a primal level he didn't want to explore, Sloan felt himself prodded by male possessiveness. It riled him to realize the schoolteacher was providing the duchess the intellectual stimulation she seemed to crave.

Sloan was almost grateful when one of the other guests interrupted his reflections and claimed his attention. Yet his senses remained keenly attuned to Heather behind him, so that he was aware when a tall, raven-haired man came up to greet her.

"Why, if it isn't Miss Heather Ashford!"

"Richard!" Extending her hand, she acknowledged the newcomer warmly, and with the intimate familiarity of old friends, allowed him to draw her aside from the other guests. "Whatever are you doing here?"

"Covering the campaign. I'm with the *Denver Post* now. I could ask the same of you."

"I'm here with my husband. I'm no longer Miss Ashford."

"Of course. . . . I'd heard you married a Westerner," Richard said with a doleful smile. "Evan Randolf told me the unhappy news when I was in St. Louis a few months ago. It was a great disappointment to a number of people, me included. I had hoped you would wait for me."

She laughed. "You did no such thing. You were far too busy breaking scores of female hearts to notice me."

Her laughter brushed across Sloan's ears like sweet music, and sent a shaft of jealousy arrowing through him—a response which only intensified as he strained to hear the man's next words.

"Actually," Richard said in a low voice, "Evan asked me to keep an eye out for you. It's not my place to say, I know, but I believe he suffered a genuine disappointment at your loss. He wanted me to discover how you're faring in your marriage, and whether you regretted your choice of husbands yet."

Sloan thought the cheerfulness of her tone dimmed a degree. "You may report that I am faring quite well, and that I have no regrets whatever."

It was then that Heather looked around and spied him. His jaw hardening reflexively, Sloan went to join her, and she slipped her arm through his loyally.

"Richard, allow me introduce my husband, Sloan McCord."

"Richard Weld," the man said, shaking Sloan's hand. "Reporter and part-time editor for the *Post*. I worked with Heather's father years ago. In fact, Charles Ashford taught me much of what I know about newspapering."

"Pleased to meet you," Sloan replied, forcing a note of sincerity into his tone.

"I've heard of you, McCord. Shaking things up down your way, are you? Word is, you have Quinn Lovell on the run."

"Not yet, but I'm doing my level best."

Weld chuckled. "I'd like to write an article about you two for my paper—cattle baron versus mining king. Human interest and all that."

"Why, that would be marvelous, Richard," Heather answered for him.

At her apparent delight, Sloan felt another spike of jealousy shoot through him, but then she turned to glance up at him with a smile softer than silk. That lovely smile trapped his breath deep in his chest and had an inappropriate effect in another part of his body as well: he felt a hardening in his loins which he found difficult to ignore.

"I'll ride down your way . . ." Weld was saying. "Let me think. . . . Would week after next do? That would best fit my schedule."

"That will do fine," he replied too tersely.

Weld turned back to Heather, and she began to question him about his career since they'd last met. Eventually Sloan left them to converse while he did his duty and mingled with the company, but he would have preferred to remain with them. In fact, what he wanted was to be alone with Heather. He hadn't cared for the reminder of the men in her past, most particularly Evan Randolf.

The evening, while politically worthwhile, seemed interminable. He found himself counting the minutes until they could politely take their leave—through a half-dozen courses and then coffee afterward.

At last, though, the guests began to disperse, and Sloan escaped the stifling atmosphere with his wife in tow. As they stepped out into the moon-drenched night, he loosened his string tie and exhaled a sigh of relief.

"Was it so very bad?" Heather asked sympathetically.

"I'd rather ride herd in a cattle stampede than attend another one of those," Sloan admitted.

Her lips curved in amusement. "I'm afraid if you're elected, you will have to attend more than a few of those functions."

"Maybe I won't run after all."

"You don't really mean that."

"No."

Her faint, sweet scent teased him as they strolled along the street, lit now and then by gas lamps. From somewhere—a highbrowed dance hall, perhaps—the tinkling sound of a piano escaped to faintly serenade them.

"There was only one thing that made the evening bearable," Sloan added in a low voice.

"Oh?"

A groove deepened in his hard cheek as he half-smiled at her. "You. Watching you in that fancy gown. Wondering what you were wearing underneath. All through dinner, the only thing on my mind was stripping it off you and seeing what I could find underneath."

"Indeed?"

"Are you wearing drawers, duchess?"

"Perhaps you should discover for yourself."

She was flirting with him, he realized, his pulse quickening. The thought of following her advice interfered with his breathing and made his loins grow heavy. The duchess was standing there calm and cool as a nun, while all he could think about was bringing her to passion. He wanted to completely shatter her control, wanted her digging her nails into his back while she screamed with pleasure. . . .

Abruptly Sloan pulled her into the shadow of a crab apple tree. His arms came around her to hold her, lightly, possessively.

"Sloan, I didn't mean here. . . ." Heather protested a bit breathlessly.

His mouth hovered over the sweet temptation of her lips. "Then where?" Preventing her answer, he brought his mouth down on hers. His tongue danced, dueling with hers, making her feel his urgent desire.

Heather repressed a moan, feeling her breasts tighten and swell. With effort, she placed a restraining hand on his chest. She could feel his heartbeat, feel his heat. "Perhaps we should conduct this discussion in private."

Drawing back, he gave her a slow wicked smile. In the light of the street lamp she caught the flare of undisguised lust in his eyes. Heat rose inside her, inflaming the tips of her breasts, arousing a heavy ache in her lower body.

Silently they turned and continued the short distance to their hotel. As they passed through the lobby and ascended the stairs to the second floor, it was all Heather could do to keep from touching him. Anticipation made her feel hot and restless, while her blood moved heavily through her veins. When they reached their room, Sloan would take her. . . . She bit her lower lip, remembering the feel of that sleek, hard body moving over her, within her.

The hotel room was white with moonlight when they entered, the damask-covered bed illuminated by a faint glow. Sloan didn't light a lamp, but turned on her, pressing Heather back against the door. His urgent kiss nearly took her breath away, while his hands came up to cover her swelling breasts beneath the stiff corset.

"I've wanted to do this all night," he murmured against her lips.

"Is it all you want to do?" she challenged, her mood reckless.

"Hell no, that's not all. . . . Take off your clothes for me," he ordered.

"I shall need help with my gown."

He obliged, making short work of the task, letting the elegant creation fall to the floor in a whisper of silk. But he merely watched as she finished undressing. Shoes and stockings went, followed by camisole and corset and lacy underdrawers. Finally Heather stood only in her chemise and the pearl choker.

"Now your hair," Sloan said, watching her through narrowed eyes.

She pulled out the pins one by one with unsteady fingers, tossing them on the dressing table. Then she shook her head till her long, golden hair swirled about her shoulders.

She smiled then, and Sloan damned near stopped breathing. With that seductive smile, so sensual and lovely, Heather was pure temptress. His dream lover in the flesh.

Possessiveness surged inside him, and for once he didn't try to fight or deny it. He felt wild. He wanted to take her hard and fast . . . no, he wanted to draw out the moment till they were both crazy with need.

He wanted to make love to her slowly, kissing every hollow and pulse. He wanted to tangle his fingers in that cloud of pale hair and savor the taste of her silken skin. He wanted to see those tresses spread across his pillow as Heather lay waiting for him, her lush graceful body bare, her eyes filled with passion. . . .

A deep ache settled in his loins. He intended to make her pay for teasing him so.

Rapidly he stripped off his coat and tie and shirt. When he was naked to the waist, he moved toward her purposefully, the image of virile strength, his bare torso strongly muscled, his bronzed arms hard with sinew. His potent energy was so strong, she could feel it wrap around her before he even touched her.

Her body tight with anticipation, Heather lifted her face to his. She thought Sloan would kiss her, but instead he put his hands lightly on her shoulders and turned her slowly to face the full-length mirror. Watching in the glass while he stood behind her, he drew down the neckline of her chemise to expose her proud, thrusting breasts.

The cool, white light was unforgiving, as was Sloan's hard assessment of her body; her skin shone as pale and luminous as the pearls at her throat.

Heather drew a shaky breath. With her breasts scandalously bare, she felt deliciously sinful and desirable. It was all she could do to remain still as the strong bronzed fingers rose to cup her ivory flesh. She was scaldingly aware of Sloan's near-nakedness, of his heat at her back, of his hard thighs grazing her soft bottom.

His splayed fingers pushed the mounded swells upward, exaggerating their already lush abundance, squeezing lightly. "So beautiful," he murmured.

His eyes were smoky and warm with desire, mesmerizing her. With excruciating slowness, he brushed the taunting crests with his thumbs, making her bite back a whimper at the sensitiveness of her nipples.

"You like that, duchess?" His voice, male and sensual, washed over her. "You like it when I play with your tits? Answer me."

"Yes . . . I like it." Weakly she leaned back against him as he fondled her, watching her own seduction. His long, callused fingers tugged on the distended peaks until her face flushed, until arousal seared through her, hot and thick.

"I like it too. I get hard every time I even think of touching you," Sloan admitted, his voice dark and husky.

"Are you hard now?" she whispered in return, shocking herself.

His eyes flared, bright and intense in the moonlight. "Why don't you find out?" When she hesitated, he murmured in her ear, "I'm tired of doing all the work."

Her senses trembling with need, she turned to face him. Her shaking fingers fumbled with the buttons of his trousers, but she managed to open them. Boldly then, her hand slid inside the parted fabric and closed over him, her palm soft and warm.

His eyes half shut, Sloan gave a soft groan. "Take it out."

Willingly she obeyed. His erection was long and hot and throbbing. Heather shivered uncontrollably as wanting flamed inside her. She could only think of how Sloan would feel when he plunged into her, how his splendid arousal would fill her.

Bewitched, every nerve in her body on edge, she caressed him, stroking the hard, hot tumescence.

"You keep that up," he rasped, "and I'll spend in your hand."

"I wouldn't mind."

His smoldering gaze met hers with a promise of burning pleasure, but to her surprise he pulled back. "I would. I've got something else in mind for tonight."

"What?"

"Punishment. You're going to pay for teasing me all evening."

"But I didn't—"

"Sure you did, duchess. I had to sit through that interminable meal while you laughed and flirted with all your dinner partners and ignored me."

"I wasn't flirting."

"But you paid me no attention. You're lucky I didn't slip under the table and come up under your skirts." He grinned. "*That* might have been interesting."

She watched him questioningly as Sloan moved to the damask wing chair beyond the dressing table. Sitting down, he tugged off the rest of his clothing and settled back, naked and relaxed, his upthrusting manhood blatantly masculine between his parted, sinewed thighs.

"Remember how I taught you to ride me?"

"Yes." The word was a hoarse whisper.

"Why don't you come here, and we'll see how much you've learned?"

His dark, husky voice beckoned to her. Her gaze fixed on his rigid, straining arousal, Heather moved slowly toward him, drawn by some invisible, irresistible force.

He flicked the hem of her chemise. "Take this off. I want you naked."

Without a word, Heather drew the undergarment over her head and let it drop to the floor. His hot eyes traveled over her slowly, boldly appraising.

Slipping an arm around her waist then, Sloan pulled her down to sit sideways on his lap. She could feel his hard length against her buttocks; he was all warm, taut muscle against her softness. Yet he remained motionless.

She twisted on his lap, seeking to nestle her breasts, so naked and sensitive, in the crisp golden hairs of his chest. He skimmed his fingertips down her arms, delicately stroking.

"Sloan," she murmured.

"Yes?"

"Don't torture me."

"Why not?"

His thumbs slid upward and brushed the underside of her breasts, sending sparks shooting through her.

"Please. . . ."

"What do you want, darlin'?" He lightly pinched her flushed, sensitized nipples.

Heather gasped, arching her slender back, taut breasts thrusting out, wanting him, aching for him. Her soft flesh clamored for release. She was fully, painfully ready for him—and Sloan knew it. Yet he refused to do anything about it.

"You. . . . I want you."

"You can have me . . . eventually. When you're hungry enough."

His fingers slid upward, sinking deep into her tangled mane, but instead of kissing her, he merely nibbled at her lips, his tongue tracing the parted outline.

A streaking heat shuddered through her. She wanted to scream at his prolonged method of arousal. She needed him to put an end to the restless, hot longing.

"Sloan . . . I *am* hungry. . . ."

"Not enough. Not nearly enough."

Her breath caught in her throat when he reached down and trailed a hand along the inside of one leg. Eagerly, her bare, moon-bathed thighs fell open to accommodate his touch. Unhurriedly his fingers raked downward through the soft triangle of curls. She was wet silk between her legs, her body already anticipating the pleasure of his possession. His lean fingers glided easily over the flushed, feminine lips, seeking and caressing.

Heather bit back a moan when he found the tiny sensitive nub of female flesh, quivering with the throbbing urgency spiraling up from his expert touch.

"You see, duchess, I want you begging me."

He rubbed her sex with a featherlight pressure, making her tremble. Her eyes closing, she let her head fall back, her mouth parted in small, panting breaths. Yet his raw-silk voice aroused her as much as his exquisite stroking.

"Are you hot for me?" His dark words only fueled her desire and left her weak with wanting. Her eyes were half-lidded against the heat coursing up through her body. She was soaking wet for him, aching for him. Almost desperate, she squirmed in his lap, seeking to get closer to the heat and promise of that swollen, rigid shaft.

"Please, Sloan . . . take me."

He gave her a lazy smile. "No . . . not yet. I'm not ready for *you*."

"Yes, you are." She couldn't believe he could make such a claim when she could feel his rock-hard erection stiff against his stomach, throbbing and pulsing.

"Touch me," he ordered tauntingly. "Make me harder for you."

She tried to obey. Her fumbling fingers slid between their bodies, down his hair-roughened chest and flat belly to his groin. She wanted him so badly, she was actually shaking. She found the splendor of his arousal, but her hand slipped on the pulsing crest.

"Greenhorn," Sloan goaded softly into her mouth.

"Sloan . . . please. . . ."

She strained against him, her taut nipples scraping his chest, and he relented.

"Easy, honey, I'll take care of you."

Sliding his hands under her arms, he lifted her up to pull her astride his thighs. "I'll give you the wildest ride of your life." Deliberately he rubbed the hard ridge of his manhood against her soft mound, making her shudder in torment. Finally, though, he lowered her onto his thrusting erection to satisfy her passionate need.

Shivering and grateful, Heather settled over him, sinking down to envelop his shaft. Her eyes closed in ecstasy as she savored the feel of the hot, sweet length buried deep inside her.

"That feel better?" he murmured, though he already knew the answer. She was on the edge; he knew he could finish right now with no more than a hard thrust of his hips.

When she rocked her body against him, seeking to impale herself harder, he stopped the soft surge of her thighs with his hands on her hips.

"No, be still," he commanded in the slow, deep tones of arousal. "I haven't given you permission to move."

Heather quieted, but it required a fierce effort. She could feel a desperate tension building in her body. There was something about maintaining that utter stillness that heightened every sensation.

Sloan seemed not to care that he was driving her mad. Indolently, he shut his eyes and leaned his head against the chair back while he grew very hard and heavy inside her. She could feel his pulsing throb like a heartbeat.

Still lazily, he bent his head to nuzzle her nipple. Heather whimpered, instinctively pushing her breast against his hot, loving mouth. When his lips closed over the aching peak, she sighed in a deep, almost painful satisfaction. Her hands closed in his hair, clutching him to her.

The soft sound of his suckling was powerfully erotic. And with every rasp of his tongue on her budded nipples, she felt a throbbing echo deep within her.

Almost without warning, then, he thrust upward, pressing deeper, impaling her to the hilt.

"Oh, God, yes . . . Sloan. . . ." Her back arched in writhing response.

"I like to hear you moan for me. . . . Do it again. Let me hear how good it feels to you."

His cupped hands moving under her bottom, he lifted her up, withdrawing almost completely. She started to protest, but when his hot mouth fastened greedily on her breast and sucked hard, Heather gave a soft cry. Her cry turned to a keening moan as he lowered her once more onto his thick, swollen instrument of pleasure. Whimpering, she clung to him, her arms and legs gripping, trying to hold him inside her.

He tortured her with exquisitely slow thrusts, driving deep, only to withdraw as he raised her up. With each surge he sucked more strongly at her, his wet mouth searing her as he slid her up and down on his shaft.

Heather writhed against him, clenching him tightly within the depth of her body. "Sloan. . . ." Her hands gripped his shoulders, she began to move helplessly, shamelessly, frantically.

"That's it . . . ride me, baby . . . harder . . . faster."

His hands gripped her buttocks, working her up and down in rough, powerful strokes, in cadence with his thrusts.

In only moments, her breath was coming in sobbing gasps. Blood surging, heart pounding, she strained wildly against him. She thought she might die from the brutal flames that licked and seared her senses, but Sloan's hands kept urging her on, moving her in a merciless, maddening rhythm that wouldn't stop.

Her body burned and shook for him; her flesh took on a life of its own, trembling and shaking and dissolving. A scream of pleasure pulsed deep in her throat as the long, endless orgasm quaked through her.

The wrenching, tearing release was violent enough to shatter her. Sloan held her convulsing body still for his thrusts, catching her sobs in his mouth, but he couldn't hold back much longer. His rough excitement matching her own frenzy, he gritted his teeth, but the sweetness of her hot, tight body destroyed his shaky control. He surged upward. His passion suddenly exploding, he rammed into her, pumping hotly, groaning his savage release against her mouth as wave after wave of grinding pleasure ravaged him.

It was a wild, delirious coming, so powerful it left him grasping for breath.

Even in the shuddering aftermath, when the fierce rapture subsided, he could feel the delicious clasping and gripping of her body around him. Passion slaked, Sloan sprawled weakly in the chair, with a limp Heather still clinging to him.

After a long moment, he managed to stir himself. With her legs wrapped around him, their bodies still joined, Sloan slowly stood and carried her to the bed, where he lowered her beneath him.

Still sheathed in her hot, moist center, he let his weight settle over her. His lips nuzzled her flushed face with a tenderness as devastating as the wild loving had been.

"You okay?"

She barely had the strength to nod. She could forgive his savagery. She had felt the same fierce urgency, the same reckless need.

"A man likes it," he murmured hoarsely, "when his woman goes wild."

She went completely still. Her question, when it came out, was little more than a whisper. "Am I your woman, Sloan?"

He closed his eyes in exhaustion. "You're my wife. That makes you my woman."

When she remained silent, he eased off her and drew her into the curve of his body, drawing her head to rest on his shoulder. In the hushed moments afterward, she could hear his heart beating steadily beneath her ear.

His woman. It was what she had longed to hear. Instead of pleasure, however, Heather felt a deep ache twist inside her. Sloan's desire for her thrilled her, yet despite his fierce loving, she knew his heart was untouched. His roughly muttered words of lust and need held little meaning.

The primal force between them was purely carnal. He needed her on some elemental, primitive, physical level, only that.

Yet she wanted more than just raw, heated passion from him. She wanted his love. She wanted the same deep abiding love he still harbored for his first wife.

Chapter 14

~~∽◯∽~~

Although the visit to Denver proved a welcome respite from routine for Heather, the return home plunged her once more into an endless round of mundane chores. One warm afternoon in early August found her out back of the house, hanging wash on the line while Janna played with her doll in the grass.

A frown drew down Heather's mouth as she attached a clothespin to a shirt of Sloan's. She couldn't explain the discontent she felt. She should be exquisitely happy. She truly didn't mind the hard work of ranch life. Nor was her restlessness due to Sloan's lack of attention. His lovemaking was everything a woman could wish. A memory of his heated passion last night echoed through her. Her nipples were still tender and swollen from his kisses. He had left a faint mark on the curve of her right breast that was sore to the touch—a lover's brand.

Turning her head, Heather lifted her gaze to the horizon, where the peaks of the towering Rockies rose in the distance, their rugged slopes shaded dark with summer forests. Her woman's time had come and gone. Perhaps that was what depressed her.

Her hand stole to her flat belly, her thoughts wistful. If she couldn't have Sloan's love, she wanted his child.

Shaking off her morose mood, she bent to choose another wet garment from the wash basket—and then suddenly went still as a faint prickling coursed up her spine. Peering beyond the wash line, she could see no one, yet she felt the unpleasant sensation of being watched.

Her heart quickening, Heather glanced at the post where she'd leaned the rifle. After the incident with the rattlesnake, she always kept a weapon close at hand.

Inching her way nearer, she grabbed for the rifle and whirled, swinging the barrel up. A man stood scarcely three yards from Janna, unmoving.

He was unarmed, Heather noted in the first moment of panic, yet he still seemed dangerous. He was watching her silently, his unwavering black eyes holding the intensity of a wild predator.

Her breath trapped in her throat, Heather stood transfixed by those dark, piercing eyes.

His tall, muscular figure sported working clothes, denims and chambray shirt and leather vest, but he was clearly an Indian. He looked a bit savage, with his bronzed skin and untamed raven hair gleaming in the August sun. His hard, striking features possessed the masculine beauty of a granite sculpture, yet there was something familiar about the high carved cheekbones and sharp nose and luminous jet eyes.

He didn't seem particularly disturbed by the rifle she had aimed at his chest.

"You gonna shoot me, ma'am?" His chiseled mouth curled with more mockery than amusement.

Letting out her breath in relief, Heather lowered the barrel. "No, of course not. But I would advise you not to sneak up on a person unannounced."

"I knocked at the front door. No one answered."

"I'm here, as you can see."

"You're Sloan's new wife."

"I'm Heather McCord, yes."

"The name's Logan."

"Wolf Logan. I suspected as much. You're Doe's brother."

"Half-brother, actually."

Heather nodded. She had heard a great deal about the Cheyenne half-breed. Mr. Logan lived up in the mountains, working his mining claim. Years ago he'd saved Jake's life, nursing him back from near-fatal wounds. It was there at the mountain camp that Sloan had first met Sleeping Doe. Indeed, Wolf Logan was no stranger; he was family.

With a polite smile, Heather moved forward, offering her hand for him to shake.

Wolf took it willingly, although one black eyebrow shot up. "You don't seem afraid of me."

"Should I be?"

"Some white women run screaming when they see a strange Injun."

"You resemble Janna—or rather, she resembles you." Heather looked around, seeking the child out. "I expect you came to see your niece."

"That, and to meet you. I heard Sloan had married again—a real beauty. I see rumor didn't lie."

Heather flushed a little at his compliment, but Wolf turned away easily, crossing over to his niece. Janna grinned and babbled a greeting as he swung her up in his arms.

"Would you care to come inside?" Heather asked when they'd become reacquainted. "I could make tea . . . or coffee." She faltered awkwardly, wondering if a Cheyenne preferred an Indian drink of some kind.

Wolf seemed amused by her hesitation. "I drink tea occasionally. I'm not entirely uncivilized. I was raised white."

"Well, then, may I offer you tea?"

"I hoped you might put me up for the night. Sloan usually invites me to stay here when I pass through."

"Of course, you're welcome to stay the night. Sloan is out somewhere on the range, but he should be back in a few hours."

"Then I'll have time."

"Time?"

"I thought I would visit Doe first."

Heather looked a bit startled.

"Her grave. She's buried up in the hills."

"Oh . . . I didn't realize."

"I'd like to take Janna with me. It's time she got to know her ma a bit."

Heather hesitated, uncomfortable turning the child over to a stranger, even if he was her uncle. "Perhaps I should come with you."

His handsome mouth curled. "I'm not going to kidnap her, if that's what worries you."

"No, but I'm responsible for her. Janna is my daughter now, and I don't like letting her out of my sight."

His eyebrow raising again, Wolf regarded Heather intently with those penetrating jet eyes, yet she sensed approval.

"I think," he said slowly, "Doe would have been glad to have you looking out for Janna."

He kept Janna entertained while Heather finished hanging the wash. When she suggested hitching up the buckboard, however, he said she would need a horse to get up into the foothills. They left word with Rusty where they were headed and rode out, Wolf with Janna propped in front of him, and Heather riding sidesaddle.

The gravesite was a natural shrine, Heather reflected when they finally came to a halt. It was protected by rugged hills, secreted in a glade of aspens. The surrounding meadow shimmered lavender blue with delicate columbine, while above the simple granite headstone towering aspens stood sentinel, their bright green leaves whispering gently in the warm summer breeze.

She watched wordlessly as Wolf dropped from his horse and carried Janna over to the grave. He bowed his head, his long raven hair falling over his carved cheekbones, his thoughts private.

After a respectful interval, Heather dismounted slowly and moved to stand beside him. An ache caught in her throat as she read the inscription: *Here lies Doe Who Sleeps, Beloved wife of S. McCord.*

"She didn't deserve to die so young," Wolf said tonelessly, yet Heather could feel his edge of anger. When she glanced at him, his bronzed jaw had hardened.

"What was she like?" Heather murmured.

He shrugged. "She was quiet mostly, but she had a lively spirit. She made you laugh . . . and just plain damn feel good."

"I understand she kept house for you?"

Wolf nodded. "Doe was five years younger. We had the same ma but different pas. Mine was white, and he raised me to be a miner. That's how I escaped Doe's fate when the army rounded up all the Cheyenne and herded them to Indian Territory." Wolf's mouth curled savagely. "They lived like prisoners on a reservation. Our ma died there. When I learned about it, I went to fetch

Doe and bring her back to the mountains, where I'd staked a claim. Doe kept house while I panned for gold."

He hunkered down, setting Janna on her feet. His voice was low and tender when he spoke to his niece. "Your ma is buried here, Janna."

"I'm not sure she understands," Heather said gently.

"Maybe not yet, but she'll learn. She should know about her mother."

Heather nodded, knowing Sloan felt as he did. Quietly she bent to pluck the fragile stem of a columbine and placed it on the grave. Picking another one, she put it in Janna's little hand, urging her to do the same.

A meadowlark trilled just then, and Wolf's head came up, like a wild animal sensing danger. Heather hadn't heard a sound, but when she looked around, she saw a horseman riding toward them.

Sloan. Her heart lurched painfully. She hadn't meant for him to find her here. She felt a little like Blackbeard's wife, prying into secrets of his past.

He came to a halt a few feet away, the brim of his hat shading his eyes. He was angry, she could sense it, even if his bright, arresting eyes remained remote and cool as he swung down from his horse.

After a brief glance at her, he ignored her and addressed his brother-in-law. "Rusty said I'd find you here."

"I brought Janna to pay her respects to her ma," Wolf explained easily.

Sloan nodded and tugged off his hat. He took a private moment before turning his attention to his daughter. He didn't speak to Heather at all, which made her wonder if perhaps he believed she had desecrated the gravesite.

They rode back together, Janna with her papa. Heather remained silent while Sloan and Wolf caught up with each other's lives. It seemed that Wolf had made a rich strike and was headed for Denver to enjoy the spoils of his find.

Sloan seemed genuinely pleased by his brother-in-law's good fortune, but he ribbed Wolf about his newfound wealth. "It's about time you came down out of your mountains and quit leading the life of a hermit, though it's hard to think of you as a mining baron."

It wasn't long before Heather realized the two men, though vastly different, enjoyed a deep camaraderie. But then, they shared a common bond— a woman they had both loved.

When they reached the ranch, Heather took Janna to the kitchen to fix supper while the two men retired to Sloan's study to resume their discussion. An hour later, she had to call them twice before they joined her at the table.

Supper proved to be an extremely enjoyable meal for Heather, with Wolf keeping her entertained with tales of life in a mountain camp. Afterward Heather put Janna to bed, while Sloan and Wolf once more settled in the study, this time sharing reminiscences over a bottle of whiskey.

"I meant it," Wolf said finally, "when I told you I made a huge strike. I'm filthy rich." He hesitated, eyeing Sloan. "I know the cattle business isn't what it used to be. Don't take this the wrong way, but I want you to have a share of my stake. It would have been Doe's, had she lived."

Sloan shook his head solemnly. "You know I can't take your money."

"Not even for Janna's sake? I am her uncle after all."

A muscle in his jaw flexed. "I'll provide for my daughter."

Wolf grinned, his teeth showing white in his bronzed face. "I know—McCords take care of their own. You told me that in no uncertain terms when you married my sister. All right, I'll mind my own business. But you damned sure better let me know if you ever need anything."

He sipped his whiskey, his expression turning thoughtful. "You know, when you first sent word about your marriage, I was ready to string you up by your thumbs, but now that I've met Heather . . . I think you did right. She's good for Janna. She'll give her advantages Doe never could, help her get accepted by the white world."

Sloan kept his face shuttered, not wishing to be reminded of the duchess's superior talents. He was in no mood to make comparisons when Doe came out the loser. In fact his mood was blacker than it had been in months. Having his brother-in-law as a guest in this house had reminded him painfully of Doe—but it was seeing Heather at the gravesite this afternoon that had brought all his former grief surging back. It had been like prodding a festering wound.

He was almost relieved when Wolf finished off his whiskey and said, "If you don't mind, I think I'll turn in. I plan to make an early start for Denver tomorrow."

Sloan downed the rest of his liquor, relishing the burn in his throat, but when he started to rise, Wolf stopped him.

"You don't need to show me to my room. I know the way. I'll just fetch my gear from the barn."

Sloan hesitated, remembering that Heather used

that bedchamber now. Wolf was like a brother to him. They shared a history that bonded them more strongly than any blood: they'd tracked down Doe's murderers together. Yet Sloan preferred not to reveal the intimate details of his marriage. He didn't want to have to explain why he and his wife didn't sleep in his bedchamber.

"Sure," he said evenly.

When Wolf left for the barn, Sloan put out the lamps in his study and went upstairs. A light shone beneath the door to Heather's room. When he knocked and eased it open, he found her sitting up in bed reading, looking lovely and virginal in a high-necked nightgown. The long-sleeved garment, he suspected, was a concession to modesty; despite the warmth of the summer night, there was a strange man in the house.

Unable to restrain his dark mood, he said brusquely, "I gave Wolf this room for the night. It's where he always sleeps. I'll help you move your things across the hall if you like."

He understood her look of surprise. There were two other rooms upstairs—one used primarily for sewing, the other for storage. Both had beds for any overflow of guests, although at the moment the bedsteads were stacked against the walls to allow more living space.

"It's too much trouble set a bed up just for one night," Sloan added more gruffly than he'd intended. "Besides, there's no reason for Wolf to know our business. He's leaving early in the morning. You can move back here tomorrow."

Her gazed searched his, but without comment, Heather rose and put on a wrapper and slippers. As she gathered her toiletries and clothing, Sloan smoothed the bedcovers, then helped her carry some of her gowns across the hall to his bedchamber.

Janna was sound asleep in her cradle, Heather noted as he lit a lamp. She found places for her things while Sloan hung her gowns in the clothespress.

When they finished, the moment suddenly turned awkward. Heather saw Sloan glance at the bed, then back at her. In the palpable silence, she could feel the tension rising off him.

He did not want her here, she knew. Any more than he had wanted her at Doe's grave.

He started to turn away, but Heather's voice, low and troubled, stopped him in his tracks.

"Sloan . . . I am sorry about this afternoon. I didn't mean to intrude on your past. It's just that . . . Wolf thought Janna should see where her mother was buried, and I didn't want her to go alone. I realize you were angry."

Aware that his brother-in-law might return any moment, Sloan quietly shut the bedchamber door. He *had* been angry to find her at Doe's grave; he was still angry. Maybe it was irrational, but he needed to keep that part of himself private, to keep his past life separate from his present. The glade was his own special place, the private sanctuary he had shared with Doe. He didn't want anyone intruding on his cherished memories, most certainly not the woman who was becoming an obsession with him. It seemed somehow a betrayal of Doe.

Emotion a hard knot inside him, Sloan clenched his jaw. "I'd rather you didn't go there again."

"All right."

"I just don't like strangers visiting there," he said by way of explanation.

Her gaze lowered, as if to mask the hurt he'd

given her. "I don't believe I am precisely a stranger. I am your wife, Sloan."

He couldn't make himself respond, so he abruptly changed the subject. "You can have the bed."

She gave him a questioning look. "Where will you sleep?"

He would take the floor. Better yet, he wouldn't sleep here at all. "I mean to ride into town," Sloan said brusquely.

She stared at him. "This late?"

"The saloon stays open all night. I thought I would catch a poker game."

"When will you be back?"

He shrugged as her hazel eyes searched his. "Before morning, most likely."

"Is that wise?"

"I wasn't aware I needed your permission, duchess."

Her lips tightened at his derisive tone. "You don't, of course. I was simply thinking of your campaign. It might not be prudent to be frequenting a saloon until the election is over."

"Maybe not back East, but this is the West. There's not a man in the territory who would change his vote because he found me playing poker."

"What about the women—the ones who are working so hard to get you elected?"

"Western women aren't like you, duchess. They don't have your prudish notions. They'll understand."

She winced at his taunting remark, yet her anger was roused. Sloan was deliberately goading her—without any real justification. Perhaps she *had* once been prudish, but she'd shed her ladylike inhibitions rather quickly upon her marriage.

That, however, was not the issue, she knew very well.

"This is not about a poker game," Heather said stiffly, "or my dislike of gambling, is it? You simply don't want me to share this bed with you. Why don't you admit it?"

"Okay, I admit it. That satisfy you?"

The hush of the room was thick and strained. Knowing he'd delivered a low blow but in no mood to apologize, Sloan started to turn away again.

Heather's fists clenched at her sides as resentment and frustration flared inside her. For months she had been patient, waiting for Sloan to accept her as his wife. For months she had tried to find a way to break through the barriers of grief and sorrow he'd erected around his heart. For months she'd hoped he would come to see her in a different light, apart from the darkness of his memories of his first marriage. It was time to stop hoping.

"Perhaps you don't want me here," she said tightly, "but I *am* your wife, Sloan. This is where I belong. Here, in this room. In this bed. By your side."

He froze with one hand on the doorknob. When he glanced over his shoulder at her, she could see denial in his hard gaze.

She went on, spurred by anger and fear. "I am your wife, Sloan. Not a stranger. Not simply your housekeeper or your daughter's nurse or your political advisor. Your *wife*. The woman whose body you take so intimately at night. The woman who loves you."

Sloan recoiled, almost as if she had struck him. The silence between them seemed suddenly deafening.

"What . . . did you say?"

Her chin rose defiantly as she met his gaze without flinching. "I said, I love you."

"Dammit. . . ." His curse was low and raw as he stared at her.

It had been an unwise thing to say, Heather thought as she saw the torment on his face. Sloan wasn't ready to hear admissions of love. His mouth was drawn in a grim line, his eyes bleak.

As if unable to look at her any longer, he shut his eyes. "I warned you." His voice was tight, knife-edged, but she heard the pain there. "I told you when we married, I wasn't looking for love."

Every bleak word dug into her heart. "I know." He couldn't let himself be loved. Couldn't let his emotions be touched. He'd set strict limits on how close he would let her come, and she had crossed that boundary. And yet she couldn't, wouldn't back down. Her future, *their* future, was at stake.

She continued unrelentingly, her quiet voice hoarse. "I am sorry, Sloan . . . for so many things. I'm sorry that Doe died. I'm sorry that you grieve for her. I'm sorry I can't offer you comfort. But she *is* dead. She isn't coming back. I am your wife now. It's time you accept it."

His jaw clenched. The silence drew out, so brittle it had an edge to it. When his eyes opened, Heather knew she had lost. The ice in his look matched the granite set of his features.

"Maybe you are my wife," he replied grimly, "but you can't take Doe's place."

Without looking at her again, Sloan opened the door, yet her soft sound of distress made him pause. For a moment he stood there, his head bowed, his shoulders rigid.

"I don't have anything inside left to give you," he said, his voice raw.

She shivered, feeling the bitter chill of despair.

"Do you hear me? You can keep your love, duchess. I don't want it."

He walked out then, leaving her alone with his slumbering daughter.

In the quiet of his bedchamber, Heather brought a trembling hand to her mouth, her lacerated heart aching with the echo of the closing door.

Chapter 15

E motion knotted like a fist inside Sloan as he stared at the amber glass of whiskey before him on the table. He hadn't bothered finding a poker game. Instead he'd ordered a bottle of rotgut and taken himself off to a corner to be alone—if being alone was even possible in a crowded saloon.

The barroom was hazy with smoke and lively with the raucous laughter of cowboys and miners, many of whom were his friends. At one end of the stage, a pretty painted dove banged on a piano and warbled a camptown song. Sloan paid them no mind.

He intended to get drunk. Falling-down, riproaring drunk. Maybe then he could forget the wounded look in Heather's eyes. Maybe then he could numb the ache in his chest.

Mercilessly pushing away the emotions that threatened him, he gulped another burning swallow of whiskey. Her profession of love had been a blow, slicing through the layers of protection he'd wrapped around himself. It was too much. She wanted too much, damn her.

He had no love to give her. The dark hole where his heart once had been was void of feeling . . . except for the guilt. All he felt was guilt. He had gotten Doe killed. He couldn't betray her memory by loving another woman.

Painful images swam before his eyes. . . . Doe in her last moments . . . her blood on his hands. Sloan squeezed his eyes shut. He could feel the blackness closing in around him.

Abandoning the whiskey glass, he raised the bottle to his lips and tilted his head back, welcoming the potent liquor's numbing power.

Goddammit, he didn't want Heather's love. He sure as hell couldn't love her in return. He couldn't bear the pain again. He couldn't face giving his heart to another woman, only to have her be taken from him again.

He didn't want the sense of peace he'd found with Heather. *Peace*, a derisive voice sneered inside his head. What was that? A dream. A dream he didn't deserve—

"How about it, cowboy? Want a ride tonight?"

Unwillingly Sloan raised his glazed eyes, trying to focus. He flinched to see a blonde woman standing over him. *Heather*. No, not Heather. This one's hair was brassy burlap, not pale silk. She wore a low-cut blue dress that exposed most of her lush breasts, and she smelled of cheap perfume. Dangling from her fingertips was a full bottle of whiskey, while her red, sensual mouth smiled in invitation.

She was a whore, his dulled mind told him. He didn't know her name—she was new since he'd last frequented the Pick & Stirrup Saloon—but she was available.

Sloan glanced at his own bottle, which somehow was almost empty. Maybe she was what he needed to make him forget, to numb the savage ache inside him. He desperately needed forgetfulness right now.

"Hell . . . why not?" he mumbled, the words slurred. He took the bottle she offered and tried to stand, but he had trouble getting his wobbly legs to support him. The blonde caught him when he staggered and wrapped a slender arm around him, pressing her beasts against his face. Laughing, she tried to turn him toward the back stairs.

Someone else blocked their way.

His head down, Sloan blinked at the female legs covered in black net wavering in his unsteady vision. He recognized those attractive legs.

Swaying, he raised his gaze to find Della Perkins standing in his path, a slight frown on her face.

"Lilly," she said to the blonde, "why don't you go see to Horace there? He wants some company, I'll bet. I'll take care of Sloan."

Lilly shot Della a narrowed glance, but allowed her to take Sloan's weight. Too far gone to stand on his own, he draped an arm heavily over Della's shoulder and let her lead him.

"Where we goin', Dell?" he murmured.

"Up to my room, so you can drown your sorrows in private."

"You gonna take care of me?"

"Sure, honey. It'll be like old times."

"I got a bad ache."

"I know, sugar."

She led him upstairs to her bedchamber. The room was familiar to him; he'd known it well in his wilder days. It was plain but serviceable . . . a brass bed, a washstand, an oak rocking chair. The sheets on the bed were rumpled from recent use and probably smelled of stale sex.

Della helped him across the room to the bed and gently pushed him down. Yeah, stale sex. With a sound that was half groan, half sigh, Sloan lay back, cradling the bottle protectively in one arm.

He felt Della pull off his boots, but instead of taking off his pants and shirt, she drew a blanket up to cover him.

He opened one eye. "Why'd you stop?"

"I'm just gonna put you to bed."

"I doan wanna go to bed. I wanna fuck."

"You're in no condition to fuck, me or anybody else, sugar. Besides, you don't really want me. You got a real purty wife waitin' for you at home."

He reached up to snag an arm around her neck and drew her mouth down to his. "Make me forget her, Dell," he murmured hoarsely against her lips.

She pulled back. "Forget who? You mean your wife?"

"Yeah . . . her."

He tried to pull Della down with him, but she resisted. "You don't want me, Sloan, honey," she repeated, "now tell the truth."

No, he didn't want her. . . . Didn't want any woman but Heather. That was the hell of it. He wanted Heather too much.

Della seemed to understand his problem. As if she could read his mind, she sat beside him and patted his chest. "Why don't you tell me about it? I reckon I'm a good listener."

Shaking his head dizzily, he struggled to uncork the fresh whiskey bottle. Della *was* a good listener, but he didn't need a confessor. He didn't want to end up telling his troubles to Della. . . .

"I doan wan' her love." He heard the slurred protest from a distance. "I loved Doe. A man only . . . fines love like that onessh in his life."

"Who says, Sloan?" When he frowned obtusely, Della smoothed back a lock of hair which had fallen over his forehead. "Seems to me, a man can love two women in a lifetime."

"No." He put the bottle to his lips and drank.

When he coughed, choking a little at the fiery effect, Della gently took the bottle from him. "I think I know what your trouble is. I think maybe you're in love with that purty wife of yours and you just don't want to admit it."

Fury surged through him, slicing through the numbing effect of the liquor. "No, goddammi'. . . . I *cannnn* love 'er. I love Doe."

"Doe's gone, sugar—may she rest in peace."

"Not gone . . . sheesh still here. . . ." He pounded his chest weakly. The pressure in his heart was sharp and heavy.

"Maybe so, but you're here with the living. You gotta get on with your life."

Sloan squeezed his eyes shut, wishing he could die like Doe had. He loved her . . . and yet her cherished memory was fading. He couldn't help it, sweet Christ. . . .

Panic gripped him. The grief, the sorrow that had once swamped him, was gone. The love he'd once felt had faded. He couldn't feel it. . . .

He breathed a savage curse. No matter how hard he tried, he no longer could see Doe's face clearly in his mind. All he could see was Heather's beautiful image, her eyes defiant and sad as she declared her love for him. As she insisted Doe was dead . . . that he had to forget her.

With a groan, Sloan rolled over and buried his face in the pillow, fighting the emotions that were strangling him.

He barely heard Della as she rose from the bed. "I'm going to send for your brother, sugar. He can take you home to your wife."

"No, doan wanna go home . . . it hurts to much."

His wife was the last thing he wanted. He'd fled here to escape her, to remove himself from the temptation of her body and the obsession he could no longer control.

For weeks he'd refused to put a name to the hunger he felt for Heather, yet it had taken hold of him in a way that was beyond lust, beyond carnal craving. All he had to do was look at her and his pulse started beating faster. He just thought of her and a fire smoldered low in his belly, swelling his groin. And when they made love. . . . He'd never before been so lost in a woman's body. What he felt went deeper than physical desire . . . damn damn damn her.

As the blackness swirled around him, Sloan mumbled another oath, despising his weakness for her. Even as he tried to shut out Heather's memory, he was assailed by an image of her heart-stopping face, her beautiful, soft golden eyes filled with pain and love.

He groaned at the terrible, unexpected yearning that swept over him. Shutting his eyes, he cursed his burning hunger for her. He didn't want her love. He wouldn't let her mold and touch his heart the way she had his body.

He couldn't love again. He couldn't bear the vulnerability. He couldn't bear it. . . .

The moon glowed down on the rugged foothills, casting a spell of silver shadows, yet Heather scarcely saw the enchantment. Her heart was aching.

She stood at the rail on the back porch, her head bowed, her throat tight with unshed tears as she remembered Sloan's parting words. *You can keep your love, duchess. I don't want it.* When a coyote crooned mournfully in the distance, she shivered, despite the warmth of the summer night.

Just then the kitchen door whispered open behind her. Her breath catching sharply, Heather turned to find Wolf Logan staring at her in the darkness with his intent gaze. Wiping her burning eyes, she closed the folds of her wrapper more tightly over her throat.

"You all right?" he asked quietly.

"Yes. I couldn't sleep. I'm sorry if I woke you."

"I'm a light sleeper."

Closing the door softly behind him, he came to stand beside her at the rail. Half-naked, he wore no shirt or boots, merely denim trousers. The corded sinews of his bare arms and torso rippled in the moonlight, brazenly masculine. Modestly Heather averted her gaze. Despite his striking handsomeness, he seemed more than a little savage with his long raven hair and bronzed skin and piercing eyes. Yet somehow she didn't fear him. On the contrary, she felt inexplicably safe with him.

"Sloan often ride into town to play poker?" Wolf asked.

She preferred not to reply. It was mortifying to have her marital problems on display. "Not often," she murmured.

"He never used to be much of a gambler. Has he changed that much since I last saw him?"

"I don't suppose so."

Wolf must have misunderstood her dismay, for he said consolingly, "I wouldn't worry too much. Sloan's not liable to gamble away the ranch. It's his heritage, after all. And he'd never do anything to jeopardize his daughter's future."

She nodded, yet it wasn't really the thought of Sloan gambling that distressed her. It was the way they had parted. She tried a careless smile. "I confess I have an aversion to gambling, ever since my father gambled away my mother's fortune."

"I heard you were obliged to pay your pa's debts after he died."

"Yes. I . . . was able to settle most of them, but Sloan assumed the remainder when we married. I didn't realize at the time, but it was a burden he was ill-equipped to handle."

She felt Wolf's penetrating gaze on her. "I thought Sloan made a mistake marrying you, but now I'm not so sure. He seems different from the last time I saw him. More at peace with himself."

"I would hardly describe him as being at peace," Heather answered bitterly.

Wolf gave a quiet huff of laughter. "You didn't know him after he lost Doe. He was like a madman then. All he lived for was revenge."

"Perhaps he has changed in *that* respect. But he . . . isn't happy. I'm not Doe, you see. He loved her so very much."

"I don't know about that."

Heather cast Wolf a startled glance.

"Oh, he loved her well enough, I reckon. They were happy together. But guilt can do strange things to a man. Shade his memory a bit."

"What do you mean?"

"I think maybe he only remembers the good parts about their marriage, about Doe herself. He blames himself for her murder, and afterward he built her up in his mind. Put her up on some pedestal, like some goddess."

"Saint," Heather murmured.

"What?"

"She's always seemed like a saint to me. An ideal which I'll never be able to live up to."

"I think he cares for you a lot more than he lets on."

Mutely Heather shook her head. Perhaps Sloan

had exaggerated the depth of his love for his murdered wife because of guilt, but she couldn't believe
he'd come to truly care for *her*. Not after tonight,
when he'd spurned her love so unequivocally.

She forced a rueful smile. "Thank you."

"For what?"

"For trying to raise my spirits."

His slow masculine smile was dazzling. Heather
felt her heart skip a beat at the display of white
teeth in his bronzed, striking face. "My pleasure,
ma'am."

The congenial moment was broken, however, by
the slow sound of hoofbeats and wagon wheels in
the distance. Several minutes later, a buckboard
swung into the yard and lumbered to a halt before
the back porch.

Heather recognized the driver. In the moonlight
she could make out Jake McCord's handsome features. She could also see the figure of a man lying
prone in the rear of the buckboard. Sloan?

Her heart leapt to her throat, while her hand
reached out to clutch Wolf's arm. "Dear God, he's
not . . . ?"

"No," Jake answered quickly as he jumped down
from the seat. "He's fine. Just had a bit too much
to drink, I'm afraid."

She couldn't reply. Instead she watched mutely
as Jake pulled his brother to his feet and caught
him around the waist.

Shaking his head groggily, Sloan roused enough
to drape an arm around the other man's shoulder.
He mumbled something under his breath but allowed Jake to support him up the steps to the back
porch.

When they passed her, Heather went rigid as she
caught the scent of cheap perfume mingled with
the stench of whiskey. Sloan had been with a

woman, she could smell it. She remembered the odor from her own visit to the saloon and Della Perkins.

The sudden slicing pain low in her stomach was like the twist of a knife.

In the kitchen doorway, Jake paused with his burden to call over his shoulder, "Should I put him to bed?"

She felt Wolf's dark gaze on her, yet she forced a hoarse reply. "Yes, please, I would appreciate it. On second thought, would you put him in the guest bedroom? Janna is asleep in his room and the beds aren't set up in the other rooms."

When she glanced apologetically at Wolf, he nodded in agreement. "You want me to bunk at Jake's place for the rest of the night? Looks like you two have some things to work out."

Heather shook her head, her throat tight with unshed tears. "You don't have to leave. Indeed, I wish you would stay. I can make up one of the spare beds."

"There's no need to go to so much trouble. I'll bed down on the floor."

"The study has a comfortable couch."

"Even better." His mouth curved in a smile of sympathy. "I'll wait in the kitchen till you get Sloan settled."

She fabricated her own smile to hide her mortification and heartache and went inside. Her pride was fiercely wounded, yet her heart was suffering more. Sloan had heard her declaration of love and gone straight to the bed of another woman.

Jealousy and humiliation scored her. He had been with a prostitute, there was no other polite term for it. She might have been reared a lady and sheltered from the seamier sides of life, but she knew well enough what men sought from saloon women. She just hadn't expected it of Sloan.

A sick ache in the pit of her stomach, Heather unwillingly followed the two brothers upstairs to her bedchamber. She lit a lamp on the dressing table and turned it down low while Jake settled Sloan heavily on the bed.

"Thank you," she said tightly. "I'll take care of him now."

"If you're sure," Jake replied skeptically.

"I'm sure."

When he had gone and shut the door quietly behind him, Heather stood over the sleeping Sloan, not wanting even to touch him. He was lying on his back, fully clothed, on top of the covers, one arm draped over his face. Her mind felt numb, but as she regarded him, her despair grew into a hard, bright little kernel of anger. After his betrayal of her, his peaceful slumber infuriated her.

For a moment she was gripped with a strangling rage so powerful she wanted to scream. She wanted to strike him, to wail and pound her fists against the hard wall of his chest. She wanted to bury her face in his shoulder and sob out her anguish.

She did neither. Instead, she gritted her teeth and bent to tug off his right boot. She let it drop to the floor with a thud.

Sloan stirred with a groan. He blinked when he spied Heather and turned his head on the pillow to peer around the room in confusion.

"What'm I doing here?" he asked in a rasping voice.

"I asked Jake to put you here. I didn't want Janna exposed to her drunken father."

He squinted at her. "You mad at me?"

Heather reached for his other boot, struggling against feelings of fury and pain. "Whyever should I be *mad*? Simply because you come home completely inebriated, stinking of smoke and liquor and cheap perfume, making a fool of yourself and mortifying me in front of your brother and your friend?"

"In-ee-brated." He slurred the word, then gave a snort of harsh laughter. "Why d'you always have to use such highfalutin' words? Why doan you jush say drunk?"

"All right, *drunk* then."

She moved around the bed and leaned over him to unbutton his shirt.

He caught her wrist. "Doan be so prudish, duchess."

Wrenching her arm away, she fixed him with a steely glare. "I'll thank you not to touch me."

His mood suddenly seemed to sober as he eyed her narrowly. "I got every right to touch you. You're my wife. I paid for you, remember?"

Her eyes blinked with the pain he'd given her, yet she kept her spine straight. "You did not pay me enough to associate with a drunken boor who betrays his marriage vows by consorting with saloon women! I've had enough. In future, you can find someone else to sleep with."

She started to turn away, but Sloan's hand captured her wrist once more. When she tried to pull from his grasp, he only held on more tightly.

"I won't be barred from your bed," he said, still slurring his words.

"*My* bed?" She was white and trembling with anger. "I seem to recall I'm the one who has been barred from *your* bed. You didn't wish to sully the memory of your precious Doe, remember?"

He winced, but Heather continued relentlessly. "You needn't worry that I'll try to force myself on you. I don't intend to let you touch me, ever again."

His blue eyes turned hard and glittering. "I think

you're forgetting something. You still owe me fifteen hundred dollars."

She felt the color drain from her face. Even on their wedding night, Sloan had used her debt to drive a wedge between them.

Dark fury burned in his bloodshot eyes as his gaze raked down her body. "You're my bride, bought and paid for."

"Perhaps so." She was trembling now. "But I've begun repaying you from my weekly salary—and I'll continue until I've returned every penny."

"At three dollars a week, it'll take years."

"Then I'll look for a job that pays more."

"I have a better idea," Sloan retorted, each slurred word cutting like a knife. "You can pay me back in services."

"What . . . do you mean?"

"Sex, duchess. You give me sex for canceling your debt. What'd'ya say to ten bucks a shot? That's one hell of a price for a few minutes on your back."

Heather clenched her teeth to stop the sudden whimper of pain that bubbled forth. His offer was not just a deliberate insult; he was deadly serious.

His hands unsteady, Sloan fumbled in his pants pocket and drew out a ten-dollar gold piece. Ignoring the stricken look in her eyes, he forced it into her hand.

"What about it, duchess?" His voice, though thick, held a razor edge that tore tiny chunks from her heart. "You wanted to repay your debt. Well, thish is as good a way as any. But I have to warn you, I believe in gettin' my money's worth."

"You want me to whore for you?" A million layers of hurt bled through her tremulous whisper.

"You could call it that—though I doan see how it's any different than what you been doing for the past five months, even if we do have a marriage license."

She slapped him them. Hard . . . with as much strength and fury as she could muster.

The blow to his cheek jerked his head around, while the gold piece fell from her hand. When he looked at her again, his eyes were narrowed and fierce. His grip on her wrist tightened.

Ashen-faced, Heather tried to pull away from him. His eyes had an icy gleam to them that frightened her.

Reflexively she drew her arm back to strike him again, but Sloan muttered an oath and wrenched her down to sprawl on top of him. Heather gasped in outrage and struggled to rise, but his arms wrapped around her waist.

"Let me go!" she cried.

She stuck out at him, letting all her frustration and pain and rage surface in a feeling of explosion; her fists swung at his shoulders, his chest, his jaw— any part of him she could reach.

Venting another curse, Sloan rolled over with her, pinning her beneath his weight. When she twisted under him and tried to claw at his face, he captured her flailing hands to hold her arms above her head.

He no longer looked drunk; he looked dangerous. His eyes seared her, smoky and furious, as he stared down at her.

Heather returned his icy gaze measure for measure. "Damn you, let go of me!" she demanded again. "You have no right to touch me."

"I'll touch you if I want! You're my *wife*."

She retorted through clenched teeth, "You can go to the devil!"

The animosity between them clashed like swords, throwing off sparks of fierce emotion.

Sloan's hard, virile face hovered over hers, the weight of his lean, powerful body pressing her down. Rage and raw tension vibrated between them ... along with an abrupt, pulsing sexual awareness.

Heather flinched, feeling the granite outline of Sloan's manhood against her thigh.

Neither of them heard the door swing open, but they both froze at the quietly lethal voice.

"You want to let the lady go, Sloan?"

Wolf stood in the doorway, his features hard, expressionless.

Sloan stared at him a moment, as if trying to understand the question. Then abruptly, he released Heather and rolled off her.

She rose shaking from the bed and fled past Wolf, into the hall.

Lying back, Sloan clutched his aching head, which had started swimming again.

The silence drew out. Wolf was still looking at him grimly, he realized. The half-breed hadn't said another word, but the disapproval on his dark features spoke volumes.

Wolf turned quietly then and picked up the lamp. Just as quietly, he left the room, shutting the door noiselessly behind him.

Sloan squeezed his eyes shut. *God, what had he done?*

The whiskey-hazed stupor washed over him once more, along with a wave of acute shame. Heather was right; he was stinking drunk. Too damned drunk to tell her he was sorry.

Sorry for scaring her. Sorry for ever letting her into his life. Sorry for trying to drive her away.

In the hallway, Heather stood with her hand clenched over her stomach as she fought tears of

despair and anguish. She heard the bedroom door
shut softly, but she didn't glance up till Wolf
touched her arm.

There was concern and compassion in his dark
eyes. "You okay?"

She heaved a shuddering breath and nodded,
though she wasn't certain she would ever recover.
"Yes, I'm all right. . . . But I can't remain here." Her
voice was hoarse.

"Do you have a place to go?"

"Caitlin will take me in, I'm certain."

"Jake's still here. He'll drive you home. Why
don't you pack your things?"

Heather hesitated. "I can't leave Janna here. Not
when Sloan is in that condition. But it wouldn't be
wise to take her. . . ." If Janna was still asleep, she
didn't want to wake her and drag her out into the
night. Nor did she dare steal the child away. Sloan
wouldn't mind being rid of *her*, Heather thought
bitterly, but he wouldn't want her confiscating his
daughter.

Wolf didn't seem to need an explanation. "I'll
look after Janna . . . and Sloan as well. You don't
need to worry."

"Thank you," Heather murmured gratefully. She
had no doubt he would do as he said, although it
was strange how quickly she'd come to trust him.
"Would you ask Jake to wait until I can pack a
bag?"

"Sure." It was Wolf's turn to hesitate. "If I don't
see you again before I leave for Denver, ma'am, it
was a pleasure meeting you."

Heather tried to smile. "I wish it could have been
under different circumstances."

"So do I." His expression was grave. "I'll stop
by on my way back from Denver in a few weeks
to check in on you."

She nodded, unable to say more.

"Here, you'll want this." He held out the lamp to her.

Accepting it, Heather went across the hall to the master bedchamber. Janna was still sleeping in her cradle, but she'd thrown off the covers entirely.

Tears stinging her eyes, Heather gently drew up the sheet. When she smoothed a lock of raven hair from Janna's sweet face, a fierce feeling of love and despair overwhelmed her.

The young child stirred then and whimpered in her sleep—almost as if she knew Heather meant to leave. Or perhaps it was simply wishful thinking.

Fresh tears clogged Heather's throat. Swallowing hard, she turned away, wondering when she would see Janna again, wondering if she could bear it if she didn't.

Chapter 16

P rying one eye open, Sloan squinted against the sunshine streaming in through the curtained windows. *Heather's room.* He groaned at the bright light. His head was pounding like a bull was loose inside his brain.

Gingerly he rolled over and buried his face in the pillow, but he couldn't escape his tormenting thoughts. The numbing whiskey had worn off, leaving behind a fierce sense of shame and a sharper remorse.

His memory flayed him more harshly than his hangover. He remembered what he'd done last night, even if the details were a bit blurred.

He'd been a drunken bastard.

With a curse, Sloan squeezed his eyes shut. What the hell could he have been thinking, a savage voice prodded. How could he have been so deliberately cruel? He had no excuse for his despicable behavior. He'd lashed out at Heather in anger, mainly because he felt so damn vulnerable. He'd deliberately tried to drive her away—and cruelly wounded her in the process. He'd seen it in her eyes . . . her golden eyes hot and bright with unshed tears.

He deserved more than the slap she'd delivered last night. He deserved to be horsewhipped.

It was a long moment before he found the courage to climb out of bed and clean himself up. Longer still before he could make himself leave the room and go downstairs to the kitchen.

Wolf was there at the table, feeding Janna biscuits and milk for dinner. The day was already half gone, Sloan realized.

"Where's Heather?" he asked, his voice dry and rasping.

"She went home with Jake last night." He felt Wolf's gaze pierce him. "Can you blame her?"

"No."

Slowly Sloan walked over to the stove to pour a cup of coffee. It was muddy and cold and strong enough to strip the hide off a sow. Wolf must have made it, Sloan surmised.

Feeling his stomach rebel, he poured the mess down the sink and glanced regretfully around the clean kitchen. There were no appetizing smells of bacon frying or pies baking. No mouthwatering pancakes with maple syrup. No warm feminine laughter, the kind that made a house a home. None of the things he'd taken for granted since Heather's arrival.

His conscience struck him another blow.

His daughter was watching him wide-eyed, Sloan realized. He greeted her, forcing a semblance of a smile to reassure her, then eased himself into a chair and propped his elbows on the table, the better to hold his aching head.

Wolf said not a word. His disappointment was palpable, his silence condemning.

"I know," Sloan said finally in a low voice. "I was a complete horse's ass."

"Worse than that, I reckon."

"Okay, a pile of horseshit. That satisfy you?"

"That's about right."

When Wolf fell silent again, Sloan lifted his head and glowered. "Why don't you just say your piece and be done with it?"

"All right," he responded soberly, "I will. You went way over the line last night. Your wife is a lady. She sure as hell didn't deserve to be treated like a two-bit whore during a Saturday-night binge."

Sloan shut his eyes. "You're not saying anything I haven't told myself a dozen times."

"What the hell got into you?"

He couldn't answer. It was hard to explain the panic he'd felt last night. Heather's declaration of love had scared him spitless—so much that he'd tried to drive her away.

"Seems to me she's a pretty special woman," Wolf murmured.

"I know."

"You should count yourself lucky to have her."

"I know, goddammit!" Sloan winced at the pain that stabbed through his head. "You don't have to tell me."

"Well, somebody should."

"Aren't you supposed to be on your way to Denver?"

"I'll go when I'm good and ready. I'm not finished having my say."

"Well, hurry up and leave me in peace."

Wolf held the cup of milk to the toddler's lips. "You say you know she's special, but you don't act much like you appreciate her."

"I do appreciate her," Sloan protested with less vehemence.

"I think you owe the lady one whopper of an apology."

He sure as hell did, Sloan agreed mutely. He would have to go crawling to Heather, his tail between his legs. Swallow whatever pride he had. Maybe then she would forgive him . . . even if he didn't deserve forgiveness.

"I'll ride over just as soon as my head settles."

"You best wait a while, give her a little more time to get over it. Maybe take her some flowers this afternoon."

"I'll take Janna with me, too."

"Good notion. She'll be more likely to see you if you bribe her."

Sloan gave his brother-in-law a baleful glare. "You're damned well enjoying this, aren't you?"

Wolf grinned, his teeth showing white against his bronzed complexion. "I am. But not out of spite. You've been like a walking dead man this last year. It's good to see you finally taking an interest in life. Even with a sore head, you're more alive than you've been in a coon's age."

"Yeah, well, that's now. What about this afternoon? Will you still be laughing if Heather puts a bullet through me?"

She had no business crying, Heather scolded herself as she stood at Caitlin's parlor window. Yet Sloan's hurtful actions the previous night had left her heart aching.

She wanted to flee. Like an injured animal, she wanted to crawl into a hole and lick her wounds. She had offered Sloan her love and he had rejected it utterly.

But then, she'd always known she was fighting a losing battle, trying to win a man like Sloan McCord, with his dark soul and embittered heart. Heather squeezed her eyes shut, struggling to swallow the ache in her throat. She would *not* cry. She had promised herself she would hold on to her pride at least.

She would do better to consider her future. She had seriously contemplated leaving. This morning she'd gone so far as to drive into town, meaning to inquire at the train station about one-way fare to St. Louis. Instead she'd stopped at the offices of the *Rocky News* to see the publisher. Not only was Gus McAllister pleased to see her, but he expressed delight at her editing of Vernon's articles. He had more work for her if she was interested.

She'd given him no answer yet—she felt too emotionally raw to make any rational decisions just then—but she would have to choose soon what to do.

Certainly there were advantages to accepting his job offer. It would give her some measure of independence for one thing, and allow her eventually to repay her debt to Sloan for another. She wouldn't have to leave Janna and the life she had made here. She wouldn't have to leave Sloan. . . .

Heather bit her lower lip to stop it from trembling. She wasn't certain she could bear to stay. Her heart couldn't stand another buffet like the one he had delivered last night.

A soft rap on the parlor door interrupted her thoughts. She took a steadying breath, and by the time Caitlin entered, Heather had herself under control.

"Sloan is here," Caitlin said. "I told you he would come."

She felt her heart wrench painfully.

"Do you want to see him?"

"No, but I suppose I must."

"He's brought Janna. If you'd like, I'll keep her in the kitchen with me while you two talk."

Heather managed a smile of gratitude. Her friend had been a pillar of strength.

Caitlin smiled in return. "Just remember, you can stay here as long as you want."

When she had gone, Heather wiped her burning eyes. The last thing she wanted was for Sloan to see her cry.

She kept her back to the door, but she could tell when he entered the parlor; she could feel the raw, sheer power of his presence.

When he greeted her in a low, rasping voice, she ventured a glance at him over her shoulder. His expression was inscrutable but he appeared to be still feeling the effects of the liquor he'd drunk the night before. He had shaved the stubble from his face, but his eyes were bleary and bloodshot. When he met her gaze, he seemed uncertain. He was fingering his hat in his hand.

As the awkward moment drew out between them, Sloan cleared his throat. He was keenly aware of her distress . . . aware of his own. At just this moment he felt as uncomfortable as he'd ever felt with a woman. He was still smarting from the tongue-lashing Wolf had given him, while Cat had looked as if she wanted to take him out to the woodshed.

And Heather seemed determined to make this harder. He wanted to apologize, to persuade her to come back home, but her silence was far from encouraging. She was still angry at him; he could read it in every elegant line of her body as she stood stiffly with her back to him.

He cleared his throat, struggling to say what needed to be said. "Heather, about last night . . . I apologize for the way I acted. I'm afraid I wasn't myself."

"On the contrary," she retorted in a low, strained

voice, "I expect you were very much yourself. *In vino veritas*, they say."

"What does that mean?"

"In wine there is truth. It's a Latin term—oh, but how reprehensible of me. You don't wish to me to use such 'highfalutin' words."

Her tone held more than a hint of animosity, but Sloan knew he deserved her scorn, so he bit his tongue. "I should never have said that. The truth is, I'm sorry for all the things I said. They were inexcusable."

"Why do you imagine I have difficulty believing your sincerity?"

"I know you're angry. You have a right to be. But please, won't you at least try to forgive me?"

For a long moment she didn't answer. Sloan tried again, softening his tone to a plea. "I want you to come home with me."

She couldn't help the leap of her heart. "Why? You obviously don't want me in your life."

"That isn't so."

"No, I suppose you're right. You *do* want me—to cook and clean for you, to care for your daughter and help with your speeches."

He took a steadying breath. His reasons for marrying Heather hadn't changed. He still needed a mother for his child, a political hostess for his campaign. But he wanted her for other reasons as well, reasons more nebulous than he could acknowledge or explain. He couldn't deny, though, that Heather had become important to him—in ways that had nothing to do with his daughter or his political ambitions.

"That's what I wanted in the beginning, yes, but over the past months I've seen what a difference you've made in my life. I want you for my wife, Heather."

She turned reluctantly to look at him and found him regarding her with troubled eyes. "Well, I don't want a husband who betrays his marriage vows with saloon women."

"Nothing happened at the saloon last night."

"Nothing?" Her tone held skepticism.

"No, nothing. I got drunk and Della put me to bed in her room till Jake could come and get me. She knew I didn't want any woman but you. Ask her if you don't believe me."

She eyed him silently for a moment, remembering the gold piece he had offered her. "You might want my body, but you made it very clear last night you don't want my love."

He didn't answer, couldn't answer. Heather felt pain squeeze her heart. Sloan didn't even realize how much he was hurting her. Her anger faded, leaving a sense of hopelessness. "Sloan . . . this isn't working. You know it as well as I."

"What isn't working?"

"Our arrangement. Our marriage. I think perhaps . . . we need to put some distance between us. For a time, at least."

Sloan stood there, unable to manage a word. He felt as if he'd taken a fist to the gut. He'd wanted to push Heather away last night, to drive her away emotionally. Evidently he'd succeeded beyond his expectations. "You want to end our marriage, is that what you're trying to say?"

"I . . . I hadn't considered that far ahead yet. But that might be best. I can't go on the way we have been." When he remained mute, she clasped her hands together, seeking courage to continue. "If you're concerned about my debt, I still intend to pay back every penny."

He made a gesture of impatience. "I don't give a damn about the money."

"That isn't what you said last night," she reminded him in a low voice. "And even if you don't care, I do. I still owe you nearly fifteen hundred dollars."

"You don't owe me a thing. What you've done for Janna is worth ten times that amount to me."

She shrugged and turned away, but she couldn't dismiss the issue. "Perhaps it's merely pride, but it is important to me that I not be so dependent on you. Gus McAllister has offered to expand my job responsibilities at the paper. He needs some book-keeping done, secretarial work, that sort of thing. It wouldn't be full-time, but it would double my salary. And Caitlin says I may live here with her and Jake."

Sloan felt a stab of panic as he sensed her slipping away. "What about the campaign?"

"What about it? You don't really need my help any longer."

"How do you expect me to explain to voters why you're living in my brother's house?"

"I can't imagine that my absence will affect your chances any more than your drunken behavior last night."

For a span of several heartbeats he didn't answer. When Heather risked a glance at him, Sloan's lean face was shuttered.

"You could at least wait till the election is over," he said tonelessly.

She looked away. Of course Sloan wouldn't want her to abandon his senatorial campaign before he won.

"You can punish me if you want," he added finally, "but it isn't fair to hurt Janna. She still needs you."

Heather closed her eyes. Even knowing Sloan was deliberately making her feel guilty, she couldn't fight that argument. Janna did need her.

She let out her breath slowly, wishing there were another alternative. Some swift painless way to break with Sloan. A way to separate herself from him that wouldn't mean ripping out her heart.

"Very well," she said, her murmur quiet with despair and resignation. "I'll return to the ranch with you. I'll stay until the election is over." She could see the tightness of his features start to ease and held up her hand. "But as your housekeeper, not as your wife."

"What does that mean?"

"I'll care for Janna and do the household chores, but I won't share a bed with you. You aren't to touch me. Is that clear?"

For a moment he didn't reply.

"And I mean to accept the additional assignments at the newspaper. Those are my conditions, Sloan. If you can't agree, then you can look for someone else to care for Janna."

Sloan took a deep breath. It was too much to expect that she would forgive him so soon after his cruelty. He would have to prove he was sincere about wanting her. But at least if Heather was living with him, he would have the chance to persuade her.

"All right then," Sloan said finally. "If that's what you really want, I won't touch you."

Heather wondered if she'd made a terrible mistake by returning to the Bar M with Sloan. It wrung her heart to realize how glad Janna was to see her, but being in such close proximity to Sloan all through supper was akin to torment. It wasn't specifically anything he said or did—or perhaps it was. He was as solicitous and agreeable as any woman could wish a husband to be. Too solicitous and agreeable. Too kind. He was trying to make up for the cruel things he'd said and done last night, she knew. But he couldn't mend the rift between them. He couldn't make it right. He couldn't tell her he loved her.

She had just put Janna to bed and escaped to her own room for the night when she found the gold piece half concealed beneath her bed.

Almost fearfully Heather bent to pick it up. Sloan's harsh words rang in her ears as she stared at it mutely. *What do you say to ten bucks a shot? That's one hell of a price for a few minutes on your back.*

The bright metal seemed to burn her fingers, but she curled her fingers around it purposely, letting the hard edges bite into her palm. She would keep it to remind her of that night, of all that was wrong in her marriage—

She flinched when she heard the soft rap on the door. Reluctantly she went to open it.

Sloan stood there in the dim hallway, looking ruggedly handsome, his blue eyes soft and questioning. His voice was just as soft when he spoke. "I thought I'd see if there's anything you need."

"No, there's nothing. I'm fine."

Sloan didn't want to accept her answer. With effort he shoved his hands in his denim pockets, reminding himself of his promise not to touch her. If he gave Heather enough time, she might relent and forgive him. Meanwhile, though, he had to deal with his male ache. With his need to reach out and pull her into his arms.

In the quiet hush of the hallway, sexual tension pulsed between them, thick and palpable.

"Good night, Sloan," Heather whispered hoarsely.

She started to turn away, but he reached out to

capture her hand, unable to help himself. "Heather?"

She flinched and pulled it back. "Don't."

"You won't forgive me?"

She wouldn't meet his eyes. "I forgive you. I just don't want you here, in this room. I want to be left alone."

"Heather . . . I told you I was sorry. All I'm asking for is a chance to show you how much."

When she lifted her gaze to him, he could see her golden eyes stark with unhappiness.

She opened her fingers, offering him the ten-dollar gold piece. "You gave this to me last night, remember? In exchange for my sexual services." Her voice trembled. "Well, I'll gladly return it if you will go away. I'll pay you not to touch me, Sloan. In fact . . . I'll double the amount if you'll only leave me in peace."

She pressed the gold into his hand. Then, before he could react, she shut the door softly, inexorably, in his face.

She avoided Sloan whenever possible. Her additional responsibilities at the newspaper took Heather into town for a few hours each day, but there were still the long evenings to get through. She felt a little more secure in her future now that she'd begun to earn a modest income, but she had yet to decide what she would do once the election was over.

Heather was almost relieved when Richard Weld arrived later in the week to interview Sloan for the Denver newspaper. Having a guest in the house meant that meals no longer must be endured in enforced intimacy.

She suspected Richard sensed the tension between them, for during the two days of his visit she often felt his probing gaze on her. Before he left, however, she found the courage to broach a question to him about possible employment opportunities in Denver for a gentlewoman of limited means.

"Do I know the lady?" he asked.

"Well . . . yes. It's myself."

"Are you and Sloan moving to Denver after the election?"

"Not . . . exactly. I was considering going on my own."

"You're not planning to leave your husband?" Richard asked, his eyebrows raised in surprise and concern.

Heather averted her gaze, though she was unable to hide the mortified flush on her cheeks. "It's possible that . . . we might try a separation for a time. Our marriage hasn't worked out the way either of us planned."

"No? You had me fooled. That night in Denver McCord looked smitten with you—like he didn't want to let you out of his sight." Richard seemed to catch himself. "But yes, of course, I'll do anything I can to help. I'll make some discreet inquiries when I get back and let you know as soon as possible. Will that be all right?"

"Yes, thank you," Heather murmured in gratitude.

As he took his leave, Richard also shared a curious piece of news with her and Sloan that might affect their futures.

"You might be interested to learn Quinn Lovell may be involved in a brewing scandal. I'm investigating his alleged bribery of a judge in a mining scheme and will be reporting in my paper over the next few weeks."

Heather knew there was nothing "alleged" about

the baron's bribing of ranchers in their district—it was undisputed fact—but she held her tongue. If Lovell was exposed for the ruthless man he was, however, it could only help Sloan's chances against him in the election.

Sloan was not as sanguine about the possibility for a shake-up in the election. Bribery, coercion, even murder had been part of district politics for decades. Nor did he appreciate Weld's visit as much as Heather did. He didn't care at all for the attentions the handsome reporter had showered on his wife.

It was the day after Richard's departure, however, when Sloan let slip the determined control he'd been exercising over himself. He came home early that afternoon to find Heather in the study, laughing with the schoolteacher over a book Vernon had brought for her perusal.

His jealousy was unfounded, Sloan knew deep down. Her intellectual conversations with the schoolteacher were one of the few pleasures Heather enjoyed from her past life. He'd asked her to give up most everything else when he married her and brought her here to live on his ranch. Still, it stuck in his craw to see another man giving her such happiness when he himself could barely get her to say two words a day unless it related directly to Janna, the ranch, or the campaign.

He restrained his urge to say something nasty to Vernon, however, and bided his time until the schoolteacher had left. Then Sloan settled on the sofa beside Heather, who was still browsing through the pages.

"What is it you found so amusing?"

"A novel by the humorist Mark Twain, about a boy's adventures on the Mississippi river. I read it when it first was published a few years ago, but I'd forgotten how delightful it is. In fact you might enjoy it," she added absently.

"I've already read it." When she gave him a surprised glance, Sloan said dryly, "I do know how to read, duchess. I just don't often have the time."

An attractive flush stained her cheeks. "I didn't mean to imply otherwise."

When Sloan leaned forward to pick up the china pot from the silver tea tray that had belonged to his mother, Heather said quickly, "It's tea, not coffee."

"I'll try it."

"Would you like me to warm the pot?" She started to rise, but Sloan pressed her down with a light hand on her knee.

"Don't get up. This will be fine."

It was the first time she had let him touch her since their fight, and Sloan considered it an encouraging sign. Not pushing his luck, however, he sipped his tea and watched Heather while she read.

The companionable silence drew out, even though Sloan's thoughts were anything but friendly. She was so beautiful, he ached. He could feel the relentless need clawing at him.

He could not have pinpointed the exact moment her awareness changed, but Heather looked up from her book to meet his gaze. Their eyes locked, and for a moment, the anger, the heartache, the despair faded away.

Sloan set down his cup slowly. He had promised to keep his hands off her, but he was about to break that promise. He needed to touch her; he couldn't help himself.

Hardly daring to breathe, he raised a gentle hand to her cheek and heard the catch of her breath. She sat perfectly still as the backs of his knuckles brushed her skin with a featherlight pressure.

Her voice was a reedy murmur. "I . . . should wake Janna . . . from her nap."

"Janna can wait," he murmured.

His fingertips moved over her skin, lingering to gently trace the shape of her face. Then, just as slowly, he reached out to take her hand and raised it to his face, pressing her palm against his cheek.

Heather held herself rigidly still, even while trying to repress the sensual shiver that ran through her at the stirring contact. When he turned his head, pressing his warm mouth against the soft skin of her wrist, her lips parted in a wordless protest.

She had feared this moment. Feared her own lack of willpower. Feared him. Sloan's gaze held hers and she saw the tenderness there—compelling, heart-stopping. She could have resisted him if not for that.

She couldn't move.

Sloan was caught in the same spell. He had only meant to touch her, then let her go. But he wanted to kiss her; needed desperately to kiss her. He wanted her to acknowledge her need for him as well.

He put his hands on either side of her face and bent to brush her mouth with his. A flame, intense and burning, licked up from low in his belly and up to his chest like a wrenching pain. God help him but he wanted her. He wanted to take her here, right now, on the sofa. . . .

The image of her lying beneath him, open for his pleasure, sent desire throbbing through him, but he knew he had to give her the choice.

Releasing her, Sloan slowly unbuttoned his shirt.

Then he took her hand again and placed her palm against his bare chest, over his heart.

"I want you." His kept his voice low and soft.

She closed her eyes.

With careful deliberation Sloan reached behind Heather to unfasten the tiny buttons at the back of her shirtwaist. When he'd opened most of them, he snagged his fingers around the high collar of the blouse and drew down the fabric. She remained as still as a marble statue, but he could see her pulse beating in the delicate hollow of her throat.

He slipped a long-fingered hand beneath her camisole and corset and gently cupped her bare breast, making her draw a sharp breath at the arousing sensation.

"I want to make love to you, Heather."

She trembled. Tendrils of panic danced through her mind, but it was edged with desire. If Sloan had tried to force her, she could have resisted. But his touch was the touch of a lover, the caress of a man who wanted to give, not take. Who wanted to please.

"Please let me. . . ." he whispered, echoing her thoughts. When he drew down her camisole and the edge of her corset to expose her bare breasts, she saw the quick tightening of his expression.

"Sloan. . . ."

"Hush, sweetheart."

Not giving her the chance to deny him, he pressed her back to lie upon the couch. Her hands closed over his shoulders, whether to cling to him or push him away, she wasn't certain. When he covered her breast with his palm, her body responded with instinctive swiftness, the nipple budding instantly beneath his touch, shooting arrows of excited painfulness deep between her thighs.

Heather drew a long, shuddering breath. "Don't. . . ."

Yet she couldn't struggle against him, didn't want to struggle as he stretched out beside her. She could feel the heat and power that emanated from that hard, magnificent body.

"You really want me to leave you alone?" he murmured, lowering his head to nuzzle a rigid nipple.

Her pulse leapt with desire as his tongue teased her. Her body was aching now, and she moved restlessly against him. When he reached for the hem of her skirts, Heather twisted in halfhearted protest, but Sloan covered her mouth tenderly, seeking to persuade. The sensual pressure was gentle, yet robbed her of breath. She shuddered, breathless and dizzy from the slow intensity of his hot, languorous kisses against her mouth.

Eventually his attentions moved lower, his lips tracing her bare throat, her collarbone, the swell of her breast. . . . By the time he found her nipple again, Heather was quivering. She moaned deep in her throat. Her longing for him was overwhelming. Nothing could help her resist the urgent demand of his lips, the hard arousal of his body, the fire that leapt to life when he merely touched her.

She trembled as he whispered against her skin, "Let me love you, Heather."

His hands cupping the lush fullness of her breasts, he took her tight, hurting nipples in turn and drew them into his mouth, biting at each hardened peak. The heat was instantaneous. It burst through her hot and bright, making her burn with excitement.

"Please. . . ."

"I know, sweetheart."

He tongued her stiffened teats until she fought back a ragged moan. Then he sucked harder, making her loins clench wildly. She had to bite her lip to stop herself screaming out for more.

Sloan himself groaned low in his throat. "God, what you do to me."

As if to prove his point, his thighs tightened, driving against her hips. Her skin aflame, Heather arched against him involuntarily, overwhelmed by the warm smell of him, the hardness of his body. She wanted him, God help her. Sweet mercy, how could her body turn traitor this way?

She made no protest, though, when he drew up her skirts, or when his hand covered her woman's mound. When his fingers found the opening in her lacy drawers, she lost the wild struggle with herself. She closed her eyes.

She could hear his sharp intake of breath as he touched her. She was shamelessly wet, and he stroked her moist cleft deliberately, trying to arouse her even further.

"This is where I want to go," he murmured hoarsely. "I want to feel you around me, tight and hot and wet."

She cried out softly when he insinuated a finger between her swollen flesh lips, but her legs parted readily for him, desire rippling through her yearning body.

As his fingers caressed her ripe sex, his burning gaze lingered on her face. "Don't fight it, sweetheart. I want you hot and wild for me."

Shifting his position so that he knelt between her thighs, he pulled down her drawers around her ankles.

Lowering his head then, he pressed his hot cheek against her bare midriff.

"Sloan . . . no. . . ."

"Yes. You want this as much as I do."

His jaw scraped her inner thigh as with brazen intimacy he eased her legs wide open. "I want to put my mouth on you."

His face pressed into her, his wicked mouth pressing against her fully in a devastating kiss. Only the shredded remnants of her pride kept Heather from moaning in wild pleasure.

Both his hands clutching the soft full curves of her bottom to hold her to him, he ravished her exquisitely, his tongue delving into her and arousing a lightning bolt of sheer sensation.

His tongue rasped her sensitive flesh, teasing and tormenting and plying the yearning kernel of feminine pleasure. Slow and tender the lashing glide of his tongue played on her flesh, then thrust inside again, pushing and twisting, deep and hot within her.

Sobbing, Heather writhed beneath him, thrashing her head from side to side. Her hands clutching his shoulders, she pleaded with him to stop, but Sloan only answered with a growling sound. And soon she no longer cared what scandalous things he was doing to her. She craved his touch, couldn't bear for him to stop. . . .

She bucked frantically against him as his triumphant mouth forced jolt after tormenting jolt from her, in a long endless orgasm that shook her to her very core.

She was still shaking when he moved upward to kiss her mouth hard. She tasted herself on his lips as his tongue penetrated deep. It was a fierce kiss that stripped away any remaining defenses, leaving only primal need.

Her arms went around his neck. She could feel the energy barely leashed within him as Sloan's mouth left hers.

"I'm so hard, I'll burst if I don't get inside you."

He gave her no more time to recover from the shattering climax. His desire, long restrained, burned hot and hard at his loins. Urgently he rose to his knees and tugged at the buttons of his pants and drawers to free his erection. When he succeeded, she could see his arousal jutting boldly between his sinewed thighs.

His blue eyes burned into hers as he lowered himself on her again. Heather gasped, feeling the rigid, heated length of his sex brand her thighs like searing steel.

"Sloan. . . ."

"I can't stop now. . . ." he muttered. "I want you too much."

He eased the silken head into her quivering flesh, groaning as he sank into the wet velvet of her. She began stirring eagerly to his touch, but with ruthless willpower, he held himself still, reveling in her helpless response.

"Tell me," he demanded in a rasping voice, "tell me you want this as much as I do."

"Yes. . . ." She longed to feel that great, thick shaft sliding between her legs, thrusting deep within her.

She wanted to cry out in despair when he withdrew, leaving her aching with loss. But then he entered her strongly again, hot and powerful and alive, sheathing himself tightly inside her. Heather gave a sob of gratitude.

Then what had begun tenderly suddenly turned wild. He gripped her buttocks, no longer in control. She gasped in welcome as he plunged home . . . arching against him as his huge shaft drove deep and hard. . . . She cried out, sobbing as his wonderful length impaled her helpless body over and over again.

They came together in passion and need. He took her with fierce, insistent thrusts, possessiveness surging through him. She was *his;* his need was almost violent, his desire uncontrollable.

She shattered an instant before he did. He held her convulsing form still for his thrusts as she clawed at his shoulders, but then the searing tumult caught him in its greedy clutches. In blind desire Sloan bared his teeth and plunged inside her, straining to withhold his soul as he gave her his body.

His surrender was as violent as his hunger. A hoarse shout dredged from his throat as he gave himself up to the powerful explosion.

When it was over, when the storm of emotion had passed, he lay against her, spent, shuddering. His skin was sheened with sweat, his heart hammering.

For a long moment neither of them spoke a word. Drained and limp, Heather lay there unmoving in his arms, while love and despair pulsed through her. She could feel the tears slipping from her eyes.

"That . . . should never have happened," she whispered finally.

His heart wrenched to realize she was crying. He wanted to hold her close, to soothe her distress and banish her feelings of regret, but she winced when he tried to tighten his arms around her.

"I asked you not to touch me."

The tension was suddenly back between them, sharp as a knife.

"You were hot as I was," Sloan replied finally. "Don't deny it."

That was the trouble, Heather thought in wretched misery, remembering her shameless reaction to his seduction. She was helpless against

Sloan, her defenses against him in tatters.

She had no protection for her heart. Her love for him made her so terribly vulnerable. And remaining here would only make the pain worse.

Chapter 17

~~~◦◦◦~~~

Heather dashed scalding tears from her eyes as she made Janna's breakfast the following morning. Her need to burrow deep and hide her sorrow and pain wasn't as strong as her need to escape. She wanted to run, as far and as fast as she could. Janna was all that had kept her from fleeing this morning.

She couldn't bear to remain here any longer.

Swallowing hard, Heather lifted her blurred gaze to stare blindly out the kitchen window. She found it a bleak thought, spending the rest of her days alone, abandoning the life she had made here, the precious daughter, the husband. . . . But she faced a bleaker future if she remained.

She loved a man who didn't want her. Desperately loved him. She had vowed to make Sloan forget the sorrow that imprisoned his heart, but she couldn't heal him. She'd been a fool even to hope to. And a greater fool to misjudge herself so completely.

She'd thought she could be content with merely being Sloan's wife, his lover, sharing a deep physical passion without his love. But she had wanted more all along. She wanted him to want her, to care for her, to feel that his life was incomplete without her. As hers was without him.

No man had ever held such power over her. Until now she had been too proud to beg him for a crumb of affection. But she feared what she would become if she stayed. She would be beyond defenses, unable to protect herself. She would be his, body and soul, accepting his unmeaning cruelties because she was so sick with love for him that she would take anything she could get.

Heather buried her face in her hands. She had to leave. Going away was the best solution for them both. Perhaps someday the doomed love that had taken possession of her heart would fade and the pain would diminish. . . .

She gave a bitter, silent sob. And maybe pigs would sprout wings.

Just then she heard Janna's exclamation of delight as the child spied her papa. Heather's spine stiffened. Sloan had silently entered the kitchen, she realized.

Swiftly she wiped a sleeve across her damp eyes. She would not let him see her cry again.

He went straight to Janna's corner and picked up his daughter. As he settled with her at the kitchen table, Heather stole a look at him. His expression was inscrutable, his attention fixed solely on the child.

She turned away without speaking.

As the awkward silence drew out between them, though, Heather felt him watching her. Self-consciously she stirred the oat porridge and scooped a small helping into a bowl, then added brown sugar and a little milk. When she carried the concoction to the table, she paused beside him.

"Would you care to feed Janna or shall I?"

"I'll do it."

She set the bowl down before him on the table, then returned to the sink, where she mechanically began cleaning the dirty pot and utensils. Behind her she could hear Sloan spoon-feeding his daughter. When Janna gave a gurgle of laughter, Heather clutched at the edge of the sink, the ache inside her chest savage.

After a long moment, she took a deep breath, trying to ease the pain, trying to gather the courage to broach a subject that would likely only kindle more misery.

Finally she said in a low voice, "Sloan . . . I think it might be best if I left. I never should have come here in the first place."

She turned reluctantly to look at him, to find him staring at her with hooded eyes.

"Where will you go?"

"I thought . . . perhaps Denver."

Sloan couldn't respond. He felt gut-punched. Heather actually meant to leave him and his daughter. He knew he was greatly to blame, but it still struck him like a blow. He sat there numbly, holding his daughter, unable to manage a word.

"What about Janna?" he said finally. "You mean to desert her now? After she's come to love you?"

She glanced down at Janna, who was happily smacking her lips as she ate her breakfast. "I love her as well. But the longer I remain, the harder it will be for both of us to part when the time comes. Children are resilient. She'll forget me in time."

What about me? he wanted to demand. *How am I to forget you?*

His mouth twisted in a thin smile. "Sure, duchess. She'll get over it. She's too young to have feelings. She's only a half-breed, after all."

An angry flush stained Heather's cheekbones. "Must you use that term to describe her?"

"Why not? That's what Janna is."

"Perhaps so, but she isn't to blame for her Cheyenne ancestry. She cannot help who her mother was."

His quick, indrawn breath was loud in the silent room; a slap would have been less hurtful.

In the awful pause, Heather bit her lip hard. She wished she could take back the words. She didn't know why she had lashed out at him like that, except that he had wounded her so deeply by rejecting her love. "I . . . I'm sorry. I should never have said that."

He ignored her apology. For a span of several heartbeats he didn't answer. When Heather risked a glance at him, Sloan's lean face was shuttered, set in harsh forbidding lines. His next question took her breath away.

"You could be pregnant, have you thought of that? You think I'll let you leave if you're carrying my baby?"

The question slipped into her heart like a knife. "I'm not. . . . My courses came last week."

"Yesterday could have changed that."

When she remained mute, he stared at her. "Even leaving that aside for a minute . . . just how do you propose to support yourself in Denver? I can't afford to do it."

"I told you, I'll find a job."

"There may be horns on that bull, duchess. For a woman alone it won't be so easy to find honest work in a strange town."

Her chin rose at his disparaging tone. "Who says it must be honest work? Perhaps I'll apply for a position at a saloon, dancing for money. I've noticed that gentlemen have a great fondness for that sort of woman."

His expression went dangerously still. She might

have been bluffing, but it outraged him to think of his beautiful wife dancing for money in a gaudy saloon. "Like hell you will," he said softly.

"Does that upset you, Sloan?" Heather retorted bitterly. "I can't imagine why. You've always known I'm not a saint like your precious Doe."

She drew blood with that barb, she could see it in his face.

"Leave her out of this," he said tightly.

"How can I, when she's always come between us?"

Sloan's fist tightened around the spoon in his hand. Heather had struck straight at that dark, empty place that had once been his heart.

"In any event," she went on tonelessly, "I have a friend in Denver, remember? I've applied to Richard for help, and he has agreed to look for a possible position for me."

Sloan remembered the newspaperman well enough. A sick sensation knotted his belly.

"At the very least I could become a governess, or perhaps a music teacher. Elite families are willing to pay handsomely for pianoforte lessons for their spoiled daughters, I've discovered."

His jaw hardening, he set his daughter on the floor and rose slowly to his feet. Janna looked startled to be so abruptly abandoned, but Sloan paid her no heed as he moved to stand before his wife.

The tension was raw, so brittle it had an edge to it. He stared down at Heather, yet he didn't realize he had reached out to grasp her shoulders until she said tightly, "Would you kindly unhand me?"

He didn't want to let her go. He felt the primitive urge to bind her to him now, so she wouldn't leave him.

"Sloan. . . ." Her eyes implored him, while her tone softened to a plea. "Let me go. You don't want me for your wife. You don't really want me at all."

She was dead wrong, he realized, his jaw locked against the pain. He did want her. More than he'd ever wanted any woman in his life.

"You think not, duchess?" Catching her wrist, he drew her hand down to his groin to feel the hard evidence of his desire. "What the hell does this feel like? Indifference?"

She winced. "Our relationship has always been merely carnal. Just sex—you said so yourself."

"Maybe so. Maybe all I've ever really wanted is your body."

She felt the color drain from her face.

For the space of a dozen heartbeats, he stood towering over her, his face as tight with emotion as hers. The strain between them was palpable enough to shatter.

"All right then," Sloan said finally, his voice as cold as a Colorado winter. "Have it your way, duchess. You can leave. You can do whatever you want once the campaign is over." His fingers opened to release her shoulders. "Don't worry that I might repeat yesterday. I won't touch you again. You have my word on it."

With no more than a glittering glance at her, he turned to scoop up his startled daughter and stalked out of the kitchen, leaving Heather alone in the brittle silence.

Her hand clenched over her stomach, she heaved a shuddering breath, fighting tears of despair and anguish, wondering if she had made a terrible mistake.

The silent and bitter war between them showed no signs of abating. They might as well have been strangers, for all the intimacy they shared.

Sloan kept his promise to keep away from her

bed, not betraying by so much as a touch or a glance that he cared whether her heart was breaking.

It was all Heather could do not to humble herself at his feet, to beg him to love her. Yet he had spurned her love in the starkest terms imaginable, and it would serve no purpose to try to persuade him differently.

She might have been gratified to know Sloan was battling his own inner devils.

They struck him hardest when he rode home at sunset one evening to find Heather beside the corral, supervising his daughter's new acquaintance with a gentle mare.

"Was there something you wanted?" Heather asked, her tone carefully even as he sat looking down at her from the saddle.

You, he nearly said. Her beauty nearly took his breath away. The setting sun made a gilt halo of her hair, while her porcelain complexion was flushed with gold and rose—a vivid reminder of how she looked in the depths of passion. A searing passion they had shared until he had destroyed the fragile bond between them.

Sloan felt his throat close tightly as a sharp pang of longing went through him. Yet he couldn't give her the love she needed.

Maybe Heather was right. Maybe it might be best if she took herself the hell out of his life. Then he could return to the cold shell that had protected him from the tormenting emotions of grief and guilt and loneliness in the endless months after Doe's death.

Maybe then he could escape the pain that hounded him now when he merely looked at Heather.

*   *   *

It was a shock to them both when Evan Randolf unexpectedly arrived in Colorado the following week. Heather had just applied herself to the mending basket in the kitchen when she heard the knock at the front door rather than the back, as was customary when neighbors came to call.

"Evan!" she exclaimed when she opened the door.

His smile was warm, his look intent as he removed his bowler to expose carefully styled dark hair. He appeared as elegant and handsome as ever in a tailored chocolate frock coat and fawn trousers.

"How are you, my dear?" When she stared at Evan in incomprehension, he prodded gently, "I trust you are well."

"Yes . . . of course." She *was* well, if well meant heartsick and lonely.

"It is good to see you after all this time. I've missed you a great deal, Heather."

She glanced beyond him to see the private carriage waiting in the drive.

"If you are wondering why I am here . . . I've come to see how you go on. Will you not invite me in?"

Heather recognized her rudeness at leaving a guest standing on the doorstep, but she wasn't certain she trusted Evan. And yet his manner seemed conciliatory enough. And it *was* good to see a familiar face from home. "Yes, of course. Do come in."

Reluctantly she stepped aside and took his hat and cane. "May I offer you tea?"

"I should like that, thank you. The drive from Denver was long and dusty."

"I shall put the kettle on." She hesitated. "You may wait in the parlor, or accompany me to the kitchen, if you prefer."

"The kitchen, if that is where you will be."

Heather led Evan to the back of the house, wondering what he could have to say to her that would warrant his traveling such a great distance. He paused when he spied the child. Janna had pulled herself to her feet and stood clinging unsteadily to the wooden leg of a chair, staring at the newcomer with wide, solemn eyes.

"This is McCord's Indian daughter?"

Heather felt her shoulders stiffen reflexively as she prepared to defend Janna from any possible slur. "Yes, this is Janna McCord. But I consider her my daughter now."

Evan viewed the raven-haired toddler critically. "Those eyes and cheekbones are striking. I expect she will grow up to be a rare beauty."

Hearing the sincerity in his tone, Heather breathed more easily. Evan Randolf was a legendary connoisseur of beauty, and it gratified her to have him praise Janna's attributes rather than focus on her mixed blood. "Please, have a seat."

Taking Janna's hand, Heather led the child to her blanket to play with her toys, then turned to fill the teakettle and set it on the stove to boil. Her guest settled at the table to watch her.

From the corner of her eye, Heather saw him survey the serviceable kitchen. When he pressed his lips together, she wondered if Evan Randolf had ever even been inside a kitchen. In St. Louis he had an army of underlings to see to his every whim.

"You have no servants?" he asked after a moment.

Heather couldn't repress a smile. "Not a one, I'm afraid. Although Sloan's ranch hands are always willing to help if I need assistance."

"It must be difficult, managing under such adverse circumstances."

"It isn't so bad. Actually I find depending on myself to be a challenge."

"Your family would be dismayed to see you thus."

Her smile turned wry. "My mother would have been appalled. Fortunately I am not much like her. She was a wealthy socialite whose happiest function was deciding which parties to attend. I grew unaccustomed to a life of ease after my father's passing. And truthfully, there is something quite satisfying about putting in a hard day's labor. Certainly it makes me appreciate more the advantages I do have."

Evan's brows drew together in a frown. "Even so, I cannot imagine that you are truly happy here. You deserve better than this, Heather."

She started to shrug and reply, "I am content"— and yet she *wasn't* content. Ignoring his comment, therefore, Heather began setting out the tea things. "I never expected to see you in this part of Colorado."

"I have business dealings in Denver, but in truth I came here out of concern for you."

"Why should you be concerned?"

"I saw Richard Weld recently. He suggested you might be in need of assistance."

Her frown conveyed her disappointment. "I never expected Richard to betray a confidence."

"He did not, not in so many words. But he had promised to keep an eye out for you, and when I quizzed him about how you were faring, he told me you were seeking employment. I've come to offer my aid, Heather."

"I am flattered, Evan, but there really was no need for you to go to such trouble."

"Ah, but there was. I am greatly worried about you, my dear. I do not like to think of you struggling under such hardship . . . although in all honesty I cannot deny hoping you would come to regret your choice of husband."

"Evan. . . ." She said nothing further, but her tone implied how inappropriate she found the conversation, and how uncomfortable.

"I warned your Mr. McCord to see to your happiness, or he would answer to me. It seems he did not take me at my word."

She glanced at Evan in surprise, but before she could reply, he leaned forward, eyeing her intently.

"Heather, I wish you to know that the offer I made you some months ago still stands."

To hide her dismay, she averted her gaze. As she set the china cups and saucers on the table, she kept her answer carefully neutral. "Evan, I am a married woman. I would never contemplate committing adultery."

He shook his head solemnly. "You quite mistake me. I would never ask you to. I would never be satisfied to have you merely as my mistress, nor would I ever insult you so. But there is such a thing as divorce."

"Divorce?" She stared down at him.

"It would leave you free to wed again."

Her lips parted but no sound came out.

"I still want you, Heather. As my wife. I want you to share my life."

"You . . . cannot mean what you're suggesting."

"Believe me, I do. I have been unable to forget you, Heather, though God knows I've tried." When she started to speak, he held up an elegant hand. "Please, my dear, hear me out. I've spent the past thirty miles working up the courage to say this. Please . . . won't you sit down?"

When she complied and sank a bit dazedly into the seat beside him, Evan took a deep breath. "I made the worst mistake of my life letting you go. And I've come to beg you to give me another chance. Believe me, I am quite serious when I ask you to consider divorce."

"But . . . the scandal. . . . Surely you wouldn't wish to wed a divorcée."

His smile was rueful, edged with self-deprecating charm. "I fancy my consequence in society is high enough to weather a scandal. But even if not, it would be worth the risk to have you by my side."

Was he truly in earnest? Heather wondered, still reeling in shock.

He apparently saw her confusion and reached out to gently take her hand. "If I thought you happy here, I would never dream of making so bold a proposal. But you aren't happy."

"That doesn't mean," she replied in a low voice, "that you and I would suit. I could never be the wife you desired, Evan. You've always seen me as a pretty ornament for your empire."

"Perhaps I once did. But with you gone from my life, I realized what a gem you were. I was wrong, not giving you the respect you deserved . . . not appreciating or valuing you properly. I should never have taken winning you for granted."

"Evan, that is all in the past now."

"But it needn't be. Please, my dear . . . can you not give me reason to hope?"

"I . . . I'm not certain what to say."

"Say you will consider my proposal at least."

"Evan . . . I can't."

His voice lowered. "Perhaps you cannot forgive me for my despicable behavior when we last met."

"That isn't the reason."

"Heather, I wish you to know how deeply I regret my behavior that day. It was unpardonable. I cannot remember that incident without cringing."

"You needn't apologize again, Evan. You did so quite adequately at the time. Lending your private railroad car for our wedding trip was a generous gesture."

"It scarcely seems sufficient after my barbarous treatment of you."

"I have put it out of my mind, I assure you."

"Then you are not sorry to see me?"

"No . . . not at all. Truly, it *is* good to see you," Heather replied, and was surprised at how much she meant it. "But I cannot marry you."

"I would understand if you don't wish to return to St. Louis. If you prefer to remain here in Colorado, I can buy you a dozen ranches."

"Evan, *please* believe me. I am overwhelmed by your generosity, but I could never wed you." She eased her hand from his grasp. "I am afraid I could never feel anything more for you than friendship, or become involved in any intimate way. I'm sorry."

His expression was pained, but his sigh was one of resignation. "I feared as much. But I had to try."

He looked down at his fingers, and Heather stood up awkwardly, unsure what else to say to convince him.

"Can you tell me . . ." he asked quietly, "if you are planning to leave your husband?"

"I'm not certain. But regardless, I couldn't accept your proposal. It would not be fair to you to have a wife who could never return your feelings. You see . . . I love Sloan."

It was a long, long moment before Evan moved or spoke. With an uncustomary air of defeat then, he reached into the inner breast pocket of his frock coat and withdrew an envelope. "I believe this belongs to you."

Curiously Heather took it and opened it. Inside was a bank draft for fifteen hundred and fifteen dollars. "What is this?"

"The amount your husband gave me to settle your debts, plus six months' interest."

"I don't understand."

Again his lips curved, but this time his smile was tinged with bitterness. "I realize I never had the right to hold you accountable for your father's gambling debts. Indeed, I only used the obligation as leverage, so you would accept my suit more readily. It was unforgivable of me."

For an instant Heather shut her eyes, contemplating how different her life might have been had Evan come to this conclusion *before* she had wed Sloan out of desperation.

"I should have canceled the debt months ago," Evan added regretfully, "when you first refused my offer. But I couldn't bear to think of McCord winning you. Call it jealousy or pride, but I wanted to make him suffer."

"Thank you, Evan. I shall put this money to good use."

"You will be able to redeem the mortgage on this ranch at least. The note is for fifteen hundred, is it not?"

Her eyebrows lifted in surprise. "What gives you the notion the Bar M is mortgaged?"

"I make it my business to know the fiscal circumstances of my opponents." Evan held up a hand to forestall her protest. "I swear to you, my intentions are entirely honorable in this case. I understand your husband is suffering rather serious financial trouble."

"No more than most," Heather responded loyally. "Many cattle ranchers are facing difficulties this year."

"Perhaps, but none of the others are wed to you." His eyes darkened. "Heather, please believe me when I say I only want the best for you, and that I would very much like to atone for my past sins. If you will permit me, I should like to provide the capital to get this ranch back on sound financial footing. No conditions attached. Purely out of friendship for you. Indeed, I would be honored if you would allow me to help. On behalf of your father's memory, if nothing else. He was my friend and I owe it to him."

"I appreciate your generous offer, Evan, truly, but I must decline. Sloan would never agree. He is a proud man, you see. He refuses even to let his family help him."

"Very well . . . but I cannot simply stand idly by while you suffer. Most certainly I don't like to think of you being forced to seek employment."

"I am grateful for your concern, but I couldn't accept your financial assistance."

"Whyever not?"

She smiled. "Besides the fact that I have a reputation to uphold, I never have enjoyed being indebted to you, or anyone else. Call it my pride, if you will."

His smile was genuine this time, and it reminded Heather why he was such a favorite with most ladies. "Very well. But if you mean to leave here, you must at least allow me to help find you employment. I have a number of business acquaintances in Denver, if that is where you choose to go. I can make inquiries . . . discreetly, of course. In fact, I know a certain affluent widow there who might be seeking a companion. If so, I could facilitate the introductions."

"Well . . . I expect there would be nothing improper in accepting an introduction."

He hesitated. "If you mean to leave here, I'm not certain why you don't simply return home to St. Louis where you have friends."

Heather gave a delicate shrug. She did have friends in St. Louis who cared for her. Certainly Winnie would always take her in. And not having to pay for lodging would greatly minimize her expenses. But she preferred Denver, where she could perhaps lead a life of anonymity, where her failed marriage would not be so obvious. Where she would not be so very far from Janna, from Sloan. . . .

"There is no future for me any longer in St. Louis," she answered evasively. "But I have a little more time to decide my course of action. I shan't go anywhere until after the election."

"It is to be held in two weeks, is it not?"

"Yes, on Wednesday after next."

"I fathom the race was predicted to go down to the wire, but that may be changing, from what I've read. Richard's articles have been highly critical of your husband's opponent."

"For good reason. Mr. Lovell's use of his wealth and influence so far has been less than ethical."

"I have a passing acquaintance with Lovell. He is as ruthless as they come. He won't take kindly to the idea of losing."

"I don't imagine so," Heather agreed.

"Your husband should be on his guard."

She nodded. Sloan's chances of winning had improved recently, thanks to Richard's candid articles questioning the honesty of the mining baron's more lucrative dealings. And she wouldn't put it past Quinn Lovell to use some underhanded means to tip the scales back in his favor.

She felt Evan's penetrating gaze on her, though, which brought her out of her reflections.

"Are you certain I have no chance with you?" he asked again, softly.

"I'm sorry, Evan. I wish I could feel something for you, but I can't."

"I know—you profess to love that cowman you wed. I just wish I knew what you see in the fellow."

"Evan. . . ."

He sighed again. "Forgive me, my dear. I'm acting the spoiled child, but I've always been reluctant to concede defeat. Very well, I suppose I must accept your answer with good grace." He straightened his shoulders and was once again the urbane railroad magnate who ruled much of St. Louis and a good deal of the rest of the country.

"In any event I intend to remain in Colorado until after the election is over. If you decide to return home to St. Louis, my dear, I would be pleased if you would consider my private car at your disposal. And if you choose Denver, I hope you will accept my safe escort there. There can be nothing improper in a friend offering a ride. My carriage can be here in under three hours, and I can even bring a female chaperone, if that would satisfy the dictates of propriety. You have only to send me word. I shall be staying at the Windsor Hotel in Denver."

Heather managed a tremulous smile. "Thank you, Evan. Your kindness means a great deal to me."

She was grateful to know she had a way to leave if she chose—and more grateful still when the kettle began to boil and she could end this intimate conversation and turn away.

Heather agreed that Quinn Lovell would not take kindly to the possibility of losing the election, but Evan's prediction proved accurate far sooner that she expected. Later that afternoon she was in the kitchen preparing supper when a gang of horsemen rode into the yard, stirring up a cloud of dust. Her heart leapt to her throat when she realized they were all armed to the teeth.

Telling Janna she would be right back—to stay there and play—Heather seized her rifle and slipped out the back door. The riders had circled the yard and the man standing beside the corral gate. Evidently Sloan had ridden in moments before and unsaddled his horse.

Her heart pounding, Heather picked up her skirts and ran. As she grew closer, she recognized one of the riders as Quinn Lovell. The others were holding Sloan at gunpoint.

Some of those same weapons swung on her as she slowed to a breathless halt.

"Heather," Sloan commanded in a fierce voice, "go back to the house."

Lovell, however, seemed pleased to see her, for he smiled and tipped his hat politely to her as he sat his horse. "Mrs. McCord. Good afternoon."

"And to you, sir." She forced the words past her dry throat. "To what do we owe the honor of this visit?"

His mouth curved slightly in appreciation of her composure. "I have a business proposition for your husband, ma'am. I've bought the bank which holds the mortgage for this ranch, and I've called in the note."

"You mean to foreclose on the Bar M?"

"I am afraid so, Mrs. McCord."

Her gaze swept the armed riders, feigning amazement. "Is this normally how you conduct business, Mr. Lovell? At gunpoint? Surely this display of force isn't necessary."

"When I'm dealing with a man like Sloan Mc-

Cord, it is. I'm taking control of the Bar M, and I don't expect him to go quietly."

No, she didn't expect he would, Heather thought with a glance at her husband. His blue eyes were as cold and glittering as glaciers.

Although Sloan's Colt six-shooters lay in the dust, Lovell evidently saw the possible peril in his plan, for he uneasily cleared his throat. "However," he added quickly, "I am prepared to offer you an alternative, McCord. You can withdraw from the election now and keep your ranch. I'll cancel the debt entirely."

Heather drew a sharp breath; the gall of the man never ceased to astound her. Lovell had already bought dozens of votes, and now he was trying to force Sloan to abandon the race when there was the chance he might lose. He must be truly getting desperate.

"Go to hell," Sloan replied evenly, his tone deceptively controlled.

Heather raised her rifle, aiming it toward Lovell. "I believe you have your answer, Mr. Lovell. My husband is inviting you to leave."

"Don't be a fool, Mrs. McCord. You could get hurt if you don't stay out of this."

"I suggest you take your hired guns and go."

Lovell's jaw hardened. "The law allows me to take command of this property. If I must, I'll return with the marshal to enforce my rights."

Watching helplessly, Sloan balled his hands into fists as Heather debated with the mining baron, but he forced himself to restrain his fury. Under most circumstances he might relish a fight with Lovell, but not when it threatened his home and family. He'd wanted to curse when he'd seen Heather running toward him. He didn't want her anywhere near the bastard. But at least she'd come armed.

Lovell couldn't know she could barely hit the side of a barn.

She wouldn't be able to hold them off alone, though. He would have to act, and soon. . . . Sloan's eyes narrowed, gauging the distance between himself and Lovell. Heather partially blocked the way, but that might be an advantage. . . .

She was shaking her head. "I am afraid you are rather precipitous, Mr. Lovell. The mortgage will be paid tomorrow."

"And just how will you manage that?"

"You are acquainted with Mr. Evan Randolf of St. Louis, I believe?"

"I know him."

"Well, Evan is a close family friend, and he has just provided the capital to allow the outstanding mortgage on the Bar M to be redeemed."

She dared not look at Sloan as she spoke, but she could sense the change in him.

"I don't believe you," Lovell replied.

"I am not in the habit of telling falsehoods, I assure you. Evan called here only a few hours ago and brought a draft to cover the full sum. It's inside the house. I had intended to take it to the bank when I drove into town tomorrow, but if you insist, I can fetch it now. It can be signed over to you, if you're willing to provide a receipt."

Before Lovell could respond, one of his cohorts called out across the yard.

"Hey, boss? What d'you want me to do with the Injun kid?"

Both Heather and Sloan turned to see a man standing on the steps of the back porch, holding Janna awkwardly in his arms.

For a moment Sloan was paralyzed by fear. Then icy rage exploded within him.

Dropping to the dirt, he grabbed for the six-gun

at his feet and rolled; when he came up, his hand was filled with iron. As he lunged for Lovell, he shoved Heather to the ground, then dragged the man off his horse. Before Lovell could even cry out, Sloan had wrapped an arm around his throat and put a gun to his temple.

It was all over in an instant. The wind knocked from her, Heather lay prone in the dust, looking dazedly up at Sloan.

Danger pulsed around him like lightning; his tone was lethal as he ordered Lovell to call his men off.

"Tell him to set my daughter down gently. If she so much as whimpers, I'll blow your head off."

His face etched with fear, Lovell rasped, "Do as he says."

When the man complied, Sloan nodded at Heather. "Get Janna and bring her here."

Climbing hastily to her feet, she ran to Janna and scooped the wide-eyed child up in her arms. Only when she had returned to Sloan's side did he fire two shots in the air to summon his ranch hands. Then he pressed the barrel again to Lovell's head.

"Tell your men to drop their guns and get off my land."

Lovell nodded slowly. "Do it."

One by one, they reluctantly but silently obeyed. The man who'd seized Janna crossed to his horse and mounted up. Then as a group, they turned their horses and rode out of the yard.

Not releasing his captive, Sloan spoke low in Lovell's ear, in a voice that was savage. "I'd think twice before you show your face here again. If I see you on Bar M land, I'll shoot you on sight. And if you ever dare threaten my wife or daughter again, you won't live to see the sunrise. You got that?"

Just then Heather heard the rapid sound of hoofbeats. She breathed a sigh of relief when, a moment later, a half-dozen of the Bar M cowboys came racing into the hard-packed earth of the ranch yard, their horses going from a dead run to a sliding stop, with Rusty in the lead.

"Mr. Lovell needs an escort back to town, boys," Sloan said almost casually. "Would you oblige me?"

"Be glad to, boss," Rusty answered grimly for them.

Looking somewhat shaken, Lovell climbed up on his horse. Without a word, he turned to ride away, leaving the cowboys to follow.

The silence that remained seemed deafening to Heather. Trembling with fear and relief, she glanced at Sloan. For a moment he stood silently watching her, his expression inscrutable. Holstering his gun, he took a step toward her. Still without a word, he took his daughter from her, but his gaze was fixed on her face.

Heather's breath caught in her throat as he reached up to slide a tangled tress from her face, the movement intimate, infinitely protective.

"You okay?"

The rough concern in his voice touched her, yet she understood his solicitude. No matter his personal feelings for her, a McCord protected his own. Even so, she couldn't resist the need for his comfort.

Nodding briefly, she let her forehead rest on his shoulder, cherishing the sensation. For a moment she was surrounded by his strength and warmth, his subtle scent, and she never wanted it to end. And yet she knew it would.

Sloan found himself torn by the same conflicting emotions. He wanted nothing more in that instant than to fold Heather in his embrace and kiss her endlessly, to taste those lips and reassure himself that she was all right. The danger to her had reminded him violently of Doe's death—and it had shaken him to the core. Heather could be lying in the dirt right now, her dark blood draining from her body. . . .

He gave a silent curse of anguish. Maybe she was right. Maybe it would be best if she left. Hell, he ought to send her away for her own safety. He couldn't bear to see her hurt the way Doe had been hurt. Until the election was over at least, he couldn't guarantee he could protect her. Maybe he never could.

Breaking the spell between them, he eased a step back and settled Janna higher on his hip.

His eyes were shadowed when he finally met Heather's gaze again. "Were you telling the truth? Did Randolf really call here today?"

The air suddenly pulsed with renewed tension as the tender moment shattered.

"Yes," she replied quietly. "And he gave me a draft to redeem the mortgage note on the ranch."

"The hell he did."

Through aching despair she saw the gathering of raw anger in Sloan's light, breathtaking eyes. Her chin came up. "I think it rather generous of him, actually."

"He has some scheme in mind that will only benefit him."

"I believe you're mistaken. He meant to benefit *me*. Evan offered his financial assistance so I wouldn't have to work in order to repay my debt to you."

Sloan stared at her, and the chill was back in his blue eyes. "I told you once, I'll be damned if I'll take money from that bastard—or let my wife take it."

"No? I suppose you would rather lose your ranch, perhaps even your life? Would you really risk your daughter's life because of pride? Can you possibly be that foolish?"

He didn't answer, but a muscle flexed furiously in his jaw.

Seeing Janna's small forehead pucker with concern, Heather softened her voice but not her resolve. "Evan gave me the money to do with as I see fit, Sloan. And I intend to settle with the bank tomorrow—unless you physically prevent me."

"I won't try to stop you," he said through gritted teeth. His expression had hardened to ice, while his eyes held that wintry look she dreaded.

"No, you won't stop me," she agreed hollowly. "Because you don't really have a choice, do you? Any more than I had when I married you."

She gave him one last bitter glance before turning on her heel to walk toward the house.

Chapter 18

⌒⌒⌒⌒

"You can't truly be thinking of leaving!" Caitlin exclaimed when Heather confessed her plans several days later. It was Sunday afternoon, and the two of them were watching the children play in Caitlin's yard after church service.

Heather looked away, regretting her friend's distress. Yet she couldn't bear to remain with Sloan, not with such bitterness and hostility between them. She hurt all the time. Sloan was never more than a heartbeat away from her thoughts, a raw ache that never left her. But he could never love her, and she couldn't live with such heartache any longer. It was best if she severed their relationship, now while she still could.

"Once the election is over," she said quietly by way of explanation, "Sloan will no longer need me."

She felt Caitlin's stare. "I take leave to dispute that. But even if you're right, what about Janna? She certainly needs you. You've worked wonders already. Just yesterday Mrs. Elwood told me she means to invite Janna to her youngest daughter's birthday celebration next month, and you know what an impossible snob *she* is. She may be rich as

331

Midas with that gold mine of her husband's, but she knows you can't buy class. She's hoping your elegance and grace will rub off on her own daughters—she told me so herself."

Caitlin paused in her argument to allow Heather a response, but she got none. "You must realize what that means for Janna's future, Heather. If a woman like Francine Elwood can set aside her bigotry, even if it's for selfish reasons, then Janna is likely to be accepted by the white community. And you're the one who's made that possible. Our neighbors are starting to think of Janna as your daughter—"

Her stoicism crumbling, Heather buried her face in her hands.

Instantly she felt Caitlin's gentle touch on her arm, a gesture of compassion.

"I'm sorry, dearest, I'm a beast. I don't mean to make this harder for you. Janna will prosper, with or without Mrs. Elwood. I'll see to that."

After another moment, Caitlin added quietly, "It's not my business to tell you how to live your life, but I feel responsible for you being here. And I can't help but think you would be making a terrible mistake by leaving."

"Perhaps so . . . but . . . I can't live this way any longer. Sloan doesn't love me, Caitlin."

"Perhaps not yet, but he will learn someday. I *know* it."

"I once hoped he might, but now. . . ." Heather shook her head, despairing of ever winning Sloan's love. "He doesn't want a future with me. He only wants to live in the past. I remind him of the love he lost." Heather drew a shuddering breath. "I've tried, Caitlin, truly I have."

But she had to face reality. No more denial and

no more hope. She could never free his heart from the chains of his past love.

"Where will you go?" Caitlin said finally in resignation.

"Denver . . . would be best, I think. I can find employment there, and I would still be able to visit you and Janna sometimes. Evan knows an elderly widow who's seeking a full-time companion. I received a letter from her yesterday, inviting me for an interview. Actually she sounds quite charming and gracious. And the work shouldn't be too difficult."

"Heather, if money is the problem, I told you, Jake and I will be able to raise some cash in a few weeks, once we sell some of our livestock."

Heather wiped her eyes. "You know Sloan won't allow you to make such a sacrifice. At this time of the year you would only be offered a pittance of your stock's worth. In any event, our situation isn't nearly as dire now that the mortgage has been paid off. Besides, money is only part of our problem."

Albeit a large part, Heather acknowledged to herself. She had redeemed the note on the Bar M ranch with Evan's draft. Not only did Sloan not appreciate her efforts, he was so furious with her, he refused to speak to her. The Bar M in the past few days had been a battleground, straining nerves and flaying already raw emotions.

Heather forced a feeble smile. "You shouldn't worry about me. If I don't find the role of companion agreeable, I could always become a political advisor. I met a number of candidates in Denver last month. Perhaps one of them will need help with a future campaign. My stock will soar if Sloan wins, and I could begin a whole new career."

Her lame attempt at humor fell flat. When Caitlin's troubled blue eyes searched her face, Heather knew her friend could see her despair.

"When will you leave?"

"I've agreed to remain here till after the election."

"But that is only a few days from now!"

"Yes."

Only a few more days to endure before she could escape the misery and heartache.

Slipping a hand into her skirt pocket, she fingered the gold piece Sloan had so contemptuously flung at her as payment for her sexual services. She'd found it on his dresser and kept it in order to remind her of his unwavering determination to reject her love—and in order to bolster her resolve to leave him.

The day of the election dawned clear and bright in the magnificent Rockies, with enough of a nipping chill to hint at autumn. In a public show of support, Heather drove into town with Sloan so he could cast his vote, but the tension between them remained higher than ever. They returned to the Bar M almost at once, since it would be the next day at least before the votes from the district could be tallied.

The following morning they again drove into town, this time for a barbecue hosted by Sarah and Harvey Baxter for Sloan's supporters.

The day proved glorious. Heather was surprised to see the crowd swell nearly to the size of the July Fourth celebration. The atmosphere, too, seemed almost as jovial, thanks mainly to the laughter and boisterous energy of the children as they played countless games in the big meadow behind the Baxters', including baseball and sack races and horseshoes.

The grownups, however, seemed more sedate as

they awaited the outcome of the election. Much of the desultory conversation centered on Sloan's chances, and whether the scandal involving Lovell would affect the voters' decisions. Sloan refused to discuss the subject entirely and spent most of the time coaching his young nephew Ryan on how to hit a baseball.

The food had been devoured and cleaned up by mid-afternoon, when Rusty came galloping across the field, waving his hat and yelling in the air like a wild Indian warrior. He'd been posted at the telegraph office to await word from the county courthouse.

Heather felt her stomach somersault when she caught his shouted words, "Sloan won! Sloan won!"

The crowd burst into excited cheers, but it wasn't until Marshal Netherson rode up at a less reckless pace and confirmed the news that Heather could breathe more easily.

"How 'bout a hand for the new Senator McCord!" he shouted.

A round of applause went up, followed by more yells and cheers.

Eventually the marshal spied Heather and rode up to the back porch, where she had been helping Sarah wrap leftover food.

"Sloan won," Luther told her in delight. "By a pretty narrow margin, but he still won. You should be mighty happy."

"Indeed, I am," Heather replied, trying to summon enthusiasm.

From a distance she watched as Sloan was surrounded by a crowd of men, all laughing and backslapping and shaking hands. A moment later he was hefted onto someone's shoulders and the rabble-rousers moved off, surging toward the front of the house and the street. She thought Sloan turned his head to search the crowd, possibly for her, but then the throng disappeared from view.

"Where are they taking him?" she asked Luther.

"The saloon, I'll bet—in order to celebrate. Which is where I should be heading, if you'll pardon me, ma'am. I've gotta buy Sloan a drink. It's not often a man spits in Quinn Lovell's eye and gets away with it. Harvey, you goin' with me?"

Luther tipped his hat to the ladies and rode off after the crowd of men.

"It'll be a wonder if a single one of them manages to come home sober tonight," Sarah complained good-naturedly as her own husband Harvey hastened after the marshal.

Most of the women stayed to finish the cleanup. Heather made the rounds to thank all of those who had been so instrumental in getting Sloan elected, and then saw the last ladies away.

Finally she collected Janna from Caitlin. Not knowing when they would see each other again, she took the opportunity to say a tearful good-bye.

"I'm going to miss you dreadfully," Caitlin said, giving her a fierce hug. "But at least Denver's not as far as St. Louis."

"I'll miss you, too," Heather replied, trying not to sob.

She was still swallowing tears as Rusty drove her and a sleepy Janna home. She had just put Janna to bed for a long overdue nap when Evan arrived a day early. She had wired him this week, accepting his offer of escort to Denver, but hadn't planned to leave just yet.

"I didn't expect you until tomorrow," Heather said as she showed him into the house.

"I concluded my business affairs sooner than expected, so I thought I would spend the night in town. Unfortunately I didn't count on Greenbriar not boasting an hotel or the saloon being occupied by inebriated merrymakers. I booked a room at the saloon, but if we left today, I might avoid the inferior accommodations. Plus the maidservant I brought to accompany us would be spared sleeping at the livery stable."

"Today?"

"Is there any reason to delay?"

Heather averted her gaze from Evan's penetrating dark eyes. "I suppose not."

"You can stay at the Windsor Hotel tonight and be fresh for your interview with Mrs. Sharp at one o'clock tomorrow. I think you will like her, my dear. She was an acquaintance of my mother's before coming out West with her husband. She used to feed me gingerbread when I was a child."

Heather smiled faintly. She found it hard to imagine Evan Randolf as a child. But she appreciated his trying to raise her spirits and divert her mind from the despair that threatened to overwhelm her. "I'll need to finish packing. And I should wait till Sloan comes home to look after Janna—and so that I may say good-bye. He is my husband, after all."

"Of course."

"He won the election," Heather said absently.

"I know. I just saw him at the saloon. He was surrounded by a crowd of well-wishers. It doesn't appear as if he will miss you greatly."

Heather winced at Evan's unfeeling remark and wondered if he was trying to console her or make her feel worse.

He seemed all business as he adjusted his bowler on his head. "I'll return for you, my dear, when I've settled my bill at the saloon and fetched the maid."

She nodded, suddenly feeling too numb to answer politely.

Sloan narrowed his eyes and squinted through a haze of cigar smoke and whiskey fumes. He wasn't drunk. He'd nursed a single glass for the past two hours of celebrating. He wasn't seeing things either. That really was Evan Randolf crossing the barroom.

A wave of fury washed over Sloan, but he clamped it down. Despite his injured pride, Randolf *had* relieved a severe financial burden by canceling his debt.

"Excuse me, boys?" he said to his friends. Rising from the table, Sloan made his way through the boisterous crowd to the bar, where the railroad baron had stationed himself.

"Can I buy you a drink?" Sloan asked, making himself heard over the clinking piano and a dozen cowboys singing off-key.

Randolf raised an elegant eyebrow. "Why should you wish to?"

Sloan gritted his teeth and forced himself to keep his tone even. "Because I owe you thanks for bailing out my ranch."

Evan smiled without humor. "I trust it hurt you to say that as much as it did me to return the funds."

"Likely more."

He inclined his head. "Very well, Mr. McCord, your gratitude is acknowledged. Forgive me, I should say Senator McCord."

"Whiskey?"

"That will do."

Sloan waved to the bartender and ordered two whiskies, then leaned against the bar. "What brings you to this neck of the mountains, Randolf?"

"Would it upset you if I said your wife?"

He went still, every nerve in his body on alert.

"Your wife asked me to escort her to Denver. Didn't she tell you?"

"No." The word was barely audible.

"We plan to leave within the hour."

Silence.

Evan regarded him curiously. "You know, Mr. McCord, you don't look witless. But you must be even more of a fool than I was. You actually had her love and let her go."

Sloan turned slowly to stare at him.

"I dislike to be the bearer of bad tidings," Randolf said solemnly, "but perhaps you should consider returning home. I believe your wife is waiting to say farewell."

She was upstairs in her bedchamber, packing her bags while Janna napped, when Sloan came in. He stood for a moment in the doorway, watching her. His first rush of panic had dulled to numbness.

"Congratulations," she said quietly, glancing over her shoulder. "You deserved to win."

Sloan made no reply. He couldn't accept her accolades, or thank Heather for her help, even knowing she was a chief reason for his victory. He should have been elated by his success. He should have cared about the election that he'd spent so much time and energy campaigning to win. He should have felt something other than the cool, dead feeling in the pit of his stomach.

"You're leaving?" he asked, forcing the words past the tightness in his throat.

She nodded. "Yes. In a short while. Evan is coming for me in his carriage."

Sloan felt his hand curl involuntarily into a fist, but he forced himself to relax. Her next comment made it clench again.

"My courses came this week."

A look passed between them, tangled with dark, churning emotions. She was not carrying his child.

"Good," he said abruptly, before turning on his heel and walking away.

She waited to say good-bye to Janna until the very last moment. When Evan Randolf's carriage arrived, he sent his coachman to the front door to fetch Heather's trunk and bags and then waited patiently for her to join him.

In the front hall, Heather smoothed on her gloves and adjusted her bonnet, postponing her leave-taking as long as possible. Finally, though, there was no more reason for delay.

Reluctantly she went to the kitchen, where Sloan had just finished feeding his daughter.

She paused in the doorway, watching the two of them together, his tawny head bent toward his daughter's raven one. She wondered if they would miss her.

"I've come to say good-bye," she murmured past the ache in her throat.

Sloan didn't reply except to nod his head. Taking that as permission, Heather moved across the kitchen. Her teeth tugging at her trembling lower lip, she lifted the tiny girl in her arms and held her tightly.

"I shall miss you dreadfully, sweetheart." She was aware of Sloan's narrowed gaze on her. "You'll take good care of her, won't you?" she asked in a voice husky with tears.

"Have I ever not?"

Even his lightly spoken words were like a knife stabbing her.

Her gaze found his, her eyes filled with love and hopelessness. She wanted him to ask her to stay, but all the crying in the world wouldn't change his feelings for her.

Sloan felt her despair echo in his veins and looked away from her unbearably sad eyes. He wanted to kiss those tears away, wanted to beg her to stay, but he crushed the urge. Lies were his only protection now. He didn't want her thinking he needed her.

"So you're choosing Randolf after all," he said in a low voice.

She shut her eyes briefly. "No . . . I'm not choosing him. My leaving has nothing to do with him."

"It's pretty clear you prefer his fortune to the life I can offer you."

"That isn't true."

"Isn't it? You expect me to believe you don't find ranch life too hard?"

"The life here *is* hard, but that isn't what's driving me away. It's you, Sloan. You're the reason I have to go."

He stared at her grimly.

"You don't understand at all, do you?"

"I guess I don't."

Her mouth trembled. "I love you, Sloan. So much it hurts. I love you . . . I love your child"—her arms tightened around Janna—"I love this land. We could have had a beautiful life together."

His jaw clenched in resistance. "So you love us but you're going to leave us."

"I can't stay. Not without your love. I can't bear to live here any longer." Her throat constricted, and a tremor shook her voice when she continued. "I can't bear the bitterness, the pain. I'm a flesh-and-blood woman. You throw barbs and I bleed. I just can't bleed anymore."

The muscles in his jaw knotted. "I apologized for the cruel things I said."

"I know. And you were sincere, I don't doubt it. But you can't say the one thing I need to hear."

"I want you to stay."

"You want my body, perhaps . . . but I'm not a whore. I've got more to give than that." She swallowed thickly. "That has always been the trouble, hasn't it? You don't want my heart. You were honest about that from the first, at least."

Her voice was on the edge of breaking. With effort, Heather strove to collect herself. "I think you've made your choice, Sloan. You love your dead wife, and you can't let her go."

He made no reply. His face was set like flint, yet she saw the dark, anguished look in his eyes.

"I can't be Doe," she murmured hoarsely. "I can't live up to her image. I'm sorry, but I can't."

"I don't want you to be Doe."

"You do. You can't help it, but you do. You insist on clinging to the past—" Heather dashed the tears from her eyes, but she couldn't banish the relentless ache. "You won't let go of your guilt, and until you do . . ."

There can be no future for us.

She left the words unsaid, but she saw the muscles in Sloan's throat work convulsively. She had affected him, Heather knew. The truth had cut deeply. . . . But not deeply enough.

"I'll tell Cat you said good-bye."

Pain lashed through her at his toneless utterance. She couldn't reply.

Without getting up from the table, Sloan took Janna from her. His own throat was achingly tight as Heather choked back a sob and fled the kitchen. A moment later he heard the shutting of the front door.

Unable to stop himself, Sloan rose from the table and carried Janna into the parlor, where he stood before the window. His jaw clenched rigidly as he watched Evan Randolf handing his wife into the closed carriage.

Yet as the vehicle drove out of sight, he couldn't explain the panic that twisted like a knife in his gut. This was what he wanted, wasn't it? Heather out of his hair, out of his life, out of his heart. Yet he felt as if a vital part of him had been torn away. The way he had when Doe had died.

He locked his jaw against the tearing grief. The past years had hardened him, like steel tempered by fire. He would survive this loss, as he had others.

Janna started whimpering just then, as if she somehow understood her new mama was leaving her for good. With a raw curse, Sloan turned away from the window.

"Want Hever," Janna murmured plaintively.

"So do I," he whispered. "But it's just us now, sweetheart. Just like before. But we'll get on. We'll comfort each other."

Still holding his daughter, Sloan wandered the empty, silent rooms, keenly aware of Heather's absence, of his aloneness. She had been gone only a short while, and already the house felt haunted by her memory.

Heather claimed she couldn't bear to stay, and after the way he'd treated her, Sloan reflected with bleak honesty, he really couldn't blame her. She deserved so much more than he could give her—a life filled with harsh challenges and grueling work. She deserved love.

Almost to his surprise, he found himself in his bedchamber, the one he had shared with his first wife. He tried to picture Doe as she'd been in life, with her quiet features and gentle brown eyes, but all he could remember was the last time Heather had visited this room, when he'd spurned her love. And later . . . when he'd offered her gold for sex, making a mockery of the tender passion that had been the mainstay of their marriage for the past few months.

He sank heavily onto the mattress. He felt numb, except for the burning in his eyes, in his heart.

He didn't protest when a squirming Janna crawled off his lap and made herself a nest among the pillows. Instead Sloan lay back on the bed, exhausted from the turmoil of the past few weeks, from the constant war between feeling and trying not to feel.

Wearily he shut his eyes, trying to summon Doe's face. All he could see was a pair of golden eyes shimmering with tears . . . Heather's beautiful features torn by despair and anguish as she said a final farewell.

She was wrong, Sloan reflected bleakly. She was wrong to think he didn't love her.

If he didn't, then why did it hurt so god-awful much to lose her?

Chapter 19

❧

He was running, his heart pounding in desperation as he chased an ephemeral vision across the sunlit meadow. Doe's shining raven hair rippled behind her in the wind as she ran from him through the columbine.

It was a game, a lover's game.

He called her name, but she refused to stop. He shouted, pleading with her to come back, but she wouldn't hear. He followed, his legs churning, his lungs laboring for breath.

She led him to her grave. When he arrived, chest aching, she was sitting cross-legged on the grass, weaving stems of delicate blue columbine together.

She lifted her dark gaze to him, and her sad smile tore at his heart. "You have come to say farewell." It wasn't a question.

He could answer only with the truth. "Yes."

The flowers slipping through her fingers, she held her hands up to him.

His own hands were shaking as he took hers and dropped to his knees before her. Her touch was so faint, she seemed more spirit than flesh.

"My love," she whispered, her image wavering before his eyes.

"God, Doe, I'm sorry. I let you die."

345

"No, the blame was not yours."

"I wish . . ." he began helplessly.

"No. No regrets." She shook her head in sadness.

"Doe . . . there is something I must tell you."

"I know. The woman . . . your new wife. . . . She loves you."

He bowed his head, unable to dispute her.

"And you love her."

"Yes. . . ." His throat was tight. *"I love her."*

"Then I must go."

When he felt her grasp waver, he looked up. Her likeness was fading. *"Doe,"* he whispered, his voice hoarse, raw.

"Farewell, my love. Care well for our daughter. . . ."

He gripped Doe's hands, trying desperately to hold on, but they dissolved in his grasp. He cried her name in anguish, but her spirit faded in a wisp of smoke and shadow.

He woke with a start, his cry echoing in the darkness, the wetness of tears chilling his face.

It had been a dream. Bittersweet, heartrending. A final good-bye.

His eyes burned with scalding tears. The muscles of his throat locked tight against the effort of holding them back, Sloan turned his head to find his baby daughter snuggled against his arm. He drew Janna into the curve of his body, seeking comfort. It brought no ease.

A sob caught in his throat.

Struggling against the fierce ache, he buried his face in the soft down of her hair. His chest heaved once, twice, before he finally surrendered to the wrenching despair. Helplessly he let the relentless pain and grief out, his young daughter's hair muffling the broken, wracking sound of his weeping.

*   *   *

It was a long while before he found the energy to stir. Amazingly Janna still slept soundly beside him.

Feeling limp and drained, Sloan rose slowly from the bed and carried his daughter to her cradle. After kissing her forehead, he turned and left the room. He made his way downstairs, through the darkness of the kitchen and out into the chill night, where the shadowed mountains stood sentinel.

Silence greeted him. Silence and healing.

Sloan took a shuddering breath. Something had eased inside him during his paroxysm of grief tonight. He'd felt a loosening, a melting. The black ice that had encased his heart since Doe's death had cracked and fallen away.

He could let her go now. He could let his grief go. There was still—and would always be—a haunting sense of loss, but it was bearable now. Because of Heather.

He raised his gaze to the rugged mountains, as always feeling a sense of his own insignificance. The Rockies would always be there, strong and immutable. Unlike life. Life was so fleeting, over so suddenly. . . .

Was that what Heather had pleaded with him to see? That he needed to accept the past and move on with his life? To make the most of what he had now, at this moment? With her?

A haunting memory, dark and sweet, swept over him, this time of Heather. Heather warming him, welcoming him into her body, filling the bleak void in his soul. Offering her love.

He hadn't wanted her love. He'd been afraid to feel again, to let her too close. Afraid to care, to need too much, for fear of losing her like he had Doe. He'd tried to keep his heart safe from Heather by keeping his distance. But it hadn't worked.

He had loved her for months and lied to himself about it. She'd made herself a vital part of his life whether he'd wanted her to or not. After Doe's murder, he had retreated deep inside himself to heal his wounds, indulging in an orgy of guilt and suffering. But Heather had slipped beneath his defenses, insinuated herself into his heart . . . making him breathe again, hurt again, feel again. Love again.

He loved her.

Sloan squeezed his eyes shut. Against his will love had seeped into his heart and into his blood, into every nerve and pore of him. He hadn't thought it possible for him to feel such emotion again. But Heather made him yearn for things he thought he'd lost forever.

An image of her cradling Janna in her arms, the golden woman and dark child, drifted into his mind. *Heather. Warmth and light and healing.*

Since she'd come into his life, the bleakness had lifted. Since her coming, he'd been alive.

But he'd driven her away.

She hadn't deserved his cruelty. How could he have hurt her so? She was giving and caring, strong and brave, everything he'd tried to reject. Sloan bowed his head, his chest aching with a fresh pain.

He stood there for a long while. Dawn stretched silver-rose fingers over the eastern sky, yet he remained where he was. Brooding, lonely. Missing Heather with a fierceness that hurt.

He had driven her away. And it might be too late to get her back.

The sun had barely risen when Sloan received unexpected visitors. He'd just finished dressing and feeding Janna when his brother drove up with family in tow and Wolf Logan riding beside the buggy.

Wolf must have returned from Denver last night, Sloan realized as he went out to greet them.

He received a chilly response from his sister-in-law at least.

"Heather's gone, isn't she," Caitlin demanded accusingly before he could say a word. The martial light flaring in her blue eyes could have sparked a brushfire. Refusing assistance, she climbed down from the buggy with her baby daughter, her jaw set with determination.

"I think a family conference is in order," she announced, brushing past Sloan unceremoniously and heading for the porch steps.

Quizzically, he met his brother's gaze, but Jake shrugged, as if to say he had little voice in the matter.

They settled in Sloan's study, with the children playing near the hearth.

"We are here to discuss finances," Caitlin began resolutely. "Wolf has a plan, Sloan, and you *will* hear him out. We're not leaving till you see reason."

Sloan looked at his friend and brother-in-law expectantly.

Wolf leaned back against the leather couch and said more gently, "Cat's right, Sloan. She told me about Lovell trying to take over the Bar M and about Randolf providing the money to settle the mortgage. Well, enough is enough. It's time you accepted Doe's share of my claim. You can finish buying out Jake's half of the Bar M and get the ranch back in prime condition. Make it profitable again."

Sloan ran a hand down his face. "You know it sticks in my craw to take your money."

"It's not my money. It belongs to Doe—and now to you and your daughter. You can accept for

Janna's sake, for her future, if nothing else."

When Sloan hesitated, Cat broke in angrily. "I can't understand why you insist on being so stubborn! You can't possibly enjoy being at the mercy of men like Lovell or Randolf."

"No, I don't particularly enjoy it," Sloan admitted dryly.

Her tone turned pleading. "Then you can swallow your pride and take the money. It isn't as if it's charity. We're family, Sloan. And if there's one thing you should have learned from that terrible range war, it's that families have to stick together. We *have* to!" When he still remained silent, her frustration exploded. "Merciful heaven, you should be grateful you have family who cares enough about you to come to your aid when times are rough!"

Sloan sighed. "I am grateful."

"Then you'll accept?"

He nodded. It would be Doe's final gift to him, to their daughter. With a share of a gold mine, he could give Janna a better life. And he could get on with his own life. Heather would approve, he knew.

"For Janna's sake, yes," he answered.

"Heaven forbid that you should accept help for yourself," Caitlin retorted with cutting sarcasm.

Sloan's mouth curved in a faint grin. "I take it you're mad at me, Cat."

"Yes, I'm mad at you! I'm furious at you for what you did to my friend."

"Your friend?"

"You broke her heart, Sloan. You made Heather love you and then you drove her away."

He looked down at his hands. "You don't think Randolf can give her a better life than I can?"

"A better life!" she yelled at him. "That is utter

hogwash! Wealth and prestige never meant spit to Heather. If you haven't figured that out by now, then you're a complete fool."

"I think you're right," Sloan agreed quietly. "I am a damned fool."

His admission took a little wind out of Cat's sail, but she crossed her arms and eyed him with a fierce glare. "So what does that mean?"

"It means that I know it's my fault she left me."

"Do you love her?"

Sloan looked away. In his mind's eye, he saw Heather, her beautiful face softly alight with passion and love.

"Dammit, Sloan, *do you love her?*" he heard Cat demand furiously.

There was only one answer he could give. He loved Heather. It frightened him how much. How much he cared for her, how much he needed her.

He needed her warmth, her healing touch. He'd kept himself wrapped in darkness for so very long, but Heather had chased back the darkness. She had fought him, fought *for* him. She'd made him remember how to dream and how to hope. How to love. Her love had unlocked the cold prison of his heart.

He felt as if he'd awakened from a long sleep. Love. The kind of love that was wild and free. The kind that seared the heart.

"Yes," Sloan whispered in a raw voice. "I love her. So much I hurt with it."

He looked up to meet Wolf's dark eyes, expecting to see regret and resignation. Instead he saw compassion, approval. Wolf knew it was time for him to let Doe go.

Caitlin raised her hands in exasperation. "Well, you sure have made a fine mess of things. So what are you going to do about it?"

"Do?" he repeated absently.

"You have to go after her."

He meant to do just that. In fact, he'd planned to set out this morning, the instant he could get Janna into Caitlin's care—though Cat had jumped the gun by showing up on his doorstep at the crack of dawn. He couldn't bear to lose Heather. He didn't know precisely where she'd gone, but he would tear Denver apart with his bare hands to find her if he had to.

"You're not going to let Randolf have your wife without a fight?" Jake prodded more gently, mistaking his silence.

"No."

"We'll care for Janna," Caitlin offered. "Heather told me she has an interview at one o'clock with her prospective employer ... Mrs. Phoebe Sharp. And I think Randolf was staying at the Windsor Hotel. That's probably where you can find her. If you go now, you can get there before they leave."

"Go," Wolf pressed, "and bring your wife home."

Sloan looked at them, his family. The people who loved him, urging him to salvage his future.

His hand shaking, Sloan raked his fingers through his hair. What if it was too late? What if he had destroyed Heather's love?

For a moment he was struck again by the raw panic that had filled him when she'd left. He rose to his feet, desperation running through him like a knife.

He had driven her away. The knowledge kept ricocheting inside his skull as he turned toward the door.

Chapter 20

The Windsor Hotel looked much as she expected, with its ornate gilt trappings and elegant gold and crimson furnishings. Yet Heather was blind to her surroundings as she sat numbly on the brocade chaise longue in her room.

Evan had been quite kind to leave her alone after luncheon, allowing her time to collect herself before her interview. The problem was, she couldn't manage it. She couldn't stop crying.

Despairingly her fingers closed around the gold piece Sloan had so contemptuously given her. Tears slipped down her cheeks as painful memories flooded her, each more cruel than the last. Sloan declaring he could never love her. Sloan seducing her body that last time, proving how quickly her resolve faded at his slightest touch. Sloan making no effort to prevent her from leaving.

Her throat closed on a sob. A soft rap on the door made her lift her head with a start. Swallowing hard, she called, "Come in."

A bellboy peered inside the room. "Beg pardon, ma'am, but Mr. Randolf says he'll be waiting for you downstairs in the lobby."

"Thank you. Would you tell him I'll join him in a moment?"

She sat there after he'd gone, her stomach clenched in knots. This step was so final. Denver was so far away from everything and everyone she had grown to love. . . .

Heaven help her, she couldn't do this. She couldn't leave Sloan. Even with all the heartache he'd caused her, the pain of living with him was preferable to the pain of living without him. She couldn't leave.

Dashing the tears from her eyes, she rose and resolutely put on her bonnet. Then she caught up her reticule and made her way downstairs.

The hotel lobby was crowded, mainly with gentlemen in business suits, although there were a few ladies like herself. Heather glanced around her uncertainly, anxious to speak to Evan. Fortunately it was only a moment before she spied him in a sitting area, half hidden by a potted palm. He was reading a newspaper, but he tossed it aside when he saw her.

"Evan, forgive me," she murmured when she reached him, "but I've made a mistake."

Rising abruptly, he took her hands and surveyed her tearstained face with concern. "My dear, what is the matter? You appear distraught."

"I am. I can't do this."

"You can't attend the interview? Mrs. Sharp is expecting you shortly, but I'm certain we could postpone it to another day."

"No, I mean I can't stay here, in Denver."

"It's that McCord fellow, isn't it? You can't bring yourself to forsake him."

"Yes. . . . Sloan is my husband, Evan. I'm sorry, but my place is with him."

"Heather . . . I fear this is pure folly. Is there

nothing I can do to persuade you otherwise?"

"No. I must go back."

Evan gave a long sigh. "Very well. I will have your baggage loaded into the carriage and escort you home."

"Please, I couldn't allow you to go to such trouble after all you've done for me—"

"But I couldn't permit you to travel on your own. I would never forgive myself if harm came to you."

Filled with gratitude, Heather raised herself up and pressed her lips against his cheek. "I can never thank you enough for your kindness."

Evan responded with a pained smile. "I only wish you could feel something more for me than mere appreciation—"

The words had barely left his mouth when he was suddenly hauled backward, his hands torn from Heather's grasp. She watched in shock as a hard fist contacted his jaw and he went flying to land with a thud on the floor.

A hush fell over the hotel lobby. Evan lay sprawled on the elegant carpet, staring up at his assaulter, who stood towering over him, his expression fierce and dangerous.

Heather had quit breathing. *Sloan.* Dear heaven. . . .

"I'll thank you to keep your hands off my wife," Sloan grated through his teeth.

"It wasn't . . . what you think," she managed to murmur.

Wincing, Evan rubbed his bruised jaw. "Indeed. I must say, Mr. McCord, this is getting to be a *most* annoying habit of yours."

Ignoring him, Sloan turned to her. "I have to talk to you. In private."

She couldn't form a reply. She could simply stare, not daring to hope.

Evan shook his head. "I don't suppose you care that you are causing a scene, Senator." When neither of them appeared to hear, he climbed to his feet and brushed off his elegant frock coat. "Very well, I suggest you retire upstairs for your discussion. I shall make my apologies to the hotel management for the disturbance. I only dare hope a man of my consequence can withstand the indignity of being tossed on his backside."

Heather glanced around her. They were indeed causing a scene. Several people were staring, including the desk clerk. Under normal circumstance she might have felt embarrassment, but just now she was too filled with anxiety to care what other people thought. She only wished to be alone with Sloan.

He must have felt similarly. Without waiting for her agreement, Sloan took her hand and pulled her up the elegant mahogany stairway.

"There. . . ." Heather indicated her room when he seemed to be searching along the hallway. He drew her into the room and shut the door behind them.

Once inside, however, he abruptly released her. For a moment he simply stared. "You've been crying," he whispered.

Absently she wiped at the stains on her cheeks. "It doesn't matter. What . . . are you doing here?"

"I've come to beg you not to leave me."

"Why?"

"Because I need you. Because Janna needs you." His voice cracked slightly. "Because I want you for my wife. Please, will you stay?"

Her disbelief showed in her golden eyes. "Why should I?"

"Because I love you," Sloan replied—too harshly, he realized. He heard Heather's soft, ragged intake of breath. At her shocked expression, his chest twisted.

"I love you," he said again, without the sharpness. "Maybe I don't have the right to ask you to stay, Heather. I know I've hurt you . . . I know I've done nothing to deserve your love. . . . But I'm asking you to give me another chance."

The naked vulnerability in his face struck her like a physical blow. That expression in his eyes, so desperate and haunted, distressed her.

She felt the same desperation. The yearning in her heart was so painful, she thought she might faint.

"You love me?" she whispered, her eyes wide with uncertainty.

"Yes." How could he not love her? Her devotion to his daughter, her fierce courage, her compassion. . . . She had faced the harsh challenges of this land, the trials of his failing cattle empire, without flinching. He loved her. Needed her. Even more desperately than she'd once needed him, when she'd been burdened by the crush of financial debts. It had taken nearly losing her to make him realize just how very much.

His heart slamming into his ribs, he took a step closer. "I want to build a future with you, Heather. I want to have children with you. I want to share my life with you. If you don't want to live on the ranch, I could sell it. . . . We could move somewhere where you could be happy."

She closed her eyes in wonder, cherishing the words she'd been longing for, waiting for, forever.

"Heather?" he asked, his voice a hoarse rasp. "God, please say something. Tell me if I still have a chance."

"I . . . never thought you could love me."

"I do. As heaven is my witness, I do." He closed

the distance between them, his face harsh with strain. "I didn't want to. I fought it from the first moment we met. I was afraid to love you, afraid you'd be taken from me like Doe was. You were right. I had to let go of my guilt. But I think I've done that, Heather. Doe doesn't claim my heart any longer, you do. I love you. I can't live without you. Please. . . ."

She gazed up at him, her beautiful eyes blurred with tears, filled with hope.

Hardly daring to breathe, Sloan reached for her, his shaking hands framing her face beneath her bonnet. He kissed her very slowly, carefully, like he'd found something fragile, precious. Like he would shatter if she turned him away. He was desperate to reclaim her, to bridge the chasm between them with wordless, unbreakable bonds.

He could feel her trembling, feel himself trembling, as he whispered, "Heather, can you ever forgive me?"

She heard the pain in his voice, heard the pleading, and her heart broke. He was so tough, so impenetrable, so vulnerable. "Yes, Sloan . . . I forgive you."

He drew back so he could again see her eyes. "You said you loved me. Did you really mean it?"

"Yes, I meant it." The tears spilled over her eyes; she knew she was crying and couldn't help it. "I love you. I've loved you for so long—"

He stopped her words with his mouth. He hauled her against him and kissed her, deep and fierce this time, telling her without speaking how desperately he needed her, wanted her. When he felt her quivering response, desire filled him, desire and joy and wonder.

He ended the kiss at last, although he didn't let her go. Instead his arms wrapped around her. He stood holding her close, molding her against him.

"I love you." His whisper was wild and low. "These last weeks have been a torment. You don't know how much."

"Yes, I do."

"Heather, I want to stop hurting."

"So do I," she whispered.

"Then you won't leave me?"

Nodding against his shoulder, she gave a tearful laugh. "I wasn't leaving, Sloan. I couldn't bear to, even knowing you could never love me. I had already decided to return home before you came. Evan had just offered to escort me when you hit him."

"I went crazy when I saw you kiss him."

"It was only gratitude."

"Are you sure?"

"Absolutely sure."

He seemed to relax, but then he drew back to stare at her, his look intense. "Heather, Wolf gave me part of his gold mine—Doe's share, he said. I swallowed my pride and took it, mainly for Janna's sake. The money will let me rebuild the ranch, but if you'd rather live here in Denver, or even St. Louis. . . ."

"But the Bar M is your home. You love it there."

"I don't want to live there without you to share it with me."

She gave a tremulous smile. It warmed her to think Sloan would sacrifice his beloved ranch for her, but she didn't want him to.

"Sloan, I love it there, too. The Bar M is my home now. I don't want to leave it, as long as you're there."

His blue eyes filled with emotion so fierce it robbed her of breath and heartbeat.

"Sloan ... I want to go home," Heather murmured. "Please, take me home."

He smiled at her, this tough, tender man who had captured her heart so completely—a smile so brilliant it shamed the sun.

"God, yes, let's go home."

She rode before him on his horse because Sloan couldn't bear to let her out of his arms. They left Heather's baggage for the hotel to see returned, and set out for home, lost in their own private lovers' world ... murmuring to each other, questioning thoughts, sharing feelings, exploring the tender, fragile dimensions of their love.

There were things that needed to be said, hurt that needed to be acknowledged and banished forever. Promises to be made and kept.

They spoke of the future: of the ranch's deliverance from debt, as well as plans for their daughter and their hope for other children. They spoke of the past: Sloan's pain at losing Doe, and of his release, like the lancing of a festered wound.

"I know how much you loved her," Heather offered, hearing the wistful sadness in his voice.

"Yes, but it doesn't hurt as much now," he admitted. "I'll always cherish her memory, always grieve a little for her, but the pain of losing her is gone. Because of you." Tenderly, his lips brushed the nape of her neck beneath her bonnet. "You fill the emptiness inside me, Heather."

Shutting her eyes, she leaned back against him, cherishing his admission and the feel of his arms around her. This was happiness, she thought.

The foothills seemed to welcome them as they grew near. A light breeze carried the fresh scent of pine and set the aspen leaves dancing, while in the distance the rugged peaks of the Rockies rose to touch the blue Colorado sky. The leaves were just beginning to turn. Soon, Sloan knew, the aspens would be coming into their full autumn glory, sending up gold and orange tongues of fire.

They were riding along a stream that bordered a wood when he saw a flicker of movement among the branches of a cottonwood. Abruptly Sloan brought the horse to a halt and reached for the rifle in its scabbard. But then his hand stilled.

In the dappled sunlight he could make out the fawn color of a deer that had come to drink at the steam. The slender, graceful animal had raised its head to stare at him, but there was no alarm in the gentle brown eyes.

Those eyes reminded him so much of Doe. Maybe it was a trick of the light, but she seemed to be speaking to him. Smiling at him. At Heather. Giving them her blessing.

The sight held Sloan spellbound for a dozen heartbeats. It was only when the doe turned and bounded off that he felt the tension in Heather's body. She thought he was still haunted by tormenting memories, he suspected.

His arms came around her tightly. "Doe would have been happy for us," he murmured emphatically. "Happy that I found someone to fill my heart. Happy that I love you."

He felt her disquiet fade as she leaned back against him.

When they reached the Bar M, Sloan turned his horse over to Rusty to unsaddle and swung a startled Heather up into his arms. Like a husband with his cherished bride, he carried her up to the house and over the threshold of the back door. The place was empty; Caitlin and Jake evidently had taken Janna home with them.

Pausing, Sloan stood holding Heather in the kitchen. "Are you hungry?"

"Not really," she murmured, struck by a sudden shyness. "Are you?"

His smile was pure sensuality. "Famished—but not for food."

He carried her purposefully up the stairs to his bedchamber, where he gently set her down. Assailed by fresh doubt, Heather searched his hard, handsome face, wondering if he finally meant for her to share this room, this bed.

There was no reservation in his expression. He looked at her as if she were the only woman on earth, the only one he wanted on earth. "I promise you, Heather," he said softly. "Doe won't be sharing this bed with us. I've told her good-bye. But if you would rather use another bed, choose another room for our bedroom—"

"No, I want to be here."

His smile was warm, heartrending. "I want you to be here, too."

"Are you certain?" she asked thickly as Sloan untied the ribbons of her bonnet and slipped it from her head.

"More certain than anything in my life."

With a tenderness he'd long denied, he raised her hand and kissed the cup of her palm, then placed it against his chest so she could feel the tempo of his heartbeat. Her lips parted in a breathless murmur of sound.

When she remained mute, Sloan took her face in his hands. "I love you, Heather." His breath was a raw whisper. "And I mean to spend the rest of my days proving it to you."

The aching tenderness in his voice reassured her, as did his gaze. She was mesmerized by the emotions playing in his eyes, the love softening his features.

The rugged planes sharpened in intensity as he bent his head and claimed her mouth, yet his kiss was so gentle, so searing, it scalded her heart. His breath filled her, warming her, stealing her soul.

His low murmur of laughter afterward suggested he had felt the same enchantment.

They undressed each other, slowly, intimately, lingering over the simple pleasure of touching. There was no hurry. They had forever. They savored this time together, the familiarity, the inexplicable newness of the moment, their hands searching each other with wonder and tender hunger.

Sloan caught his breath when Heather stood naked before him. Her pale-gold hair fell in rich, deep ripples over her shoulders and down her back—the way it had in his first dream of her.

But she was no dream this time. She was gloriously real. His dream lover in the flesh. She was, he thought, drinking her in, the most beautiful thing he had ever seen or ever would see. She was strength, she was courage. She was joy and triumph. She was his heart.

Longing filled him, as strong, as desperate as the need to breathe.

"I dreamed about you, did you know that?" he said softly. "Before I ever knew you. You haunted me even then."

Her answering smile was so lovely it made his heart ache.

Needing to touch her, he stepped closer. He wanted to fill his hands with her, to feel her delicate shiver, to hear her uneven breath. He wanted to see wonder and blind pleasure in her eyes. He wanted to see love and trust. He wanted to heal the hurt he had given her. . . .

Only touch could convey his repentance. Reaching for her, Sloan enfolded her in his arms. He felt the sigh whisper through her body as she stood contentedly in his embrace.

"Do you feel the same fire I feel?" he murmured as his hands came up to caress her naked back.

"Yes."

"It's been like this since the first moment I saw you." Quietly, Sloan drew back. "I'm sorry I never told you how much you meant to me."

Reaching up, she touched her fingers to his lips. "Hush . . . no regrets. Not now."

To his surprise she took his hand and led him to the bed. When he lay back, he tried to gather Heather to him, to fit her warm body to his, but she seemed to have other notions.

His breath checked sharply when she knelt on the mattress above him. For a moment his heart almost didn't beat. Heather held his gaze as deliberately, her knuckles brushed the surging, hard, silky flesh of his erection.

"I want to please you," she said almost shyly.

Sloan met the soft fire in her eyes and it triggered something primal in him. Desire, heavy and urgent, curled in his loins.

"You always do," he replied, his voice suddenly ragged.

A tantalizing shudder passed through him as her fingers closed around him. His breathing deepened in quick, steady arousal as she stroked him, caressed him.

Then she bent over him, letting her lips claim his straining flesh. The muscles of his chest contracted, his skin suddenly felt hot and tight.

"Heather. . . ." He was already hard and near to

ursting, but her gentle ministrations sent desire ri-
ting in his veins. Her hair spilled like a curtain of
lvery silk over his skin as she continued her
arm, sensual seduction, her tongue caressing him,
ormenting him.

Sloan groaned aloud at the sensation, his face
ontorted with pleasure and pain. But Heather re-
used to stop. He moaned her name again, his voice
oarse, dark, just this side of pleading. Her burning
ps slid over him, drawing him into a sweet tem-
est of pleasure.

Blindly Sloan caught his hands in her hair while
is hips surged up to meet her feasting mouth.

She was a woman to drive a man crazy. . . . He
as crazy. He was filled with the pounding need
o possess her, to please her, to love her.

Suddenly he couldn't bear to wait. He needed
er to take him deep inside, to drain him, renew
im.

Capturing her shoulders, Sloan shifted her body
nd rolled over her. As he stared down at her, he
vas unsurprised to realize his hands were trem-
ling, his body shaking. "Love me, Heather. Please
ove me. . . ."

"Yes. . . ."

His eyes took on that fierce, intense expression
hat was so much a part of him as he eased her legs
part. When he pushed into her, she caught him in
leek rippling velvet, gloving him so hot and tight
hat he felt as if he would come apart.

He moaned raggedly.

With brutal effort, he forced himself to restrain
he violence of his desire, but the molten heat in his
gaze seared her. "I'm still not close enough," he
aid harshly. "I want to share every breath, every
eat of your heart."

He thrust harder, pressing deeper, impaling her.

Her body shimmered with fierce response at h
savage tenderness.

"Do you need this as much as I do?" he raspe
as he began to move.

Those were the last words he spoke for a lon
while. He took her tenderly, wildly, possessing he
completely, until she wept soft, mindless cries o
pleasure, of pleading and surrender . . . until h
shook with the force of his desire and love.

It was beyond lovemaking. The melding of the
bodies was like a mating of souls, fiery and des
perate and joyous with need. And when her explo
sive release at last came, everything within hir
shattered. He gave her his soul, and she took it wil
ingly.

Afterward, when their slow, shuddering gasp
were spent, she lay with her cheek pressed over hi
heart, her hair spilling like a curtain of silver-gol
silk over his skin. As their steady heart rhythm
mated with their languorous breathing, Sloan mar
veled at the frightening, exhilarating experienc
he'd just endured. Making love to Heather alway
stunned him. Every time he felt as though he los
a part of himself, because he did.

And yet this time was different from all the oth
ers. A deep sense of peace flowed in his veins. Th
kind of peace he'd never expected to find again.

He'd found it in Heather's arms. She had giver
him resurrection.

His frozen heart had thawed under her warmth
She'd taught him to love again, banishing the
bleakness in his life. She had brought him alive
again. He was alive, furiously, wildly alive. . . .

His arms tightened around her reflexively. This
was the woman he needed, the woman he loved
She had become his heartbeat.

"God, I love you," he whispered fiercely.

Raising her head, Heather returned his gaze mistily. Her heart felt recklessly open and unbearably full. She believed Sloan completely. She could feel it, the love in his touch. Could see the desire and need rampant in his face.

"I love you, too." He was her husband and she loved him utterly; so much she trembled with it.

"For always?" he demanded huskily.

"Yes," she whispered. "For always."

His chest tightened with longing, and when she raised her lips to his, need came crashing into him, more immutable than before.

His mouth closed on hers, claiming her irrevocably. His hands clenched in her hair and he kissed her hungrily, a kiss raw with desire and tenderness, fraught with promise. A promise of tomorrow. Of peace and joy. A new start to their marriage.

They would begin their life together again, in passion and love this time, as true husband and wife.

Dear Reader,

Here at Avon Books, we're thrilled over Stephanie Laurens, author of this month's Treasure, DEVIL'S BRIDE. Stephanie, a bright new voice in historical romance, has written a sensuous, witty love story with an unforgettable hero. When an intrepid governess is caught in a compromising position with a dashing duke he proposes marriage. But is this a match made in heaven?

The MacKenzies are back! Fans of Ana Leigh's MacKenzies series, will be happy to know this unforgettable Colorado family is back. And if you haven't yet discovered the MacKenzies, what are you waiting for? This month, don't miss THE MACKENZIES: DAVID . . . and get to know the rollicking MacKenzie cousins.

Fans of dark and dangerous heroes won't be able to resist Cassian Carysfort, Lord Bevington, hero of Margaret Evans Porter's THE PROPOSAL. Cassian has decided that Sophie Pinnock will become his mistress, but she is not easily persuaded in this sensuous love story set in 18th-century England.

For lovers of contemporary romance we present Curtiss Ann Matlock's IF WISHES WERE HORSES. Curtiss Ann's special ability to create emotional, heartwarming love stories between strong, steadfast heroes and down-home, delightful heroines is unsurpassed. Discover why best-selling author Susan Elizabeth Phillips has said, "Her books are wise and wonderful."

Happy reading!

Lucia Macro

Lucia Macro
Senior Editor

Avon Romantic Treasures

*Unforgettable, enthralling love stories,
sparkling with passion and adventure
from Romance's bestselling authors*

EVERYTHING AND THE MOON *by Julia Quinn*
78933-7/$5.99 US/$7.99 Can

BEAST *by Judith Ivory*
78644-3/$5.99 US/$7.99 Can

HIS FORBIDDEN TOUCH *by Shelley Thacker*
78120-4/$5.99 US/$7.99 Can

LYON'S GIFT *by Tanya Anne Crosby*
78571-4/$5.99 US/$7.99 Can

FLY WITH THE EAGLE *by Kathleen Harrington*
77836-X/$5.99 US/$7.99 Can

FALLING IN LOVE AGAIN *by Cathy Maxwell*
78718-0/$5.99 US/$7.99 Can

**THE COURTSHIP OF
CADE KOLBY** *by Lori Copeland*
79156-0/$5.99 US/$7.99 Can

TO LOVE A STRANGER *by Connie Mason*
79340-7/$5.99 US/$7.99 Can

Avon Romances—
the best in exceptional authors and unforgettable novels!

SCARLET LADY
by Marlene Suson
78912-4/ $5.99 US/ $7.99 Can

TOUGH TALK AND
TENDER KISSES
by Deborah Camp
78250-2/ $5.99 US/ $7.99 Can

WILD IRISH SKIES
by Nancy Richards-Akers
78948-5/ $5.99 US/ $7.99 Can

THE MACKENZIES: CLEVE
by Ana Leigh
78099-2/ $5.99 US/ $7.99 Can

EVER HIS BRIDE
by Linda Needham
78756-0/ $5.99 US/ $7.99 Can

DESTINY'S WARRIOR
by Kit Dee
79205-2/ $5.99 US/ $7.99 Can

GRAY HAWK'S LADY
by Karen Kay
78997-3/ $5.99 US/ $7.99 Can

DECEIVE ME NOT
by Eve Byron
79310-5/ $5.99 US/ $7.99 Can

TOPAZ
by Beverly Jenkins
78660-5/ $5.99 US/ $7.99 Can

STOLEN KISSES
by Suzanne Enoch
78813-6/ $5.99 US/ $7.99 Can